A Wish Upon Jasmine

A Wish Upon Jasmine

by LAURA FLORAND

Chapter 1

The street tried to ease her heart, with its hushed heat and shadowed old stone, and Jess braced warily against it. She never knew what might come out of her heart, when she loosed that stopper on it. Sometimes still it was this great wail of grief. Sometimes it was something even crueler, like hope.

Papa loved this town. He'd carried Grasse inside him all his life, like a knight's bastard son, exiled from Camelot.

Too late for him to claim a place here now. Could she? Did she even want it?

The iron key refused to turn in the stubborn lock. She pulled it free of the gold-painted oak door. The key had seemed ancient when she first removed it from an envelope in New York. But the streets of this old perfume capital probably remembered when it had been the latest in high-tech security.

She took a breath, rubbing the key, and a sense of quiet grew in her, like the hushed heat in the shadowed old stone street. The scents in this Provençal street were working their way into her braced heart like water into tiny cracks in a dike. She was afraid of all the emotions that would flood out, if she didn't stop those scents. And yet, at the same time, she wanted to press her face against the stone and just breathe in the scent of baked time. She wanted to press the key to her nose and see what old iron smelled like.

She tried to fight scents and their emotions with briskness, the way she had learned to do in New York, during those two years of her father's dying. Briskness was a default solution to all problems, in the big city. But here, the attempt at briskness only made her fingers fumble on the key.

1

What's your rush? the key's scent said. The stone of the street said. The bright young sun said, seeking its way onto the color-washed walls through cracks and crannies and shirts hung out like flags between balconies to dry.

I've got all day.

You've got all week.

We've got a half-dozen centuries.

She pushed her phone into her back pocket, tucking away the GPS that had guided her here, and focused. The key slid in, jiggled, and this time turned smoothly. Scent burst out at her as she pushed the door open, rich, thick, old, stirred like dust, layers of it loosening and rising up off the floor.

She grasped the door handle, still on the threshold, staring into the dimness. A gleam of old brown glass here, shadowy bottles on the walls. The scents woken by the door gathered around her in long fingers twining through her hair, settling onto her, some grasping, some caressing, some sighing in relief as they sank down.

She glanced back into the shaded street. Her hair stung, as if the scents trailing through it were trying to pull her head back around to focus on them.

She stepped inside, leaving the door open for light, her eyes adjusting enough to make out old cut-glass bottles decorating shelves like dusty jewels in a forgotten royal treasure chamber. She found a light switch, but of course the electricity had been turned off. She opened the panes on the big windows, found the latch on the shutters, and pushed them wide. Scents swirled and leapt in that great current of air like a joyful fountain. Sunlight crept in, second-hand, and mingled with them, making them giddy.

Now she could make out a counter, with a cash register that could have come from the turn of the last century. On the wall behind it was a great, framed ad from what must have been the 1920s, a lady with short rippling hair and a negligée of a dress, leaning into bursts of violet like a kiss. *Eau de Violette.*

This had been left to *her?* She might as well have been walking down the street, had a package thrust into her hand, and opened it to discover she was holding a fairy kingdom. Something stirred in her, so unexpected in a heart used to grief that she didn't quite know what to do with it.

A strange, archaic, wild and puzzled joy.

She moved through the room slowly, stretching up her fingers to touch one of the old cut-crystal bottles with its silver stopper. It slid soft and dusty under her skin.

An old shop that sold perfumes in the heart of Grasse. God, some people in this city would have a fit when they realized it had been given to the maker of Spoiled Brat. Her mysterious benefactor, Colette Delatour, must have meant it for her father, only...it had been too late.

Grief lanced through her, and she turned away from the shelf, leaving a trail of fingerprints in the dust.

Another old door in a corner past the counter. She tried the key again. Door and key alike seemed to hold still one last second—and then they yielded, in a rush, swinging open.

She stepped into a completely dark room, the only windows a narrow bank high on one wall, all shuttered now. She fished for her rental car keys and pressed her tiny travel flashlight.

Shelf after shelf of brown bottles, yellowing labels curling off them, names written in a firm hand with just here and there a tendency to flare, to soar. Her little light tracked over them, found alphabetical labels like *amande, jasmin, rose, violette,* and other names only perfumers knew: *fructone, hedione, indole.* Vials of all shapes and sizes glowed dull with dust under the flashlight, packed into racks of small shelves in the middle of wooden islands. The same handwriting marked

3

cardboard boxes stuffed under shelves: *Pompes Or—15mm, Capots fleur.* Gold pumps. Flower bottle stoppers.

She caressed the roundness of one brown bottle and picked it up, carrying it with her into the shop, which now seemed almost brightly lit compared to the depths from which she had come.

Setting it on the counter where the best light came from the windows, she rubbed it again, savoring that perfect curved smoothness, fingertip tracing gently the curling edges of the label. *Amandes amères*, this one said. The hair on the nape of her neck shivered. Bitter almonds. One of the most beautiful scents in the world.

Caressing the bottle one more time, she eased the stopper out.

A shadow blocked out the sun. "What the hell do you think you're doing?" The voice vibrated through her bones, dark and powerful, and she looked up with a gasp, her hand knocking the bottle.

A dark form lunged toward her, spearing through scents straight toward her heart—

A hard hand caught the bottle halfway to the floor, oil sloshing out. *Almonds. Christmas and Easter and everything delicious. The scent of happiness. The scent of...*

The shadow straightened, towering over her. "Who the hell are y—" His voice stopped as if it had slammed into a wall.

...him. Oh, good God, it was him.

Black hair, broad shoulders, lethal, fast reflexes, the way he filled and filled the room, seeming to grow bigger with every second that passed.

She reached out suddenly and put the stopper back in the bottle he held. Nothing happened. Too late. He was out.

Gray-green eyes swept over her face. Everything in him went absolutely still.

And it stilled her, too, that much stillness in him, this great, excitement-packed stillness, swelling bigger and bigger in too little space, trying to get out.

"*Toi?*" he said low. *You?* But it was more than *you*, it was *toi*, this intimate, possessing *you* that said *I already know you. We are not strangers. We can come right into each other's verbal space.*

She took a step back, tugging at the bottle. But her back hit the counter, and he held on, staring at her.

Her breath was coming too tight in her body, and she couldn't think. She scrambled for that cynical shell that she'd grown for the perfume industry, hardened specifically for people like him. But she couldn't shake the scents of this place out of her fast enough. She felt stupid and soft and real, like a girl who wore something flowing and romantic to a perfume launch party and didn't realize until she got there that she wasn't as beautiful as a princess, she was just naïve and ridiculous amid all the sleek gorgeousness around her.

A girl who still believed in wishes and magic in a world where everyone else knew those were just marketing tools.

He wouldn't release the bottle, their hands tangling with each other around it. "It's you," he said very low.

She shook her head. *No, it's not. I'm not that girl. I'm sleek and cool and successful. I'm not that stupid girl.*

His lips tightened. Sensual, firm lips that pressed quite easily into a disciplined line. "*Tu ne m'as pas oublié? Tu me comprends?*" *You haven't forgotten me? You understand me?*

In New York, he had spoken English, this gorgeous British-on-French accent that had dissolved her right down to her bones, turned her to putty in his hands. But her father had always spoken French with her, so of course she understood him now, too, as much as she could ever understand someone like him, all elegance and money and luxury pleasures and bottom line.

Having him appear out of a bottle had robbed her of speech, though. If only he had been a little...bluer. Or tinier in the legs. His broad shoulders did narrow to a lean, hard belly, but the tanned skin and that elusive, magical green hint in his eyes, the faint sun-lines around their corners, the slashing black eyebrows, the straight, hard, elegant lines of his face, and the black hair all added up to something compelling. The scents that had caressed over her twined around him, checking him out, vying to see which one got the right to settle on his skin.

"Certainly." She tried for that bored elegance with which he could speak, when he wanted. Tried to layer under it that same promise of lethal sharpness, that panther message that he gave out: *I am sunning on a tree right now, but if I choose to wake up and extend my claws...it's all over for you.* "Hello, Damien. Rosier."

Wasn't stating his name one of the rules for taking control of someone who popped out of a bottle? Such an important name, that last one. She hadn't known the Rosier part that night, and learning it had ruined everything.

Gray-green eyes traveled over her face—and then down and up her body. That tiny flicker of his lashes packed a wallop. Her body shifted for the look, before she could stop it, asking: *Did you like what you saw?*

Jess. No. Not again.

"Jasmin Bianchi," that even, precise voice said, with that latent purr of a hungry panther about to pounce on a bunny. He did it better—said her name as if he was taking possession of *her.*

As he recovered from his surprise, his game face returned, distant and a little ironic, but a restlessness filled his body, as if a thousand urges to assassinate his enemies rode just under the surface of his skin.

"Fancy meeting you here," Jess said absurdly. Grasse was a Rosier town. She'd known perfectly well she was going into the heart of his territory. *You knew you'd see him again if you came here,* a voice in her head said, this painful, stupid hope. *What were you thinking, that somehow he would make everything that happened afterward a lie and turn himself back into your fantasy prince again?*

Shut up. She shoved that hope back in its bottle, where it kicked and fought to break free.

He switched to English. "The surprise is mine."

A wave of heat hit her, at that blend of clipped British English with the French accent still clinging to it. It made her skin remember that French-British accent caressing all up and down her length. It made her want to try to capture it like a scent, lure it into that bottle along with hope, so that she could un-stopper it and listen to it in her bed every night. And never take the risk again of letting the source of that accent in her bed be the actual him.

The man before her.

"I, uh...my father came from here," Jess said. *I'm not chasing you. I'm not following you around the world like some groupie, just on the hope I can catch a glimpse of you walking through the streets.* "This is my inheritance."

"Your inheritance," Damien repeated flatly. And then, under his breath, "God damn it, Tante Colette."

Jess hesitated, confused. Her whole body felt confused. His arrival had thrown it into a whirl, over-exposed, over-aroused, longing for cover. It wasn't the type of body made to survive naked in front of that cool gaze, and it knew it.

"This shop," Damien said, with that crisp, tight, romance-brushed accent of his, "has been in my family since the Renaissance. One of my ancestors had a glove-making shop in this same spot, and she probably inherited it from her father. It's where our dynasty was founded."

Oh, crap. Jess's heart congealed into some unpleasant glop and sank cold and slimy through her body right down to her toes. This magic, special shop, this gift of joy that had shone for a moment like a light

7

at the end of a very long tunnel, was a treasure for which she would have to fight Damien Rosier?

Damien, who'd already stripped her bare and exposed all the writhing, aroused, lost, hungry heart of her for his evening's casual lay? And who'd capped that off by stealing her company. Her *company*, that thing she'd held onto with all her might while her father was dying, that great risk and dream, her one chance to make magic and wishes out of perfume again and not some new version of Spoiled Brat over and over until it killed her. Her one chance to be what her father had dreamed she would be. What *she* had dreamed she would be.

Damien had destroyed her so ruthlessly when he had kind of *liked* her, or at least thought she was worth a hook-up or two. What the hell would he do as her enemy?

Damien, who right now, looking at her, probably carried super-imposed over the sight a vision of her hot and wide open and reaching for him. Who could probably remember what her sex felt like, flushed and slick and clinging to his fingers as he cleverly, cleverly...

Control, Jess. Make yourself cynical, amused, hard. Like Spoiled Brat. If you can make a perfume that belongs in this world, surely you can fake belonging in it, too?

"I got a letter," she said. "From Antoine Vallier."

"I am going to kill that bastard," Damien said, between his teeth.

Okay, no more names. She didn't want to expose a host of more innocents to his destruction. She took a step back, but ran into the counter.

His eyes flickered over her recoil and hardened. "I didn't mean that literally."

Well, how would she know? He was Damien Rosier. And all her beliefs in his tenderness, in the sensuality and wish and wonder of him that night, were stupid dreams. Trying to catch a prince by singing into a well. God, she hated this industry.

"I had my own lawyer check it out before I came," she said. "Somebody really did give it to me. She probably meant it for my father, but..." She couldn't finish that thought.

"My great-aunt Colette Delatour," Damien said grimly. "That's your somebody."

His great-aunt? What the hell was going on? And how had she gotten dragged into the middle of it?

"She made and sold perfumes here during the war." Damien pivoted away from her, like a man who just had to move before he started taking out the perfume bottles with karate chops.

Or possibly taking out her. She'd already proven what an easy target she was.

"So my great-grandfather deeded it over to her, and they tried to emphasize her different last name, that she wasn't a part of the family, so that if the Gestapo moved in against the Rosiers and started arresting them all, they might not include her and this shop in the sweep. She was a stepchild—my great-grandfather married her mother when she was six."

Jess didn't even know who her great-grandfather was. This man had *history*.

Damien smiled a little, an up-swelling of old pride. "So she and my grandfather pretended that they couldn't stand each other, that Pépé couldn't forgive her for receiving some of his inheritance, and she used her perfume shop to send coded messages in perfume all over Europe. Only another nose could read them, the kind of person who could memorize and identify thousands of molecules on scent alone and never have to refer to notes. The Germans never cracked it. They never even suspected it."

The hair rose on her arms. She stared around the shop, the power in those bottles now so great it made her shiver. The Rosiers really were a dynasty of power. Influencing the entire course of a war seven decades ago.

In a shop that had already been in their family for centuries back then.

When her father used to warn her about the Rosiers, he hadn't even been exaggerating.

She rubbed the goose bumps on her arms.

His gaze flickered down over her again and back up to her face. His lips pressed together. "Jess—"

"Well, maybe it's time to shake things up," she said suddenly, lifting her chin. Just because she was shy and wistful and romantic, just because she was lost right now and vulnerable, didn't mean that *he* had to know it. Not again. This time, she could fake that tough, sophisticated shell.

She *could.*

Just spray on your own Spoiled Brat and wave it under his nose. That will help.

She'd do it, too, if the damn perfume didn't give her a migraine.

He stared at her. "...Shake things up?" His voice sounded odd, compressed.

"Stir things up." She made a gesture with the hand that had gotten splashed, and the scent of Christmas and happiness washed all around them again. Rich and sweet. Somebody needed to take control of those bitter almonds and bind them down with other molecules, moderate that blithe happiness with a little hardcore sense. Civet, maybe. Something pissed off and ready to fight back.

He folded his own arms across his chest, gazing at her. His eyes really should be black. Merciless. Instead they were this beautiful gray-green, like a deep sea in the quiet privacy of early morning, when no one was around to disturb her peace and all that sea was for her.

Those eyes tricked a woman in all kinds of wrong ways.

"I prefer the situation as it is," he said coolly. "Not stirred." But his gaze flicked up and down her body once.

"Of course you do. You're a Rosier. The aristocrats always hated it when the starving peasants rebelled and overset their world order."

Those sea eyes could be as cool as...well, the sea. "I come from a long line of peasants."

She snorted before she could stop herself. Yeah, right. The Rosiers' nepotistic perfumocracy held sway over this region as if it was their own city-state and they the Borgias. Her father had talked about it some, when she asked him if he ever wanted to return to France to escape the American perfume industry he had had a tendency to curse. And Damien Rosier was the heir apparent to Rosier SA, their Chief Assassin, the one who took out his family's rivals without a second thought.

Heartless. She'd been a tiny, tiny fish in the school he ate for breakfast. She'd had that one bright dream to nourish her through a dark time, and he'd gotten bored one day and had the munchies.

"So did the kings of France if you go back far enough," she said. "Let's get real. My father warned me about you."

A faint narrowing of his eyes. "Warned you? About me?" He searched her face. "Was that before or after—"

"About the Rosiers," Jess said quickly. "You probably weren't even born when my father left Grasse."

His face closed, once again a perfect shield over his emotions. *Never play poker with this guy.* Except she already had—strip poker. And she'd lost the last of her heart, while for him it had been a casual game.

"I already knew about you," she said recklessly. Or she should have. Who didn't know about Damien Rosier? *Nobody* wanted to mess with him. No woman should blithely let him pick her up at a party as if he was going to save her heart.

The corners of his lips tightened. He dropped his hands in a slashing movement that took them to the pockets of his suit. God, he looked like such a prince in that suit—so elegant and so masculine, the lack of tie

11

and the buttons undone at the throat the only indication that he, too, could get a little overheated sometimes.

"And what," he said precisely, "did you know? Already?"

Keep it cool, Jess. Don't flush. Don't let him see that it mattered more to you than it did to him. Don't let him see your wounds, don't let him see your hurt, don't let him see anything that would make a predator go for the kill. God, she wished she wasn't so frizzed and stale from the international flight. She'd kill for a little supermodel gloss right now.

She shrugged, trying for his tough cynicism. "All I needed to. You took over my company. That same weekend."

Too bad her father hadn't raised her in France, so that her lips could make as tight and sensual a line as his did. Instead of her own stupid poetic bow that made her lips look vulnerable when she least wanted it. Of course, if her father had raised her in Grasse, she'd probably never have gotten her big break in the perfume industry, either, not even to make perfumes like Spoiled Brat. You had to be a Rosier, or from one of the other big perfume families, to make it here.

"And that told you all you needed to know about me?" He picked up the bottle of bitter almond oil and gazed at it.

"With the help of a little bit of research." Which had produced photo after photo of him, handsome, cool, wealthy, a different beautiful model or actress beside him in each one.

So that the discovery of him at the next night's perfume event, less than twelve hours after she'd left his New York apartment, leaning over supermodel Nathalie Leclair, her back against the wall, her beautiful, sexy face turned the few inches up to his that was all her height needed, had just slid its knife so deep into Jess's gut she still got sick from the wound.

So get over it. This is the industry. Tough the fuck up.
He sure as hell hadn't been so affected by her. As he'd
proven conclusively that Monday, when she'd walked
into her little dream company to discover he had taken
it over.

Lines of tension showed at the corners of Damien's
lips. He was too young to have those lines, but that was
what a man got, when he devoted his entire being to
cutthroat, heartless business.

"I didn't know it was your company," he said
abruptly. "When I took it over."

Oh, yeah, right. As if he didn't know the name and
important information on every single person who had a
stake in that start-up artisan perfume company before
he bought it. "Ignorance isn't your reputation."

Those lines at the corners of his mouth hurt her,
deep down. They hadn't been there, that night. Without
his last name to anchor her in reality, she'd been totally
lost in his sensuality, in that quiet, courteous romance
of him leaning beside her against the terrace wall,
talking, in that curious fascination in his eyes as he
looked at her and lured her in closer to him. The way he
seduced, as careful of her as if he was being seduced,
too. She hadn't seen any lines at the corners of his
mouth that night *at all.*

"I knew Jasmin Bianchi held ten percent of the
shares," he said tightly. "I didn't know you were Jasmin
Bianchi. The same woman who made Spoiled Brat." His
gaze ran over her again, as if trying to unravel her.

No. No more unraveling. "A full name changes
everything, doesn't it?" She tried for ironic, a little
dangerous, like him.

God, the shock of it, when she'd realized he was
Damien *Rosier.* That her wish-on-a-star Prince
Charming was an *actual prince*, at least as far as the
perfume industry was concerned, and way the hell out of
her league.

Why hadn't she let herself realize it before? It wasn't as if there were that many thirty-ish, black-haired, sardonic, elegant, French-accented Damiens likely to be running around a perfume launch party.

"I still can't believe you're the woman who made Spoiled Brat." His lip curled involuntarily over the name of the perfume, and it felt as if he was curling his lip over *her*. After the way his hands had been all over—and inside—her body, that curled lip made her *writhe*. "*You* did?"

"I was being sarcastic at the time." And she'd never again been allowed to be anything else. Every brief that demanded romance, sincerity, dreams, wishing—those went to other perfumers. She got the briefs for perfumes that were supposed to pitch temper tantrums or rake beautiful, polished nails down everyone else's chalkboard.

Until by the time her father died, she hated her career so much that the death of the man who had inspired her into it, coupled with the loss of that dream of a company, had left her huddled on the edge of a precipice, staring into a great void.

"Sarcastic." That fine masculine mouth of his, which gave such a lovely tightness to his vowels, could also form the subtlest, most expressive moue, when it didn't like the flavor of something. She *loathed* being the distaste in his mouth.

Damn Rosier snobs. Her father's stories should have warned her. "Jealous?" Rosier SA commissions were solidly at number four and number seven in perfumes this year, while four years after its release, her Spoiled Brat had only dropped from number two to number three.

He raised an eyebrow. "Well, you've successfully proven that there are no depths to which people's tastes can't sink. I suppose that's a feat to inspire some kind of envy."

From the man who had fit a night with her in between all the supermodels he hung out with. Yeah, he probably thought his own tastes had sunk to new depths, didn't he? *What in the world was I thinking when I slept with her?*

He'd probably been drunk. God, in that milieu, he might have been drugged.

She hadn't been. She'd just been...sad. And so eager to grab onto happiness.

Such a stupid, female thing to do, to let that wish for happiness latch onto the nearest hot guy and imagine that happiness was bottled up in him. That all she had to do was rub it a few times to set it free and let it wash all over her.

And yet, for just that night, that happiness had seemed so damn real. Sometimes, even today, if she didn't pay attention, hope snuck out and she still wanted to believe in that happiness again. Wanted to follow it to France and see if she could wish so hard she could make it come true.

But she was paying attention now, and she shoved that hope down *hard*.

"I really think it was the marketers who proved how low people's tastes can go." *AOS sent me the brief. I was fresh out of perfume school, and ready to prove myself in a cynical industry that had eaten my father alive. So I did it. And did it so damn well I cemented my reputation forever. Nobody believes I can do anything else. Not even, sometimes, me.* She bared her teeth at him. "*I* was making a little industry commentary."

"Congratulations. The industry is suitably destroyed."

Temper flared. Why was she letting him get away with this? She was a perfumer, an *artiste*. He was a moneyman. *She* was supposed to be looking down on *him.*

"At least I don't kick kittens into traffic if I need to, to expand my family's business empire."

His face closed immediately. He stepped back from her, with a tight curve to those fine sensual lips. "Only puppies and baby strollers. I draw the line at kittens."

She wished his eyes matched that ironic expression. That they didn't keep flickering over her and searching her face, as if he couldn't forget what she looked like when he was making her come.

God.

Suddenly she hated everything about the way men and women worked, that no matter how much a woman might try to fight it, somehow it remained true: he had been inside her body, but she hadn't been inside *his.* No matter what now, no matter where, whenever they met, he would always look at her and think about the ways he had owned her, taken her, and she would never, ever own any part of *him.*

She folded her arms. "You know, you can go back into your bottle."

"What?" He blinked.

She reached out again to take the *amandes* bottle from him. His hands tightened on it, the edge of his fingers pressing against hers. "Now that we each know who we really are, I would like you to hand my property back to me and leave. I own this place now." A space. A magic. Something that had lasted for centuries. Something that could be *hers.* As long as she held on tight to it. "Which means that, contrary to what you Rosiers like to assume, you can't possibly."

Their eyes locked a long moment. "You don't think we have anything else to catch up about?"

What, was he bored and thinking another quick lay would be fun?

"*No,*" she said between her teeth, her own lip curling in revulsion. He could take that disdain and arrogance and shove them where the sun didn't shine.

His lips pressed tight together, and it was ridiculous how that hard line emphasized their sensuality. All the things that mouth could be disciplined to do. The scent of bitter almonds rose between them like a physical force, a battle of wills. The glass curved cool under her hands, his warm, taut fingers pressed against hers...

"As you wish," he said finally, with that gorgeously sensual-on-crisp accent of his that seemed to reach right into all her pink parts and tickle them unmercifully. With a tiny ghost of a bow, he loosed the jar, turned around, and walked out.

Wait. "That did not count as one of my wishes!"

He paused at the doorway and glanced back, his eyebrows raised again. His gaze skated up and down her body once, leaving her head to toe in flame. With a shake of his head, he was gone.

Chapter 2

"Tante Colette." Damien paced, which was a damn hard thing to do in that garden. The August sun of Provence warmed it all through, so that even the great medieval walls could not keep it cool, and bees buzzed in rosemary and lavender and every other possible herb a ninety-six-year-old woman could grow in her garden in Provence, the heat releasing the familiar blend of scents into the air.

His family was always doing that to him. Surrounding him with silk and scent and sensory pleasure and expecting him to be the hard one, the merciless one, the one silk slid right off without touching. He made a sharp motion of his hand, trying to slash that warm scented air away from him, but it only waved the scent of bitter almond into the mix. He couldn't get that almond scent off him.

Idiot. You didn't even try. He stopped under the fig tree and stared up at the big brown fruit, just splitting to allow its red richness to peek out. He smelled like the damn Feast of Kings. Like somebody should combine him with those figs and make a tart out of him.

"Did you have something to say, Damien?" Tante Colette asked coolly from her stool in front of the jasmine growing up one wall. Ninety-six, and she was weeding.

They'd tried to do the weeding themselves, but Tante Colette had kept weeding anyway. Until they finally realized that by doing too much of her gardening for her, they were stealing something essential to her happiness. She was exactly like Pépé, their grandfather, who needed to be present at the harvests, who did not want, while living, to yield all the usefulness of his life into younger hands.

Damien hardened his heart. That was his heart's job, right? To stay hard. Untouchable. Every member of a big family had to make his niche for himself, and ruthlessness was his. "Yes. You've crossed the line here, Tante Colette. You gave away *Laurianne's old shop*? To the perfumer who made *Spoiled Brat*?" He knew he was supposed to be the cousin who only cared about money and the bottom line, but, God...Spoiled Brat. It made his skin cringe.

"She came?" A leap of light in those old eyes.

"What is she, another of Léo Dubois's descendants? Or did you decide to give away our heritage to every descendant of every child you rescued during the war, or...what the actual hell?"

Tante Colette's brow wrinkled still more. "And...*you* were the one to discover her first? Not Tristan?"

Damien stiffened, his chest tightening around his heart to keep it still, that old, ulcerous knot lodging in his belly. "Tristan?" His matchmaking aunt had planned Jess for Tristan?

Who, by the way, had a fit and died every time Spoiled Brat was even mentioned.

"Well, I just thought..." Tante Colette searched his face, perplexed. "She seems so...soft for you. At least in her photos."

Damien wasn't his cousin Matt. He didn't have a soft heart, and he didn't need to cover it with folded arms and growls as if it was vulnerable when it clearly wasn't. But sometimes it hurt anyway, as if his family had stabbed him in it, and he couldn't even explain why. "Soft for me?"

Maybe she'd thought so, too. That he was too hard for her, too cold, something. He'd thought...well, yes, that she was all softness and he was all hardness, that night. But it hadn't been a *bad* hard, had it? It hadn't felt that way to him—hot and eager and hungry hardness and wondering, at how much she smelled like happiness to him, at how her pale brown hair lay in such soft, loose curls around her head and slid through his fingers, as if softness and happiness could be real, could come true, could belong to him, too.

Not just the expensive pleasures that money could buy, but real, down deep, utterly free happiness.

He sure as hell hadn't felt *cold* that night, or thought he had been cold to her.

But if she'd agreed on the way that night felt to him, then she would have...wanted to see him again, right? Instead of shutting him away with that cynical mockery, as if he couldn't be trusted in that close to her and she'd made a mistake, letting him get near. It had been like trying to get inside a mirror, when he'd found her again after that night. As if, instead of all that wistful, hopeful sweetness into which he'd sunk that first night, he kept hitting instead against a reflection of himself, of who she saw when she looked at him, until her irony defeated even his.

He reached up and touched the split fig, with just one fingertip.

"I just thought you needed someone more...sardonic." Tante Colette waved a dirt-stained old hand in the air. "Cooler. Tougher."

"She made Spoiled Brat when she was barely out of perfume school," Damien said. "Trust me, she has a strong sense of satire."

Wait, what were they arguing about, exactly? That Jess Bianchi was a better match for him than for Tristan? How did Colette manage these things? They were supposed to be arguing about her insane urge to give away parts of the family inheritance to random pseudo-descendants who had no idea of their value.

And unlike Matt, he was *not* too soft-hearted to fight off threats to his family. His aunt, clearly losing it at last, had given away part of the valley to a rock star semi-descendant of hers only a few months ago, and instead of fighting that threat off, Matt had gone and gotten engaged to the rock star instead.

And that did not make Damien feel wistful at all, damn it.

"Plus, she's a perfumer," Colette said. "I see you with someone more...business-like."

Damien's mouth set hard.

"Or someone long and cool and sleek."

Since old photos indicated that Colette had been long and cool and sleek herself as a young woman, this shouldn't seem like an insult. But somehow it did.

"We seem to have gotten off the subject, Tante Colette. We're not really talking about whether that woman is my soul mate. We're talking about the fact that you gave away a vital part of the family's heritage."

Colette gazed at him for an enigmatic moment. Take a woman who could outsmart the Gestapo when she was only twenty-three and give her seven more decades of experience, and God, but she was a hard read. "Well. If it bothers you so much, Damien, maybe you should get it back."

And she returned to her gardening.

The fig fell off the tree, and his hand whipped out and caught it before it could hit the ground. He stared at it until all he could do was eat it. The sweet pulpiness yielded to his teeth and burst in his mouth as the scents of jasmine and almonds and all the herbs and sun and stone of Colette's gardens crowded in the air around him, as if those scents wanted to eat him, too.

***

Jess stood in the middle of the laboratory, her head tilted back, her eyes almost closed, breathing in its past. *Daddy, make me a cloud.*

And he would bring home the scent of a cloud in a bottle.

Make me a dragon flying. Make me a baby star, that I just picked up and am carrying back up to the sky.

In high school, she had wanted different things. Scents that would make her the most popular girl in

21

school, scents that would make the boy she had a crush on dream only of her. Her father shook his head at those, so she tried to make them herself, experimenting with all the power of the perfume molecules her father let her play with.

He'd warned her that the best scents really only helped you be...you. It was hard, as a teenager, to accept that, when she didn't like *her* and wanted to be someone more glamorous, someone fabulous. A female version of the elegant Damien Rosier, perhaps—cool and collected, her heart impenetrable, always in control. Jane Bond.

She was an idiot still. And she missed her father.

Missed someone who would make baby stars for her.

She rubbed a small bottle wistfully. Jasmine.

She'd made her own wish for happiness once out of jasmine and almond and vanilla. A simple, silly wish no one could ever have believed came from the maker of Spoiled Brat. She'd been so tired of being sad. So she'd snuck a spray of it at the door onto the terrace of a glamorous party, like some stupid child blowing bubbles and hoping they'd bring magic. What kind of magic had she really expected to find at a party like that, full of the image-obsessed luxury crowd, all gathered for the launch of a perfume?

Yeah, it was a dumb place for a woman to try to find happiness, but it was hard for her to figure out where else to hunt for happiness in a big city. Bars? Nightclubs? Bookstores? Parties were where friends pushed introverted people like her, so they would meet people.

She'd sprayed a tiny bit more into the air around her as she tucked herself into a corner of the terrace, her quiet space in the night away from the headache of the party.

She knew that happiness didn't work that way. She knew it didn't follow a woman down elusive trails until it found her. She knew you built your career out of being tough and cynical and that no one cared about your perfumes that smelled like baby stars. But her father had been dying, and she'd felt so incredibly lonely, as if all the baby stars were going to fall from the sky and never be picked back up again.

When a black-haired prince of a man with a fine, ironic pair of lips and an elegant assassin's way of moving had appeared in the terrace door, she hadn't asked too many questions. When he'd gazed at her a moment and then moved slowly over to her, his eyebrows drawn faintly together as if something perplexed him, when he'd leaned beside her against the terrace wall to comment on the view of the city in the night, she'd...let herself believe in wishes.

Just for a little while. Wishing on a baby star.

Her thumb circled against the small glass vial wistfully, once, twice, thri—

A shadow darkened the door between the shop and the back room.

And a long, lean form filled it, the grace and economy of muscle veiled in a business suit, a man who would probably assassinate baby stars if he found them, if they stood in the way of his family's empire building.

Her whole body tightened against the memory of his hands on her, that intent absorption on his face as they stroked down her body, and she set the vial down. "You've got to stop doing that," she said.

One eyebrow went up. If ever a man had been born to raise one eyebrow it was Damien Rosier. Except his eyes were so...not hard, on her. So searching and intent, and so deceptively *not* hard in that hard, controlled face. The color of his eyes was just criminally misleading.

"Doing what?" Damien said coolly.

"Nothing." She shoved the bottle away from her. And bit her tongue on the urge to say, *I wish I had a...* and see what happened.

I wish you would kiss me. I wish I hadn't seen you with that supermodel the next day. Or on all those celeb websites with other models and actresses. I wish I was

23

someone different, the kind of person who could wrap someone like you around my little finger.

I wish you were my happiness, the way I thought you were that night.

I wish that so bad.

Damn you.

"You're in my shop," she said. *Mine. My space. Not yours. This is one thing I'm going to keep.*

His lips took on that lethal line that made them seem so sensual she wanted to take every Disney film and beat it to death to teach that damn company not to make a girl dream of Prince Charming. "Do you really want to push that right now? I can guarantee you that I can get a court to revert this property back to my family."

Oh, yeah, of course. Just as her father said— *everything* had to belong to the Rosiers. She put her hands on her hips. "Then why don't you?"

He turned and moved restlessly through the workshop, his strides slicing too quickly to the end of the room where he paused like a race car on a short street with no outlet. He pivoted back. "I'm not looking forward to hiring a psychiatrist as an expert witness to my aunt's dementia."

"She has dementia?" Jess asked uneasily. That would explain this gift, at least. Maybe, like that night she wished her very own dark-haired prince to her, the shop was just an illusion of happiness that she'd have to give back.

"No," Damien said. "Thus the reluctance." Something brooding and dark shifted over his face. He shoved his hands into his pockets.

"Wow," Jess said wonderingly. "You'd actually hesitate to groundlessly call a family member's sanity into question just to get what you want?" She was intensely proud of her light, ironic tone. *Yes, see? I am tough and cynical, too. I'm the kind of woman who can handle a hook-up just fine and never fall into any trap of dreaming for more.*

24

A slicing, dangerous glance. His hands closed into fists in his pockets.

"Don't let it get out," Jess said. "It would ruin your reputation."

"Don't let it get out that you play with almond and jasmine oil like a kid at Christmas," Damien retorted. "It would ruin yours."

Their gazes locked. Jess fought down the sick sensation in her stomach. She could handle this. She could. Maybe she'd go buy a bottle of her own Spoiled Brat and spray it into the air every time he came near her, to prove that she was *not* the girl who'd worn a flowing romantic dress to a perfume launch party and believed, right up until she got there, that she was as pretty as a princess.

Damien's hands flexed in his pockets. "Jess—"

She turned toward one of the work counters, pretending to organize bottles. "I suppose if you do decide to go after me and destroy me, I'll know. Once it's too late for me to do anything about it, of course."

He gazed at her. A little muscle started to tick in his jaw. "I didn't know it was your company. Jess."

"I didn't know you were a Rosier. Damien."

He shifted away again, gazing at old dusty bottles on a shelf, their labels peeling. "I know."

"What?"

"I know you didn't know who I was. It was…obvious."

She stared at him, not understanding how it could have been obvious or what that hint of brooding around his mouth meant. "And you didn't think it would have been at least polite to correct that?"

"You didn't tell me your last name, either. You didn't even tell me your proper first name."

She tightened her stomach muscles and lifted her chin. "What, if you'd known I was the one who made Spoiled Brat, would you have held your nose while we made 1—?" She bit the word back. Stupid, screwed up vocabulary, always letting slip her secret wishes.

"Had sex?" Damien said flatly.

Yeah. There was the right vocabulary word. She swallowed, trying to force the sickness down into a tight ball inside her where no one could find it, particularly not herself.

"I don't know what I would have done." Damien picked up a delicate perfume bottle—this fantastical romantic whimsy of crystal and fragility—and stared at it in his masculine hand. "Perhaps worn armor."

What did that even mean? Was he talking about condoms? "Good God." She pressed a horrified hand to her belly. "You didn't wear—yes, you did." She definitely hadn't gotten *that* stupidly romantic.

He gazed at her for a blank second. And then, very ironically: "Don't worry. I remembered that kind of armor. Jesus." His hand closed hard on the little crystal bottle.

"Well, yeah," she said. "You must be in the habit."

He'd been gazing broodingly at his fist around the perfume bottle, but his head turned and he stared at her. "What?"

"I mean, it must be an automatism. Otherwise, you'd have a disease by now."

That muscle started to tick in his jaw again, just this fine, subtle proof of tension. "Well. Sex ed in the States must be better than its reputation."

She was growing so sick to her stomach she was afraid that any second she might do something horrible, like cry. She pressed her hands into the counter. "I need you to leave now."

He made an abrupt move toward her, stopping on the other side of the counter from her. "Jess—"

She fisted her hands on the counter. "This is my space." She asserted it adamantly. *Damn you, I don't care what you do, there is one good thing in my life I'm going to keep.* A magic little shop where she could hide away and make scents out of the world. Dream. Wish again. "I know you don't like it, but until you bring that court case, that doesn't change the fact that it's true. I want you to leave."

She couldn't make him, though. Hell, she didn't even know what number to dial for the police in this country.

Black eyebrows drew slowly together. "Jess—"

"I wish you would leave," she said desperately.

He stilled, taking a deep breath. Slowly, he released it, searching her face. And then his fist unfolded from that delicate crystal bottle, and he set it down in the middle of the counter. She caught a glimpse of red indentations from the pointed facets before he slipped his hands in his pockets. He nodded briefly and was gone.

She stared down at the counter, his big handprint in the dust pressed just across from her two small ones. And the exquisite, fragile, gleaming perfume bottle, polished by the grip of his fingers, set precisely halfway between them.

Chapter 3

The morning started soft, dew on the jasmine, the first day of the harvest. They really didn't need all hands on deck in this way, but all the Rosier cousins always turned out the first day, the same way everyone always turned out for Christmas and the harvest of the roses. It was special. It reaffirmed who they were.

Damien's hands moved automatically, a pinch of a jasmine flower, dropped into the wicker basket. The jasmine that they harvested from August into October was more delicate than roses. It required care not to damage the fragile, precious petals. It was also backbreaking, because the plants were so low you had to bend or sit on a stool all the time. This should have been familiar, reassuring work to him. They'd been working these fields since they were children, when they'd been the perfect height for the jasmine and too small to properly reach the roses.

But he couldn't calm down. Tension ran through him, this tight, angry urge to fight a battle, this incipient headache, as if someone had locked him in a room not with fresh jasmine but with that damn Spoiled Brat.

He lifted a handful of his flowers, breathing deep to clear his head, and a bee stung him on the knuckle.

Aïe. Damn it. He went to the truck for some spray.

His grandfather snorted. "Still say lavender oil works the best. Smells better, too. Sure you don't want some?"

With a wry smile, Damien held his burning knuckle out to his grandfather. Pépé dabbed lavender oil on it, and he brought his hand to his face a second, breathing in the blend of jasmine and lavender, tension unknotting all down his back. Sometimes you didn't even know you were tense until the first day of the jasmine harvest, when that smell hit you and everything loosened and the world made sense again.

28

Even down to the bee stings.

All the battles for dominance with other businesses around the world, all the boardrooms and meetings and accounts...it all comes back to this. These petals sliding over my fingers, this scent in my hands. This is where it all started. And this is what it's all about.

Even if his job was always the boardrooms. The business. Taking out family enemies, building empire. While Raoul and Lucien ran off to explore the world, while Tristan spent his life sunk in perfumes, while Matt pretended this valley was what the family could depend on for centuries more, Damien did what had to be done: fought the business battles and won them.

That was his job. No threat to Rosier SA got past *him.*

While other businesses shrank and closed doors, left their empty, broken windows in the heart of Grasse, he spread the power of Rosier SA to every continent on the globe, anchoring not only Grasse's economy but local economies everywhere. While fragrance producers in the valleys around Grasse gave up, sold out to real estate developers because they had no other economic choice, Damien gave his family choices. Power. Wealth.

He, like his father before him, froze his heart and got it done.

And no one, no one in this world, believed he had any softness or warmth to his heart. He looked down at the jasmine flower, delicate and scented against his tan hand. White as his sheets, across which soft, pale brown curls had spread like a gift. As if she trusted him with sweetness and softness, vulnerability and hope.

Raoul came up to them with a basket of jasmine on one arm, his fingers running gently through the flowers before he emptied them into the larger basket at Pépé's feet. The expression on Raoul's face was profoundly eased, like a man who had just sat down in an old comfy armchair in front of his own fireplace after years away at war. Since there was no urgency to the first morning and *they* weren't getting paid by the weight of what they picked, the other cousins drifted up with their jasmine as an excuse to join the social gathering, the way some men might show up with a couple of extra beers in one hand.

Matt, big and growly, turned to watch his fiancée who was incompetently picking jasmine flowers at the end of a row, picking one or two, then pausing to bury her face in her basket and breathe the scent, obscuring the basket so completely that it looked as if her basket had turned into a hedge-hog of bronze-tipped curly hair. Across from her, Raoul's fiancée Allegra picked, and beside them, a couple of bushes farther down the row, Léa and Jolie. The four women had hit it off so well that they turned just about every event into a social occasion, where they talked about anything from careers to politics to silliness and occasionally the men.

Damien looked down at the jasmine in his basket. No woman was over there gossiping about him.

And that didn't bother him in the slightest. Of course not.

Tristan held a single jasmine flower in his hand, twirling it, breathing deeply of its scent, then lifting his head to gaze across the fields and up into the hills. Tristan swore that if he could ever manage a scent that captured, truly captured, the jasmine harvest and not some weak, bloated version of it in a bottle, he would have made his life's contribution to posterity—bottled happiness and strength to pass on to the world.

But even Tristan hadn't managed that. No one had— the ephemeral gorgeousness of reality in a bottle. These days, it wasn't even fashionable to try—perfumers focused on creating works of abstract art, and striving to capture reality made it seem as if your art had been stuck in the Renaissance.

Hell, in the current state of the industry, Spoiled Brat could hold the damn number three spot on the bestseller lists. Clearly, some people's definition of *art* was more abrasive and shudder-producing than others.

"I don't understand why Tante Colette is doing this to us," Damien said abruptly. "I mean, what the actual hell? Okay, fine, so Jasmin Bianchi is presumably another of Léonard Dubois's descendants. That doesn't excuse..." *disinheriting her own family,* he'd been going to say. Except, fuck, maybe it did excuse it. After all, maybe the grandchildren of her adopted son, even if she did have him for only eight years before he ran away, did count as much as the grandchildren of the stepbrother with whom she maintained such a combative relationship. Except that both the part of the valley she had given Layla and this shop were *Rosier* heritage. From centuries past.

"Spoiled Brat." Tristan clutched his head. "She gave *Laurianne's shop* to the perfumer who made *Spoiled Brat.*"

"I told my father," Pépé said. "I *told* him not to trust any of the family heritage into her hands."

"Laurianne's perfume shop," Tristan said. "*Spoiled Brat.*" He yanked at his own black hair.

"She gave away a chunk of my valley," Matt grumbled. Damien's big bear of a cousin was supposed to be heir to all the valley around them, the family patriarch in training, and he practiced for it by growling all the time. "We need to sit on that damn Antoine Vallier until he learns to quit doing this shit."

Antoine Vallier was the new lawyer in Grasse who kept helping Tante Colette deed over her property to random strange semi-descendants from the other side of the world. Every single one of them—besides Tristan, who had gone to school with the guy and anyway didn't do that kind of thing—had gone and threatened him personally with the consequences of making enemies out of the Rosiers.

And he still kept doing it. The guy must be suicidal, there was no other explanation.

"Are you still complaining about that?" Layla asked, coming up with a wicker basket brimming with jasmine flowers over one arm. Despite her Lebanese blood and the sun-friendly skin it should have given her, Matt had covered her with so much sunscreen that white patches marked her face under the big floppy hat Matt had settled on her head. She looked entirely delighted with herself, though, and if she kept bringing great handfuls of jasmine to her face like that, she was going to get stung on the nose.

Matt looked down at her, and his expression softened. He framed her face to rub the white blotches of sunscreen in better with the most incredible gentleness in his big, callused hands, shaking his head slowly.

Damien looked away, embarrassed. He could not get used to Matt's heart being all exposed like that. He kept wanting to tell his cousin to put some damn clothes on the thing.

Thank *God* Damien didn't have such a tender, easily wounded heart. A memory of a night in New York lanced through him, just like that, and he stamped it down. *Shaken, not stirred,* he made his heart say. *My name is Bond, James Bond.*

Or would it be better if his heart had been stirred not shaken?

It was just a cocktail, God damn it. My heart wasn't affected at all.

Just like hers wasn't.

"Why don't you just ask her?" Raoul's girlfriend Allegra said cheerfully, and Damien almost said, *Because every time I try she makes it clear she thinks it was a mistake, letting me in that close.*

"Why she's doing it," Allegra elaborated. "You could try *talking* to her. She's your aunt."

Oh. She meant Tante Colette.

Allegra stopped beside Raoul to smile up at him. Raoul had returned from Africa quite adamantly at Christmas, his russet hair streaked with a premature charcoal, looking and acting like a wolf come in out of the cold to inspect the contents of the nearest warm barn. But Allegra fed him cookies, and all of Raoul seemed to ease into calm whenever she came near him.

In fact, even when she wasn't around, you could tell when he thought of her by the way his face relaxed.

Something about it twisted Damien's middle into a tight, jealous pang, and he didn't even know why. Allegra was not remotely his type. And unlike Matt and Raoul, he wasn't grumpy or wild. He didn't need anyone to help calm him down—he had control of *himself.*

"*You* could ask her," Damien said, disgruntled. "If I ask her, she'll say something cryptic."

"You could ask her," Layla said sweetly to their grandfather, Colette's stepbrother. "She's your sister."

Pépé gave her the look he used to crush insolence.

"Well, she might tell you," Layla said, friendly and about as uncrushable as her exuberantly curly hair. She brought a handful of jasmine to her face and breathed deep. "In honor of all those times you two worked together to save children during the Occupation."

"If I were you, I wouldn't go burying my nose in any pretty thing you decide is supposed to smell sweet," Pépé told her. "It's a good way to get stung."

"Pépé," Matt said, low and growly.

"Anyway, if this girl's last name is Bianchi, she's probably some kind of cousin of yours," Pépé told her. "I know perfectly well who that Bianchi boy's real father was. I don't need to ask Colette. I'm the one who told her that boy was getting girls pregnant around here." He grimaced. "Léonard had a mother who would give her life to save others, and her boy turned out...like that."

Layla just stood there, dumbfounded. "I have a cousin?"

A cousin? Merde. Damien had four first cousins on his father's side—three of them standing right here—five more on his mother's side, and so many second and third cousins that he couldn't even begin to count them. He knew, technically, that Layla had a much more limited family than the Rosiers did, but the stunned, hopeful expression on her face at the idea of having *a* cousin really brought the difference home.

"Given the way that boy of hers behaved, you might have several. Maybe more than we even know about," Pépé growled.

All his grandsons just stared at him. This was a little bit beyond their capacity for imagination, children trailing around who weren't solidly embedded in the expectations of family, particularly step-cousins who might show up out of nowhere and claim all the family heritage Tante Colette held. Hell, there was her house in Sainte-Mère still, too. And God knew how many family heirlooms. She'd produced Niccolò Rosario's war-lost seal for Matt, and an old Renaissance perfume box Niccolò's mother had had made for him for Raoul, but so far she hadn't shown any inclination to trust anything as heart-precious as their family heirlooms to Damien.

Even though he spent his whole fucking life fighting to protect everything that was fragile and precious to his family.

"Well, in that case, you might, too," Layla said sweetly, not looking away from Pépé. "After all, you had a son run off, too." Lucien's father, although he'd done it at forty-five and not sixteen. "And are you one hundred percent sure that all those boys of yours always used their heads about contraception, starting way back in the fifties?"

Now not only might they have unnumbered step-cousins, but Layla was peopling their family with any number of unidentified half-siblings, too. When they already felt they couldn't all quite fit together in the same valley. They stared at her, appalled and fascinated.

Matt bent his head to her ear to mutter: "He's older than the Pope. Catholic country. Maybe let's not talk about contraception?"

"Well, *you* know how to use con—"

Matt covered her mouth with his hand and turned beet red. Even Damien had to grin. Layla made Matt so damn happy. That happiness seemed to fill this whole valley with a radiant rose- and jasmine-scented luminosity, so that it was all he could do not to pull out

34

his phone and start cementing another business deal right that second, to wall more money and power around that valley and keep that happiness safe.

Pépé frowned at Layla. "That is just about enough out of you."

"Pépé." Matt folded his arms across his chest. "She can say what she wants." And, sotto voce to Layla, "Will you behave?"

Layla grinned.

"So who's on this one?" Pépé asked. "Not you," he told Matt severely. "You clearly couldn't battle a flea." He gave Layla a crushing look.

"I'm tougher than I look," Layla told him sweetly. She made fists and pretended a boxing stance.

Pépé had to firm out a twitch of his lips.

Matt folded his arms and growled. "I got it back, didn't I?"

"You got lucky," Pépé said. "This time I want someone ruthless. Someone who can go for the kill and not go soft over a pretty face." He turned and said that thing that always iced Damien's heart: "Damien. It will have to be you."

Chapter 4

Damien moved through the empty shop, where the scent of Christmas played with the scent of jasmine and vanilla and rose, and older scents sulked in corners, wondering when their new owner would rub them awake, too. Traces of her fingerprints were everywhere in the dust on bottles pulled down from shelves and left on counters. And there, on that bottle of bitter almond oil, were the marks of his.

He made a sharp motion of his hand, trying to cut through the scents that came for him. But they curled around his fingers like a woman's soft wavy locks.

Jess did the exact same thing his family did—surrounded him with silk and sweetness and expected him to be the hard one, who didn't give a damn.

And yet that night, she hadn't seemed to expect cynicism from him at all. As he leaned beside her on the terrace, they'd talked about the view like two ordinary, unsophisticated strangers trying to make a connection. About the way the sky flipped upside down in New York so that all the dazzle of the night was human, below, tense and greedy and a little harsh, for all its beauty, and about other places in the world, where the night softened human stresses away and the stars came out above. *Have you ever been to Morocco, the desert, at night?* No, but she'd driven through Texas, talked about feeling that she could reach her hand into the sky and pluck a handful of stars.

That quiet way she talked, a little shy, a little hungry for stars, and the way he'd laid his words under hers like a firm, sure path closer to him: *You can trust me with this shyness, this dreaming. I like it.* The way her forearms had pressed against the terrace wall so close to his, and the way he'd let the itch build and build in his palm to cover her smaller hand before he finally, barely yielded to it, lightly stroking his fingers up two of hers and over her knuckles. The way she'd drawn a little breath and looked up at him, dusky eyes wide.

And wanting.

As if she thought he was her wish come true.

It had felt as if he'd found his heart. That heart that he'd stashed away somewhere long ago, in the service of his family, suddenly, it was his again. As alive and beating as it once had been.

Or maybe it had felt as if *she'd* found his heart. Dug it out of its secret evil sorcerer hiding place, only she wasn't on a quest to kill him with a dagger through it, she was holding it in gentle, wondering hands.

Yeah, right.

Nobody did that with him. Gave him gentleness or trusted him to have any of his own.

And it turned out, she hadn't trusted him with it either. Fuck, maybe that softness was because she'd had a glass too many of champagne and he hadn't even realized it.

He stopped in the door of the workshop.

Jess Bianchi stood on her tiptoes on the very edge of a counter, reaching for the highest shelf, her thumb rubbing away the dust that covered the label on a jar.

Her legs looked fantastic in that whimsical white sundress, her bare feet arched, the dress clinging to her torso and butt as she stretched, a wobble away from falling and cracking her head.

He moved under her and had to take a second to enjoy that round, firm butt just above his head before he could bring himself to mess up the view. "Jess."

She gave a startled cry, clutched for the bottle as her toe slipped off the edge of the counter, and fell with a scream.

He caught her, of course, pulling her in hard to his chest. *I've got you. You're okay.* The dress was a more informal style than the one she had worn that night, but the skirt had that same romantic flow of fabric over his arm, that pale color, as if he'd caught something as young and innocent as a dream.

Even though it had taken him no effort at all to catch her, the heart he wasn't supposed to have started to beat too hard. Waking up, hopeful, like a child half asleep but just starting to remember from the scents in the air that it was Christmas.

And she yanked away from him as hard as she could, putting a good two meters between them, clutching the jar that had fallen with her. "What the hell was the point of that? To scare me? To let me know I'm in your power?"

He checked a tiny second. Not too long, he didn't think. He just had to stop his heart beating, had to put that damn organ back away, buried under some great tree in an ancient forest, where she couldn't get at it. It hurt, putting it back. The hole for it felt dark and small and damp.

A child being stuffed into a closet when all the other kids were opening their presents.

He had to press his lips together hard. "I was just—" His gaze got distracted on her hair, a lock pulled free from that loose knot between her shoulders and tangled over her face. He rubbed his thumb over the side of his finger, trying to scrape the sensation of that hair away. "I thought you would fall no matter where I said your name, so it was better I be right under you."

She stared at him distrustfully, the dusk of her eyes all dark gray now, no blue.

His fingers curled into his palm. "I'd hate for you to die when I was on the premises," he said sardonically. "Even the Rosier name might not get me off for that one."

Jesus. Were they actually talking about whether he might *murder* her? When she...that night...that way she'd seemed to *trust him.* With everything that was soft and sweet and true.

Fuck.

38

He wanted to hit someone.

Maybe a mirror of himself.

"I brought Mace," she said, and pulled a little bottle out of her pocket.

He took a step back, in a reflex against actual Mace, and then made out what she held: a small bottle of perfume. A perfumer of her caliber could definitely find oils in this shop that would blind a man or leave him coughing uncontrollably if sprayed into his face.

Then he recognized the shape of the bottle and laughed before he even realized that laugh was going to happen. It was Spoiled Brat.

Humor sparkled across her face, this flash of self-satisfaction. She waved the bottle menacingly.

"You wouldn't dare." The joke of it eased something in him like a flash of light. He'd always liked to laugh. He used to do it with his cousins all the time, until they started giving him migraines. "Spray that crap in this shop? Ruin the air in this place?"

She pressed her finger on the spray button, her eyebrows arching. He liked the way mischief and menace brought out the strength in that heart-face of hers. "Are you going to leave quietly?"

"Centuries of our history. A family heritage. And you're going to ruin that with one twitch of your finger?"

"I thought you said Laurianne was a glove-maker. Meaning descended from tanners. This place has had worse scents in it than Spoiled Brat."

"Hardly," he said dryly. He liked battles of wits, liked using words as rapiers, and he liked the edge of humor that ran along the blades here, a flickering glimpse of a night of happiness...kept back at sword's point. But he wondered what he'd done that night that had made him seem so untrustworthy in close to everything soft and vulnerable of hers. When he'd thought...he'd thought...*fuck.*

She drew the bottle back a little. "Did you just say my perfume smells worse than animal skins soaking in urine?"

"At least the urine was an honest scent. True."

She looked at her bottle a second. "You know, if you're not careful, I really am going to spray you with this stuff."

"Jesus." He shuddered. "It probably doesn't wash off for days. The molecules you used in that thing."

She gazed at it another moment and then at him, a scary look in her eye. He backed up a step. "Seriously. Don't."

She gave a slow, wicked, lopsided smile that was so exactly what he'd *hoped* to wake up to that morning after, instead of an empty apartment, that he got caught by it. "It will make it easier for them to find the culprit if my dead body turns up."

He got ready to drop behind the counter. "What are the police going to do, sniff the wrists of all the suspects?"

"They'd have to call in your own cousin as an expert witness against you," Jess agreed mournfully. "One Rosier pitted against another. Imagine the scandal."

No prosecutor around Grasse would be idiot enough to expect one Rosier to testify against another. "If you inflict that thing on me, I'm going to grab it from you and spray you all over with it."

And *that*, maybe, would convince his heart to go back into that damn, dark hole. At least then, she'd smell like what she wanted him to think she was—spoiled and hard and careless, of her own heart and everyone else's.

She lifted the bottle, narrowed her eyes. "*Are* you going to leave quietly?"

He resigned himself to the torture and put on his game face. "No." *Show your true colors now. Spray me.*

She stood there, stuck, for a long moment. And then she frowned in something close to a sulk and looked down at the little bottle. "Damn it." She set it down. "All those self-defense lessons are right. Never draw a weapon unless you'd be willing to fire it."

His hand snaked out to snag the bottle and pocket it, so he didn't have to run *that* risk again. Spoiled Brat. Hell.

"Hey. I just spent a hundred dollars on that thing."

He removed one of his cufflinks and set it on the counter where the bottle had been. "I'll trade."

She stared not at the cufflink but at his wrist where it had been. Color appeared suddenly on her cheeks, and with it a slow heat swept up through his body. He wanted to lose another cufflink. He wanted to find an excuse to trade away every single item of clothing he wore, one by one, in this slow, deliberate striptease until she was blushing all over her body.

That night, he'd stopped with his shirt off so that she didn't catch fire. And he'd loved it, loved the flame and fascination in her, loved pulling her into his bare chest and kissing her in little toying kisses, seducing her, until she forgot to be unnerved.

He fingered his second cufflink. "Not good enough? You want the full set?" She could pawn the pair of cufflinks for ten times the cost of that tiny bottle of Spoiled Brat, but who cared about the bottom line? Their value was in the blush on her cheeks.

She swallowed and took a step back, color deepening.

Well...*well.* He removed that second cufflink and set it beside the other with a little click.

She stared at his wrist. Then her gaze tracked up his torso helplessly until she reached the open collar, when she closed her eyes tightly. She swallowed again.

At this point, that night, he'd abandoned his cufflinks on the dresser and moved toward her, running his hands down her arms. *I've got you, you know. Thank you. Thank you for trusting me with your wishing.*

Now he fingered his watch. She could pawn *that* to buy a car. A nice car. His father had given it to him when he orchestrated his first smooth takeover of a dangerous Rosier SA rival.

He unfastened the band.

"Don't!" she said, strangled.

"I don't want to cheat you." His voice came out silky and a little mean. *You're always the mean one, Damien.* Matt, pissed off and growling carelessly that way he did, as if his damn temper bounced off his cousins. *Machiavellian.*

"Are you kidding me?" Her breasts were shifting in beautiful little pants, her face flushed and panicked. "That's worth way more than a bottle of Spoiled Brat! For something like that, I'd have to make you your own custom perfume."

His fingers froze on the watch, as the fantasy of it caught him—her making a scent for him, testing it on his skin to see how it blended with his natural scents. The time it took to do something like that properly, as she tested it through top notes, middle notes, bottom notes to make sure it was perfect for him all the way through…time in this shop, under her hands, fulfilling whatever fantasy she made of him.

And then his gut clenched around the reality. God knew what perfume she'd make to represent *him.* Something mean. Machiavellian. Some masculine variant of Spoiled Brat, maybe. Maybe she'd call it *Assassin.* The kind of perfume a woman made for a guy whose apartment she snuck out of while he was still asleep, and to whom she spoke with arch, light, flippant indifference ever after, to make sure he knew that nothing of value had been offered by her that night.

And nothing of value received by her either.

He swallowed down the tightness in his throat. And then just ripped the watch off, making himself do it.

He set the watch down in the middle of the counter by the cufflinks, dark, brushed titanium, a gauntlet thrown down.

You can't break me, that watch said.

Or did it say, *I yield.*

***

The dark titanium band curled on top of the counter amid those bottles of scents. All the hair on Jess's body lifted. She couldn't breathe. Shallow sips of air got stuck in the top of her lungs.

"What are you doing?"

"Not enough?" His hands shifted to the lapels of his coat. "This is Dior, hand-tailored. Will that be enough?" He held her eyes, his glittering with...anger? Why would he be angry? "How much of me are you worth?"

All of you, that stupid hope in its bottle tried to whisper. She shoved it back down. Of course he did not think she was worth all of him. That was her fantasy. But she got to decide her own worth, and if he couldn't pay it that didn't mean she had to give herself to him cheaply. Not again. She firmed her chin. "More than that."

He peeled off the coat, his eyes locked on hers. She couldn't hold his gaze. Her own wanted to dart all over the place—his chest, his shoulders in that fine white shirt, the lean waist and flat stomach that she remembered touching—

The coat draped over the counter, beside the watch.

All the scents in the shop exploded in her brain like fireworks, leaving nothing but colors and longing. "Stop!"

He reached for his cuff. "Tell me," that mean, velvet panther's purr, "when I've bid high enough."

"None of that's worth any of me!"

Deft, tan, masculine fingers rolled up his cuff to reveal half his forearm.

43

"Then what's worth you, Jess?" That dangerously sensual menace, like the soft pad of a panther's feet as it backed a mouse into a corner.

"A heart!" she said wildly. His fingers stilled on his cuff. His eyes lifted suddenly to hers, the sea just before dawn.

Oh, God, what had she just admitted about her romantic, wistful insides? She yanked herself back from the counter. "Nothing *you* can give!"

He didn't move a muscle. Not the fingers on his cuff, not the taut, strong forearm half-revealed, not even a shift of his chest to breathe. And then the fine muscles at the corners of his lips pressed down, revealing again the tiny lines he was too young for, and he dropped his left arm.

"Well, obviously not if you want a heart," he said sardonically. "You're sure you wouldn't accept a more practical form of currency for one of your perfumes? Hard to deposit a heart in a business account."

Oh.

Oh, they were talking about...a perfume. How had she gotten so confused as to think they were talking about her? About him? Her face flamed.

Daddy, make me a baby star.

Daddy, make me a dragon's call.

"They are worth that, though," she murmured wistfully.

"What?"

"Somebody's heart," she said, hopelessly. "A real perfume is." A perfume made out of the perfumer's own heart.

But that kind of exchange didn't work, as her poet-perfumer of a father had learned, as work of his art after work of art got eaten up by accountants in the designer houses or floundered and failed to attract any but a niche group of buyers once released. Nobody wanted to give their hearts. They wanted Spoiled Brat—their own scent version of a selfie. *Look at me! It's all about me! Love me, but don't expect me to ever turn this camera around and point it at you.*

"Well. Since I obviously don't have one of those," Damien said with a dark, vicious irony, "perhaps we could agree on some other price."

"For...a perfume?"

"That's right."

"A custom perfume...from me?" She didn't mean to put that incredulous emphasis on *me*, but...well, Spoiled Brat had permanently condemned her in the eyes of most perfumers. Like a top chef who launched a frozen food line. The nose who had made Spoiled Brat was not exactly the kind of nose the financial elite of the world went to for their unique, classy, bespoke perfume. Heads of marketing, on the other hand, practically kissed the air every time her name was mentioned.

Of course, he *was* the moneyman. And Spoiled Brat made money.

"Yes." He rolled up his right cuff.

God, she wished he would quit undressing. Or maybe just...start on the buttons running down his chest. Undo them, like he had that night, one...by one...by one...

"To sell?"

"Oh, no." The danger and power of him filled the room like a scent that obscured all the others. "Only for me."

She blinked down at the cufflinks, watch, and coat on the counter. She didn't even know what they were worth. Twenty thousand? Probably a fair price for a custom, unique perfume from a top perfumer.

Which she of course *was*. Spoiled Brat had hit number two, no matter how much that infuriated the academy of good taste.

She'd had such a hope of breaking out of the Spoiled Brat role with the start-up niche perfume company she'd helped found with quixotic actress Tara Lee, but then...well, he'd happened to that dream. Just snatched it right up without a single person even needing to talk to her about it, leaving her with ten percent of the shares in a start-up that had just been swallowed whole by one of the major fragrance companies. *Exactly* what she'd been trying to get away from.

"Shall I write you a check?" Damien said.

"No." She put her hand over the items. "No. I'll take these."

Exactly what she'd gotten from him the last time. The removal of a few items of clothing for the chance to touch him, while she, like an idiot, had thought they were reaching for each other's hearts.

Her hand closed around the titanium watch, and she picked it up. Scratchproof sapphire crystal, a black sapphire for the crown, dark gray titanium case and band. Unbreakable. Impenetrable. Merciless.

It would be a good reminder to her, when dealing with him.

"Who gave you this?" she asked ironically. "Your last model girlfriend?" Good God, it was a Cartier. Had her guess for the worth of the items placed on the counter been a full zero too low?

"My father. On behalf of the family." He held out his upturned wrist.

Chapter 5

That bare wrist made jitters grow in her stomach and then stretch out in leaping pulses through her body as if she'd drunk far too much caffeine. She tried to breathe deep, but she couldn't get the jitters to calm down. Strong wrist, upturned to offer its most vulnerable point to her. Strong masculine hand, closed against her, in a fist. White sleeve turned back.

The watch that would have made any attack bounce off that wrist now lay in her hand, abandoned armor.

He'd taken it off once before for her. Forgotten on his wrist, it had caught in her hair, and he'd disentangled it and tossed it to the side of the bed as if it was worthless, compared to the moment he was caught in. He'd stroked his fingers through her hair to ease the sting from the pull of the watch, and kissed her in this tender, intense apology that had felt so...precious...

She swallowed, setting her jaw against the urge to sink her head into her hands and cry. Exactly as she had done after she had seen him with that model, after she had learned of his takeover of her dream company, after she'd wanted to confide in her father that she'd met a guy but was afraid of getting hurt...and hadn't been able to confide in him, because he was dying. Her wish had failed, and all the stars in all the world were winking out, leaving nothing but the harsh lights of the city and her standing looking down at them, all alone.

God, it had been such a bad time.

"What, do you expect me to come up with something perfect for you on the spot?" she demanded.

"You did before."

Her gaze flew to his. Unbelievably, his lashes lowered, black veiling his eyes. His jaw was so hard.

He couldn't possibly be talking about a perfume, since she'd never worked for Rosier SA.

She didn't know what else he could be talking about. Not...well, not *her*. That didn't make any sense at all.

Even if *he* had felt perfect to her. Utterly, vulnerably, heartbreakingly perfect, so perfect she'd been scared of how brutal the morning after might be and run away.

You didn't want the prince to wake up and be, well...the vice president and official assassin of one of the major fragrance companies of the world, in charge of expanding empire and cutting down opposition at any cost, so entitled and so hardened that he hooked up with a new model or actress at every event he went to. In short, she definitely didn't want to wake up to find out her night prince was him.

Leaving him sleeping had let her keep her illusions for, oh, nearly twelve hours more.

Like letting a doctor's call go to voicemail because if she could just not answer, she could pretend for a few more hours that the world was what she wanted it to be.

"You're the nose," Damien said dryly. "I'm just the man who makes money off people like you. What do you think the first step should be?"

Her first step should...should probably be to touch that wrist. To smell his skin. To close her eyes and relax her brain and let herself sink into him—into who he was and who he wanted to be to the world. To understand both the deepest heart of him and the face of himself he preferred to show, and to make from that understanding the perfect blend that would allow him both to be true to himself and yet only give what he chose of himself to the whole wide world.

God, that sounded dangerous.

"Put your wrist down," she snapped. "You make me feel like a damn vampire." Except...not. He made her want to lower her mouth to his wrist and...not bite. Not take. Instead of fangs, she wanted to stroke that vulnerable, strong wrist with the softness of her lips, wanted to close her eyes into the sensation of his skin against hers, wanted to steal a little taste with her tongue...

Heat burned in her cheeks and in her breasts.

"You don't need to revisit my scent, then?" Damien lowered his hand. Ruthless eyes locked with hers. "You can work with it from memory?"

She glared at him. "No." *Yes.* Her face was so pitifully hot, exposing all her vulnerability to him. "It's not as if you're going to wear it on your wrist and wave it around for everyone to smell." Women did that, so desperate to change what the world thought of them by the perfume they sprayed on their wrists.

"Suit yourself." He slipped his hands into his pockets. And she felt bereft, as if she'd just lost a precious chance. "I want you to fail."

What? Her spine straightened against the words, and she didn't even know what he was talking about yet.

His mouth curved faintly, a smile that could strip a woman naked and toss her out in the snow. "You think you deserve *this* shop? In my family since the Renaissance? Where one of the greatest fragrance dynasties on the planet was founded? Just because your father told you poor-pitiful-me stories about how tough it is to make it in our world? Then you'd better show me what you can do. Before I have you kicked out of this shop and out of this town so fast your head will spin."

His tone froze her skin. Her heart panicked, as if she'd just broken through ice and plunged into the deathly cold beneath the surface. When she'd just been twirling in her skates across the surface. Oh, yes, *that* was why he didn't have ice-blue eyes. Because that gray-green water under the ice was much, much more deadly.

Damien Rosier.

She'd bought that reputation of his. She'd believed it. She'd pulled back from him and his business takeovers and different-model-a-night life, and she'd thrown up every barrier she could to protect herself. But she hadn't realized that somewhere, deep down, she still believed in that dream of his gentleness and sweetness.

Because that was all that she herself had truly known.

"You think I *can't* come up with a scent for you?" she asked between her teeth. "That's why you asked? So you could set me up?"

His eyes were so cold, uninterested. He ran his gaze over her, checking for weak spots and finding so many she bored him. It was barely worth his time to take her out.

"*I made the number two perfume when I was only twenty-four years old.* And it's still at number three!"

He shrugged, this panther's move of *God, this mouse is dull.* "That's why I bought out your little start-up. So I could have you and you could make that kind of fortune for us."

Yeah. Shutting off her bright, daydreaming path away from her reputation, ending her great, financial gamble that was supposed to allow her to make *art* again, perfumes that made her proud, that made her happy. Baby stars.

He'd stolen that from her.

And *hell.* Was it really her name that had attracted the sharks like blood would and brought that dream of theirs down?

"I sold my shares! You *don't* own me!"

"So you got away." He opened one hand, a glimpse of calluses through the elegance. "And now you're right here." He didn't have to add what rang through every street in the town and echoed in the valleys all around: *In Grasse. In the heart of my power.*

Her fists clenched. Ghosts of her father danced in her head—how he'd had to leave Grasse to even have a chance of finding a place in the perfume world when he wasn't part of a family like the Rosiers, how he'd always felt like an exile.

"And if you want to stay here," Damien said, with the bored ease of a man who knew she didn't stand a chance against him, "then you have to make a scent that *I* would wear." His lips curled faintly, pure disdain. "When you don't even know your art well enough to smell my skin."

She reached across the counter to grab his wrist in both hands and yank it to her.

He locked his arm, making it clear that if he didn't want to give her a second chance at his wrist, then she wouldn't get one. And then he relaxed his muscles and let her pull his hand out of his pocket to her.

The counter lay between them. Thank God.

When she bent her face to his wrist, her heart beat so hard in her head that she could barely even *smell*. His palm was right there, big and warm as it had been that night. With the slightest move of her head or his hand, he could cup her cheek.

But he didn't.

And she didn't.

She closed her eyes and took a slow breath of his wrist. "Cheap citrus. You must have washed your hands last at a restaurant or something. You can't tell me Rosier SA stocks that in their restrooms."

He said nothing.

The back of her head, where his gaze must rest, burned. The whole line of her back burned. Her butt even burned, and he couldn't possibly see that from his angle.

"Lavender," she said curiously, turning his hand over to follow it to his knuckle. "Under the citrus. A nice lavender, too bad you had to wash most of it off."

"It's good for bee stings," he said, and she opened her eyes to note the red swelling over one knuckle. Ow. That must have hurt.

A sudden urge swept through her to kiss that spot to help make it feel better.

She turned his hand back over quickly, to hide the sting from her lips, and angled her head up his wrist, away from the distraction of that soap. A smile wanted to cross her lips at the faintest wisp of scent that she caught, that scent of happiness, and she fought it back. "A little almond, still."

A vision of him in the shower, quick and indifferent to himself, in and out so fast that he hadn't really soaped his arms, so that the scent of almonds from the day before still clung wherever he hadn't rubbed.

Oh, damn, that vision of him in the shower. All that lean, hard body of his...

She swallowed and angled her head up the veins and tendons of his forearm. Such a strong forearm, and yet if she cut him there, he could bleed his heart out just like any other human. A leap of sensual curiosity. "Jasmine?"

He wore jasmine?

Fresh oil, unadulterated, as if it came straight from the plant or somebody's wishful thinking. She'd made her wish for happiness once out of almond, jasmine, and vanilla.

"I was helping with the harvest this morning," he said.

"The harvest?" She lifted her head to look at him. His face was too close. As close as it had been that night just before he kissed her. There had been so much...courtesy in that kiss. *I want you*, that kiss had said. *But let me know if I'm going too fast.*

"That's how Rosier started," he said in that ironic way, as if nothing he said could give his auditor purchase on him. "With a glove maker in this shop who needed scents to perfume her gloves. And with an Italian mercenary who got her a valley and filled it full of flowers. We still have that valley. We still harvest those flowers."

And, yes, August would be the start of the jasmine season here. She tried to wrap her mind around Damien Rosier, the cool, lethal businessman, carefully picking the fragile white jasmine and laying it flower by flower into a basket, so that its precious petals would not be harmed. She could only imagine it if...she remembered the way he had treated her, that night.

Believing that he could pick jasmine was kind of like believing...that night had been true.

Her heart seized, terrified.

"She made him the most exquisite pair of scented gloves as a wedding gift," Damien said. "The family preserved them forever, until they got lost in the war. Or until Tante Colette stole them, according to my grandfather. Which would be better—at least she wouldn't have let them get ruined."

Scented gloves. Jess knew the history of perfume, of course, knew how the power of Grasse in the perfume world had grown out of its tanning roots, the hunger for the Renaissance world to find ways to sweeten the scents of leather gloves, knew the vital status symbol gloves had been. But it was still odd to hold Damien's very masculine hand in hers and imagine a similar hand, an Italian mercenary's, and scented gloves.

"I wonder how Niccolò felt," Damien said, unexpectedly low. "When Laurianne took that hard, mercenary hand and slid over it that softest kid leather that she'd embroidered with silk and scented with ambergris and roses, just for him."

Jess looked down at his hand in hers. A line of calluses showed subtly at the base of his fingers and more visibly at the tips.

"They must have been scarred everywhere, his hands." Damien's voice dropped to a pitch that made her very skin vibrate for it. "From fighting everyone's battles for them. For money. And she gave them warmth, and softness, and sweetness, and beauty. As if they deserved that."

Jess couldn't stop looking at his hand. The *beauty* of that masculine hand, of that strong wrist, of the way the rolled sleeve contrasted with the tanned skin that grew paler there at the inside of his wrist.

That hand fisted slowly in her hold, tightening the tendons and muscles of his forearm under her fingers, and he pulled his arm away from her, stepping back from the counter. When she looked up at him, his face was completely closed.

Only those gray-green eyes looked as dark and brooding as the sea.

"Sit down," Jess said.

His eyebrows shot up. Apparently people didn't give Damien Rosier orders that often.

She pulled a folding chair away from the wall, an old thing made of wooden slats, leaning on top of a little round table also folded against the wall. Once Colette Delatour or some employee of this place must have set this chair and table out in front of the shop every day to eat or take the air and chat with passersby, just like everyone else in this town seemed to do.

"Sit," Jess said. "If I'm going to make you a scent, then I need to get at your skin."

"Or under it?" Damien said ironically.

She looked at him quickly.

He looked away. And then sat, still not looking at her. Was it her imagination, or did he not like letting her stand above him? His self-control gave so little purchase on him that it was hard to tell.

Her heart beat so hard she felt light-headed. It was all she could do not to reach out and grab one of those straight shoulders for support. Or at least just rest her hand lightly there, caress the shape of muscle and strength through that fine veil of white.

She moved behind him, where at least he couldn't see the flame in her cheeks.

He held still. The tension in him as she came behind him and he refused to turn his head grew palpable.

"Are you wearing any scent now?"

"*Non.*" His word came out too crisp, bitten off.

"This is where you would wear it, if you did." She bent.

Mistake. Coming behind him had seemed safer than approaching from the front, turning *him* into the vulnerable one. But now, to reach the open collar of his shirt, she had to bend her head past his shoulder, until her hair spilled over it, until her face was essentially nuzzling the side of his neck and hollow of his throat. Her hands pressed against his shoulders to keep her balance. They were steady as steel under her fingers, but warm and resilient.

The shirt got in her way, despite the open collar. His fingers shifted against her hair and a knuckle brushed her cheek as he undid another button.

And then another.

She kneaded her hands into his shoulders, trying not to fall into him. Her brain fogged, lost in this warm, human maleness of his scent that held a hint of...citrus again. Lemon verbena maybe. A much nicer quality than the scent that had been on his hands.

"What soap do you use?" *In the shower. All over your naked body.*

"My Tante Colette makes soaps for us for Christmas." His voice sounded rough.

There was something oddly sweet about his words. This wealthy, ruthless businessman...who got homemade soaps from his old aunt and used them.

She pulled back before she could just bury her nose in the hollow of his throat and maybe even nibble at it. See how rough his voice grew when she did...

"Okay." She moved away quickly, back to the other side of the counter. "I've got it. I'll have to start running some tests of things today."

Damien didn't move. The small chair emphasized his size—tall, broad-shouldered, almost lounging. A panther. Even to the green in his eyes as he pinned her with them, just waiting for weakness to show. "That was fast."

"I'm just getting started," she said brusquely, spreading papers and bottles in pretense of work. *Please go away now. Let me pull myself together.*

"And here I thought you were a trained perfumer," he said, so infuriatingly she clutched a bottle and pressed it hard onto the counter to keep from throwing it at his head. "Men have layers."

"Like onions," she agreed solemnly, flexing her fingers on that bottle.

He checked, and then laughter flashed across his face. He tried to catch it back, but it curled up the corners of his lips. "Like parfaits."

Laughter. That leaping, hot humor, as if he held so much of it he could barely keep it down. Or as if *she'd* woken it up in him. She wanted to wake it again. But her brain had frozen in utter delight and arousal as she stared at that laughter, and she couldn't come up with another clever thing to say.

That laughter of his seemed to catch on her face and hone in on it. The laughter faded, leaving only a trembling in her stomach in its wake. He stood, stepping toward her. "Layers." His voice dropped into that dangerous purr. "We heat up, for example."

His finger rubbed the hollow of his throat, where her nose had been, drawing her eyes back to that strip of flesh and the four undone buttons.

"We sweat a little. We get dirty."

Holy crap, would her mind stop taking his words as verbalized sex. *Gets dirty...playing rugby! Or something!* Not *as in dirty sex.*

"We have sex," he said, and her brain fried.

Stop. Stop. Stop. And for God's sake, quit saying all this in that French-on-British accent. I can't take it!

"You can't make a scent for a man unless you take into account how his own body scent is going to change through heat and arousal." His finger drifted down his chest to a still-fastened button. "After all, when else

56

should a woman even be able to smell a man's body, except when she's in close enough that he's aroused?"

Thank God for the counter between them so that he couldn't smell *her* arousal. She hoped. Oh, God. "So when I test the scents on you, I'll make you do fifty push-ups to warm up!" she snapped.

"In your professional opinion, there's no difference between the scent of sweat and the scent of sex?"

Oh, God, yes, there was. Sweat was part of arousal, but there was so much more. The scent of *his* arousal, the scent of hers, the way they had blended together on her hands, on her body...

"Well, maybe you could see if one of your models could accommodate you for a quickie just before you come by," she shot at him. The words cut across her own skin, they hurt so bad.

He drew back.

His face shut down.

And that fast, he was impervious, dangerous Damien Rosier again. "I could do that, yes." He rolled down his left sleeve. The deft move of his fingers rubbed over all the points of arousal in her body and drove her out of her mind. "Or I could use you."

She jerked back.

"Just in fantasy, of course." Such a clipped, perfect voice, with that sensual brush of French that drove her skin *mad*. "Dreams. I wouldn't want to sexually harass someone who'd taken me on as a client."

Not sexually harass her? He wasn't her employer. She'd quit any possibility of *that* position just as fast as he'd taken over her company. And *they'd already had sex.*

"But I could think about you." He rolled down his other sleeve. "Just to get in an aroused state." He gestured downward and...oh, lord.

He *was* aroused.

Like...it was...he was...

She couldn't move.

He—

"For example..." His gaze traveled over her leisurely, as if he held the mouse's tail firmly under one paw and could take his time. "I could imagine pushing you back on that counter. You'd probably say no, of course. But this is my imagination. So I could just cover your mouth with my hand until you couldn't say a word."

He rolled down his right sleeve. "Your eyes would be so big just above my hand, and you'd try to grab my arm to push me off, but it would be too late. Because you can't fight a man off in his imagination. And I'd already have my other hand sliding under that pretty white skirt of yours. And then you wouldn't want to fight anymore."

He buttoned the fourth button of his shirt. "But I'd hold you down anyway. Maybe I'd let go of your mouth to hold your wrists, so I could hear all the sounds you made while I played with you any way I wanted to."

He buttoned the third button. "And I'd make you come," he said softly, viciously, "until you couldn't take it anymore." The second button. "Until you begged me to stop." The last button, the collar snug around his throat. "And I still wouldn't stop. Until you were so weak from coming that you couldn't even pull your thighs together when I finally let you come back down. You'd just lie there, with your skirt all up around you and that counter damp with you, while I did this."

He picked up his coat and slid it back on.

"And this." He picked up his watch while she stood frozen and fastened its armor back around his wrist.

"And this." He picked up the cufflinks and neatly threaded them through his cuffs, not even fumbling.

"And walked out."

He turned and walked to the door of the workshop and paused to look back at her. "Want to see what I smell like?"

She could only stare at him, aroused and slapped and utterly undone.

"Well." A crisp tug to adjust his sleeve. "I suppose I could always come up with another fantasy tonight, when you're ready to test your first blends."

"Get out!" she yelled. "And I don't have to work on a damn thing for you! You just took back all your down payment!" She gestured wildly at his suit coat, watch, cufflinks. Somehow, of everything that had just happened, that hurt the worst of all—that those superficial parts of him that he had given, he'd taken even those back, too.

"I'll pay cash," he said evenly. "It's cheaper."

And he walked out.

Chapter 6

Damien had barely gone halfway down the street when he met Tristan coming up it.

Fuck.

"Are you okay?" Tristan rocked to a stop, brown eyes searching. "You look kind of...emotional." His voice on the last word was dumbfounded.

Imagine that. I had an emotion. Don't have a heart attack.

"I'm fine," Damien snapped. He felt hot all over. He wanted to hit someone or something, slam his fist against glass to see it shatter...and here was one of his cousins. So convenient.

Tristan leaned to the side to peer past Damien up the street. "Did something *happen*?" he asked. "I mean, you act..." He waved a hand to try to capture the implausibility of the way Damien was acting. "...upset."

"I don't get upset." Damien adjusted his cuffs. Tristan, of course, was in a T-shirt on this hot day and eating a damn ice-cream cone. Damien had business meetings. "Don't you have work to do?"

"I'm stuck. I need to go windsurfing and clear my head. Want to come?"

God, it was so hard not to hit Tristan right this second. "I've got work."

"Plus, I wanted to see this Jasmin Bianchi Tante Colette gave her shop to. You think Tante Colette might have given her Niccolò and Laurianne's perfume recipe book, too?" Tristan's tone grew hungry. That missing perfume recipe book from the founders of their family had gotten them into all kinds of escapades as children and teenagers, as they thought of ever more dangerous places to hunt for the war-lost heirlooms. But this past year, Tante Colette had given both Raoul and Matt family treasures that proved she had had at least two of those missing heirlooms up in her attic all that time. Either they had been really crappy at hunting in the attic when they were kids or else their Resistance-honed aunt was wilier than five wild boys raised in peacetime had ever started to imagine.

"I'm taking care of Jess Bianchi." Damien used his mean voice. *You're the mean one.* "If she has anything else that belongs to this family, just leave it to me."

"Yeah, but I want to meet her." Tristan angled to see beyond Damien again, up the street to the shop. "The woman who single-handedly destroyed an entire art form. Spoiled Brat." He shuddered.

"It's an industry, Tristan," Damien said, annoyed for no reason he could define. Heat and frustration still wanted to explode out of him everywhere. "And she makes money."

Tristan rolled his eyes. "You would say that. She's probably just your type."

Damien's fingers curled slowly into a fist on the far side from Tristan. "I'm in the middle of—negotiations—to get back that shop. Stay away from her. I don't want you to screw anything up."

Tristan's eyebrows went up a little. He flicked a glance over Damien's face that made Damien tamp down on his expression all the harder. Of all his cousins, Tristan was by far the most difficult to beat in poker. Matt he could completely fleece, and with Raoul he was pretty evenly matched, but Tristan *saw* things, even when Damien didn't have one single damn tell.

"I can play good cop," Tristan said. "Hell, if she's been negotiating with *you*, she'll probably throw herself into my arms as soon as I walk in the door. I bet you I can have her selling it back to us by the time I finish this ice cream." He took a step forward.

Damien blocked him. "I said leave it, Tristan."

Tristan's eyebrows flew higher. He savored his ice cream, gazing at Damien. The two were the same height, both black-haired, both with a similar long, lean strength, as they'd grown up doing the same sports together—rock climbing, windsurfing, dirt biking. Strangers assumed they were brothers, not just cousins. But Tristan played through life, and it showed in all the relaxed lines of his body. Whereas Damien...Damien suddenly wanted to grab that cone from Tristan and walk off to eat it himself, in private, sucking cool sweetness down his throat until he could calm down.

"Okay, now I *really* want to get a look at her," Tristan said. "What is she, gorgeous?"

No. She was pretty. Like a child's bouquet of handpicked wildflowers in the middle of a host of hothouse roses. Funny. Most of the famous actresses he knew could look past all the bouquets sent them on opening night and clutch to them their own child's handpicked, wistful bouquet as the truest, most beautiful thing there. But nobody thought *he* could.

Like...what the actual fuck? Who on this whole planet was so jaded and indulged as to actually prefer two dozen roses to a fistful of wild flowers picked with great hope just for you?

Yet people thought *he* wouldn't know the difference. *He'd* crush the wildflowers in his fist. His own family fucking thought that.

Yet she...hadn't. Leaning on that terrace beside her over New York that cold February night, the fragile cocoon of warmth from the patio heaters battling the chilly air, he'd felt almost as if they were holding a single daisy between them, taking turns plucking off petals to see what dream they could find. *She likes me a little...I like her a lot.*

She had a sweetheart face, and a pensive mouth, and soft, long light brown waves and curls that looked as if she just caught them in a knot at her nape when she stepped out of the shower and called it a good hair day. When she dressed up, she liked flowing, romantic dresses, as if the little girl in her had never quite gotten over playing at princess.

And ever since they'd slept together, she looked at him with a cynical curve to her lips, an ironic eyebrow, and a flippant briskness that didn't suit her at all.

It made him want to do...well, pretty much everything he'd just been so insane as to tell her. Even the part where he walked out in a fucking temper because that flippant, cynical barrier she'd put up made him want to rend things.

Himself, maybe.

"Stay the fuck out of this, Tristan."

"Hmm." Tristan savored his ice cream as he contemplated Damien. "My curiosity is now killing me."

Damien was going to shove that damn cone down his throat. "Do you want my job?"

Tristan recoiled. "No. Shit. Do you need another raise?"

"Then quit interfering with the way I do it."

Tristan hesitated, glancing from Damien past him toward the shop up the street. "So you were working just now? That's what got you so—"

"I'm always working." *No heart in me ever.*

"Hmm," Tristan said, over his ice-cream cone.

***

Jess simmered. So much energy zinged off her all those molecules of scent in the shop danced in the ozone.

She would show him. Oh, yes, she could give him *exactly* the fragrance he deserved. She was perfect for it. She'd spent her entire damn career creating perfumes that drew nails down the olfactory chalkboard.

He was *not* getting this shop from her. She had lost too much already. She would go down kicking and screaming, holding onto this shop with all her might. This magic was *hers*.

Usually, when she started work on a brief, that initial blank space made her stomach drop out of her, the moment when she didn't believe she could do it, she would never get it right. She had to fight through it, doggedly start putting ideas down on paper. This time, anger surged her right past that moment of doubt.

Oh, yes, she would get him right, that bastard. She knew *exactly* what to make for him.

She needed to get some supplies. She opened bottles and sniffed them and banged them on the counter. Some molecules could survive more or less intact for decades in the right conditions—thus the trade in treasured long-discontinued or formula-changed perfumes—but for Damien she wanted all her substances to be so new they *shone.* Sunlight glittering off dark, brushed steel.

She wanted scents that rang against your knuckles if you rapped them, they were so hard, she thought as she drove to Laboratoire ElleFleur on the road outside Grasse. She wanted the kind of scent that took a woman's butterfly dream and didn't even use a pin to stab through it, just crushed it down with a bare thumb, sneering as the butterfly died.

Just that faint moue of a sneer, as if the butterfly was pathetic for being so vulnerable to a man like him.

Oh, yes, she would show him. She felt *singed* with the need to show him. *And that whole fantasy of yours about pushing me back against a counter? You can just look at me and salivate, you bastard.*

She parked the car in the steep parking lot near the factory doors and strode up, cherishing a vision of herself as textured and real-seeming as the scents dancing in her head: her, sleek and gorgeous, in some tight little skirt, her expression imagination-brushed to be beautiful and glamorous, giving him his own moue back, making him eat his heart out.

Or whatever excuse for a heart he had. In her imagination, she didn't just *smell* like Nathalie Leclair, she looked like her. And he was begging on his knees.

She pressed a button for entrance and waited, tapping her foot, for the factory door to open.

***

"You won't work with me." The muscle in Jess's jaw felt very like Damien's looked, when his lips got that line.

The thirty-something commercial director, a lean man in glasses, gave her a cool, assured look of dismissal. "I'm afraid we just can't provide small samples to every perfumer who comes by."

"I'm *Jasmin Bianchi.*" If she specified any of a laboratory's products in one of her fragrances, and it went on to sell anything close to her Spoiled Brat, she could double a laboratory's revenue for years.

"Yes, so you've said."

She resisted picking up some of those bottles off his desk and throwing them at him, at that tone.

"Unfortunately, we can't sell in smaller amounts than five kilos."

"Five *kilos?*" The man had lost his mind. "That's 150,000 euros, if I want Grasse jasmine." Not to mention, what the hell would she do with five kilos of jasmine absolute? Those were production quantities. No independent perfumer could go through that much during concept phases.

"*Je regrette,*" he said, immutably polite.

Jess put her hands on her hips. "You're a Rosier SA subsidiary, aren't you?" she finally realized. Damn it, she should have done more research before she came out here.

"Yes, we are," the commercial director said coolly.

And so they wouldn't even let her smell samples, let alone take some with her. It was just like her father had always said—the Rosiers and the other big fragrance families held a lock on this town, and screw anyone who wasn't part of them or who made them her enemy.

She pivoted and strode out, yanking out her phone.

She'd be damned if Damien would beat her this way. Worse, *block her from access to scents.* Drive her back to New York and the bowels of some giant company that could make sure she was provided with everything she wanted, as long as she worked on commercial caricatures for the rest of her career. The Rosiers may have shut her father out of this town, but they could not exile her.

There had to be some small laboratory trying to make its way here. Or a subsidiary to one of the rival families. The Rosiers couldn't own *everything*.

***

The metal steps gripped at his shoes as Damien climbed up to the platform five meters above the concrete floor, huge machines all around him. Hell, the equipment needed an upgrade. And—"Where are their protective glasses?" He pointed at a group of three workers.

Cédric Lambert, the very young and working-on-a-dream CEO, looked guilty. "It's hard to get everyone to wear them. They're, ah, not very stylish."

Damien cut him an incredulous look. "Oddly, the French government is not going to take that into consideration when they fine the hell out of you. Bureaucrats. And, you know, we are entirely surrounded by corrosive chemicals being processed at high pressures and with extreme heat sources. So those bureaucrats *might* have a point."

"If only they weren't so *big*," Cédric said, pulling his own glasses down off his head. Where they did, indeed, look ridiculous.

Damien knew he was a hypocrite for not wearing his own protective glasses while he gave this lecture, but it was true that they were the nerdiest looking glasses known to man, and nobody could sue him for not protecting his *own* eyes.

He slipped his hands in his pockets and gazed out over the factory, thinking about its profit-loss statements. Although why Lambert put the word *profit* in the name for those statements was beyond him. Optimism?

He glanced sideways at the twenty-five-year-old CEO. But then, that was what the region needed, wasn't it? Sheer, blind, stubborn optimism.

With that and a dose of actual business sense, you could possibly save an economy.

Unfortunately, Cédric, like his recently retired parents, had been determined to make a go of it without any of that actual business sense, just conviction and his training in chemistry. Laboratoire Lambert had been floundering along that way for years. Until Cédric faced facts and came to see Damien in his office in Grasse and essentially begged for a takeover. Well, Cédric had tried to put a good face on it, as if he was offering Rosier SA the opportunity of a lifetime, but since Damien already knew all about Laboratoire Lambert, that hadn't really worked.

"A hundred and three employees?" Damien said. Local people. Who passed him on the street, whose kids bought ice cream at the stand just down the street from him and made *that* business possible, who bought houses and filled schools.

"Possibly a hundred and seven," Cédric said. "We have four women on extended maternity leave."

French law required that positions be held for three years for any woman who took time off to have a baby. It was one of those many laws that sounded great in some ideal world in the Assemblée but put a hell of a burden on a company.

One hundred and three. Or seven. And a profit-loss statement that had not actually seen the word *profit* in years.

His grandfather wouldn't have done it, when he held the reins of the company. His father wouldn't do it. Hell, given their father-son communication skills, this was going to mean another damn fight and then a month or two of the cold silent treatment, everything between them reduced to crisp one-sentence emails. His father had long since dismissed the previous generation of Lamberts as "idealistic hippies with a chemistry degree".

"We have this new hay absolute we're working on," Cédric said, with that same light in his eye that Tristan got over one of his damn thirty-thousand-euro ingredients. "You have to smell it. It's like grass and gold, all in a bottle. Liquid sunshine, fresh-cut." He pulled a small brown bottle out of his pocket, clearly having carried it this whole time as his *pièce de résistance*.

Artists. God.

Or chemists. In the perfume industry, the line between the two was never very clearly drawn.

Damien accepted the bottle and smelled it. He had to agree it was nice. Tristan had raved about it. *Damien, if you let that company go under before they can go into proper production of it, the world will be a darker place.* And, with that wink of Tristan humor, *Or at least my world will.*

"And it's got fantastic staying power," Cédric said. "We've been testing it. It's not one of those absolutes that smells good early but breaks down in a few months. And we've just started working on this absolute of narcissus that is going to be stunning. Wait until you smell it!"

"Right." Damien rubbed the bridge over his nose. But his head didn't bother him, right this second. No vice tightened over his forehead, no screws into his temples. One hundred and three—or seven—people. Living on a dream.

Sometimes, it was really nice to give a dream actual substance. He started to smile as he extended his hand to shake Cédric's. "Let's get some paperwork started."

***

"I think you would have to talk to Monsieur Lambert, *mademoiselle*," the assistant said nervously. At least Jess assumed the young woman was an assistant. Surely a commercial director would have more assurance? That said, the way this operation was run and given the younger woman's white coat, she might actually be a chemist who had happened to be standing closest to the door when Jess buzzed for entrance.

"Fine," Jess said with great patience. When she had been working for AOS, supply issues had never been her problem—reps brought her samples, and an assistant placed her orders—but when they'd been setting up Amour et Artisan, she'd been the one who visited laboratories to talk about supplies. She had been the only one on their start-up team who could properly evaluate whether she thought a laboratory's products were good enough for her. "I'll talk to him."

"Well," said the chemist-assistant-student-intern-whatever-she-was uneasily, as she led Jess between massive machines into a meager office area, "it's just that right now, he's a little busy."

Jess stopped stock still as she spotted a black head through the glass walls and cheap blinds of the office. Damien, pen in hand over papers, glanced up at the movement.

For a second, their gazes locked through glass. Then he came to his feet just as she yanked open the glass door. "What the hell are you doing here?" she demanded.

The chemist-intern-whatever gasped behind her.

"Working," Damien said crisply. How could eyes that cool hold that much heat?

"This is the one laboratory in Grasse that the Rosiers *don't* own!"

Damien capped his pen with a thin smile. "Past tense."

For a second, fury strangled all speech. And then she exploded: "What is *wrong* with you?"

That mockery of a smile faded away. He just looked at her, his lips that straight, hard line. "Doubtless infinite numbers of things."

"Are you just so damn empty inside that you have to buy up everything that *matters* to other people to try to fill yourself up? Like some damn vampire, sucking all the blood out of everyone else to see if you can find out what life tastes like?"

Damien's expression went grim and blank. He stared at her, the only motion in his body the twisting of his pen in thumb and forefinger.

The nervous assistant hugged herself in embarrassment, and the other man in the office stood awkwardly to the side, looking between them.

"My father was so right about you people," Jess said bitterly. "One freaking perfume shop in Grasse escapes your grasp, and you tell all the laboratories around town to refuse supplies, just so you can freeze me out. What's wrong? Did I insult your pride by not staying to kiss your feet the next day? Was I supposed to beg you to marry me and let me have your babies?"

The corners of Damien's lips were white. His hand closed around the pen. He didn't say a word.

"You *bastard*," Jess said viciously, bitter and hopeless and caught. By cutting off her supplies, he might as well have bound her in duct tape in a dark room, all sensory input cut off except the struggle against the bonds that held her. It was an incredibly effective way to destroy a perfumer's ability to work. She turned around to stride away.

"What supplies?" Damien's abrupt voice cut like an ice shard.

"My *perfume* supplies!" She spun back around on him, outraged. "You know damn well what I'm talking about! You told every laboratory around this town to shut me out!"

He gazed at her, eyes narrowing, for a long moment. And then, flatly, "I'll have to deal with this later. I'm busy right now."

Oh, that bastard. The dismissal, firm, from a position of power, was like a dash of acid from one of those machines. She had to make herself stride out before she started breaking things in impotent fury.

Chapter 7

"Where should I put them?" a cheerful voice asked, and Jess looked up and started at the juxtaposition of the cheerfulness and the black hair and long, lean, male body. Then her eyes focused, and she realized that this man who looked very like Damien also looked nothing like him at all. The eyes were brown, the smile too amused, his way of moving too relaxed and easy.

Jess straightened from the lower cabinet, where she'd been trying to see what else this place might have that she could work with. She'd have to beg a friend in New York to overnight her collection of materials, there was no help for it. Her father's were boxed up in New York, too. Not that she wanted to waste her father's ingredients on someone like *Damien.*

"Where should you put what?" She eyed the giant cardboard box the man carried. "You're Tristan Rosier, aren't you?"

He beamed at her. "My reputation precedes me."

"Indeed," she said dryly. Tristan Rosier's star reputation drove the average serious perfumer crazy—the way the media honed in on him just because he was hot, flirted well, and was a Rosier. Making perfumes was geek work, might as well face it, and Tristan refused completely to fit into the introverted social expectations of his colleagues. He acted more like he belonged with the models and actors, the marketing team and executives, at those blasted perfume launch parties. All perfumers thought they were the real star of the show—they were—but Tristan actually got everyone else to treat him like one.

He gave a little bow. "Yours precedes you, too."

Touché. She narrowed her eyes at him. "What's in the box, stink bombs?"

He looked delighted. "While that is a *brilliant* idea for driving an enemy out of territory, and I once did it to my cousins when they tried to claim I was too little to join their pirate club, no. Well...I'm not saying it wouldn't stink if I dropped these things, but that's not the goal." He advanced into the room and forced space for the box on a counter.

Jess looked into it at the tops of very familiar brown bottles, packed in tight and several layers deep. Wariness grew. "What is this?"

"A present." Tristan smiled at her.

"Why would you be giving me presents? Those look like perfume supplies." And if they were quality perfume supplies, as she must assume they were coming from the Rosiers, that big a box of them was a very expensive gift.

"Well...I *am* the good cop, but as a matter of fact, just to keep you confused, the bad cop sent these."

Her eyebrows drew together. "You mean Damien?"

Tristan looked smug. "It's funny how when I say good cop, bad cop, people *always* know which one is which."

"Why should Damien tell you to bring me these?" Jess asked, increasingly wary and also annoyed. Because if Damien started making nice gestures to her after she had yelled at him in public like that...well, that made her seem like a pretty crappy person, didn't it? And she was already well aware of how bad a start she had made in this tight-knit perfume community by yelling at one of its scions in public. That little display was going to have a ripple effect, and she'd started to feel sick to her stomach as soon as her temper had died down enough for her to realize it.

"Well, to be precise, he didn't ask *me* to bring you these. I am under strict orders not to get anywhere near you. However, I am quite terrible at obeying orders from my cousins, and when I caught one of the lab techs in our perfume division packing these up to bring to you at his orders...obviously I couldn't resist."

She folded her arms against the gift. "So he freezes out all my access to supplies and then generously lets me know that he can grant me largesse when and if he chooses? Am I supposed to develop the Stockholm syndrome or something?"

"Oh, is he holding you hostage?" Tristan asked brightly. "Why does no one ever share all the juicy details with me? How did he get your passport?"

Jess glowered at him.

Tristan smiled back. He didn't laugh *at* a person, she noticed. It was this warm *come-on-let-go-of-your-temper-and-laugh-with-me* kind of humor. "Is he really freezing out your access to supplies? I'm not saying he's not capable of it, but are you sure it isn't just the local laboratory managers being a little over-achieving in their kissing up?"

"He just took over another laboratory this morning so I couldn't get any of its supplies!" Fine. It might be a *leetle* self-centered to assume he had taken over a whole company just to get at her, but...he did have a record of crushing her hopes. Although she was more like the accidental road kill in the process. A flower that fell off a bush and got stepped on while he was reaching for what he really wanted.

"Did he go take over another company?" Tristan shook his head indulgently. "He really is insatiable about that. You wonder how much energy and time any one man can spare to saving the whole world. Which one did he take over this time? Not Laboratoire Lambert by any chance?"

Jess parted her lips and stopped. "How did you know that?"

Tristan's face lit. "Did he really? Hot damn. Uncle Louis is going to be so pissed, but *damn* I want their hay absolute."

"You couldn't just buy it from them like most people? You Rosiers had to take over the whole company?" Jess asked angrily.

"Well, yeah. It was going under. Even Damien's going to have a hell of a job saving it, and his father is going to act hard and impatient over it for months. Uncle Louis hit his business stride in the eighties." Tristan thought about it a second more and then just grinned and pumped his fist. "*Shit.*" It was a delighted curse. "And Damien acted so tough when I asked him about it, like he wouldn't even think of making such a stupid business move."

That didn't even make any sense. "Why would Damien Rosier buy up a company that was a dead weight?"

"Well…it's a Grasse company and employs around, what, a hundred people here. Don't worry, he'll eventually make it profitable. That's what he does."

Jess stared at him, trying to process this.

Tristan flung out his hands. "He turned that Amour et Artisan company around for you, didn't he?"

"*Turned it around?* We'd barely gotten started! We had big plans for that company." *I had big plans for that company. Dreams. The only dreams I had to hold onto.*

Tristan snorted. "I've met Tara Lee. All charm and conviction, to get people on board, and no business sense. You dodged a bullet on that one. Now you can see what your dream company can become when you have someone with real business acumen behind it."

This whole conversation was like looking up at the sky, expecting to see its ordinary blue, and discovering that you were instead staring at the ground high overhead, and the sky was actually what you were standing on upside down. "Except that it's not mine anymore," Jess said tightly. "I left. I sold my shares."

Tristan's eyebrows flexed together. "Well…I'm sure you turned a nice profit on them, once people knew Damien was taking over. But it seems kind of an idiot move on *your* part. No offense."

"He would have made me produce the same crap as Spoiled Brat again! I wanted to do *niche* perfumes. Something *good.*"

"Did he actually tell you he expected the commercial stuff? He's backed quite a few niche perfume companies. And the name Amour et Artisan does wave your niche perfume ambitions like a bright pink flag. Did you talk to him before you left?"

Well...no. She had just left. And buried her father. And...despaired.

Yes. Despair. That was the place she'd been in.

She gazed down at the box of perfume supplies, and then reached out a hand to slowly stroke their caps. Had she finally climbed out of that pit of despair?

"This is one of my favorite greens." Tristan touched a bottle at the corner. "The scent is amazing. Like sunlight on grass, you know? And the way it blends." He kissed his fingertips, in a gesture so French it reminded her painfully of her father. "Let me know what you think of it."

"Thank you," Jess said slowly, still not quite sure what to make of all this. But if Tristan's own favorite greens were in this box, then he had taken over from the lab tech and selected the essences and molecules himself. So he deserved her thanks. Damn it, *Damien* deserved her thanks. That really went against the grain.

"It's that hay absolute I was telling you about," Tristan said. "From Laboratoire Lambert."

"Thank you," Jess said again, feeling very stiff.

Tristan shrugged. And smiled. "Sure. After all, Damien's my cousin. And I'm very interested to see what you do with him."

***

"Making yourself at home?" a cool, velvet-dark voice asked, as Jess struggled to drag her heavy suitcase over cobblestones.

Jess's head came up sharply. Damien hadn't come by the shop the day before to harass her. She'd started to wonder if Tristan's box of supplies had been some kind of peace offering.

Until the hotel that morning informed her that her room had been booked, in fact all rooms had been booked, indefinitely. *It's the tourist season,* the woman had explained with a smile that clearly communicated the real message: *No Rosier Enemies Allowed.*

"My idea of a comfortable home includes electricity and running water," she said sharply. "But since you had the hotel kick me out, I guess I'm going to be camping at the shop and hauling buckets from some of these fountains that fill this city."

Damien's expression turned inscrutable. "I had the hotel kick you out? Is this the same way I had all the local laboratories refuse to supply you?"

"And I'd started to think I might have misjudged you about the laboratories," she said bitterly, and yanked at the suitcase, stuck once again on cobblestones.

He picked it up as easily as if the giant suitcase weighed nothing. "You packed for a long stay, didn't you? What's in this thing, your whole apartment?"

"The length of my stay is none of your business."

He said nothing for a few steps, expression impenetrable, except for that little glitter of anger in his eyes. "How long until your water and electricity are turned on? What date did they give you?"

"They didn't," Jess snapped. "Apparently both accounts are in your name, and the only lawyer I know of who might be willing to face off against the Rosiers and get that straightened out, Antoine Vallier, is out of town."

"Just as well for that bastard," Damien said darkly.

"If you think you're going to drive me out with discomfort, it's *not* going to work," Jess said. The more he gave her a hard time, the more determined she got. Despair and old grief just faded back into the shadows

76

at that vivid instinct to *fight*. He'd taken enough from her. Life had taken enough from her. This shop was hers.

Damien pulled his phone out of his pocket, slid his thumb across it a couple of times, and then spoke into it. "Fréd? You still have the account records for the water and electricity at Tante Colette's old shop? Get those turned back on for me today, will you? Don't throw weight around, but you might want to mention that I'm a little impatient to have to intervene to deal with this myself. Maybe throw in a reference to my efforts to turn Grasse into a place where new businesses feel welcome to set up and thrive."

Jess blinked as he hung up. Her eyebrows drew together. "Are you trying to place me in your debt or something?"

He cut her a chilly glance and stopped in front of the old door, suitcase still in hand, and waited while she unlocked it. Then he carried the suitcase up the narrow back stairs to the old rooms above the shop. They were dusty still—she hadn't even started to clean them—and the mattress on that old dark wood bed probably held mice. Jess cringed to think about dealing with it, or, even worse, trying to sleep on it. But the alternative—making the rounds of the hotels begging for a room—pissed her off.

"That will be five dollars," Damien said.

She stared at him.

"For the suitcase." He held his hand out, like a doorman waiting for a tip. "So you won't be in my debt."

His eyes glittered, and she felt her own lips tighten. She had to take a deep breath to get the words out: "Thank you."

He just watched her ironically.

"And thanks for the supplies," she said stiffly.

He didn't say anything. She didn't know why he had helped her with the suitcase. He looked as if he could barely stand to be in the same room with her.

"You'll have to tell me how much I owe you," she said.

His jaw tightened. "Don't worry about it. I may be *empty* but my bank account isn't."

Shame brushed her. That had been a nasty thing to say on her part. Not to mention that, in her anger, she'd revealed to their audience—and thus to the entire gossip network of Grasse—that she and he had slept together.

"Why are you fixing my problems?" she demanded, rather than try to apologize for something she wasn't quite sure she wanted to.

"Because apparently I'm causing them."

Well...he *was.* Stealing her company, the whole laboratory-supply issue, the hotel, the water and electricity.

"Just by existing," he said.

Yes. Just by existing, he made a tumult rise inside her that made her feel far too alive. Like she could get hurt again.

But he made her want to *fight,* too. Like she was a resilient person who knew she could survive a few hurts.

God, it felt good to feel alive.

"I don't owe you anything," she insisted, folding her arms across her chest.

"You owe me a damn fragrance," he said sharply, and left.

***

The water and electricity were on by noon, a rapidity that suggested the mayor might have gotten involved, and Damien himself carried in a mattress right after she got back from lunch. He didn't speak to her, his expression cool and closed when their eyes met briefly. He and a big man with charcoal-streaked russet hair carried the mattress up the stairs and, before she could even make it to the landing after them, came back down with the old mattress and disappeared with it down the street.

And Jess lay back on the bare mattress, which smelled of factories and newness, and stared at the ceiling and didn't know what to think or feel about any of it.

The new smell of the mattress wasn't a hospital smell, but it was closer than anything else she had smelled since she got off the airplane. Close enough to take her mind back to a place it didn't want to go...

***

New York, six months ago

Her phone was ringing. She shifted on the uncomfortable chair in the ICU waiting room, where she'd gone while the nurses changed her father's catheter, did those last care-taking things. She should have left him in his apartment, like he'd wanted, but she just couldn't watch him die without seeing if there was one last thing the hospital could do.

By now, of course, she realized she'd been wrong. She shouldn't have done this. Grasped onto him so hard that she hurt him in her fear of letting go. She should have just let him...die.

She shoved water off her face, yet again, and tried to focus on the phone screen.

She didn't recognize the number, but she often didn't recognize numbers these days. It could be test results or insurance, a new doctor, or, rare-to-nearly-never anymore, someone calling to see if she needed help, could they bring food, do a load of laundry, drive her somewhere.

She'd read on a website the things people were supposed to do to help someone in her situation. Almost no one ever thought to do them for her. After two years, maybe they'd gotten tired of it.

She was tired. So tired her hand fumbled on the phone as she answered.

"Jess." The male voice was calm, assured, sexy French-on-British. Her heart tightened in this confused, mushy way, like it wasn't actually a muscle anymore, it had been pulverized too much. She couldn't deal with Damien Rosier. Not tonight. "How are you doing?"

She stared at the waiting room television while tears filled her eyes just at the question. She had to hold the phone away from her a second to sniff hard and cram all those tears back.

For that moment, she wanted to turn to him so badly. Wanted to just fling herself into his arms, *make him*, through sheer desperation, be that man she had imagined him to be—someone tender and careful and strong, able to hold her through this terrible, terrible night.

The same way she'd wanted to *make her* father stay alive.

"Now that you've had a bit more time to adjust to everything, I wondered if we could talk. Could I take you out to dinner?" He named one of the top restaurants in the city.

Oh, God, of course he wasn't asking if she needed help. He was bored or something. Ready for another hook-up. He wasn't the man she had wished he was, that night. He was the man who hooked up with a different model every night, the man who had slept with her while stealing her company, without a second thought.

Jesus, she must be in Damien's little black book now. One of his resources of women in New York who might be up for good sex when he was in town and had the urge.

A wild vision of herself at that restaurant, crumpled and stale from the hospital, no shower in two days. She stank of dying.

"No," she said.

A tightening of frustration in his voice. Women must not tell him no that often. "Jess. Don't you think this is *important?*"

More important than her *father dying?* How the hell self-centered was he?

God, of course she couldn't throw herself into his arms and ask for help. Of course she had to handle this all alone.

The nurse came to the waiting room door and nodded to her. Jess's hand tightened on the phone.

"Jess. I know you have a lot going on right now, but don't you think it's at least worth seeing each other again?"

At least it put things into perspective. *Was* it important, a hook-up that had seemed beautiful and had turned out to be with one of the industry's ruthless players? Was it even worth thinking about, right this second? Let alone risking repeating in a desperate grasp after a fantasy?

"No," she had said as she shifted her thumb to disconnect. *No,* although it hurt her heart, added one last Gordian twist to the knot in her stomach. "I really don't."

Chapter 8

"Nice skirt," Damien said. It wasn't. It was a perfect little pencil skirt, featured in the display window of a shop just down the street, which she'd paired with a tailored white blouse, exactly the kind of thing newly hired women at Rosier SA wore to prove how professional they were.

Of course, they also usually carefully curled or straightened their hair, a step in glossy perfectionism she seemed to have entirely missed in her education in things feminine, and most of the time they remembered to put on their shoes when he came into their office.

Jess was moving very briskly among the bottles, test blotters, papers, and moleskin journal she had laid out on the counter, but she'd forgotten she was barefoot. She was such a geek. Way worse than Tristan, who'd learned to disguise his own nerdiness with social skills when he was very young. She'd probably played at being Galadriel when she was a teenager. Her perfumes were her magic potions or something.

"Did you get it just for me?"

A tiny streak of color on her cheeks. So, yeah.

Instead of, say, the soft, playful, romantic sundress she'd been wearing the day before.

He was going to break one of these damn glass bottles around him. Just strike out and slash its head off.

"I've put together a couple of things I want to test on your skin," she said briskly. Her fingers tightened around one of the bottles. She tried to spear him with a look. "I expect you to stay professional."

Hell, he could see why she'd hidden in a perfumer's lab instead of taking on the business world as a career. She couldn't spear a marshmallow with that look.

Which made it all the more pathetic that he, the man whose heart was made out of titanium, felt as if he'd not only been speared but was now being roasted just a little too close to the fire and was about to go from burnished gold to crispy black in a sudden catch of flame.

"Do you?" he said coolly.

Her flush deepened.

So no.

She didn't really expect that.

And yet here he was anyway, instead of knocking on a locked door she refused to open to an asshole like him.

Interesting.

He pulled out a checkbook and a pen made out of platinum that had been somebody's idea of what he'd want for Christmas. "How much did we say?"

A bottle clicked on the counter. Suddenly her eyes did spear him. It was the oddest sensation. Where everyone else's much sharper looks bounced off his shield, hers just sank right through him and held him. "I don't want your *money*."

It pissed him the hell off when people said *money* in that tone. He'd made a shitload of it in his life, both for himself and for his family—not to mention all the people who depended on Rosier SA for a living.

And what he'd spent his entire career managing and growing for his family wasn't fucking *crap*. It was what allowed the rest of them to act so precious and entitled over their perfume art and their valleys full of roses. Because somebody wrapped a great wall of money around them and made sure the real world couldn't penetrate it and get its money-grubbing hands on their dreams.

"You know what we said." Jess put her chin up and tried a cynical curl of her lips, even while color deepened in her cheeks. "Take them off."

He froze. Arousal and *nakedness* swelled up through his brain, taking over his thoughts. Removing his coat and cufflinks and watch that morning to disturb her, and wreck himself, had been one thing. Repeating the same striptease *at her command* turned it into something far more exposed and vulnerable.

And Damien didn't do vulnerable.

Well, he'd done it once.

With her.

And the day after she'd...taken herself back. The trust, the sweetness, the magic, the wishing. As if she'd made a mistake, giving it to him.

As if he couldn't possibly deserve a handful of wildflowers.

If it wasn't hothouse and expensive, he wouldn't know how to appreciate its worth.

His fingers were stiff on his cufflinks.

"Do you need help?" Jess asked.

"No," he snapped.

And then he realized, too late, what he'd slashed back from him—her fingers on his cufflinks, the soft hair just a bend of his head away, as she focused on that first step of getting him naked.

Damn it.

He got the cufflinks off and set them on the counter.

"Cash would have been more practical." He made his voice ironic. His back-up tone.

"I'm not practical," she said, as stiff as his fingers on his damn watch.

No kidding. *So you need me. You really do. I'm exactly the perfect person to protect all your impractical dreams.*

Something knotted in his chest, there, just below the hollow of his throat. He tried to swallow past it, and it wouldn't go away.

He got the watch off and set it beside the cufflinks. Hard and expensive and she could live a year off it, if she had the practical sense.

But then, if she'd had that, she'd have taken a check. Idiot perfumers. All fairytales and whiffs of twenty-thousand-euro absolutes they wanted to play with as if they were free.

It had been laughably easy to take over her little artisan company. Basically, he'd noticed rainmaker Jasmin Bianchi was part owner, raised an eyebrow, and thought, *I'll take that. She might be useful.* And a few hours later, he'd had it.

He pulled off his coat.

God, he felt so much more naked doing this at her orders than he had the other morning. No, it wasn't quite that. He'd felt naked that morning, but powerful in it— pushing *her* around with his stripping, instead of growing more and more exposed.

She pressed her hand down on his coat as soon as he laid it over the counter, gathering it and the watch and cufflinks to her. "If you try to take these back again, we're done," she said, hard. "I'm not playing this game, where you promise part of yourself and then take it back the next minute because your mood changes."

"*You're* not playing that?" he asked incredulously.

She checked, her fingers flexing into his coat, her eyebrows drawing slowly together as she searched his face.

He closed his expression hard, as hard as if he was trying to beat Tristan at poker and Tristan was getting that gleam of too much perception in his eye.

"What do you mean?" she asked, those damn dusk eyes fixed on his face.

"*You* turned it into a game," he heard himself say harshly. "Where you pretended to give something, and then you changed your mind and took it back. *I* wasn't *playing.*"

She stood very still on the other side of the counter, blinking slow, great blinks at him.

Fuck this. He threw himself in the chair, stretching out his legs, lounging there, the man in power waiting for his enemy to beg. Yeah, he knew body language and how to use his own. Essential in power plays, every time. "Let's have it."

She hesitated another long moment, until he almost started to believe she might actually *say* something to him, instead of just shutting him out, but instead she pointed wordlessly to his cuffs and his collar.

He had to flip this situation somehow. So he raised his eyebrow at her, lazy and ironic. And slowly rolled back each double cuff, one, two turns. Slowly, holding her eyes, unbuttoned four buttons on his shirt to expose his throat.

She looked down. And suddenly shifted awkwardly and grew five centimeters taller.

Damn, she'd noticed her shoes.

And it really wasn't fair that she was just a tiny bit awkward in them as she came around the counter toward him, either from unfamiliarity with those particular heels or because he was getting to her.

It got to *him*, that awkwardness. Made him want to push all this stupid game of rapiers and shields away and pull her into his lap. Say, *Shh. Come here. Let's talk. I'm not as bad as you think.*

The instinct ground to a halt, this great, screeching of brakes and rebellion against having to say those last words. Against having to *defend* himself against her assumption that he was a heartless asshole. Even after he'd held his own heart out to her like...

...like a pitiful bouquet of wildflowers.

Lured into believing that she would see how much more valuable they were than the hothouse flowers. Or diamonds, or whatever the hell he was supposed to have given her instead.

She stepped to the side so that she didn't have to stand right between his sprawled legs, dipped a strip into a tester, and held it out to him. "What do you think?"

He made sure his hand brushed hers as he took the *touche* from her. Masochist.

The scent smelled...like his damn titanium watch. Hard, impenetrable elegance and perfection, no softness in it anywhere.

He kept his expression exactly like that scent.

"It's a bit harsh," Jess said. "It will need a long maturation period. But this can give me an idea."

Damn her.

"Remember, you're just getting the top notes right now," Jess said uneasily.

His jaw set. "I know how perfume works."

"Can I try it on your skin?"

He held out his wrist, not looking at her. Fuck, she hadn't even *tried* to get at him. None of that evening on the terrace, none of that *night* was in that perfume at all.

Or was he really just so titanium hard that what had seemed like magical warmth and sweetness to him had seemed this cold and shallow to her?

Granted, his behavior since she'd gotten here probably hadn't been the best demonstration of the soft side of his character, but...

Just fuck.

A cold spritz of that heartless juice on his wrist. She hesitated. "What about—?" She gestured to his throat.

Merde, he hoped the synthetics she'd put in the thing weren't the kind that would cling to his skin for days, no matter how hard he tried to scrub them off. He pulled aside his shirt, still not looking at her.

Like exposing his throat to a cobra bite. Another spritz, at the hollow of his throat.

She stepped back.

They stared at each other, her eyes uneasy, his jaw set and hard.

"Are you going to do your, ah, fifty push-ups?" She waved toward the floor.

Oh, sure, hell, why not. He needed something to do.

He stood, and she immediately retreated to the other side of the counter. Rage rode under his skin at how different her reaction was from the last time he'd unbuttoned his shirt in front of her, how she'd been a little shy and a lot wondering and so carefully trusting. Not like she trusted easily. Like she trusted rarely—and yet he had been the recipient of that trust.

He yanked his shirt off and tossed it on top of his coat.

He felt ridiculous, and then he felt mad, and then he felt mean, as he dropped to the floor and hit those push-ups. One, two, three, four, he couldn't work his mad out, no matter how many he did, it just built in him, with every breath of that steely scent being woken by the growing heat of his body.

By the time he'd worked up the hint of sweat that she wanted, he was feeling so mean that he shoved himself to his feet in one hard lunge, ready to stride out of there before he did anything else he could regret.

And then he got a look at her face.

The deep pink in her cheeks, the vulnerable plumpness of her lower lip, as if she'd been biting it, the way she'd pulled one lock free of the knot at her nape and was twirling it around her finger, her eyes dark and dilated and locked on his torso...

The mad went right out of him. His mouth curved. But the mean—oh, yes, the mean still held. *You think this scent is me? Well, let's see how you like it.*

"What do you think?" He held out his wrist to her.

"It's really about what *you* think," she said, but she leaned across the counter and brought his wrist to her face, her nose brushing his skin as she took a deep breath.

Her eyebrows crinkled together. She shook her head. "Maybe it needs more citrus."

"What about here?" He touched the base of his throat.

She swallowed.

He waited, increasingly conscious of his pumped muscles, naked torso, and the faint glow of sweat over his skin.

That night, he'd taken off his shirt before he started undressing her at all. Exposing himself first. Making it easier for her to expose herself in turn, luring her in. And also just because...he'd really liked the look on her face as he took off his shirt. It had made him feel...pretty damn hot, to tell the truth.

Like now.

She came slowly around the counter. He didn't sit down, and her breath grew shorter and shorter as she came in close to him.

Just for a second, standing a few centimeters from his chest, she looked up at him, so vulnerable that he wanted to soften. *It's all right. Remember? Remember me?*

She went up onto her tiptoes and rested her hands on his chest to balance as she took a breath of the hollow of his throat.

And after that he didn't have a soft cell left in his body.

Everything about him went hard and hungry and determined to get what he wanted.

Chapter 9

"We've still got the arousal test," Damien said, with that dark velveted steel voice of his, like a black panther's paw just before the claws sprang out.

Jess's fingers curled into her palm as she stepped back. "Well," she said sharply, "after whatever hook-up you've got set for tonight, send me a text and let me know what you think."

His teeth snapped. He took a breath.

"I don't even have a date," said the man who had a different top model on his arm in every single photo Google had produced of him. He prowled away from her to slouch in that little folded chair, elegant pants and naked, faintly gleaming chest, the muscles of his biceps and chest more sharply defined than ever after the exertion. He smiled at her, a mean curve of his lips. "I'll have to make do with you."

"Like you did in New York?" Jess said through a tightness in her throat.

The tension in his body grew palpable. If she stretched out her hand, the air around his body might be too dense to reach his skin. "Is that what you think I was doing?"

She turned away, going to the counter to pretend to take notes.

"Go ahead." The steel under that velvet was making his voice vibrate at a pitch that buzzed all over her skin. "All those actresses and models, and I...*hooked up*...with you because...what? I got lazy? *Is that the story you're telling yourself?*"

His voice whipped across her. She looked up from her journal and had to brace. His eyes glittered with anger.

"Maybe," she said defiantly. "Maybe you just wanted to go with what was easy for once. It happens."

His hand clenched into a fist. "*Fuck* you," he said incredulously.

She flinched back.

He dragged his hand over his face. "God damn it." He stood abruptly and turned toward the door, then grabbed the jamb and held himself there a moment. "I'm sorry," he said curtly to the doorjamb. "That was out of line."

She said nothing, the words having shocked her deep enough in her stomach that she still hadn't swallowed them down.

"I have four male cousins," he said roughly. "I forgot myself. I shouldn't talk that way to you."

Well, she'd lived in New York. She knew perfectly well how easily some people said *fuck*. But...he hadn't seemed to have any trouble with manners the night they met. In fact, one of the things that had most enticed her about him was his courtesy—the way he curled his quiet and thoughtfulness around her until she no longer stood cold and alone on that terrace. She stood wrapped up in him.

He turned his head. His lips twisted, his eyes dark. "God forbid I should have done something sincere. Or meaningful. Or real."

Her heart beat too hard. Everything about that time came back and clogged her throat and pressed stinging against the backs of her eyes: the wish of him amid loneliness and loss, seeing him with that model the next day, walking in Monday morning to discover she'd lost her company and hope of becoming something different to his casual avarice, and all of that, all of it, against the backdrop of her father dying. He'd been dead two weeks later.

Loss and loss and loss and loss.

All her candles blown out and not one single wish come true.

"I'm not good at that kind of thing," she said through the tightness in her throat.

"Sincerity?"

"*No.* The...casual hook-up."

His lips pressed so hard. "Not as good as I am, for example?"

Regret twisted her. "Exactly."

His eyes blazed once and then went so chilly she felt plunged into that water under the ice again. "Well. As fun as this is, I'd better get moving if I want to find someone more comfortable with my style in time for dinner. Fortunately, modern technology has gone so far beyond the little black book these days. I can actually rate potential women for ease, looks, and availability, all right here at the touch of a finger." He held up his phone.

She gaped at the shock of it, sick to her stomach. Oh, God, what was she on that phone? A one star?

The glitter in his eyes cut like being abraded with emeralds. "You know what? I take back that apology. *Fuck you.*" He grabbed up his shirt and strode to the door and pivoted back. "And no one who produces this shit"—he touched his wrist—"is getting to keep this perfume shop, so try again."

***

"What the hell is wrong with you?" Tristan sought a grip in the rock. "Damien, you can't take this attitude up rock. You need to calm down before you get yourself hurt."

"Or somebody else hurts you," Matt growled from the other side of Tristan.

"Any time you want to try, Matt," Damien snapped.

Tristan closed his eyes briefly. "You don't know how much I love being in the middle of these discussions."

They clung halfway up the limestone cliff at the end of the valley, spread out, Matt on one end, then Tristan, then Damien. The cliff face offered multiple possible routes to the top, from easy to challenging. They'd cut their climbing teeth on it, as kids.

"Can I just climb the damn rock already?" Damien asked tightly. He hadn't asked for company. He'd just acquired it somehow, because he had to drive through the valley to get to the cliffs, and his cousins, of course, noticed his car and didn't want to miss out on a good climb. Or else they lived to give him headaches.

"Fine," Tristan said. "Don't fall on your head."

So they climbed, and it did help. You had to focus on rock, Tristan was right. You couldn't fling yourself up it mad. Eventually you had to slow down, put yourself into the moment—suspended between limestone and sky, over the valley that had nurtured his family for centuries and that now he defended.

At the top, quieted—Matt's growling, Damien's temper, Tristan's frustration with them all worn out— they sat on limestone and dirt, gazing out over the valley.

The steeple of the church stood above their little village of Pont-le-Loup. Beyond it lay hazy hints of the Mediterranean and the great mass of populace and land development that crouched between this valley and the sea, ready to swarm up into the valley and devour it, if ever they lost their battle to defend it.

If *Damien* lost.

Because that was the fact of the matter. It was all up to him.

His grandfather had lined Matt up as their future patriarch. Matt got to growl and act bossy as if the whole heart of his existence wasn't as vulnerable as those ephemeral rose and jasmine petals. Tristan, as the youngest, got to pretend none of these issues even existed—he was an *artiste*. Lucien and Raoul got to run off and be the adventurers.

But Damien defended the ramparts.

He went out into that brutal, cynical, dog-eat-dog world beyond this valley, where every man who ever tried to cut a deal with you might have a knife ready for your back. Out there where every woman who smiled at you was calculating your income or ability to advance her career. Or possibly had her own knife ready for your back.

Or couldn't believe in him at all.

He'd been in the thick of that world since he finished at the London School of Business seven years ago. Expanding their empire, conquering their enemies, building Rosier SA into something *nobody* could ever take out. Giving this family their *next* five hundred years.

Making sure Matt could keep this valley which Damien's own children would never even inherit, and—

His brooding hiccupped. His eyebrows drew slowly together, and he glanced at Matt. Matt had his arms loosely around his knees and was gazing out at his valley with that hungry pride of his. *My valley. On me. All mine.*

But...Matt had said that he wanted to make it into a trust. That he wanted to make sure this valley was all of theirs, and their children's. All by himself he had said that, two months ago, without anybody forcing him, as if...Damien rubbed his fingers over limestone, the callused tips of a climber.

As if Damien belonged here, too.

Inside the valley with its sweetness, *inside* this heart of their family that still beat true.

He took a deep breath that expanded his lungs and let it slowly out. Tension wanted to release out of his neck when he did that, and he didn't like to let it. He might need that tension. It was a mistake to relax when someone else could see him.

A flashing memory of the long, slow drift of his body into sleep, his arm over the waist of a woman who had lured him into wishing upon a star, the blissful fall of peace...

Fuck.

"Do you *ever* relax anymore?" Tristan said suddenly from his left, and he looked over to find Tristan not watching him at all. Just gazing out over the valley as if all was right with his world.

"I'm fine," Damien said, as if all was right with his world, too.

As if there wasn't an emptiness the size of this valley inside him. And no matter how much he tightened himself, vice-like around his head and heart, no matter how much he squeezed that emptiness, it just compacted, got denser and heavier and yet still somehow empty.

"Are you just so damn empty inside that you have to buy up everything that matters to other people to try to fill yourself up? Like some damn vampire, sucking all the blood out of everyone else to see if you can find out what life tastes like?"

Was that what he was doing when he agreed to take on Laboratoire Lambert? It had felt...different, on his end. Like doing something good. But the artists couldn't see that, ever. Maybe nobody could. Maybe he really had gone over to the dark side, his notion of what was good and warm and special so divorced from reality that he got sucked into his belief in it while no one else even noticed it at all.

Sometimes, he thought that he'd had an emptiness the size of a valley inside him all his life. But he knew exactly when that emptiness had condensed in him in that cold, icy way so that he couldn't ignore it anymore.

Monday morning. All weekend, an anxious, temper-edged emptiness had been growing in him. What had happened to her? Why had she left like that, before he even woke up? Was she cheating on someone with him or something? The perfume industry was a small world, but he hadn't seen her in it before. Would he be able to find her again? Would she want to be found, or the next time he saw her, would she be on her husband's arm and desperately beseeching him with her eyes not to say anything?

Had it not...had it not seemed *special* to her? Was it just some kind of dream? Those dreams like other people had, that got away from them in the morning because they were so careless and impractical with them, dreams that no one ever gave substance to.

But that didn't make sense, because...*he* gave substance to dreams. That was what he was in life, the person who put something solid into the crazy dreams and made them come true. While everyone else floundered when their wishes were exposed to reality, unable to protect them in the harsh light of day, he toughed it up and did whatever the hell was necessary to make the wish come true.

Which would make it the ultimate irony if the most beautiful dream he had ever had escaped *him.* Left him empty.

But he'd had to put the emptiness aside, of course, to stride into that meeting room. All the founding team of that business gathered, and Tara Lee smiling at them and acting charming, which was when he learned that she hadn't even discussed the sale with the rest of them before she did it. She had the majority shares, and she'd sold them all to him and with it left the others who had built the dream with her high and dry.

And there she was. Jess. Sitting there staring at him. His Jess, only today she was in jeans and a pretty shirt, and her face had this stunned blankness on it. When he tried to meet her eyes, she looked down at the table in front of her. For a second, he was so sure she was about to cry that his instincts tried to shred through all his self-control and make him commit one of the worst faux pas a man could make when he took over a company— go up to a female employee and pull her into his arms so that everyone could see they had a past.

He'd managed not to do that. Long enough for the introductions, when he'd found out that she wasn't just Jess but Jasmin Bianchi, the reason he had been excited about this company in the first place. That had been a shock. *She'd* made Spoiled Brat? Hell, that was an unexpected facet to her character.

And he wanted to go discover all those other facets right then. He'd kept the meeting upbeat, brisk, telling them about his ideas for how to make the company viable, that he was there to help them flourish not uproot them, that Rosier SA was interested in seeing this venture come to full flower. The type of people who could found an artisan perfume company without a lick of business sense ate that kind of flower language up.

Afterward, he almost hadn't managed to catch her. She was leaving quickly, her face this blank thing that hurt him, as if she had been drugged and was being dragged off to something terrible.

"Jess." He managed to catch her in the lobby downstairs, just shy of the door.

She braced before she turned. Then she looked at her phone and texted something, as if she barely had her mind on him, glancing at him up and down with this amusement that just *grated*. "You again?" she said, like a jaded socialite having to deal with the unwanted consequences of a one-night stand. Her eyes were odd, though. Her eyes seemed glassy. Maybe she *was* drugged.

Fuck, could she have been on drugs that night? Did *that* explain that misty magic feel to her?

"Jess." He could feel his eyebrows draw together, that wide-open feeling she produced in him drawing in, trying to fold back up tight. "Jasmin."

A bored lift of her eyebrows. She looked like a thirteen-year-old trying to produce ennui. It was ridiculous. It was as annoying as it was from a thirteen-year-old, in fact. Worse.

"Jess. Let me—can I take you for coffee? Lunch?"

She gave him an ironic smile and shook her head. "I'm busy, I'm afraid."

And that was a slap in the face. Too busy to have coffee? When he'd—when they'd—he took a breath. "Dinner?"

97

"I've really got to go," she said, looking at her phone. She texted something, and he suppressed the urge to wrench the phone out of her hand and throw it across the lobby.

"But Jess—"

Her eyebrows stopped him. She made him feel as if he was some teenage nerd trying to declare his undying love for the most popular girl in school. Made him feel that in more ways than one—like he really wanted to do that—grab her, tell her she must not understand, he lov—

"What was it, *droit de seigneur?*" she said. "Is that how you always seal the deal? I got to be your little bottle of champagne to toast yourself in your victory? Did you sleep with Tara, too?"

He stopped stock still staring at her. This sick, great hollowness opened, and he felt like he was falling into it. That whole night of tenderness and wonder, and... *that* was what she thought of him? "No," he said. "I wouldn't do that. Jess, the company doesn't matter—"

Her eyes lifted from her phone and locked with his. "It does to me."

"I'll buy you a new one," he said roughly, impatiently. "It's just a company, Jess, *merde.* I—"

"I've got to go." She pocketed her phone.

"I didn't know you were Jasmin Bianchi, Jess," he said quickly, struggling not to just grab her and hold her in place. "Not that who you are matters, none of this matters, Jess, but—"

"Ciao," she said, and walked out.

And this great hollow emptiness had expanded inside him, icing him everywhere, this loss, this incredulous *wait, what? What? How could this have just happened? Either it was just a hook-up or it was life-changingly special, but it can't—surely it can't have been both?*

And yet it had been both. One thing to her and one thing to him. He'd tried several times—tried to initiate a conversation the next day as she packed up her supplies and walked out, tried to call her two weeks later after she might have had time to think—but he'd never gotten through to her at all. She'd been crystal clear on it: *You're just not that important.*

Everything that he had thought so special—not worth her time. Because she thought he was just a bastard with money, a taker, a user.

Sitting on the limestone now, with his cousins, he rubbed his bare left wrist. When he slid behind the wheel of his car dressed for business, just the assets within that space—the Aston Martin, the watch, the suit, the cufflinks, the damn platinum pens people gave him—were worth half a million dollars.

So it was stupid to feel so empty. As if he had nothing that was actually his.

Chapter 10

Shit. Jess clenched her fist on the counter the next morning, restless with a rage that had kept her tossing on that new mattress half the night.

He'd called this scent *shit?* When she'd captured so perfectly that steel quality to him that he liked to show the world. It should be *exactly* the kind of scent he would want to wear as he strode into a meeting to let those present know that he'd bought up all their dreams and ambitions because they'd made such easy, stupid targets out of themselves.

Not that anyone in a boardroom should be able to smell his scent, of course. It wasn't the Renaissance. A man these days must wear fragrance with restraint. A touch of it at the base of his throat or the nape of his neck, a spritz perhaps in the lining of his jacket, so that when he took it off, you got just an elusive waft of the man he wanted you to know.

A vision of Damien Rosier, removing his suit coat in a boardroom as he moved in for the kill.

A vision of Damien removing his coat in a restaurant and turning to offer his arm to Nathalie Leclair.

A vision of Damien removing his coat in his bedroom, his eyes on her...

No steel in that moment, or at least none that he'd wanted to telegraph.

Seduction then. Was that what a fragrance for him needed? Did he prefer to soften what he was with his scent rather than advertise it?

Her fingers sank into the folds of his coat, and she lifted it to breathe inside the lining, around the collar. Her whole body clenched as everything came back to her—the way his body had felt, braced over hers in his bed, the hunger in his eyes, the care of her, that *This is our first time and I don't want to scare you away* care, how much he held himself in check, and how that restraint honed his cheekbones and made his mouth severe and passionate, his eyes glittering with so much intensity. The way his lips had felt, as he buried his face in her throat and kissed her all...down...her...

"Excuse me," said a voice from the door to the old-fashioned laboratory, and she jerked out of the memory, dropping the coat.

The woman who stood there had bronze-tipped hair so curly that it was the first thing Jess saw. The second was the raised eyebrow and the curious way the woman's green eyes rested on the coat. With intrigued recognition.

Jess just managed not to shove the coat guiltily behind her back. "May I help you?"

"I'm Layla Dubois," the other woman said, and Jess thought: *I know that face.* She'd seen it just last night, while researching the Rosiers online to give herself greater knowledge of her possible enemies here. *That's Belle Woods. Yet another of the glamorous, famous women the Rosiers date.*

Before Damien's cousin Matthieu Rosier had started appearing on celebrity sites with Belle Woods, he'd been on them a lot with model Nathalie Leclair, which was...nauseating, if *both* cousins had hooked up with the same model. But confusing, too—like...what was Damien's relationship with Nathalie? Had he possibly not been hitting on the model that evening Jess had seen them?

If so...if so...she couldn't think about it. It hurt her stomach too much to think that she might have actually had a chance at something beautiful and destroyed it because she was too afraid to believe.

"I like your music," Jess said to Belle Woods, instead of any of this, with more dryness than that music deserved. "Wish for Me", which hadn't even been released yet but which had gone viral on YouTube from a recording made at a festival, was the kind of song that made an already lonely woman just want to hang her head and cry.

The irony of a musician who'd had all her wishes in life come true having the musical ability to twist lonely hearts like that. She'd probably win another Grammy for the damn thing. And God, did anyone in this family ever date someone ordinary?

The rock star smiled wryly at having her incognito immediately blown. "You're Jasmin Bianchi, right?"

"Most people call me Jess."

"My family call me Layla," the other woman said. Her head tilted. She kept studying Jess in a way that made Jess want to check a mirror to fix her hair and make sure she could support such a searching gaze. Layla took a deep breath. "Which, um, I think we might be. That is...I think we might be related."

What?

Jess stared at her.

"Have you talked to Tante Colette yet?" Layla asked.

Colette Delatour? The woman who had given this to her? The ninety-six-year-old woman Damien didn't want to accuse of dementia in a court of law? "I should," she said uneasily.

She should have done it *already*, before she got caught up in this shop and a battle with Damien. She just wasn't used to having...well, relatives. Generations. Someone behind her to whom she could and should turn and talk.

"Do you want me to take you to see her?" Layla asked.

Jess hesitated. That felt so...supported. To have someone there for her, when she faced an unsettling time. She tested the idea, but it felt like pressing her feet into sand while standing in the waves. "There's no need," she said quickly. "I can go on my own."

"Oh." Layla's expression flickered. "You, ah...you don't get lost around here? I always used to," she said ruefully. "In fact, I still do, half the time."

"No, I'm fine on my own," Jess said.

Again Layla's expression flickered. "Oh. Okay." She hesitated, visibly uncomfortable, and then shifted to look at the shelves. "What an amazing place. I didn't know the family had this. Tante Colette never showed it to me."

"You thought it should come to you, too?" Jess asked warily.

"What?" Layla gave her a confused look. As if Jess didn't quite make the sense Layla had expected her to make. "No, not at all. I'm still trying to adjust to the inheritance she gave *me*. I just didn't know Tante Colette had more of these shocks for the family up her sleeve. Her idea of a magic wand is more along the lines of a cattle prod."

Jess waited, trying to figure out what in the world Layla meant.

"Fairy godmother hardened Resistance war hero style," Layla said, waving her hands. "You know?"

Jess looked at her blankly. Maybe Layla would start making sense if she kept talking long enough.

"I also didn't know I had a, you know, a...cousin." Layla peeked at her, keeping her body facing the shelves of bottles but her glance lingering, studying Jess again.

"A..." Jess stared at her.

"I'm pretty sure," Layla said. "That is—I mean...well, we should ask Tante Colette. If you're descended from Léonard Dubois, too. If that's why she gave you this place."

Jess's eyebrows crinkled together. "My father was illegitimate. I think it was part of what drove him to the U.S. That sense that he could never find his place here where...the big perfume families hold sway." Notably, the Rosiers.

"Monsieur Rosier says Léo was a very wild teenager, running around a lot before he ran away."

"Monsieur...? Louis Rosier?" Damien's father, the formal head of Rosier SA, who got his son to do all the dirty work?

"Jean-Jacques Rosier. Matt's grandfather. And Damien's," Layla added, with a little gleam in her eye as she glanced at the coat Jess still held.

Jess shoved that coat farther down the counter. "There are a lot of Rosiers around here," she said dryly. All that mass of family and power against...just her. All by herself. Her father had made his way in life alone, too, and she'd been luckier than he had. Until six months ago, she had at least had him.

She couldn't even imagine what it must be like for Damien to have a support system reaching out infinitely, through centuries of networking and extended family, so that on that damn phone of his he probably had five hundred people he could call for help removing any given problem.

A problem like her, for example.

"Yes," Layla said happily, hugging herself and then spreading her arms. "So much *family*."

Well, somebody certainly felt welcomed into that family, didn't she? Jess rubbed a cufflink between her fingers, feeling exposed and alone.

She glanced up to find Layla eyeing her wistfully again, sidelong. Layla looked quickly away.

"Thanks for coming to meet me," Jess said awkwardly. She could feel it, that effort on Layla's part to reach out to her. And yet trying to reach back across the gap between them with her own hand extended felt so risky. Like...to not be exposed and alone, to create a new family, she would have to try to believe in the scariest and most impossible things.

Expose herself to infinitely greater possibilities of hurt than the one of being lonely.

"Of course," Layla said, confused and uneasy. "I mean, I...I've never had a cousin."

Oh. Jess stared at the other woman a moment. Layla knew what it was like to be alone, too?

Jess hesitated, rubbing her hand over the counter. Memory stirred, all the times her father had made her perfumes that smelled like dragon's wings or fairy dust, all the ways he had reached from his world into hers as a little girl, to hold them close.

There was something Jess could do. Something that could reach out to this alien cousin. It was its own kind of risk, but it was a risk she knew how to take. "Would you like me to make you a perfume?"

***

A great, bare vine climbed up the street of stairs like a banister, or like massive roots leaving a path for humans to follow as they reached for the sun. In the hush of thick medieval walls, the stairs lay in shadow. Jess's stomach hurt as she stopped in front of an ancient oak door with a rose-shaped brass knocker.

You're just hungry, she told her stomach sternly. She hadn't yet had lunch.

She took a deep breath and grasped it, knocking with the flower on that ancient door to let her in.

Yeah, and *that* didn't feel like wishing on a star at all.

There was no answer. Of course not.

She swallowed finally and turned away, the hurt in her stomach relaxing into something more empty.

The door opened. "Yes?"

She turned around so fast she tripped on the stairs and had to grab the old vine for balance. An old, old woman stood in the door. Straight and tall, with white hair and a face as wrinkled as paper that had been crumpled in a fist time after time and then spread out. She wore a thick rust-colored tunic over dirt-stained black yoga pants and held gardening gloves in one hand.

Jess's heart started to beat too fast, and she gripped the vine more tightly. Thick as a man's wrist and more reliable, that vine. "I'm...I'm Jess Bianchi. Jasmin Bianchi."

Light flared in the old woman's dark eyes. "Jasmin." She held out her hand.

Jess clasped it carefully, afraid of delicate bones, but the old woman's grip was strong. She smelled of lavender and lemon, a hint of dirt and a little bit of onion, as if she'd been pulling onion grass in the garden or cooking in the kitchen.

"You look like him," the old woman said. "Like her."

"Are you...are you Colette Delatour?"

"Of course. Come in."

Jess followed her down a hall of dark old wood hung with photos, past a kitchen in which she glimpsed orange-red pots hanging on the wall and a window full of light, through to a garden in the back.

Jess took a wondering breath when she stepped into it. Entirely surrounded by great, old walls, one of which must be the medieval fortifications of the town, it was like stepping into a witch's garden out of an old tale. Pick a plant without permission and you might find yourself owing your firstborn child.

A fig tree grew in one corner, laden with ripe figs around which a few wasps buzzed. Herb beds lined the walls, thick with green and silver and the purple sprigs of late lavender. A clothesline was hung with washing.

"Oh," Jess said very softly as scents—living, vivid scents—rushed in and embraced her. As if life itself had surrounded her in one great hug.

"Oh, the smells." She moved toward the beds with her arms outstretched. She'd grown up in New York. She visited gardens, of course, to study scents, but for the most part, the scents of herbs and flowers she held in memory were wishes she pulled together from bottles, sending formulas down to labs to have her latest idea sent back up to her for testing, in the hope that this time she would hit on the formula that would make that wish of a scent come true.

Her hand brushed over the—ah, this was the scent that Damien had from his soap. Not lemon verbena but lemon balm, with soft but faintly rough leaves. It smelled *heavenly.*

Bees buzzed in the lavender. She ran her fingers up the sprigs, and they buzzed gently around her hand as the lavender scent released into the air.

"This is beautiful," she whispered. She could smell the stone. It framed this place, held all these scents safe in a thousand years of strength. She could smell the dirt, rich under the brightness of the herbs and the buzzing of the bees.

"You're just like Tristan," Colette Delatour said, amused but gentle about it, and Jess looked back at her.

"Is that who you said I looked like?" Although what resemblance there was between Jess and any of the sexy Rosier cousins, she had no idea.

"Oh, no," Colette Delatour said. "No, you've no blood shared with Tristan. Or with Damien," she mentioned, so unnecessarily that Jess flushed. "You look like *him.* My son. Or I tried to—be his mother." That old, strong, quiet voice faltered unexpectedly. But when Jess looked at her, her eyes were steady, her body straight.

This woman was ninety-six? Geneticists should be in here begging for DNA samples.

"And you look like her," Colette said quietly. "His real mother. Élise Dubois. Those same soft brown curls and that tender mouth that let her go everywhere, because soldiers always forgot she could be strong. She forgot it, too, sometimes, even when she was in the middle of acts so strong and courageous they cost her life."

Jess stared. Was this part of her history? She carried the blood of a woman who was a hero? "In the Resistance?" she hazarded.

Colette nodded. "He had them, too, her son. That tender mouth and that soft hair. He wasn't a bad boy, you know. He was just a boy who had been very hurt. Most of us were, by the war. Trying to heal, to grow back to normal, but sometimes it was like trees that had been broken in a storm trying to grow up straight no matter how many other fallen trees were holding them down."

Jess kept one hand curled loosely around a lavender stem for strength as she faced this old, strong woman. "I'm sorry," she said quietly. "I'm sorry you had to live through that."

"I'm glad you didn't," Colette Delatour said simply. "But it makes your generation hard to understand sometimes."

Yeah, she bet. They must feel like freaking marshmallows to an old Resistance war hero. Jess looked down at the herbs, petting the lavender with one hand and the lemon balm with the other, and then knelt to breathe them in, drawing in her own strength before she asked for more details of this story.

A thump and a step. "Tante Colette, is this what you wan—" The male voice broke off abruptly.

Jess flushed dark as she stared at Damien, just stepping out of the door into the garden, an old trunk that made her think of steamer trips braced on one shoulder, his head angled to accommodate it.

He stared at her, not moving.

The moment drew out and out, Jess on her knees with her hands in plants and her hair brushing the leaves, Damien tall and strong and with a great weight balanced on his shoulder. A position that made his biceps look fantastic.

"Yes, that's the one," Colette finally said calmly. "Thank you, Damien. You can set it on the picnic table."

Jess came to her feet as Damien moved jerkily, crossing to the table and setting the dusty trunk down with a thump. His hands rested on its handles, as he stood without moving.

Jess found she'd approached the picnic table somehow, and she stopped abruptly before she let herself walk right up to him. "You've, ah, you've smudged your shirt," she said absurdly.

He wore dress pants but only a white T-shirt with them, as if he'd stripped down for his aunt's trunk-fetching task.

Damien brushed at the smudge on his shoulder indifferently, eyes still fixed on her.

"Here." Colette Delatour handed him a drape of white fabric that had been lying on the other end of the picnic table. "I fixed that button while you were up in the attic."

Damien looked away from Jess at last, focusing on his aunt. That hard mouth softened just a little. "Thank you, Tante Colette." He squeezed the tips of her old fingers gently once and took the fabric, which turned into one of his white dress shirts as he shook it out and started to pull it on.

"You make your aunt do your mending?" Jess challenged dryly, just for something to weaken this moment, to make it safer. *Stupid.* Of course Damien Rosier, with his Dior tailoring, didn't *need* his aunt to do his mending.

At least...maybe he did need her to do it. Maybe she needed to fix that button for him. But it was a different kind of need. A need that could be satisfied by the little act of making five or six strong stitches, the little act of squeezing old fingers to say thank you.

Her throat tightened inexplicably. She wanted to sew on a button or have someone sew one on for her.

Damien shot her a dark glance, but he didn't respond, buttoning his shirt. God, every time she saw that man he was dressing or undressing in front of her.

She swallowed, fighting back hot and insistent memories.

"What good timing that you could stop by," Colette Delatour said. "Damien was just telling me that he had a free hour before his next meeting. Let's have lunch in the garden."

***

Damien didn't want her here. He didn't know what to do with it—this woman to whom he had felt as if he could offer himself like a fucking falling star, caught mid-fall and held out carefully, with hope. And she'd seen nothing but...titanium.

A man with no heart, who used everyone he saw.

He didn't know what to do with that opinion of him from her here, in this garden, where he already felt like one of those damn ripe figs half the time—splitting open while the wasps zoomed in. His aunt always made him feel that way.

But he had a duty. They used to be a little more lax about visits, letting a few days slip by between them, but Raoul had chided them when he came home, woke them up to how old their aunt was growing. An ironic reprimand, given that Raoul hadn't been around for visits for fourteen years, but still...he'd been right.

Now at least one of them checked in on Tante Colette every single day at lunch, and another swung by in the evening. Not just him, Matt, Tristan, Raoul, but also Gabriel and Raphaël Delange, who had their restaurant only a couple of medieval streets away, and Layla and Léa and Jolie and Allegra, his own parents, Tristan's parents, more distant cousins. They stopped by. They helped with whatever needed helping. They gave her their company and soaked up hers like a precious resource that might one day run out.

And just because his aunt's opinion wounded him didn't mean he left her on her own. Hell, if he avoided everyone in his family who treated him as if bullets bounced off him, he might as well act like Lucien and run off and join the Foreign Fucking Legion.

Maybe that would get rid of these damn migraines his family brought on so often anymore.

Or teach him what real bullets felt like. *Damn you, Lucien. Are you ever going to come back?*

"Are you all right, Damien?" Tante Colette asked, laying pressed, hand-embroidered napkins on the table. Of course she had made them use the little round table instead of the rectangular one, so that he wouldn't be able to shift without his knees bumping into Jess's or his forearm brushing hers.

"I'm fine." He set the tray down, unloading wine glasses, a bright yellow Provençal pitcher of cold lime-infused water, the crisp cucumbers that Tante Colette had just had him slice for their first course.

"You don't need anything for your head?"

Damn it, he should never tell his family anything. "It's fine." He refused to look at Jess, his lips pressed together.

"What's wrong with your head?" Jess asked.

Yeah, right. As if you care.

"Migraines," Tante Colette said. Traitor.

Traitor was too dirty a word to use around an old Resistance fighter, though, so Damien just had to lock the temper up there where it could pound on the inside of his skull with the rest of his tension.

Jess stood looking at him with her eyebrows pleated as if he'd suddenly confessed to being half-unicorn. Damn it. He turned to lean the tray by the base of the fig tree.

"Do you need a cool cloth for your eyes or something?" Jess asked. "Should you go lie down?"

He shot her an incredulous look. "I'm fine." He jerked out her chair and his aunt's and stood behind his aunt's, slipping it forward correctly as she sat. Jess took her own seat before he could move to her chair.

He took the pitcher and filled their glasses, and it was all he could do not to press the cold condensation on the ceramic against his forehead. He did *not* have a migraine. He just had this incipient pressure against the back of his forehead, running in a line toward his temples and tightening around his skull.

111

Jess dug in the small purse she had hung over the back of her chair, twisting so that his gaze followed the curve of her neck, the stretch of her bare arm, the soft curls twisted loosely at her nape. She was wearing golden-pale capri pants today and a sea-green drapey thing that looked romantic and wistful. She must not have expected to see him.

"Here." She held out a small plastic bottle, its contents rattling.

He took it. Advil. He recognized the brand from his time in New York. "Modern medicine? Tante Colette won't approve."

Tante Colette gave him an ironic glance. "I approve of modern medicine very much, as would anyone who went through a war. But in your case, you'd do better to just take the afternoon off and go windsurfing with one of your cousins. Then you wouldn't get the migraine at all."

Yeah. For a second, the thought of the waves and the wind filled him, of laughing with and challenging his cousins as they raced, and he took a slow breath, that line of tension easing.

When he opened his eyes, Jess was leaning a little forward onto her elbow, nibbling at her thumbnail, studying him as if that unicorn horn was sprouting from his head. Which was about what his skull felt like it was fighting to contain, when he got a migraine. She had eyes the color of dusk, a little blue, lots of dark gray.

He looked away.

"To finding my family again," Tante Colette said, lifting her lime-water glass, and he sighed at the reminder of her familial priorities but made the toast and did it properly—meeting her eyes and then Jess's as he clinked glasses, because it was rude not to. Most people thought not looking into the eyes of the person you clinked glasses with brought bad luck, like a subtle curse of the other person.

Jess flushed a little as their eyes met and drank a long swallow from her glass, and that flush for some reason made the tension in his forehead ease again. Maybe the migraine was going to stay away after all. Maybe all it had needed was a quiet lunch in this garden.

With the bees buzzing, and the cool water, and the scents, and the thick medieval walls wrapping them in peace. "I'm sorry, did you want some wine?" he thought to ask Jess. Tante Colette drank very little these days, and he never drank alcohol during a business day. He won battles by having the sharpest wits in the room. "I can open a bottle."

"No," she said quietly. "No, this is...nice." Her fingers stroked the condensation starting to form on her glass.

Was it? He hesitated, not sure how to feel. It was going to sneak into him, this quiet garden. Its scents and calm and the way she was looking at him were going to get to him. And then he'd have to go back out and be her bad guy. She'd tricked him that way before.

But, God, it was so nice to let the tension relax out of his temples.

He slowly set the small bottle of painkillers by his plate, not yet opening it.

"I was telling Jasmin—Jess—about her great-grandmother and her grandfather," Tante Colette said as Damien started to serve the cucumbers. Jess first, as the guest, Tante Colette second as the oldest—and only other—woman present, himself last.

He glanced at his great-aunt. She had been sixty-six when he was born, three months after Matt's birth, and he'd grown up on stories of her and his grandfather's exploits during the war. And never realized how much wasn't being told. How many parts of sixty-six years of life he never thought to ask about, and no one dug out and told him, perhaps because they were too painful.

Matt had heard the story of Tante Colette's adopted son with Layla and filled the rest of them in, and of course after what she'd done to Matt—stealing part of his

valley like that and giving it to some random rock star—
Damien had tried to find out everything he could, so he
would be ready to protect the family the next time.

But he'd never heard the story from Tante Colette.

She told it simply, the story of a schoolteacher who
saved one Jewish child in her class and then found that
she had to save another, and another. Élise Dubois had
ended up helping them save dozens of children whom
Tante Colette and Pépé and their cell had ferried across
the Alps into Switzerland. And when the Gestapo had
arrived at her house, she'd taken cyanide and died,
rather than risk torture and her ability to withstand it.

At this point, according to Matt, Layla had been
sobbing in his shirt. Jess was biting the first knuckle on
her finger, her eyes red, but she didn't turn to him for
support.

Damien looked down at his hands, strong and flat
and empty on the table, his left wrist naked. He needed
to get a new watch.

"So I took her boy," Tante Colette said. "I took him
and tried to raise him."

"Where was his father?" Jess interrupted softly.

"He died in the first six weeks. On the front, before
the surrender."

Jess's face worked. "Oh." She bit hard at that
knuckle.

"Léo was a sweet boy," Tante Colette said. "Tender.
Very bruised. He was only eight when his mother died.
She'd sent him to hide up in the hills behind the house,
and he'd crept back down after the SS left, and of course
one of them was waiting for him. An eight-year-old child
who'd just lost his mother. They took him in. The local
SS captain made a pet of him, and you can only imagine
how that might have affected him, when the SS was
responsible for his mother's death. And any information
he let slip about his mother's friends, they used that, of
course. It was six months before we could get him back,
when the war was ending, and we never knew how much

guilt that little boy let eat him up, for things he might have let slip that he never dared tell us." The old woman stopped and shook her head, silent a moment, before she took a breath. "If he went wild, then that's on my shoulders, that I couldn't save him. But yes, he had an affair with one of the teenage perfume factory workers here, when he was sixteen and she was fifteen."

"That's not wild," Jess said. "To make love to someone and mess up when you're wounded and lonely. That's just...hungry."

Damien slanted a swift glance at her. She twisted her hands. It was insane how hard it was for him not to just lay his own hand over both of hers and calm them. *It's okay. Shh. It's me. Remember?*

"Thank you," Tante Colette said quietly. "But it was wild for the fifties. Her father was furious. And Jacky lit into him for failing to uphold the family honor, and he ran away." That old, dark gaze fell. She stared at her own hands, wrinkled and spotted and still capable of weeding a garden or sewing a button or making a soup. "And he kept running. Once in a while, he'd send something to me, you know. A postcard from California, a mask from Papua New Guinea. I would never know what to expect. He never told me anything in them. It took a professional heir hunter to track down the children he had left behind."

Did that plural *children* mean two, and now they were done, or were there more?

"But he kept running. He never came back here. I guess there was just too much he needed to get away from." Tante Colette's gaze was straight and steady as she said it.

"I'm so sorry," Jess said unexpectedly. She closed her hand over both of Tante Colette's, exactly as Damien had restrained himself from doing for her. Both he and Tante Colette stilled in surprise. "That must have been so hard for you. I'm really sorry."

"Thank you," Tante Colette said slowly, staring down at Jess's young, slim hand over her old ones. If Damien hadn't known his Tante Colette better, he might have thought that quick breath she drew, the flicker of her eyes, was to fight off the threat of tears.

He stared at his own hands, wishing he had offered that gesture of consolation. Wishing he could offer it now—one arm to Jess, one to Tante Colette.

Maybe Jess was right in her belief that he was shallow, hard titanium.

Probably, in fact, the reason Layla had cried into Matt's shirt was that Matt had pulled her into his arms. He could imagine Matt doing that, the big, growly bear, who pretended to be so tough and was actually a damn marshmallow. He wanted to be able to imagine himself doing it, too.

"I wish I'd tracked you down earlier," Tante Colette said. "I wish I had been able to meet your father, too, before he died."

Jess gave a soft intake of breath, and her eyes filled, her free hand clenching into a fist on the table.

"I'm sorry no one was there for you," Tante Colette said.

Jess pushed back quickly from the table, grabbing her purse. "Excuse me."

Damien rose automatically, reaching too late for her chair, and stared after her as she went into the house. Something about the threat of her tears, the sudden departure, made his stomach hurt.

Wait. He still thought of Chris Bianchi, with his fascinating niche perfumes, as a living contemporary. How recent was his death?

"Excuse me," he said to Tante Colette and went after Jess.

He found her in the kitchen, splashing her face with water from the kitchen sink. Then she curled her hands around the edge of the sink, just standing there, her back to him, her shoulders slim but straight, as she took long, deep breaths.

116

"Are you all right?" Damien asked.

She whirled so fast he might have been trying to stab her in the back. Her fingers clutched the edge of the sink behind her. "I'm fine."

"Fine like my head?"

"What?" she asked blankly.

Here in this kitchen where he'd been fed so much soup all his life, with its dark wood and sunlight and cheerful red pots, he felt oddly vulnerable. Shakily vulnerable, almost sick to his stomach, as if he was exactly as vulnerable as a woman in a strange land who'd just been splashing her face with water to hide tears. He took a step closer. "I didn't realize your father had died."

Her head drew back a little in shock. Then her eyebrows crinkled in disbelief. "Did your *secretary* send those flowers?"

"What?"

"The flowers you sent! For the funeral!"

He couldn't conceive of his executive assistant sending flowers for somebody's funeral without alerting Damien to the death. Frédéric knew better. "Are you sure it wasn't some other Damien? A friend of your father's?"

Her face worked, and then tears spilled over again. She dashed her hand angrily across her eyes. "It wasn't even *you*?"

"Jess. I didn't know. This is the first I've heard of it." *Why the hell didn't I know? Couldn't you have—* "I'm sorry."

Her face crumpled, her skin so splotchy and red. She didn't cry prettily. It was wrenching his stomach apart. He couldn't handle this. He couldn't handle being her bad guy right this second.

She grabbed her purse off the counter and dug into it, and he looked around for Tante Colette's box of tissues. But instead of a tissue, she pulled out her wallet, digging out a business-size card from among the credit cards. "This wasn't you?"

She thrust it at him and then shoved both her hands across her face again, trying to scrape away the tears.

A florist's card. He turned it over. *If you need anything, anything at all, this is my private number. Damien.*

He pressed a fist to his heart. "Good God. Your father died—then?"

Right after they'd slept together, right after he'd walked into Amour et Artisan that Monday and realized she and Jasmin Bianchi, whose company he had taken over, were one and the same, right when she'd kept showing that brittle, cynical flippancy whenever he tried to talk to her, until it had hurt so much to keep trying that he'd sent her those flowers and stopped. Sent her those flowers with his phone number because...fuck, what if she ended up pregnant? Sent her those flowers because...well, he would have kind of liked to send her flowers that next day, if he'd known her full name then and where to find her, if by the time he'd found out her name she wasn't making it obvious that she didn't want anything to do with him again. Sent her those flowers because...he'd wanted one last excuse to give her his number. And never once when he'd jerked his phone out of his pocket at the ring of that private number had it ever been her call.

She stared at him a long moment. And then she turned her head away. "He was dying when we met," she said wearily. "It's the kind of thing that makes a woman *stupid.*"

Fuck. He reached out and gripped the doorjamb. Everything she had just said hit him too hard—what she must have been going through. And the fact that he was her *stupid.*

That she thought sleeping with him had been that bad a thing to do.

When he'd thought it was possibly the best thing he'd done *for himself* in his entire life.

"I'm sorry," he managed.

"He'd been dying for two years," she said. "But it was...the end. And he...finished two weeks after you—took over Amour et Artisan." So two weeks after that night, too.

Fuck.

Fuck and fuck and fuck.

"Jess." He moved toward her, his hands stretching out.

She started as his hands closed around her upper arms and stared up at him.

"I'm so sorry," he said, because what else was there to say, with her face so splotchy red, her pain so visible. It was worse than his pain. It made his pain feel like self-indulgent whining. Kind of the standard opinion of any of the male cousins' pain when they were growing up, in fact, so dismissing his own feelings was a familiar comfort. "I didn't—Jess, you should have told me. You were *alone?*"

He couldn't even conceive of facing his father's death alone. *Everyone* would be there. People would hug him or grasp his hand or kiss his cheeks, over and over and over. His body would almost never stand untouched, the whole funeral. He wouldn't even be able to move, the church would be so packed with family, his cousins' shoulders pressed tight against his as they crowded together to fit everyone into the church for the ceremony. Their strong shoulders would lift the casket for him, to help carry his burden. His shoulder still sometimes felt the imprint of Raoul's mother's casket, six years before.

"Why didn't you *call* me?" he asked incredulously. How could anyone face that kind of thing *alone?*

Her face crinkled in confusion. "Why would I call you?"

It stabbed right through to his heart. He couldn't breathe for it. Couldn't move his hands on her arms. Couldn't speak as his throat tightened and tightened.

Her eyebrows crinkled more, her dusk eyes turned bluer by tears, searching his face as if he was some new, fascinating molecule and she was trying to figure out how to turn him into a perfume. "Did you think you *mattered?*"

He released her arms as if they'd turned red hot and took a step back. His fists clenched over the burn in his palms.

"I mean..." She fumbled. "I mean, that I mattered? I mean...I don't know what I mean."

He shot her a savage glance. "Of course you fucking mattered, Jess." God damn it.

She stared at him. And all at once her eyes filled again. "I can't even imagine it," she whispered. "I can't even imagine having someone there who would make me feel not alone."

Oh, hell. He just reached out and yanked her into his arms, holding her tight. It hurt him everywhere. The burn of her up his body, the pain in his palms against her back. All those fucking things that *did not matter.*

Not from him.

Not to her.

She held very still. He could feel the shakiness of her breath, little gasps that fought tears.

Fuck.

He lifted a hand and stroked her hair. So soft. Those little, gentle ripples of curls. The twist of it into a knot at her nape. His thumb worked into that knot without him even realizing he was doing it, until her hair loosened and fell down her back. He stroked the length of it. *It's all right. Shh. I'm here.*

I'm not all right, but I'd like for you to be.

"You'd have cared?" she whispered into his chest, and he felt wetness through two layers of shirt.

Her tears, while she questioned whether he would have cared *that her father died.*

"Jesus, Jess." His throat strangled any other words. What the hell was the point of even trying, against an opinion of him like that, when he'd thought...he'd thought...

Hell.

"Of course I'd have cared," he finally managed. He still couldn't even let go of her, although the hurt had sunk all the way into his bones now, turning them achy and old.

She opened one hand against his chest, spreading her fingers over his pec. "I didn't know you could do that," she said slowly. "Have a little black book full of women and still actually care about someone you hooked up with at a party."

He closed his eyes. The instinct to say something ironic and cold, to fight her back from him, was so powerful, and yet...how could he add hurt to a woman who was crying over her father's death, which she had faced all alone? "I don't have a black book full of women," he said through his teeth.

"A phone. Whatever."

His hands closed into fists, against her back. "You were supposed to recognize the phone as irony."

"Irony?" She lifted her head. She looked an utter wreck. It made him want to do everything sappy. Stroke all those tears off her cheeks. Give her himself again.

"A lie," he said tightly. "A stupid lie, because you believed it."

Her eyebrows drew together again. "So I'm not in there as a one star?"

Jesus. He let go of her. He couldn't do this anymore. He just couldn't. "No."

She folded her arms around herself, making him feel like a jerk because she was once again having to console herself alone.

But I would have been there. If you'd believed I could be.

"Jesus. A *one* star?" he said suddenly. "*Fuck*, Jess." He shoved his hands across his face. He needed longer hair like Tristan, so he had something to yank out. He needed his watch, his coat, his cufflinks.

"Can I ask you something?" she said suddenly.

"God. Please don't."

"How often do you hook up with someone like that?"

So much for denying her permission to keep stabbing him.

"I mean...for example...how many women have you slept with since me?" she asked, her voice dropping as if maybe some of her questions might actually hurt her, too.

He turned abruptly for the kitchen door, wishing he could walk straight out of the house and didn't have to go back to the garden and his aunt.

"For me it was none, see," she said suddenly, and he stopped still in the door, his back to her. "None before, not for a long time before, and none since. See? I told you I wasn't good at it."

He stood very still for a long moment. And then strode two steps down the hall toward the garden. And then stopped.

He came back just enough to show half his body in the doorway, his hand gripping the doorjamb until it hurt his fingers. "Me neither." Her eyes widened. He held them. "None since."

He jammed one of his own knuckles with the force of his grip on the frame before he jerked his hand loose and strode back into the garden. Maybe for once in his life, he could hide behind his ninety-six-year-old aunt.

Chapter 11

"Did I ever tell you about the time Damien tried to catch the moon?" Colette asked, and Damien coughed on his soup.

Jess, spoon in her mouth, looked over it from Colette to Damien, then awkwardly swallowed the lemony chicken orzo soup Colette had had ready for their main course. The soup seemed an incongruous, cozy winter choice for this hot August day, but in the quiet shade of the garden its lemon and comfort worked oddly well. "Uh—no."

Obviously, since she'd only met Colette Delatour forty minutes before. Of course, Colette was ninety-six. Maybe she genuinely couldn't keep track of what stories she'd told anymore.

"I think I'm going to have to go." Damien looked at his left wrist, then curled his fingers into his palm when he found that wrist bare. "I'm sorry to rush out in the middle of lunch, Tante Colette, but—"

"His mother wished for it," Tante Colette said, and two streaks of color appeared on Damien's cheeks.

Jess stared, spoon locked in one hand. Was Damien Rosier *blushing*?

If her opinion of him got overset much more, she might have to start from zero.

Grief squeezed her. This nascent suspicion that if she had believed in him, after that first night, she might not be starting from zero but from something far richer and more beautiful. God, what if in all that loss the world had visited on her, some of it had been her own fault?

"Tante Colette—"

"For her birthday. It was her little joke, you see. Damien kept trying to get her to ask for something *special* for her birthday, instead of just hugs and kisses from him."

Definite color on Damien's cheeks now.

"And she finally told him she wanted the moon and the stars. She said later she thought he would *draw* them for her. Make them with glitter. Something like that."

Damien pressed fingertips hard into the table. "I was seven," he pointed out abruptly, almost a growl.

"Aww," Jess said involuntarily, lifting her hand to her lips. Then *she* blushed as Damien glared at her. But...this sudden vision of Damien as a child hit her, a little, black-haired seven-year-old trying to give his mother something more than hugs and kisses. Because he wanted to be *bigger*, of course, he wanted to give her something wonderful, while his mother almost certainly thought hugs and kisses from her little boy were the best thing any woman could ever have.

God, he must have been *adorable*.

"But Damien, he wanted to capture the *actual moon.* So he made this elaborate trap at the top of a tree, with a big mirror he managed to rope up there with Tristan's help—Tristan was five—and even a cage he built out of sticks. Tristan stood at the base of the tree with a rope to pull at the right moment, which was supposed to close the trap, and Damien climbed to the very top to hold up the mirror, and—when he fell, he cut his chin wide open."

Jess looked at the scar on Damien's chin. So that was what it was from.

"He might have fallen on a shard of the mirror, but we don't know for sure, because he and Tristan tried to bandage it themselves and cover it up. It was the middle of the night, and they didn't want to get in trouble. Plus, we raised those kids to be self-reliant. And in the morning his mother came to wake him and screamed and screamed. The wound had been too big to close easily, and in the night it had soaked all through the towel they used, all over Damien's face, all over the bed around him. Twelve stitches, he needed. The sight of him covered in blood in his bed still shows up sometimes in his mother's nightmares."

"It does?" Damien said, startled.

"She thought he'd been murdered for a moment, before her screams woke him up. For weeks after, she would sneak into his room to sleep on the floor, just to make sure he was okay." A flicker of confusion crossed Damien's face. Apparently he'd never heard that detail of his own story before, and it jarred with his understanding of it. "And Damien? He was upset that he'd fallen just before he managed to capture the moon."

Damien glowered across the garden, not looking at anybody.

Jess pressed her fingers to her lips. *Oh, my God. You must have been so sweet.*

"From which the saying in our family: Be careful what you wish for. Damien will get it for you."

Damien closed his eyes, looking very put upon. Jess found herself wishing she hadn't destroyed a possible right to reach out and stroke the inside of his wrist to tease him into a better mood. God. Was it possible she would have had that right, if she hadn't run away that morning and kept running from him ever since?

"I wish I had some of those figs for our dessert," Tante Colette said, and Damien rose immediately, then stopped and gave his great aunt a dirty look.

Colette smiled a little.

Jess found herself fighting a smile, too.

"Maybe you two young people could pick us some," Colette said.

"I'll clear off the table," Damien said, and did that instead, so that Jess picked figs alone.

She'd never seen an actual fig tree before. The green, dusty aroma embraced her, faintly milky, fresh and almost too sweet. The figs felt firm and smooth in her hand, even as they split open, showing their pink flesh. The wasps alarmed her, and more so when one buzzed to her hair to investigate the new scent. She held very still, a fig in one hand, cringing from the possible sting.

A firm breath puffed against her head. The wasp took flight. Damien appeared from behind her, moving to the other side of the fig tree without a word.

Jess tried to keep picking, but she kept looking at him, through the dappled shade and the wasps and the hanging fruit.

None since.

Of course you mattered.

Why didn't you call me?

Her heart was starting to hurt her. It had hurt so much this past year, but this hurt was different, crueler—as if she might have snuffed out her own wish.

Such a sexy, handsome man, with so much power and so much wealth and such a reputation for ruthlessness. Who had once been a seven-year-old who tried to catch the moon for his mother, because he didn't think his hugs were good enough.

"I saw you with Nathalie Leclair," she said suddenly, painfully. She spoke in English, just in case their words might reach Colette Delatour.

He looked at her blankly, one hand frozen around a fig above his head. "With my cousin's ex-girlfriend?" The British in his accent was very clipped, the Rs a rough breath.

"The next day. I don't usually go to two perfume parties in a row. I don't usually go to *any*. I don't like them, and other than your cousin Tristan the actual perfumers don't get invited to them that much. But I...guess I half hoped to run into you again." Half hopes could be hard to kill. When she'd come to Grasse, that same half hope had *still* been struggling to come alive again, the hope that she would see him again and somehow he would make everything she knew about him

126

not be true so that she could believe in him again. "But when I did...you seemed pretty occupied."

He just stared at her a moment. "I don't know what you're talking about. Nathalie Leclair—the model? She used to date my cousin Matt. It was a disaster."

Jess called up the painful image again. It had definitely been him and not one of his cousins. She wouldn't mistake him for anyone. "You had one hand braced by her head, and you were leaning into her. You might have been arguing. The two of you appeared pretty intensely engaged. Then you took her arm, and the two of you left together."

Damien's lips pressed tight. "And that was all it took?"

Well...Nathalie was so beautiful and glamorous. Exactly the kind of person who fit with Damien Rosier, unlike Jess herself. And everything had seemed so hard then. Grief and loss drowning her at the bottom of a well. Of *course* the one beautiful, magical night had turned out to be a grasp at a straw.

Damien had that steel look again, except for the tic of a little muscle along his jaw. "I was always trying to damage control Nathalie back then. That would have been not too long after Matt broke up with her. She was a loose cannon, and he had no idea how to defend himself from her style of attack. I don't really remember that party, since I had to deal with her so often, but I certainly never *left* with her. You might have seen me leading her into another room, away from cameras."

Oh. This stupid garden must be stealing all her strength, because Jess wanted to cry again. Had she destroyed something that truly could have been, so stupidly?

"You know what I would have done, if I'd seen you with another man leaning into you at the next night's party?" Damien asked.

She shook her head.

"Stabbed him and smiled over his corpse."

She blinked.

"Or in some other way cut him out of that picture. I sure as hell wouldn't have watched you walk out with him and not said anything. We have a very different approach to life."

Indeed. How did one *manage* that—so much ruthlessness, so much self-assurance? She knew perfume, but even with that, every start of a new fragrance was its own kind of anguish, that whole blank page of scent to fill and so many ways to never quite succeed with what was so beautiful in her head. And when she worked on perfume, it was in spaces of quiet, where she didn't have to impose herself on other people. That self-confidence that could cut through other people like a knife—no, she didn't have that.

"But most of all, I wouldn't have believed it," he said. "I would have thought, 'What's going on? Picking up another man twelve hours later doesn't fit with what I know of her.' And I would have made sure I did know what was going on, before I made any decisions to ditch you from my life."

He'd tried to get through to her multiple times, after that boardroom meeting that Monday when he saw her again and realized he'd taken over her company. He'd tried to figure out what was going on. She'd had to shut him out repeatedly, his eyebrows drawing more deeply together each time she pushed him back.

"I wasn't feeling very strong back then," Jess said, low. "I *already* felt as if my whole world was crumbling down, before I saw that."

Damien looked down at the fig he held in his hand, rubbing his thumb over its skin. He didn't say anything, but for the first time since she'd seen him in Grasse, his lips weren't pressed in a firm line. Softened, they looked incredibly sensual, his eyes brooding, his eyebrows drawn very slightly together. She wanted to ruffle his hair, to make that brooding look complete.

"And, you know, you're a little bit out of my league," she said roughly.

His eyebrows went up. "What do you mean by that?"

A flush started to climb up her cheeks. She should have kept her mouth shut. "Come on. You know what I mean."

"No." His eyes lifted from the fig and met hers. "I don't."

Her cheeks heated painfully. Of course ruthless Damien would make her spell this out, pin her mercilessly well outside her comfort zone the instant she accidentally stepped beyond it. "You're gorgeous and sexy and powerful and wealthy, and...I'm just me."

"One of the top perfumers of our generation?"

She dropped a fig into her basket and pushed her freed hand across her forehead, shoving strands of hair back from her flushed face. "Besides that. I'm just...me."

"Underneath who you are to the rest of the world, you're just you?"

She nodded. He was holding her eyes as if she was supposed to understand something, and almost, almost...she thought about him as a sweetheart of a seven-year-old, trying to catch the moon. And she thought about that ruthless steel surface of his, that casual *I'd stab him and smile over his corpse*. And she thought about the way his skin was revealed that night as he slowly unbuttoned his shirt, watching her. Kissing her. Running his hands up her arms in this stroke of reassurance and seduction...

She picked another fig quickly, too ripe.

The wasp that had been feasting unnoticed on its split flesh buzzed around her hand angrily. Damien reached out and offered his hand to the wasp instead, distracting it toward him. It buzzed around his fingers a moment and then flew off to another fruit. Damien took the over-ripe fig from her—calluses on his fingertips brushing her palm—and tossed it into the corner of the garden.

"Which of those things that you just said about me do you care about?" Damien asked. "Gorgeous, sexy, powerful, wealthy?"

None of them, that was the thing. Sure, a couple of them had been nice little pluses, but what she had *cared* about, actual care, was the way they talked, like a tale out of time, the gentle, quiet, sexy care in *him.*

She wished she could just plunge into some icy pool and hide her hot cheeks. But she'd already been enough of a coward with him, hadn't she?

"I liked the gorgeous and sexy," she finally admitted. Kind of. Except that it was like sleeping with a movie star. Hard to believe it was real. If he'd been a little more geeky, a little more ordinary, he would have made *sense.* She could have still believed in her luck the next day. "The *powerful* and *wealthy* are a little unsettling."

He was silent a moment, turning a fig in his palm with a little stroking motion of his thumb that was bringing back far too many memories. "I'm quite comfortable being powerful. And the wealth protects my family. Plus, it's essential to power."

Of course.

A one-sided curve of his mouth. "I find you thinking I'm *gorgeous* and *sexy* a little unsettling." The French layered over the British in his accent, roughening the R in *gorgeous*, softening the G.

Her skin prickled at the thought of unsettling him.

This faint gleam in those sea-green eyes of his as they flicked over her body, and...was that a hint of color on his cheeks again? Surely not. "But I might be able to get used to it."

She turned hastily with her basket toward the table where Colette Delatour sat waiting for them.

"Not comfortable with it, no," Damien said in her ear as he followed her, the French-on-British accent rubbing all up and down her spine. "But I might enjoy it, just the same."

Chapter 12

It was shadowy and quiet in the back room of the little perfume shop. Damien closed his eyes, breathing in the aromas of dust and shade, the forgotten scents that layered with the bright, pushy ones that had just been awoken. If he followed the threads of scents, if he took his time, he could piece together what Jess had played with that day, after she'd left Tante Colette's house. Tristan, who had finely trained his Rosier nose, would have already known. Damien had been destined for business so young he'd never had that training.

He'd chosen that destiny, of course. Yes, it had pleased his father, but it had deeply disappointed his mother, who would have whole-heartedly backed him if he went into an artistic career like Tristan. It was just that...Tristan thought what was vital to Rosier SA was the perfume he made. Matt thought it was the valley and the flowers he grew. But Damien had always known that it was the money, the business deals, the knowledge of behavioral economics, the control. *That* was what determined their lives. That was where the real power lay.

He could hear Jess shifting around, shoes forgotten again, her feet making almost no sound. Slouching in this chair while she was on her feet working felt oddly intimate. Like a man might stretch out on a couch after a hard day and not come to his feet when his wife entered the room but just smile at her and maybe form his lips into a kiss to invite her to come to him, to bend down, to brush his lips with happiness.

I'm here. You're here. It's been a long day, but now we're together.

But at the core of that shadowy, quiet intimacy, his stomach knotted. He kept his breath calm, his eyes closed, his body slouched. No need to let anyone else see his nerves as he waited to see what fragrance she had made for him this time.

He almost hadn't come, he'd dreaded the moment of truth so much. The slap when every raw ripping open of himself at lunch was thrown back in his face. He'd gotten to the shop so late that she'd been visibly surprised to see him, coming down from upstairs where, apparently, she had been making the bed with the pressed sheets Tante Colette had given her after lunch.

He thought about helping her spread those lavender-scented sheets. Thought about looking at her across the bed as their hands swept over cotton, tucked it under corners, made that bed ready...

He tried to channel *gorgeous* and *sexy.* So sexy that the next time she walked near him in that damn wannabe-a-model red skirt she had put on sometime that afternoon, he could just catch her by the waist and pull her down astride him, shove that tight skirt up and find her panties...all...wet. Oh, yeah, and he'd—

A scent wafted under his nose, the strip brushing his lips, and he jerked, his eyes flaring open.

"Sorry." Jess drew back. In French, her accent was almost perfect, thanks to her father, but America slipped into it in the stretch of certain vowels. "Were you falling asleep?"

"Of course not." Because this wasn't an intimate moment full of trust, this chair wasn't a couch at the end of a long day, the brush across his lips wasn't a kiss, and so he couldn't do that. He couldn't relax.

"Do you want something for your head?"

Yes. He did. He wanted her to dampen a cloth with cold water, he wanted her to fold it and lay it over his eyes and rest her hand on his forehead, he wanted to just sit there, like that, with the cold on his eyes and the gentle, shaded warmth of this room in the hot August, the scents stirring while she moved around him, letting him soak up the peace. "I'm fine."

His head didn't hurt at all, in fact. He just wanted that cloth anyway.

"Did you take that Advil?"

"My migraines have been greatly exaggerated," he lied, and took her wrist, bringing the scent strip back to his nose.

He braced just a second before he breathed. Titanium again.

God damn it.

He started to release her wrist.

"Wait," she whispered. "Wait for it."

His jaw set. But he brought the strip back to his nose, forcing himself to learn this salutary lesson on opening up.

And then...his hand slowly relaxed on her wrist, his thumb stroking her pulse unconsciously, as his head cocked. And then his stomach tumbled, and something vulnerable tried to escape, as this sweetness reached him, politely hidden by that titanium. This elusive, dancing breeze of sweetness, like the whisper of coolness in the shade on a hot Provençal day, protected by walls.

"Is that fig?"

"Maybe a tiny bit." Her eyes were large in the dim room. He hoped to God he didn't look as vulnerable as she did.

"Lavender?"

She smiled a little and didn't answer. *Merde*, her mouth looked so sweet when she smiled. It made his own lips so hungry.

He couldn't figure out all the scents. But the heart notes of the perfume were starting to come out, and unlike that titanium head note, it was this rich and yet simple heart, this gorgeous pure dappling of sun and shade, with steel still running through it like a sword plunged into dirt after a battle, and it made his throat tighten. He fought his own vulnerability, wanting to yank that sword out of the dirt and hold it up to ward everyone off.

"It will take a good thirty minutes for the base notes to come out," she said. "Can I try it on your skin?"

His stomach clenched, at the thought of what the base notes might reveal, some deep-rooted betrayal of this moment of peace, and yet...he might be able to risk it. He held out his wrist for a spritz, tilted back his head for another, there at the vulnerable base of his throat. "Push-ups again?" he asked ironically.

Her gaze flickered to his torso and arms in a way that surged slow and hot through his blood.

His voice went deeper. He held her eyes. "Or shall we go straight to the arousal test?"

Yes. I want to do the arousal test. Pull you down astride me right here, shove that skirt up your waist, push your legs wide with my body, leave you all exposed to me.

Let's go back to what we were good at.

Sex. Naked. When everything seemed possible and everything seemed true.

"We could go for a walk," she said, soft and rapid.

It came from so far outside the box of his thinking that he stared at her. "A walk?"

A little flush touched her cheeks. She turned to neaten up her workspace. "Around town."

A walk. Around town. Around his town—his beautiful, happy, stubbornly defended town. "Together?"

Her jaw set a little. She looked down at the bottles on her counter.

Come here, even that hint of wounded vulnerability immediately made him think. *It's all right. Come sit on my lap.*

Preferably astride. Preferably with his hands insi—

"A walk." His stomach eased. His head eased. Maybe even his heart. Slowly, his lips relaxed and even curled upward. He rose. Oh, thank God. She still had to tilt her head back to look up at him. He still could cling to that primitive, desperate power of being born a man. "It's a nice evening for a walk."

***

He was doing it again. Seducing her. With these exquisite manners and this quiet care, as if he was picking a jasmine flower, trying to hold the flame on a candle without putting it out, cupping a dandelion without knocking away all its seeds before the wish could be blown.

As evening fell, the old Renaissance streets of Grasse were quietly active, shops shutting up while restaurants spilled their life and warmth into the street, everyone dining at the outside tables. No, not dining yet, Jess realized, except for a few tourists. Mostly hanging out with drinks or coffee with friends, before it was time to shift to meals.

People collected around a stand that served gelato-style ice cream of all flavors, including the flowers and herbs of the region—jasmine, lavender, rose, thyme. Damien glanced at her and opened a hand toward the stand, but her stomach felt full of flickering candle flames, tickling and scary, and she shook her head. Her heels and little skirt were hard to walk in, the skirt shortening her stride, the heels wobbling on cobblestones. She half wished she had worn a knit sundress and sandals and half wished she could just carry off sexy and sophisticated like one of his models, even when strolling on paving centuries old. Sexy and sophisticated required so much work and attention to unimportant things, like how much you ate and how you fixed your hair. It was a particular skill, requiring a certain amount of luck in your genetics and then, exactly like most other accomplishments, at least seventy-five percent hard work, practice, and persistence.

And she'd chosen to practice something else, something that mattered to her more. Those models who looked so great as they marketed her perfumes to the public could no more have made a perfume than she could have looked that sleek and alluring. They worked in symbiosis, she and those models, but she was the secret element of that symbiosis, the elusive magic, and they were the glamorous show.

So naturally, it made sense to assume that the elegant Damien Rosier might prefer the glamor.

And yet...here they both were. Together.

A couple of times, Damien caught her arm as she wobbled. His fingers would curve, warm and strong, around her upper arm or her elbow, for just one moment, holding her up. And then, always, they dropped away.

His hands slid into his pockets, where they could never accidentally brush hers.

People sat at tables under plane trees along the great Cours Honoré Cresp, children riding on a merry-go-round. Damien led them down the long esplanade to stop at the parapet, and they stood there, looking down at the more modern town, the great spill of lights toward Cannes.

The memory of standing on a terrace above New York, leaning against a railing as they talked, looking down at the dazzle of city lights, came back vividly. *Yes*, she thought. *Let's go back to what we were good at.*

Talking. Quiet. Care. Two strangers slowly offering each other sincerity.

Sex, also. She had to admit that they'd been *really* good at sex. Or Damien had, at least. Maybe she'd seemed pretty ordinary to him. A star or two above a one star rating, but nothing phenomenal.

The lights below were beautiful against the pink and dusk blue of the sky over the sea some ten miles away. Their arms on the parapet braced that careful distance apart, just like that night in New York, when they were strangers. Damien gazed toward the horizon, his profile so perfect he could have been built by Disney, except that there was too much real strength to that jaw, to the scar on his chin, the straight black lashes, the strong cheekbones and the way his lips seemed to default to a firmness that left those little lines at the corners. As if allowing them to soften was what took conscious effort.

No tension at the corners of his mouth that night in New York. None at all.

"It would have been like believing in magic, to believe in you," she said suddenly.

"Yes." His breath released roughly. "I know exactly what you mean."

"In the morning. At night, it's easier to believe in dreams."

He glanced at her once at that and then looked toward the horizon again, where the pink grew thinner and thinner. She remembered his multiple attempts to speak to her, after the takeover announcement, the way he withdrew, his expression closing, from her attempts at cool sophistication. She remembered her father dying, and her company lost, and her whole world coming all to pieces while she tried to play it cool because, of all the stupid things, she cared what he *thought* of her.

"It's night." His voice was as velveted as darkness.

"Almost." Her own voice felt like velvet, too.

A feeling grew in her, as if she was standing in the wings, getting ready to shove herself naked out on stage.

It would be nice if he took her hand, to lead her out on it.

That night, he'd seduced her, no question about that. All the moves had been his.

But this time, he made no moves at all. He was seducing her effortlessly...just by being him.

She stared at her fingers, stretching them to see if they held any courage.

So much courage in the history of her family. And she was afraid to touch a man's wrist?

Not a villain of a man. Not a superficial player. But a man who carried chests down from the attic for his old aunt and tried to catch the moon for his mother and who may not have understood how easily wounded she could be six months ago but who hadn't meant her any harm at all.

She took a breath and touched that strong forearm. It tensed under her fingers.

She curved her hand around it and lifted his arm, bringing his wrist to her nose. It made her a little dizzy to take for herself that right to touch him.

Was that scent him? Had she gotten him this time? "What do you think?" she asked him.

An artist's question, always vulnerable. Lesson after lesson in the perfume industry had taught her cynicism—not to put her heart into her work like her father. To approach it like a chemistry formula, plug these notes in for success. To keep her critical distance. But this afternoon, working on this scent...some of her heart had snuck into it.

It was the fault of that little shop. It was the fault of that lunch in a garden with a woman who had risked her heart and her life time and again. It was...his fault. His fault for yanking her into his arms when she was hurting.

Damien braced. Why would he brace? But then he brought his wrist to his face and breathed the scent.

The tension eased from the corners of his lips. His gaze swept over her once, searching. "It's got...stone in it," he said, low. "Stone and sun and time."

So that had worked. She bent her head, smiling a little.

"Depth."

She nodded.

He focused on the view again. No lines at the corners of his mouth. In profile, that mouth even looked...uncertain.

No. Hard, elegant, ruthless Damien Rosier? Uncertain?

"Do you like it?" she asked nervously. An artist's most painful question.

"I might."

Not exactly enthusiastic awe. But his caution touched her, somehow. It gave her the courage to lift her hand to finger his open collar. "May I?"

He turned to face her, leaning on one elbow on the parapet, the angle of his body bringing his throat more easily to her level. She stepped in close and nestled her face between the panels of his shirt to breathe deeply.

The sweet warmth of his body. *A man should wear his fragrance wherever he wants to be kissed,* one of her mentors had once said. She wanted to close her eyes and let her head sink forward, just stay there forever, breathing his scent. Except...

"It's not right."

"No?" his voice sounded husky.

"It's still not you!" She drew back, frowning up at him. "Damn it."

He raised his eyebrows. "I think I like it."

No. If she'd gotten it right, he wouldn't *think* he liked it. His whole body would vibrate like a chord struck just right when its scent was on his skin.

"Well, what do you know about it?" she said crushingly. "Are you a perfumer? No. It's *not* right. There's something missing."

His lips curved in the most aggravating way. Like a moneyman indulging an artist. "I guess you'll have to try again."

She frowned at him. "Damn it. I was so positive."

"I'm not sure I'm flattered, that you were convinced you knew me already."

Ah. *Touché.* The idea caught her: that there might be more and more of him to get to know.

Oh. How...beautiful. Like this shimmering path twisting into the heart of dark, mysterious lands, luring her down it. She wanted to dance down it. She wanted to pick her way with cautious fascination. She wanted to clutch her dog Toto and watch out for witches.

And she wanted to be a little mysterious and fascinating to him.

"My father could take six months of trials on a perfume to get it right. There were some ideas he would play with for years before he did anything with them." So many ideas left in his journals unfinished, when he died, so many small bottles of trials strewn across his desk. Once her career had been filled by the "Spoiled Brat" type of briefs, she'd grown more mechanical, getting the brief done and moving on to another. Once in a while, she'd try against all advice for another brief, something magical, but it got harder and harder to do every time the executives shook their heads and sent her back to the Spoiled Brat realm, giving the brief to someone whose name suited it more.

"Six months or years, hmm?" Damien smiled a little, with no suggestion at all that years was too much time to spend on his scent. He took her hand and brushed her fingers gently against the hollow of his throat. Frissons ran from her fingertips down her arm into her body, shivering everywhere.

"Why don't you ever wear a tie?" she asked suddenly. Even in a tux at that party, no tie.

He shrugged, still playing her fingertips against that vulnerable point of his body. "They're old-fashioned."

Stroke and stroke of her fingers against himself. His skin was silk-smooth there, fine, over that strong curve of bone. His hand felt sure and warm around hers.

"They make me feel like I'm suffocating," he added suddenly.

She stepped forward again, all at once, and kissed the hollow of his throat, there where he sought freedom from suffocation. She didn't know what in the world came over her. Once there, she froze in embarrassment, and his arms came around her, one hand cupping her head.

The gentle rub of his hand against her hair, the shift of his chest in a quick breath. Such a strong, warm chest. It felt utterly delicious to be held against it.

She closed her eyes. "I wish..." A whisper that trailed off against his skin.

"What do you wish?" His voice, vibrating in his chest against her ear, rubbed her as gently as his hand on the back of her head.

But she couldn't say it. She shook her head, losing her nerve.

He shifted her so that she leaned back against the parapet, his hands on either side of her. His eyes were dark and serious in the falling night. "I wonder if I get to make wishes."

"What would you wish for?" she whispered.

He shook his head. Maybe he lost his nerve, too.

Her mouth felt too soft, too tender. Like it was begging for a kiss.

His gaze ran over her face and lingered on her lips.

"This," he murmured. "I'd wish for this."

But even as he bent his head, she couldn't shake the sense that he was being chary with his own wishes, keeping them small. Asking for a drawing made with silver glitter instead of the actual moon.

His lips brushed her cheeks, the corners of her lips, his body rubbing subtly against hers. There and gone. His breath passed lightly over her lips as he shifted to her other cheek. A gentle, teasing test of skin to skin, lips brushing down to the corners of hers again.

She closed her eyes, lifting towards him, bringing her fingers to his shoulders. Broad, strong shoulders. Fine, pressed cotton.

His lips, closing over hers. Firm and sure and sweet and hungry.

But not pushy. Not demanding. Not taking her over. *Come. Come dream with me.*

He'd kissed her like this that night on the terrace in New York, only a little more certain, a little more wondering, a little less in check.

I'm sorry. She went up onto tiptoe, into the kiss. *I'm sorry I made you afraid to believe in this again.*

Arousal pushed him past caution quickly, faster than it did for her. His hand firmed on her back, pressing her in harder, his kiss deepening, and the scent of stone and sun and time and steel and dappled shadow was lovely against his skin. She wanted to sink into it, sink into him.

Even if that scent wasn't quite right.

He lifted his head, his breathing deep and fast. In the growing darkness, strings of lights shone in the plane trees that lined the esplanade. Café-goers sitting under those trees nudged each other and watched them, visibly, gleefully gossiping.

"Do you know a lot of people there?"

Damien didn't even glance back over his shoulder. "Even if I don't, they certainly know me." He shifted his hand to her lower back and led them away, back into the windy streets. "Are you hungry?"

She'd been hungry the night she met him. Hungry for love, for hope, for happiness. He'd wrapped that hunger all up in sex and fulfilled it. And now...yes. She was hungry for more.

"This is a nice little restaurant," Damien said.

Oh.

"Not as fancy as Gabe and Raphaël's or Daniel's, or that new place near here, Leroi's, but if you don't mind something simple..."

"Oh, please," she said quickly. "Simple."

That was what had been so perfect about that night, wasn't it? How simple and true it had all seemed.

Damien had to greet several people as they moved through tables, their curious but friendly glances scoping her out as he politely introduced "Jasmin

142

Bianchi, a perfumer". They were seated on a terrace on a *place* where a fountain played and more lights sparkled in plane trees before she added, for something to say: "I don't know who those people are, whose restaurants you mentioned. Gabe and...Daniel?"

"Gabriel and Raphaël Delange are my second cousins on the Delange side, and they have a three-star restaurant in Sainte-Mère, near Tante Colette. Daniel Laurier married my cousin Léa, and has his own three-star restaurant near here. Leroi's just opened, to a lot of attention. His chef de cuisine isn't that well-known yet, but Luc Leroi came down here from Paris, a very famous pastry chef."

She shook her head ruefully. "Is there anyone in your family who isn't an over-achiever?"

He lifted his eyebrows. "Is there anyone in yours who isn't?"

Fine, maybe she and her father could be called *high* achievers. Not over. Just pursuing their art with passion. There was nothing *over* about that.

"I'm the only person left in my family." She forced down the lump in her throat.

"No, you're not."

She stared at him.

"You have a cousin, Layla, who has already won one Grammy but claims she's just 'average'. You have an adoptive great-grandmother who, with the help of your blood great-grandmother, saved thirty-six children during the Occupation. Their photos and stories hang in museums as heroes not only of France but of all humanity. And by adoption you have all of us. The Rosiers. The same cousins and ruthless elders I have."

She couldn't wrap her mind around it. The attempt made her nose and eyes sting. "I thought you didn't consider Spoiled Brat an achievement."

"If your anti-achievements stay at the number two and three spot in perfume sales for four years, it would be interesting to see what your achievements do," Damien said dryly.

"Probably not as well. When you put your heart into things, they never sell as well."

He shrugged. "I thought you were worth taking over a company so I could scoop you up as mine."

The wording rippled through her. But she stiffened against it. "That didn't work out for you so well, did it? I'm not that easily bought."

His eyes narrowed. "Because you don't like *money*." He curled his lip over the word. "God forbid we care about a dirty word like that."

"There's nothing wrong with money."

"Thank you." That dark flash to his eyes in the night. "You relieve my mind."

"I bet it's distracting, though," she said suddenly. "From what really matters." A vision of those perfume launch parties—all those expensive dresses, expensive watches, hair, skin, shoes, cars, jewels. The infinite inflation of cost, as everyone tried to out-perform each other in success.

"And what really matters, Jess?"

"I don't know," she said slowly. She looked around, at the tables full of people talking in low contentment, at the groups and couples that passed through the plaza, at a cat balanced on a balcony and a little girl coaxing it inside, at the strings of lights on great, old trees with peeling bark, at the Renaissance and medieval stone. At him, across from her, watching her as if he was going to think about every word she said. "This does."

His mouth eased.

"Time. People. Doing what you love." From a very little girl, she'd known a perfumer was what she wanted to be. But perfume had become such a flat, cynical act. Until she walked into that little shop. There, playing with concepts for perfumes for him and for her newly-discovered cousin Layla, she felt alive again. It was terrifying, actually. Like working on perfumes *used* to be, when she still tried to make them magical. Like trying to believe in something when you knew it could never come true. "What matters to you?"

"I don't know," he said, as if he really didn't. And then, after a moment: "My family. Success. Strength. Here." He gestured.

"Grasse?"

He nodded. "If we walk much in that direction, you'll see the broken and boarded up windows, the men hanging out on doorsteps for lack of anything else to do. It's a fight, to keep Grasse and the surrounding villages alive. Most of the flower production has gone out of this region, and that was what the economy depended on for centuries. We, Rosier SA, had to expand, become a global company with headquarters here, in order to be big enough to survive."

"Good for you," she said softly. *Really* good for him.

"My father and grandfather were the first ones to see we would have to change."

"You're the one who does it, though. Leads the battles, takes out the enemies, earns the scars."

"Only one scar." He touched his chin.

Every time Jess's attention was drawn to that scar now, she wanted to press a kiss there for the little boy who had tried to capture the moon. Capture it for his mother, the woman who, at that point in his life, he must have loved most in the world.

"That's what money does," he said. "It keeps alive the places where people can take their time, do what they love."

She reached out suddenly and touched the back of his hand. "Do *you* do what you love?"

He fell silent long enough that she thought he wasn't going to answer. The waiter came and she withdrew her hand as they gave their orders, an interruption that could have let Damien change the subject. But when the waiter had gone, Damien turned his fork over, again and then again, running his finger down the back of it.

"Yes," he said suddenly. "I do love it, actually. I love it every time I win. Every time I can say, I've made my family and my people—all the people who depend on us—safer and more powerful still."

That made so much sense out of him. Not a shark, not an assassin. A *warrior*. A hero.

Exactly like generations of his family before him, adapting to the demands of the times, but always fighting for their family and their people, even if that definition of "his people" now included people all over the globe. *You wonder how much energy and time any one man can spare to saving the whole world,* Tristan had said. And, *Now you can see what your dream company can become when you have someone with real business acumen behind it.*

"You wanted me to say something different, didn't you?" Damien said. "That I hated it, that at heart I was really just a misunderstood artist trapped in a business suit."

She shook her head. She was an artist. Business acumen like his was exotic, incomprehensible, and *hot.*

She'd just never truly believed someone as hot and capable as he was would find an artist-geek attractive himself.

But one thing gnawed at her. "Then why do you get migraines?"

He stared at her.

"If you love what you do...then why can't you do it for more than a few hours without it splitting your head?"

His expression changed, several times—these flickers of half-processed and indecipherable emotions. He sat back. "I don't know."

"Did you get it checked out?"

"I don't have a tumor or an aneurysm, if that's what you mean," he said dryly.

A fast punch of shock into her belly. "Thank God."

He dipped his head a little. "Thank you."

"Did you just thank me for being relieved you don't have a *brain tumor*?" It reminded her of his reaction when she'd been surprised to realize he would have cared about her father's death. "You don't expect much from me, either, do you?"

His expression was so puzzled. Like the expression on his face when he'd learned that his mother had snuck into his room every night for weeks to make sure he was okay. As if he'd forgotten to expect care from *anybody*.

Kind of...kind of like her.

"Is your mom still alive?" she asked suddenly, and far too bluntly if his mother wasn't.

He nodded.

So he didn't expect care despite the fact that he was entirely surrounded by family members, including the mother who, that moon story suggested, loved her son very much.

"Do you still get along with her?"

"Of course," he said, as if her question insulted his manners.

"What does she think of what you do?"

"She stays out of the business world." He made a small gesture with his hand, pushing his mother off the conversational table. But then he added: "She's artistic, and tried to get me to take after her and not my father. She regularly reminds the world that I was such a cute, sweet little boy."

Ah. So she loved her son but didn't understand him as an adult. Didn't see that he was still trying to catch the moon. Or maybe it just broke her heart to see her little boy grown up and out in the harsh world and so she avoided facing it any way she could.

"She's delusional, of course. My cousins and I were hellions."

"Were you?" Jess said enviously. She'd been a very well behaved little girl, introverted, which, in the social

147

pressures of middle and high school, had turned her very shy. It had taken college for her to grow back into a certain confidence, and Spoiled Brat had been her first real act of defiance. "It's not necessarily a contradiction in terms."

He looked at her a moment, and then a smile broke across his face unexpectedly. Wow, he had a crease in his cheeks when he smiled that was close to a *dimple*. "I was a cute, sweet hellion?"

"You should really smile more often," she said involuntarily. "It looks *good* on you." Human. Alive. Happy.

The smile faded as he gazed at her, his eyes growing serious and searching. His fingers stretched to touch her knuckles. The graze of callused fingertips shivered through her. "I could say the same of you. I just realized how little you've smiled for me."

"I think I might be kind of serious by nature."

"How would you know? If you spent two years watching your father die, it might take you a while to recover your sense of humor."

Oh. The sweet pain of his understanding. It shot through her and then eased her more open as that pain relaxed, like a deep massage that had hit on her most knotted muscle.

"What happened to your mother? You said you were all alone."

"I had friends," she hastened to correct herself. "And he had friends. There were people at the funeral. I wasn't *all* alone."

He didn't argue with her, but he didn't make any noise of agreement either. He just watched her, his fingertips rubbing gently back and forth over her knuckles.

"I don't really remember her at all," she said wistfully. She'd constantly invented mothers for herself as a child, tried to throw her father in the path of every woman with a kindly smile in the park, whether the woman had her own kids or not. She'd have stolen a mother for herself right out of a happy family without a second thought, she'd been so single-minded about it. And if siblings came with, so much the better. "I was so little—only two."

He lifted her hand and kissed it.

Oh.

"You shouldn't do that," she whispered.

He turned her hand over, and kissed the palm. "Why?"

"It—I don't know how to handle it." She pressed her free hand to her stomach.

He smiled. That faint, rather dangerous smile. "You know, Jasmin, you really shouldn't tell me your weaknesses. I'll find them and exploit them fast enough without your help."

Oh, yes, he definitely would.

"I told you I was out of your league. What am I supposed to do that throws *you* for a loop?"

He considered a moment. An eyebrow went up. "Breathe?"

At which, of course, she forgot how to. Her breaths caught high in her chest.

"Breathe *deep*," he said, with that secret flash of humor. "I particularly like the deep breaths."

Her breath came in fast and deep.

He smiled.

"*And* you know how to *flirt*," Jess protested. "It's not *fair*."

"I'm the mean one. I don't play fair."

He'd played fair that night. Clear and sure in his attraction to her, in his approach, but careful of *her*— her right to say no, to withdraw, to be cautious. And with that care, he'd let her forget all caution entirely—she'd felt entirely safe in his hands.

"You're the mean one?" The mean one of whom? His cousins? "What are the others? Teddy bears?"

He tilted his head just a little, a wry smile curling one side of his mouth. "Maybe one of them."

"You're not very good at it, being mean."

Both his eyebrows shot up.

"I mean, you try, but you're really inconsistent. You forget all the time."

He just stared at her.

"What, I'm the first person to ever tell you that?"

"Other than my mother," he said wryly. He shook his head. "Pépé is going to be so disappointed in me."

"Pépé. Your grandfather? He likes you to be mean?"

"He's counting on it. That's why he hasn't sent another of my cousins after you. I'm the one he can count on not to go soft over a pretty face."

Jess tried to digest that. The whole idea had such an odd, pointy shape, she wasn't even sure where to take the first bite of it. "Your grandfather sounds kind of...tough," she said eventually. She wasn't touching the "go soft over a pretty face" bit.

He gave a little crack of laughter. "Ah...yes. I believe that's been mentioned about him before."

Jess waited. She liked getting him to talk to her just by waiting. They'd used that technique on each other quite a lot, that first evening.

"He and Tante Colette have been feuding, or pretending to feud, or God knows what with them, for a good seventy years. They got those thirty-six children over the Alps, and they held their cell together, and blew up supply depots and more things they won't ever tell us. But once the war was over, they took their energies out on each other, I guess. Maybe they had to take all that post traumatic stress disorder out on someone, and they could only count on each other to be tough enough to handle it."

Jess gave that some thought. "So he and your aunt are so tough and hard...that they saved thirty-six children? Risked torture and their lives for strangers when most people were keeping as low a profile as they could?"

"They smuggled a lot of those kids out in wagon loads of rose petals."

What a heartbreaking image. "I see where you got it from then." The toughness, but also that care.

Damien was silent for a moment. "You, too, in that case."

"What?"

"Both your adoptive and your biological great-grandmother were doing it, too."

"*I'm* not tough." When she'd met him, she'd felt as fragile as a match flame, like any rough breath could blow her out before she could even light a candle. Funny to realize, even as she thought it, how much stronger she felt now. As if that flame wasn't a match after all, but embers, huddled under ashes, ready now, after a few warm breaths, to catch on some good, seasoned oak and flare alive again.

"Élise did it from sweetness," Damien reminded her, with a squeeze of her hand. "Her heart was too tender to let her just watch others suffer. That was her courage."

"I'm not sweet either," Jess said, confused. *Your Tante Colette and your grandfather must have had sweetness, too, to save children. They just learned to be too tough to show it. Like you.*

One of his eyebrows went up a little, and he gave her an odd, searching glance. "Ah."

The waiter brought their wine, and Damien tasted it and then handed his glass to Jess. Apologetically, the waiter moved to pour a sample into her own glass, too, but she was already drinking from Damien's. Crisp and light, a rosé perfect for the summer evening and the Provençal air. She nodded. The waiter glanced involuntarily at Damien, who seconded her nod, and the waiter poured.

They sipped good wine and ate good food and talked, surrounded by lively happiness and the age of the town.

Damien had beautiful eyes. Every time he smiled and that crease showed in his right cheek, she wanted to kiss it. Between courses, his hand always came to rest strong and sure over hers, those callused tips brushing the back of her hand, stirring all her nerve endings.

The walk through the old, stone streets to the little shop was quiet, like their move from that terrace to his apartment that night. He still didn't take her hand, but his breathing roughened, out of all proportion to the easy pace.

When she turned to face him at her door, he was very close. Close enough that only his hands on the door to either side of her face kept him from brushing her body.

His deepened breathing made her prickle with hunger and nerves. In the lamplit street, his eyes were dark.

"What do you wish now, Jasmin?" That dark, deep voice, like a brush of velvet night. A scent of jasmine reached her, from vines climbing up the wall between her shop and the next.

"I—" She shook her head. *I can't wish it out loud. I can't say it.*

A flicker of anger in his eyes.

"Nothing you want?" His hand slid down her arm and took that big iron key from her.

Not that I can say.

"Nothing at all?" His thigh brushed hers as he unlocked the door behind her and pushed it an inch ajar.

Why was he doing this? Challenging her? Everything had been flowing so smoothly. Why wasn't he making it all easy for her, as he had that night, so that the move from conversation up to a bed flowed like thick, inexorable desire, uninterrupted by any thought?

She stared up at him. His lips compressed, and then were deliberately relaxed.

"I want something," that dark panther voice said. He pressed his palm against her midsection, just below her belly button, just above where the touch in public would have been obscene. And then he ran that hand slowly, slowly, slowly, up her ribs, bunching her top until it wrinkled against her breasts. His hand stopped on the last rib, the edge of his palm barely grazing the underside of her breast.

Her heart beat so hard it rang in her head. Her breasts hurt, and her sex clenched.

He bent his head to her ear, nestling it into the fall of her loose curls. A deep breath drawn close to her ear, the slow release of air that brushed over her lobe and the side of her throat. When he spoke, his voice was the tenderest caress, like black silk sliding over her body: "I want to fuck you."

The verb penetrated, just *penetrated*, like it was meant to do, as if she was being held back up against this door by his hot body and being very tenderly fucked.

"I want to push you back on those lavender-scented sheets my aunt gave you and stamp my scent all over them." His hand stroked down her body, over her butt and thigh, pulling her into him. His voice got even lower, till it vibrated in her fingertips and her toes and between her thighs.

"I want to rip that damn skirt off you, which I hate, and slide my fingers under your panties and straight up into you."

She jerked, as if he'd done it in fact. Her thighs pressed together, and her nipples ached, all her pink parts waking with erotic panic. His words took possession of her. Tied her up in the black silk of them, held her still for whatever he wanted to do. And she *liked* it.

His mouth brushed back up to her ear. That delicate, delicate caress of breath there, his voice the absolute of darkness. "And I want to fuck you with them until you have lost your mind."

She sagged against the door. His lips followed the curve of her ear. "I want to wrap my hand in these curls of yours and hold you down to the bed with them and kiss you so deep it's like I'm fucking your mouth."

She made a little sound, turning her head into his shoulder. Black silk everywhere, running all through her, caressing and binding every part of her body.

His fingers stroked down her thigh, lifted it to his hip, as he rocked his erection so-much-too-gently against her. "I want to spread your legs so that you can't squeeze them together while I do whatever the hell I want to you."

Her head fell back against the door. His lips grazed across her bared throat. "And when you've come enough"—his hand flexed into her thigh—"when you're exhausted from coming"—his teeth grazed against her collarbone—"when you're limp and vulnerable and all mine"—his fingers threaded through her curls and spread them over her breast as he straightened away from her—"maybe, maybe I won't be so damn pissed about the way you treated me the morning after."

He drew back, his arms bracing him off her.

Jess stared up at him, shocked not only by his words but by how much she had liked them. She ached so badly it was all she could do not to grab him and rub herself against him to try to satisfy that ache, there in the public street.

"I'm sorry, Jess. I know you had your reasons. But I can't do the same damn thing I did last time and still lay myself out there, while you don't even trust me enough to say what you want out loud. While you still think I'm—this." He touched his throat where she had sprayed that steel and stone scent. "Part of me is still angry. And if I went upstairs with you right now, I'd make you beg."

154

He pushed the iron key into her hand and closed her fingers around it. Then he turned and strode away into the night.

Chapter 13

Fuck. Damien gripped the edge of a stone fountain in the dark street, drops of water from the stream into the basin cold against the back of his hand.

What the hell was that all about? You idiot.

Reacting on emotion. No strategy, none of that cool assessment that made him feel like some Hollywood superspy, scanning a situation and spotting every single weakness that left him a path to victory. Just a fucking emotional loose cannon, careening across a deck in self-destruction.

What the hell did he expect to accomplish that way, acting how he *felt?*

Not even any properly rational feeling, either, just gun-shy cowardice. *I get it. I get that she was going through a rough time. I get that my reputation preceded me. Or followed me. Whatever.*

But I'm still so damn pissed.

Not always. Not constantly. It had been going so damn...beautifully. Just like the last time. Everything flowing so easily, he'd had her in the palm of his hand. And it was just his own stupid fault that this time, it hadn't felt like this wondering reveal of his heart to this magical stranger who would keep it safe. It had felt like stripping the bandage off a raw wound and trusting her not to pour salt on it.

So that when he'd locked her back against her door and thought about that bed of hers upstairs, so intent on her when she couldn't even trust him enough to tell him what she *wanted*, damn it, after that whole evening of careful courtship...when he'd done that, the memory of waking alone in his own bed, of the dull, blunt shock when he'd met her again and she'd brushed him off as if he was nothing, had kicked rage alive to stop him.

A destructive rage. *God,* what an idiot.

The last two times he'd reacted so purely on what he *felt* had been that night in New York and earlier today when he couldn't stand to leave her alone with the memory of her father's death and had to pull her into his arms. Both of which times he'd gotten fucking burned.

Although...although...something good had come of this afternoon. He drew a slow breath and sank his hand into the basin of water—cold against hot skin.

Some degree of understanding. Of forgiveness. Of willingness to try again.

Which he had just screwed up.

He couldn't believe he'd said *fuck* to her.

God.

Not just said it, but said it as a *verb.* Put it together with objects, turned her body into this crude field of his victory, and *told her about it.* Some fantasies a man should shut the hell up about and *never* let out.

He wanted to wind back time, put them back at a table with a chilled rosé in his hand helping him stay calm, put them back at the parapet of the esplanade, talking as if they were starting over.

Way to screw up a do-over. In some self-immolative punishment for the past.

He splashed a handful of water over his face, dragging his wet hand down slowly until his chilled fingers rested on the hollow of his throat. Just where he had dragged her fingers. See, *there* he'd been on the right track.

Now his pulse there beat hard and frantic. He lifted his wrist to his nose again. The sun and stone and time still lingered.

Like his life. The great old bones of his world—the land, the old medieval and Renaissance buildings, that had seen the rise of his family and might one day, if he or his cousins or their heirs ever lost their battles, see it fall.

He closed his eyes a moment. She'd gotten *something* of him. Something important, too. It was far better than that first shallow titanium. Couldn't he have been content? Did he have to wreck everything in his desire for more? In his desire to have her look him in the eyes and say, as if she could believe in him, *I wish for you.*

Idiot.

He let himself into his building on the *place*, climbed up steep old stairs to the top floor, which was all his. He pushed open the gray-blue shutters and stood with his hands around the iron railing, gazing toward the distant sea. Then he turned around and looked at his empty bed.

What a damn idiot he was.

***

Jess gazed warily at Damien through the window beside the old shop door early the next morning. She kept seeing that brooding mouth shape the word *fuck* over and over. Sensual, controlled, *fuck* and *fuck* and *fuck* until the panties she'd just pulled on fresh two seconds ago were already getting damp.

She swallowed, blinking his actual, unmoving lips back into focus, and his black lashes lifted so that he met her gaze through the panes.

Brooding, wary, almost sullenly apologetic.

She hesitated, then unlocked the door, stepping onto the threshold rather than letting him in. "You own jeans?" Well-worn ones, too, that rode low on his tight hips with a casual affection, as if he and those jeans had been friends a long time. His T-shirt, a sea-green that brought out the green in his eyes, clung to broad shoulders and tight abs, the sleeves riding the swell of his biceps. His shower-damp hair did unfair things to her erogenous zones.

His lips did that pressing thing that she'd learned indicated she'd flicked his temper. "It's Saturday."

Well, that explained the number of people in the streets late the night before. She'd lost track, with the travel. "Thanks for the update. Now go find some other woman you think you can get to beg."

Her own words jerked through her, the thought of some other woman—a beautiful model, of course—begging him for every fuck he wanted to give. The image wrenched her stomach to nausea.

Damien shoved a hand through his wet hair, his lips tightening. "I'm sorry about that."

He should be, of course. No man she knew had ever said *fuck* like that to her. Like a verb, with her its object. The men she attracted were *sweet*, quiet. She'd never known a word could heat her entire body like this, for hours and hours, make it heat again the instant she saw him.

"You apologize to me a lot." And there was something to be said for a man who had the grace to apologize.

"And you never apologize to me at all," he said rather grimly.

Oh. She folded her arms over her chest. Under the hoodie she'd pulled on when his knocking woke her, she wore only a cami and yoga pants and no bra. It was a very disconcerting state of attire, for facing off with Damien Rosier. Even, or maybe especially, when he was in a T-shirt. "*I* didn't say I wanted to fuck *you*," she said angrily, before she thought.

One corner of his lips twisted up. "If you had, trust me, I wouldn't be asking for an apology."

It clenched in her stomach, rubbed over her nipples as if the words were his two thumbs taking control. She tightened her arms, desperate to get a bra on as some token armor. "Just spit it out. Why did you drag me out of bed at this hour?"

His gaze swept over her hoodie and messy hair, until all she could think about was a bed. Her body being dragged across one by strong masculine hands taking her over...

"Funny," Damien said dryly. "I thought you were an early riser."

Why in the world would he think tha—a memory of sneaking out of his bed at dawn while he was fast asleep, his arm still stretched over the part of the mattress where she had been. The sight of his full name on an envelope on top of a stack of mail by the door, as she let herself out, and the shock of the realization. *Oh, good God, he's that Damien.* The whole walk of shame home in her heels and silly flowing evening dress, in New York at six in the morning. The calls and knowing commentary from men, until she found a taxi. Taking a shower, when every inch of her body felt sensitive, and getting dressed in jeans, and hurrying to her father's apartment so she would get there in time to talk to the hospice care nurse.

"It's six hours earlier, in the time zone I was in until six days ago," she said, to avoid all that.

"So you must have had a hard time falling asleep," Damien purred. "Tossed and turned until all hours of the morning."

Well...not exactly. But only because she'd cracked under the torment of the images and dragged her own hand down her body and...She glared at him. "Don't make me bring out my Mace."

Dark, dangerous humor. "Don't make me rub you three times to see if I can get my wishes to come true."

Oh. She took a step back, on the impact of it. Damn it, her body was already frantic for him. And it had taken him less than a minute. "Go to hell," she said, which was a total lie. That wasn't what she wanted to have happen at all. *Fuck*, those chiseled lips said in her head. *I want to spread your legs and do whatever I want to you.*

"I've got flowers," he said.

What?

"That's what a man offers, right, when he needs to apologize?" Something still faintly sullen around the press of his lips, as if that need to apologize went against the grain.

"You think *flowers* can do it?" she said scathingly. But she scanned for his flowers nevertheless, with a little kick of hope in her heart. She didn't see any sign of anything but hot male in a T-shirt, empty-handed. "Go to hell."

"You haven't seen the flowers yet."

She drew her eyebrows together suspiciously.

"Your namesake." He reached out to pick a small white flower from the thick mass of them growing near the door and held it to her in two fingers. "Jasmine."

Okay, that was kind of lame, as an offering of flowers went. He could have at least brought a proper bouquet. She did love jasmine, though. Her scent. But if he tucked that flower behind her ear, she was going to bite his fingers. Hard. "Thanks," she said very dryly, not taking the flower.

"A whole field of jasmine, in fact," he said. "The biggest field in France."

She blinked at him a second. And then an inkling of what he might be talking about started to work through her, and her eyes widened.

"It's the harvest. And we are its biggest harvesters. Come see. Better yet"—he brought the little flower to just below her nose, caressing her with its rich, sweet, moonlit scent—"come smell."

Oh. She stared at him with her lips parted. Oh, that was just...impossible.

Utterly impossible to refuse this, no matter how much she should throw his flowers back in his face.

"The jasmine harvest," she whispered.

The corners of his lips eased upward. He nodded once.

"The actual jasmine harvest." Flowers stretching everywhere, full of their rich, whole scent, before the distillation process changed it. If she had been a visual artist, this would have been like giving her a glimpse of the actual sun instead of just paintings of it. As she was a perfumer, there was literally no greater or more sensual a gift he could have offered her. "Can I touch the flowers?"

He slipped his hands in his jeans pockets, the waist tugging down against his hips, drawing her eye to flat abs and—she yanked her gaze back up to his face. That subtle, dangerous smile. "Jess, *chérie.* If you've got the guts to reach for it, you can touch anything you want."

Chapter 14

"Are you going soft on me like your cousins?" Pépé demanded, locking faded blue eyes on Damien as if he was looking at him through the scope on a rifle. A talent Pépé had not lost, in seventy years of *not* holing up in the hills with a rifle.

"Me? Soft?" Damien barely bothered to raise his eyebrows. When family didn't believe it was possible for him to have emotions, it took astonishingly little to dissuade them of any doubts.

Pépé narrowed his eyes. Smooth away the wrinkles, change the white hair to black, and those blue eyes could have belonged to the head of a Resistance cell realizing one of his operatives had been subverted. Actually, hell, if his country got occupied again, Pépé would be right back at the head of a Resistance cell today, white hair and wrinkles and all. He'd kick some serious *ass*. "You brought your aunt here."

It had been an easy matter to stop and pick up Tante Colette, giving pleasure to both her and Jess. Jess's aloneness scared the hell out of him. As if she was just floating in this dark void, with no human connection to keep her from being lost in it.

His family might drive him crazy, but without them, he would be completely adrift, no meaning to his life at all.

"I knew how much you missed your sister," Damien said dryly.

Pépé gave him one of the looks he used to sit on his upstart grandsons. "*And* you brought that girl she's using to get to you."

"Admit it, Pépé. Secretly you and Tante Colette exchange texts in plots to get us all matched up. We all know what's really going on here."

Pépé...wait. Did Pépé blink? Hell. Seriously? Damien typically overestimated his opponents' ability to strategize—it was one of his greatest weaknesses, in fact, his tendency to assume his opponents actually had a chess-master level of strategy behind their actions—but in his grandfather's and great-aunt's cases, overestimation might not be possible.

"You can't bluff me, kid," Pépé said grimly.

Yeah, and Damien also probably couldn't outsmart two people who had saved thirty-six kids and fought the German occupiers all while pretending to the world that they couldn't stand each other and that Tante Colette wasn't even considered part of the family.

Hmm.

Damien narrowed his own eyes at his grandfather. The crossing of steel blades.

A very faint smile touched Pépé's mouth. He pressed it out immediately. "So. You're going to just let this girl steal Laurianne's shop from our family? The shop where we all started? That's been in our family since the Renaissance?"

"I'm working on it." Humor flickered. "Of course, Jess would say that we've had it much longer than our fair share."

Pépé transferred that narrowed gaze to Jess. Her head was buried in a jasmine bush, her hair, still damp from her shower, spilling against the green leaves. Her sensual happiness charged through Damien erotically. He'd given this pleasure to her. He'd thrilled all her senses.

A faint smile curved his mouth. Knowing perfumers, she might even prefer it to an orgasm.

But just in case, he'd liked to give her a few orgasms, too. Press her back up against an oak tree in the *maquis* and make her come surrounded by scents of sun and time and shade and pine and herbs. Pull her down on top of him between these rows of jasmine tonight, while the moon gilded over their white petals, and make her come surrounded by the rich, sweet scent of her namesake flower and the scent of her own sex. Take her up those stairs above the perfume shop and crowd her backward onto that bed and make her come amid lavender-scented sheets that had been embroidered a hundred years ago...

He dragged his focus back to his grandfather. The last thing a man needed to do when dealing with Pépé was get distracted.

"And I hate to point this out, Pépé, but I believe the shop was passed to Tante Colette before my parents were even born. Now whose watch would that have been on?"

Pépé gave him one of those sharp glances that said, *Oh, are you doing battle with me? Good.* "You boys have no respect."

Damien smiled. "And here I thought that lying to you and acting as if you couldn't fight your own battles anymore would be a lack of respect. Getting old?"

That curl to Pépé's lips. Damien's mother said he smiled just like his grandfather. A statement that was always accompanied by a resigned shake of her head. "I can still take you, kid."

Damien glanced from his grandfather to his great-aunt, at some distance from them and busy ignoring Pépé completely. Tristan had just tucked a jasmine flower into Tante Colette's hair.

Again, a little caution ran through him. Sometimes, he couldn't shake the feeling that out-plotting their descendants while pretending not to even speak to each other would be child's play for two Resistance veterans.

"Pépé." He opened his hand in the nearest thing a man of his generation could come to a bow. "Losing to you would be an honor."

***

Jess had died and gone to heaven. No wonder her father had always lived New York like exile. No wonder some part of him had always missed his homeland so badly. The *scents*. They had *texture*, they had feeling, they had *life*.

The silk of the petals and gloss of leaves brushed her face, and the oils, when she carefully picked a flower and placed it in the basket Damien had given her, caressed scent onto her skin. Dirt under her feet released its own scents, and she wanted to take off her shoes and sink her toes into it.

Shaky and vulnerable with sensuality and pleasure—as if she'd just been experiencing multiple orgasms—she looked up to find Damien and a tall, old man approaching her and tried to pull herself together. She had changed into a sleeveless top and capri pants for this excursion, but now she wished for her hoodie again—just to be able to pull it over herself and not show how naked she felt.

"Jess. May I present my grandfather to you? Jean-Jacques Rosier." A small smile curved Damien's lips. "Your great-uncle."

Jean-Jacques Rosier shot him a sharp look. "By adoption," he said firmly.

"So you still have your limited view of family, Jacky?" a cool, rusty voice said, and Jess looked around to discover Colette Delatour coming up on them.

Jean-Jacques Rosier glared at his stepsister. "Laurianne's shop is all the proof I need of the danger of not keeping what's of value to us in the hands of the real—the blood family."

Damien's hand curved under Jess's elbow. "You know how in films someone pulls the pin on a grenade and everyone dives for cover? This would be a similar cue."

Those old sniper blue eyes snapped back to Jess before she could go a step. A man whose experience of live grenades probably wasn't confined to films. "Running?"

Her backbone turned to adamantine just at the glance. She lifted her chin. "No. I think you Rosiers have shut out enough people who didn't fit your ideas of family."

Colette smiled faintly.

"You think you deserve a shop that has been in our family for centuries?"

Jess locked eyes with Jean-Jacques Rosier. "Just call me Robespierre."

Damien made a little choked sound, his hand flexing on her elbow. "Told you," he said to his grandfather.

"Besides," Jess added, "if I'd risked my life day after day for five years in that shop making perfumes to send messages across Europe in a fight to save my world, I guess I'd think I had the right to do exactly what I wanted with it, when I was done." She turned and inclined her head to Colette. "I'm honored." And, as she thought about it more and it really hit her, this choked feeling grew inside: "Deeply."

Both sets of white eyebrows went up a little, not quite in surprise or doubt, but in some kind of thoughtfulness. Colette and Jean-Jacques glanced at each other and back at her and Damien.

Damien's hand was warm under her elbow. "On that note," he murmured, and led her down the row of jasmine, "would you like to meet any more of my family? I promise that they're exactly as difficult as our elders might lead you to expect."

Jess tilted her head back, still adjusting from the impact of the previous meeting. "That's amazing. You look *exactly* like him."

"White-haired, blue-eyed, and wrinkled like a note from the past?"

"It's in the bones. The mouth." The lean hardness. And most notably in that ruthless, do-whatever-it-takes look in the eyes.

"In my defense, then, can I mention that he also helped get thirty-six children over the Alps, and that he met our grandmother while doing it—she took them on into Switzerland. He was faithful to her until the day she died, and still is."

"You'd do that," she said definitely.

Damien actually tripped. Just this barest stumble on a clump of dirt, quickly smoothed out. "Be faithful?" he asked oddly.

"If your country was occupied by a deadly enemy, you'd organize a cell to fight them off and save everyone you could. And you'd do it *well*. You'd outsmart them over and over. I can see you doing it."

He stared down at her a moment. He looked utterly confounded—embarrassed and honored and completely confused. Finally he rubbed his hand through his hair. "What about the part about falling in love and loving that one woman for the rest of my life?"

Heat flushed up her cheeks. She felt vulnerable and full of wishing. "I'm sure your grandmother deserved it."

"Very much so, yes."

She loved how much he loved his family. It made her intensely hungry. "*Have* you ever been in love?" she asked wistfully.

His expression grew distant. "I fell in love once."

A little pang in her heart. She shouldn't have asked.

He looked away from her to hold out his hand to a big man who needed to shave before he turned into a bear. "Jess, my cousin, Matthieu Rosier. Your cousin Layla's fiancé."

The bear bent and kissed her cheeks, brown eyes assessing, and then Layla appeared, slipping under his arm. Layla hesitated over her greeting, but then went with the French cheek-kissing thing.

A happy scent, Jess thought as Layla's exuberant curls brushed her nose. For her cousin, she definitely needed to make it a happy scent. Full of life and joy.

My cousin. She tested the phrase again. *My cousin Layla.*

"My cousin Tristan." Tristan's brown eyes leapt with laughter as he leaned down.

Jess, who had started to reach for his hand, which was how she usually greeted professional colleagues, adjusted wryly to kisses. Tristan straightened, winking at her. Any woman who dated this guy had to have more hormones than sense. He was *obviously* trouble.

"You know," Tristan said, with that gleam of laughter in his brown eyes, "I am *very* intrigued to meet you." He glanced at Damien.

Damien gave him a blunt *back off* look.

"Make that fascinated. Riveted. Compelled."

"Tristan," Damien said between his teeth.

"Words fail me," Tristan said, holding his cousin's eyes.

"They will, in a second," Damien retorted. "Or at least the ability to speak will fail you."

Tristan grinned. "You know, I wouldn't have matched you with Spoiled Brat in a thousand years," he told Jess, as if they were meeting for the first time. "There's something about an unexpected streak of cynicism behind a sweet face, isn't there? That perfume was brilliant. The most brilliant send-up of modern society in our generation. And you were only twenty-four."

Damien stared at Tristan as if he had dropped off the moon. And Damien was about to punch him right back to it.

"*Enchanté. Tout à fait enchanté.*" Tristan bent over the hand she had offered for a shake, as if to kiss it.

Damien grabbed his cousin by the shoulder and shoved him back two steps. Tristan laughed out loud.

"Excuse him." Another big man stepped in front of Tristan. "It always did take all four of us to sit on him. And even then he usually wiggled free."

"Raoul," Damien said to her.

Amber eyes and slate-streaked russet hair and an edge to this big man like a feral wolf. The man who had helped Damien carry the mattress in. He bent his head and kissed her cheeks.

"His fiancée, Allegra." A small woman with glossy dark hair and bright brown eyes.

"Aren't you forgetting someone?" a voice asked behind Damien.

He started. "Maman?"

A woman in her fifties, trim and tanned, her sun lover's skin older than her physique, smiled at Jess, lifted her eyebrows at her son, and then kissed Jess on each cheek, four times total. Gold bracelets chimed faintly on one wrist, and large, artsy red glass earrings caught the sun. Her short hair was dyed a stylish, gold-streaked brown.

"Véronique Rosier," his mother told Jess. "You can call me Véro. I'm sure Damien was planning to introduce you to his mother first but got distracted." A minatory sidelong glance at her son.

Damien let out the slow, restrained breath of a man dealing with far too many family members at once. Kind of the pained breath of a man who was...worried what the girl he was bringing home might think of his family?

"Maman," he muttered, in the tone of someone who really wished he could discreetly kick his mother's ankle under a table to make sure she behaved. "I didn't see you were here." And quite possibly might have turned that Aston Martin of his around and driven them the other way if he'd spotted her before he parked.

"So *you're* the woman he tried to catch the moon for!" Jess realized all at once, delighted.

"Oh, please, don't remind me," Véro said, with a dramatic flinch.

Damien closed his eyes briefly, that tiny touch of color returning to his cheeks.

All Jess's caution and reserve dissipated when he looked like that. It made her want to tickle his ribs. Tease him. Just *relax* with him and make him relax with her.

"I thought you and Papa were in Paris," Damien said.

"Oh, I can't run up to Paris every time your father has a business meeting." Véro dismissed the idea with a perfectly manicured hand that had paint splotched across a knuckle. "I'd never get any of my own life lived. But we'll have you both over to dinner as soon as he gets back, how about that?" She smiled at Jess.

Damien stared at his mother a second. "I—"

His mother kissed him firmly on his cheeks, four times, and then pinched one of them for good measure. "Next Saturday. I'll make your favorite."

Jess found his inability to handle his mother so adorable that it was all she could do not to kiss him. "That sounds wonderful," she said firmly, before she realized that she'd essentially just assumed a place as Damien's date before his family. A place he might have been trying to refuse her—that might have been the reason he found it so awkward to handle his mother's assumptions.

She hesitated, uncertain all at once.

Damien slanted a thoughtful look down at her, but he didn't say anything to argue.

Of course, he *did* have exquisite manners when he wasn't angry. So what could he say, now that she'd accepted?

"I'll have to check my calendar," Damien said. "I may be out of town."

Oh. That. That was what he could say.

All her pleasure deflated like a limp balloon.

"Then check it." His mother reached into his pocket to pull out his phone.

"Maman." He locked his hand over his pocket.

"Hey, if he's busy, you should come hang out with us," Tristan told Jess.

Damien pivoted like a knife striking.

"All of us," Tristan told Damien guilelessly. "That concert Layla's friend is doing, remember?"

Jess bit her lip on a surge of amusement. "Are you by any chance getting a migraine?" she murmured to Damien.

"Not quite yet," Damien said, while Tristan's mobile eyebrows shot to the top of his head, and Véro Rosier frowned in surprised concern at her son.

"You get migraines?" Tristan said to his cousin.

"I internalize the desire to give you a headache," Damien retorted.

Tristan gazed at him a moment. "You know, that explains a lot about you."

"Oh, for God's sake," Damien muttered.

"So," Tristan said cheerfully to Jess, "are you helping him relax?" A teasing lasciviousness in his eyes.

"I'm not sure he does that," Jess said wryly, and Damien shot her a sudden sideways glance.

Images ran through her: Damien, his eyes closed on that uncomfortable chair in the little shop, the expression on his face as she had been preparing the fragrance strip. Damien, asleep on a big white bed, his lean, muscled body so lax it was almost innocent, as if all his muscles had lost their tension.

"Not even for you?" Tristan looked disappointed in her.

"Tristan," Damien said between his teeth.

"Want me to sit on him?" Matt asked Damien in a growly voice.

Tristan sighed and shook his head. "Never," he told Jess firmly, "be the youngest of five cousins. They gang up on me."

"It's the only way to beat him," Matt growled. "He's uncrushable."

Tristan looked smug.

172

Which she supposed he could be, if all four of his older cousins had to gang up on him to beat him.

Where was the fifth cousin? "It looks kind of fun," she said wistfully. "I mean, I know I'm not supposed to like you Rosiers, but..."

"Why are you not supposed to like us?" Tristan demanded, with the offense of someone who was liked by most of the world.

"Snobs," Jess said. "Think you own the perfume industry. Shut everyone else out."

Tristan looked indignant. "That's what people say about us?"

"My father couldn't even stay in Grasse. He had to go to New York to have any chance, and he always felt exiled."

"Okay, your father must be twice my age," Tristan protested. "I take issue with the claim that my cousins or I drove him out of Grasse. My uncles...I don't know. It's true about the old-boy network around here. But hell, Chris Bianchi is one of my role models. I love his work. It's not commercial, but *merde*, it's fascinating. If he wants to come work in our perfume division, it would be an honor to have him as a colleague."

Damien made a little motion with the hand on the far side of Jess. Tristan's gaze flickered to it, and his eyebrows flexed together as he gave Damien a quick, questioning look.

"I'm sure he would have been honored to know that," Jess limited herself to saying, her throat tightening.

"Would have—" Tristan broke off. "Oh, hell. Is Chris Bianchi—"

"Six months ago," Damien said, again with that motion of his hand, as if to push this conversation away.

"Fuck," Tristan muttered, and looked to Jess, a quick, sincere sympathy in his eyes. "I'm so sorry."

"Oh, *ma pauvre petite*." Damien's mother reached out to clasp both her hands.

"Thank you," Jess said to both of them, her eyes stinging.

"I only met him a handful of times, but I admired your father a great deal," Tristan said, all the laughter gone out of his face, replaced by regret.

Damien put his arm around Jess's shoulders and pulled her in snug to his side.

Warmth and strength. Her throat tightened more, and she breathed carefully through it, focusing on the support, pushing past the urge to cry. "Thank you," she said again.

Tristan and his other two male cousins all looked helplessly at Damien. Layla reached out and laid a hand on her arm.

Damien squeezed her shoulders. "Come here," he said quietly. "Come pick jasmine."

He led her down a row away from all the other pickers and away from his family to sit her on a little gardening bench with a basket. "Here." The masculine gentleness both undid her and gave her strength at the same time. "When you get tired, let me know."

It was the best thing she had ever done to process the grief for her father: pick fragile white flowers rich with the scent he had loved so much he had named her after it, this long, rhythmic meditation on life and ephemerality, with support nearby but not intrusive— just strong and warm and willing to be there. Her eyes prickled again, and the prickling gently subsided.

He'd lived a good life, her father. He'd inspired a next generation. He'd inspired *her*.

She took a deep breath of the flower she had just picked. Some things, you captured as much of their essence as you could, to carry with you, but life wouldn't let you keep forever the actual flower. She set the jasmine gently down to rest on top of the other fragile white blossoms in her basket.

A hand gave her shoulder a little squeeze. Damien, passing back by. Her head turned instinctively toward his hand, and his fingers smelled of jasmine, too. Such a strong masculine hand, and such a feminine smell. Just a kiss away.

She picked another jasmine flower and offered it to him in two fingers. His own peace offering from that morning.

And you never apologize to me at all.

Callused fingertips brushed hers as he took it. "I am sorry," she said, looking up at him. "For what that's worth."

He twirled the single white blossom slowly in his fingers. His other hand squeezed her shoulder again. He nodded once, brushed the blossom across her cheek, and then walked on down the row, still carrying the flower.

Chapter 15

"This is part of your family history, too?" Jess asked wonderingly.

After lunch with his family, Raoul and Allegra had volunteered to take Tante Colette back to Sainte-Mère and Damien had driven Jess deeper into the valley, to where it narrowed toward the gorge through which the river entered the valley. He'd parked on a gravel shoulder, and they'd hiked down to the river. On the steep slopes, olives had once been planted, their silvery endurance still visible among the other trees and vines and vegetation that had grown up once that olive grove was abandoned, maybe centuries ago.

The slopes here must be kept verdant by the river and by what Damien described as a wet winter and spring, although now the dry air sipped the sweat straight off their skin as they walked, before a bead could form. The heat drew out scents of oak and herbs, and cicadas sifted their dry, timeless chorus through the air. Here and there, they had passed old walls that braced the terraces of the abandoned olives. Damien barely spoke during the walk, and this curious, prickly tension had grown in her as he followed her on the trail in silence.

But the *pièce de résistance* came when they reached the river. Chalk-filled from the hills, it flowed milky green under a small, stone bridge that looked... "Is it *Roman?*" Jess asked.

"Originally." Damien's face looked honed, brooding, as if he wasn't thinking about what he said at all. "It was destroyed at some point during the fall of the empire. There's mention in records of a Nicholas Rosier rebuilding it, but we're not entirely sure if that was Niccolò Rosario himself or his son or grandson, since they were both named after the first Niccolò, and recordkeepers often transformed Italian names to French here. That's how Rosario became Rosier in the first place."

"Incredible." To have that much history, right there, as part of his blood, his heritage. How did his skin *hold* it all? Jess felt close to bursting just at being part of it secondhand.

Damien shrugged. "The valley goes to Matt."

Jess cut him a quick glance. He said that as if it was a given of his life, but there was something about the line of his mouth that made it hit her: that so much of his history and heart was held in this valley, that he fought the capitalist fight to defend it, and that he was exiled from it. It made her want to go smack some people, and unfortunately she was pretty sure no amount of frustration would really allow her to smack a man who was ninety years old.

Damien's head tilted, and he glanced back up the valley, obscured from view by the trees. "Unless he..." Damien broke off and shook his head once firmly, turning to swing over a great, fallen trunk and then down to the flat sandy bank of the narrow river. Jess followed him as he ducked under more low-hanging branches, laden with brown fruit, and found herself in a little private alcove formed by the wild fig tree arching over them and the sandy bank. The river ran just beyond the drape of the fig branch, a vivid milky green, and the bridge arched above it and them, some ten yards away.

"Beautiful," she murmured. "I could sit here for hours." Sheltered by the fig tree, nibbling on its fruit, watching the green flow of water under a Roman bridge. Oh, yes. With a book and maybe a comfortable pillow, she would stay here all day.

Except for the tension Damien brought into the space. Or maybe by himself, he would have brought no tension. Maybe it took both of them to create tension, inside this cocoon of peace.

She focused on the figs in front of her and the river beyond them, turning her back to Damien. The figs were irresistible. She plucked one and brought it to her mouth, but almost regretted it, too conscious of Damien watching.

"Figs are a sex symbol," Damien said, as her lips closed around the round fruit.

Didn't that figure. She closed her eyes, her tongue touching the roundness.

"Male," Damien said, as her teeth sank into the sweet fruit, "and then you bite into it and it's female."

She drew the other half of the fruit away from her lips to look at it. The inside could, indeed, evoke the idea of the female sex. "That's just nasty," she muttered. "I never thought of figs that way at all."

"No? Lots of other people have. From the Greeks at least. What an innocent mind you have, compared to the whole rest of history."

He made that sound dirty, her innocent mind.

Or at least like something he could dirty up.

She took a deep breath, her body heating until she might soon split like that fig, and started to bring the other half to her mouth.

He caught her wrist. His eyes locked with hers. "Feed it to me."

The hot, dry air whispered around her, and the cool stream taunted with its rushing song just behind her. In the peaceful shelter of the draping fig tree, nothing was at peace. And yet...it felt oddly safe. A safe space for testing their limits, for fighting something out.

"Feed it to me, Jess." His eyes compelled her, tantalizing and promising.

Her hand trembled and brushed his face as she brought the fig to his lips. He took his time eating it, as if he was savoring the most luxurious of pleasures. She had to turn away, walking toward the edge of their little green cave, where fig branches draped between her and the river.

Silence. Peaceful and yet dangerous. The kind of protected space where anything could happen. And everything was so *sensual*. As if you could pick up time and caress it in your fingers. Sink your toes into it, curl them into its clinging grains. Take a bite of it, and it would burst sweet and lush on your tongue. Once upon that time, a young Roman soldier might have tempted his girl with a fig, as they curled up here, in peace and desire.

Even in the restful shade of the fig tree, it was still a hot afternoon. The water promised coolness, just a strip of clothes away.

Something about it reminded her of that beautiful moment of wishing above New York, but the arousal at the heart of it was bigger and dirtier, older than that newborn arousal that night six months ago. It had gotten scarred and grimy, lost its fresh baby face, but it was also a hell of a lot less fragile. Nobody needed to protect this arousal or nurture it. It could come right out and dominate its situation.

Movement behind her, large in that little cave of figs and green leaves and filtered light. Damien's fingers brushed the top of her head.

"Wasp?" she said warily.

Without a word, he stretched his arm past her body to show her his hand. Some harmless-looking tiny black beetle crawled on his finger. He flicked his thumb, and it flew away.

Jess focused on a fig splitting with lushness, just in front of her.

Damien brought his hand back to her head and stroked it down over her hair. She took one long breath and didn't want to release it, as if she could lose this moment if she didn't hold on tight to every molecule of it she breathed in.

He closed his hand around her hair right near the roots and held it there, the back of his knuckles against the nape of her neck.

She went still. The soft, reassuring sound of water filled their haven of figs.

He wound her hair around his wrist, pulling her back a step, himself forward, until his body was one long promise of heat just behind her. But it didn't quite touch.

In the heat of the day, that promise of heat shouldn't have tempted more than the cold water in front of her. And yet she wanted to step back far more than she wanted to step forward.

His head bent to just behind her ear, as he held her captive. "I'm still angry." The dark words burred over her, something that came out of the night into this dappled daytime space.

"I said I was sor—"

His hand tightened on her hair, enough for a tiny sting. "I know what you said. I know how a nice person should feel now. I'm telling you how I really feel."

Oh. His words moved through her in this rush of erotic promise, as if his honesty was as sensual as a slide of silk the length of her body. She tilted her head back into his hold, easing the sting. She couldn't really see him—this barest glimpse from beneath his chin. But she didn't try, her eyelids going heavy, too much sensation all around her for her to need vision.

"How do you feel, Jasmin?" A courteous question turned dangerous, a challenge threaded through with anger.

She closed her eyes completely and concentrated on feeling. She felt...she felt...like she wanted him to tighten his hold. Like she wanted him to do something with it. Like his hold on her hair was the grip that would finally haul her out of the quicksand she had been caught in, breaking her free once and for all. Her voice dropped lower than the sound of the river and the cicadas. "As if I could make a wish. And it would come true."

"I've been a wish, thanks. This time I'd like to be something you actually believe in." Fingers brushed just faintly over the nipple of one breast, through her shirt and bra. The touch teased all through her, this curling, hungry sensation that woke her body from head to toe.

"Maybe I went about it the wrong way last time. Matching myself to what you *wanted* instead of matching myself to what you could actually believe was true."

What she'd *believed*, the next day, was that he was ruthless and focused on money and power, that he couldn't possibly be a safe place for her wounded heart. And yet...when he'd learned her heart had been wounded, he had pulled her into his arms and held her hard. He'd taken her to harvest jasmine. He'd wrapped his arm around her shoulders as she spoke about the loss to his family. He'd tried his best to take care of her, all the ways he knew how.

"I'm sorry," she said again.

"Yes, I know." His fingers grazed, barely touching, over the slope of her breasts to the other nipple and hovered, his touch so light it might have been her imagination. "I'm sorry, too. But you haven't forgotten what I'm sorry for, just because I've said it, have you?" His fingers trailed down her belly, teasing with that almost-touch against her navel. His voice dropped into infinite darkness in her ear, some demonic creature who had come out of a bottle to consume the whole daylight world. "You haven't forgotten that I said I wanted to *fuck you.*"

She shivered, on a little gasp, her head pressing back against his hand.

"You haven't forgotten that I said I wanted to slip my fingers here." His fingers grazed, almost-touching, down over the zip of her capris, hovering with this hint of heat where her thighs tightened instinctively. "I'm sure you haven't forgotten what I said I wanted to do with my fingers. Even though I've apologized."

She squeezed her eyes tight, just to make sure she didn't accidentally wake up. Little shimmery trembles of excitement weakened her bones. She could feel her own sex softening, and no amount of tightening her thighs to control it helped at all.

"What did I say, Jess? That no amount of apologies can erase?"

She couldn't answer, throat dry.

A tiny sting as his hold tightened on her hair. His palm shaped the space of her sex, as if he would cup her fully, but he held it just a millimeter off, all heat and no pressure. "Tell me. What did I say?"

Thank God she could keep her eyes closed. And just feel. His heat against her back, his grip of her hair, the sound of water and cicadas, the dappling of light and shadow over her face, the sand under her toes, the milk-sweet scent of figs, and the dry, summer green of the forest. The heat and promise of his not-quite-touching hand. "You said you—you—wanted to...do things to me with your fingers."

His fingers teased against the seam of her pants and withdrew. "So you do get over insult faster than I do. You've already started to forget. I told you that you were the sweet one."

She shook her head slowly, against the hold of her hair.

"But that's not exactly what I said, Jess."

She swallowed. "I—I remember exactly what you said."

"But you've released it. It's not important to you. You don't brood over it and let it affect you." His hand gave pressure at last—rubbing slowly down her thigh, pushing her back against his body, so that she could feel the pressure of his own arousal and the hardness of his muscles everywhere. "Because you're too sweet."

She closed her eyes very tightly. Her sex felt abandoned, jealous of his choice of her thigh. She tried to squeeze those secret lips together, but the act only brought more dampness. "Damien—"

"What did I tell you, Jess? What exactly did I apologize for, that you've found so easy to let go?"

Her voice sounded as rough as a fig leaf. "You said— you said—you said you wanted to slide your fingers straight up into me." Moisture released in her body, dampening her panties. "You said you wanted to"—her voice went almost inaudible—"fuck me with them until I had lost my mind." Her body sank back against his, powerless, except for those inner muscles that kept trying to clench on emptiness.

"How rude. What inexcusable language." His hand rubbed back up her thigh. "The kind of thing I could apologize for over and over, and you still wouldn't get over it."

"I—" She tried to turn her head into his chest. His hand tightened on her hair, so that she couldn't seek refuge in him and she couldn't escape. She couldn't see him, but he could do whatever he wanted.

"Straight up into you?" He stroked a delicate finger over the seam of her pants. "With no preliminaries at all? What a bastard."

He must be able to feel her dampness through two layers of cloth. He could definitely feel the way her hips arched for more pressure from that finger and her butt pressed back hard against his body when he drew that finger away.

"You—you didn't specify. About the preliminaries," she managed.

"No? Well, you know the male mind. We always fantasize straight to the damn point." His sarcastic fingers grazed away again to draw little circles over exactly where soft curls lay, on the other side of the cloth. This incredibly sensitive area of her skin that was so close and yet so far away from the...*damn point.* "You don't, though, right? Because you're female. You fantasize long, soft caresses that go on forever."

Right this minute, she was fantasizing something a lot less frustrating, more immediate and more intense. She swallowed, even her mouth craving texture. *I want to kiss you so deep it's like I'm fucking your mouth.* Insidious words. They made her want *both*—the kisses and the actual fucking of her mouth. Her body twisted against his again before she could stop it.

"That's it?" He petted her zip. "That's all I said? I didn't make matters any worse? There's nothing else I should apologize for?"

"Damien—"

"You'd better tell me, Jess. So I can get it all out of your system."

"You said you wanted to spread my legs." She whimpered a little as his hand cupped her sex fully, in reward. The heel of his palm rested just over her clitoris. She tried to press into it. He almost let her. Almost— maybe—he moved that heel of his palm side to side in a lazy, taunting rub. "So that—so that I couldn't squeeze them back together again. While you did whatever the hell you wanted to me." *Oh, God, please. Please do whatever the hell you want to me. Please do something. And do it over and over and over.*

And—hard.

And long.

And..just do it!

"Ah, yes." Three fingers rubbed leisurely up and down the seam of her pants. "You know, maybe you weren't so wrong in deciding I must be a bastard, six months ago. Because I'm starting not to feel sorry for what I said at all."

"Jesus, Damien, *please.*" She bucked against his hand and back against his erection, twisting her butt against it.

"Did I say something rude about making you beg, too? That's turned into something of an obsession of mine."

She grabbed his hand in both of hers and pressed it hard against her. Oh, God, she could feel her own moisture, where their fingers interlocked. "You said you wanted to fuck my mouth," she managed, and it sounded like a moan.

His hips jerked once against hers, his hand grinding down involuntarily as he pressed her back against him.

"I said I wanted to *kiss* you like I was fucking your mouth," he corrected.

She risked opening her eyes, and yes, it was still daylight, they were still out in the open air, and his cheeks were dark, his head turned down to her as he watched her every expression like a cruel sultan watching Scheherazade spread for his pleasure.

"But I like your re-interpretation."

She'd take about anything at this point. Anything. Any kind of pressure or intrusion into her body, any way he wanted to touch her or take her, as long as he actually *did it.*

"See, you hold a grudge, too," he said. "You're the sweet one, and I'm the mean one, but even though I've apologized, you haven't forgotten or forgiven a word I said."

"You bastard," Jess said weakly.

"Darling," he replied. In French, of course. *Ma chérie.* It brushed all over her, different, less trusting, more charged, than that night in New York, when he'd said it with such intensity and wonder. Of course, she hadn't called him a bastard that night, either. She'd felt aroused and fascinated and seduced, but she hadn't felt like she was going to climb out of her own skin and claw him out of his. "Take off your clothes."

Heat and heat and heat everywhere, the August afternoon, his body, hers.

"You see that fresh fallen tree just up the bank?"

What?

"It's not lavender-scented sheets. But I want you to take off everything but your panties. And go lie back on it. Do it with me watching you, without me touching you, without me making you—and if you do, then from now on this afternoon is mine. This is as real as it gets. I will do whatever I want to you, and you...all I want to hear out of you is *yes* and *please.*"

He released her hair and stepped back. She almost slid to the sand at the sudden removal of his heat and support. She turned slowly to stare at him.

His eyes glittered as he folded his arms. And waited. Hard. Predatory.

She swallowed, curling her toes into the sand. And then she dropped her hand to the button of her capris.

His chin came up sharply.

She unbuttoned them. He drew a hard breath, his mouth sensual and sullen and dangerous.

She unzipped them, so aroused it was all she could do not to press her own fingers against herself even as he watched.

He looked like—he looked like a man who was going to fuck her any and every way he wanted to, if she made one more gesture. She licked her lips. And pushed her capris down her hips. Nakedness washed over her, this sudden and utter nakedness, her butt in flimsy panties as she bent to push the pants off her feet, her bare thighs. She closed her eyes as she straightened and pulled her shirt over her head in the same movement, so she could just *do it*. Be naked. Get him to actually do all those crude, sexual things he had threatened.

He didn't move. His cheeks were darkly flushed.

She turned toward the trunk.

"Your bra," Damien said, clipped.

She stopped a second. And then turned back to face him, lifted her chin, and unclasped her bra, dropping it on the sand.

Damien's arms unfolded. He breathed as if he had run a race.

Jess climbed over the tree trunk and lay back on it. Bark pressed against her bare skin, this faint, rough underlining of how real and gritty and out in the open air this was.

"Jess." Damien's voice had gone guttural, gravel on a dark night. "Spread your legs."

Chapter 16

She couldn't believe she was doing this. She couldn't believe she would do it *anywhere*, follow his orders like this, let alone do it out in the open air. This was *nothing* like that night in New York. It was impossibly, dirtily real. And yet there was something there that was the same—this passionate hunger and...trust. She didn't trust him enough to reach for him herself and count on him being there, but she trusted him enough to let him do whatever he wanted to her.

Do things to me. The tree bark pressed against her back and butt, through the fragile cloth of her panties. *Do a lot of things to me.*

Shadow and light played over her eyes, through the thick green leaves. Her thighs kept wanting to clench closed, but her knees ran into the tree trunk, keeping her wide open. Only her toes touched the ground, so that she barely had any purchase at all.

She could hear Damien approaching, and she closed her eyes.

Silence.

The brush of warm skin as his hand pressed into the bark beside her body. She opened her eyes to meet the dark intensity of his. The flush on his cheeks. The face honed by arousal and hunger until his expression could be mistaken for cruelty. A willingness to eat her up to satisfy his own needs.

An idea that shouldn't arouse her, but *God*, it did. This flooding, relentless arousal that made her butt cheeks clench against the tree trunk, made her fight not to squirm.

His gaze ran over her body. With a very faint, cruel smile on his mouth, he pinched her wet panties between his thumb and forefinger, pulling them a centimeter or two away from her skin.

Instead of pushing those panties *against* her. Rubbing her. Doing *anything.* She bucked. "Damien. Jesus."

He slid his fingers under the panties, playing with her lush fullness. Arousing, maddening to stare at his face and realize how much he *liked* tormenting her. He was really getting off on it. "Tell me again what I said I wanted to do to you here, Jess?"

"You bastard." She bucked against his hand.

"*Ma chérie,*" he replied sweetly.

"You said you—wanted to—*slide your fingers straight up into me and fuck me until I lost my mind.*"

"I guess that shows the value of an apology, because"—his arm flexed against the trunk, lowering his face right to her ear—"I still want to do that, Jess. And I'm going to do it right now." Two fingers slid into her.

Oh, thank God. She clutched around them with all her inner muscles, her knees tightening against the bark, her hands reaching for him.

He caught her wrists and bore them back against the tree trunk over her head. His fingers thrust and thrust again. She whimpered. They were so forceful, those fingers, and her body was so wet, and she liked it so much.

"My God, you're about to come already, aren't you?" he said. Ruthless. Merciless.

She tried to twist her wrists free to reach for him, but he tightened his hold. "Please, Damien." All he had to do was slide his thumb just a centimeter over...

"No," he said harshly, and removed his fingers, bringing them slick with her own moisture to her breasts. "I want to play with you some more." He squeezed her breast in his hand, rubbing her nipple between a slick thumb and forefinger. "Give you somebody you can *believe in.*"

She whimpered a little, her bare toes digging into leaves and dirt as she tried to press her hips up.

"You could beg me. I've fantasized about you doing that for six damn months. You're so sorry you threw me away and you beg so damn hard."

"Damien." She was going to go out of her mind.

"You get exactly what you ask for, in my fantasies," he said cruelly. "Me. Ruthless. Superficial. Heartless. You get exactly what you want."

Damn him. "Damien, please."

"Yeah. That's a start." His hand slid damp down her stomach, and he paused at her navel just to torment her, playing with it. She writhed and tried to jerk her wrists free, but he held them hard, her forearms rubbing against the bark. His voice so rough and dark in that bright, shadowed day: "Say please again."

"Anything," she whispered, trying to compel him with her eyes, since she couldn't control him with anything else. "Anything you want."

He bent his head low until his mouth brushed her ear. "I told you." Warm breath against her skin, voice like gravel. "I want you to say please."

She *was* saying it. She twisted her head until her lips brushed his ear in turn. And bit his lobe. "Is that all? Please?"

His hand tightened on her wrists. His hand came down between her legs and hovered there, cruelly just out of reach.

"Nothing else?" she whispered desperately. "Nothing at all? Not *fuck* maybe?" She flinched a little to say it. But after the flinch came excitement, a great hungry rush of it. That world held *power*.

He went very still. A hard breath shuddered through his body.

She cast around for more, pushing aside the silky French for the rude, crude, blunt Anglo-Saxon. "Or

189

cock?" She had never said that word out loud in her life. But it jerked right through him.

His fingers thrust straight into her again. She whimpered, but it wasn't enough. She needed more. Harder and faster, and she needed his damn pressure just a little bit higher, and—

"Not *please, Damien, fuck me with your cock*?"

God, the power of those words together. The *taste* of them. Dirty and rich, like sinking her hands down into the black dirt from which flowers grew, after a lifetime of playing only with those flowers' elusive scents.

His breathing was ragged, his face still buried in her hair. His body vibrated like something strained to snapping. "You can't talk like that. You're too...sweet." He pulled back enough to stare at her mouth. His hand came to hold her chin, his thumb dragging the scent and moisture of her own sex across her lips. "Your mouth is too sweet for...those...words."

She caught his sex-drenched thumb in her lips and sucked it in hard, sucking and licking and biting just a little. "Are you sure?" she whispered as she released it. "Absolutely sure my mouth is...too...sweet?"

"Damn you." He was shaking. He brought his hand back to her sex again.

Oh, God, she was so close to coming. "*Fuck,*" she whispered. "*Cock.*" The words were addictive. They worked on him so hard.

"Shut up." He thrust two fingers into her, then opened them, pressure against her walls. She squeezed back, as hard as she could.

"*Fuck me* with your *cock.*"

"You're too easy," he said harshly. "Damn you, Jess. I swear to God that if you come already, I'm going to make you do it again. And again."

But *he* was easy, when she went to work on him. She could see it, his decimated self-control, the way each word she spoke broke him on his own savage hunger. "Fuck me *hard,*" she breathed.

He twisted one hand between them and pressed the heel straight over her clitoris, pressing down, down, until her hips were driven back against the tree trunk by that pressure. "I'll make you shut up, Jasmin."

"You can try," she taunted, and slowly licked her lips. "*Fuck.*"

He thrust his fingers under her panties, thumb going unerringly to her clitoris. "I can make you shut up in five seconds."

"I wonder if your *cock* tastes good?"

He jerked all over, thumb driving against her clitoris.

She whimpered. Her head tossed to the right, as she lost control of her taunts. "Oh, God, Damien, *please.*"

"Just shut up." He rubbed his thumb over that swollen, begging little nub, slick with the moisture on his fingers.

"*Fuck,*" she whispered valiantly, as her body jerked and jerked again. Waves of pleasure were crashing down on her at last. Cresting, coming, almost there, if only he didn't pull his thumb away just at that moment. "Damien, *please.*"

His hold on her wrists loosened as he focused on the movement of his other hand, of his thumb, his mouth utterly ruthless. Oh, thank God, he was going to let her come.

He was going—

She was—

The waves were—

She grabbed him hard as they crashed in on her, managing three final coherent words. "Damien. *Fuck me.*"

And then her body jerked, taking her past thought or speech, into this realm of moaning, whimpering pleasure. Which he rode and rode. He kept her coming, the shocks of it running through her over and over, almost like a punishment, until she truly couldn't bear it anymore and twisted half off the trunk to knock his hand away. He pulled her back, coaxing one last shudder out of her. Until she curled around his hand, pressing it against her and tightening her thighs around it, panting and still shaking with aftershocks, slowly falling, falling, falling back.

To the grain of a tree's bark under her skin. To the dark face of a man who looked ready to bite her.

Her muscles all felt limp as she turned into him, trying with weak, soft holds to grab for him, to pull herself into him. She twined around his hard, braced body.

He pulled her into him and held her still, but he didn't bring his thumb back to her over-sensitized sex, letting her shuddering subside at last, her body slick with sweat, until she was limp and exhausted.

Then he picked her up. "My turn."

Chapter 17

Damien knew he was a bastard. Scores of people had told him so. But he'd never gloried in it quite so much as right then, with Jess's pliant, sweat-gleaming body in his hands, yielding to his every command.

He'd reduced her to this with that first extended orgasm, and the memory of her shuddering, helpless body filled him with a plundering satisfaction. Now she wanted nothing more from him, she only wanted to give. And he kept her in this dazed, docile arousal, stroking breasts and back and thighs gently as he pulled her astride him on the tree trunk.

He took a hard, luxurious grip on her bottom and thrust her down on him, just exactly as hard as he wanted to so he could feel that first fierce plunge of his dick—his *cock*, damn her dirty, dirty mouth—into her body. *Merde.* That felt so good. So glorious. So victorious. He wanted it to last for fucking ever, and he knew it wouldn't. He was too damn aroused. It might last for five seconds.

But he thrust her down on him hard again, pulled her up, pulled her back down, grinding her hips against his, angling his body as deep up into her as he could. Her lips were puffy and parted, her hair hanging all about her face, her breasts full and still begging for more attention, but he couldn't give them more attention and keep this thrust of her body onto his, and damn but he wanted the thrust. He caught her mouth with his, kissing her, biting at her lips, using his tongue like he would use his dick. *You said you wanted to fuck my mouth. I wonder if your cock tastes good.*

Oh, hot hell yeah that—her mouth—her on her knees as he gripped her hair as he—oh hell yes and he—

He pulled her off him. "Kneel down." His voice must have sounded like something dragged out of hell.

She shivered all over, this visible shudder of her body, the moisture gleaming down her thighs, her eyes huge.

"Here." He picked her up and carried her back to the tiny beach. "On the sand." She'd asked for this. It was her fault, not his. A woman couldn't talk like that to a man and expect him to keep any shred of decency in his body.

She stared up at him, entirely naked but for the panties, which she was still wearing because he had only shoved them to the side before. And then, oh God, God, she closed her eyes and tilted her head back, her lips parted.

Fuck. Hell.

What a bastard. What a fucking bastard he was. She was his sweet *wish*. She was his romantic *promise*. And arousal blinded him, so that his hands shook as he wrapped both fists in her hair *so that she couldn't yank her head away* and guided his cock between her lips.

She gasped. He knew immediately that she'd never done it, and it filled him with this savage triumph, like a ravaging soldier. God, he could be. He could be a Roman soldier taking his tribute from some roadside woman who needed his money, only, only—

She did something with her tongue. Clumsy and elusive. She was trying to figure out how to do it. His brain fused. His mind could hold nothing, nothing but the need to push his cock deeper into her mouth, to flex his hands in her hair and hold her for it.

"Good." He panted, his breath seeming to fill his body from his heart to his dick, shattering and hard. "That's right, sweetheart. Just...easy. Just let me..." He pushed deeper into her... "Just...you don't have to do anything, just relax your—oh, God, can you suck? Just a little? Please?"

She brought her hands up to cup his balls and circle around the base of his penis, like she needed something to hold onto, and oh God she tried. A careful, sucking pressure as he pulled himself back. His brain seared.

He literally had no thoughts at all. Just this flame-streaked blackness, and her willingness, and clumsiness, and still *trying*, and he thrust slowly back into her as deep as she could let him go before her eyes widened in panic, and out, and—shit.

He yanked out of her mouth just in time, twisting away from her, as he shuddered and shuddered again in one hot, glorious blindness of pleasure.

***

Shame attacked within minutes. He couldn't look at her as he came back from washing in the stream, and when he did...oh, fuck. She was naked except for panties on the sand, her arms wrapped around her knees, and a couple of pink marks from the bark on her back.

"Here," he said roughly, spreading out his T-shirt. "Sit on this. You'll get sand—" *in uncomfortable places.*

"I might mess it up," she said of the T-shirt, her flush deepening. She ducked her head. She might—oh.

Oh, *yeah.* Because she was so wet between her legs.

And some of his shame retreated before a thick, sticky, greedy pride. That wet was all him.

He picked her up and set her on the T-shirt. Damn it, her back. His fingers grazed over the pink traces the bark had left where it had rubbed her skin. He didn't know what to do about them. He'd rubbed and scraped his skin much more as a child climbing trees and never thought twice about it—no one in the world, not even his mother, would ever have even noticed—and yet those tiny pink marks still made him feel an utter bastard.

So finally he bent and kissed the uppermost one, on her shoulder blade. And then he just knelt there, with his forehead against her nape. A much safer position to be than facing her.

*Bordel de...*he had fucked her mouth. Damn it. All that effort in New York, to be her prince, all the beauty of being *thought* a prince. And he'd just put his dick in her mouth.

He'd just been as crude as it was possible to be.

(And his brain sparked awake with a few cruder things he could do to her. *Shut the hell up*, he told it.

But what if she likes those, too? his brain taunted. Maybe that wasn't his brain. Maybe his dick had gained sentience. Just revolted against its overlord and taken control, like it had tried to do when he was thirteen.)

"I'm sorry," he said, and it was an absolute lie. He wasn't sorry. He was just ashamed. Give him a half hour and another proof of her low opinion of him to flick his temper, and he might do it again. (Deep in his body, greed re-awoke, intrigued at the possibility of a repeat. Or maybe one of those other raw visions of sex...)

Jess ducked her head into her arms, but not before he saw how deep her blush was. "Quit apologizing," she said, muffled. "You're kind of Machiavellian in your apologies."

He sat back, raising his eyebrows a little. That didn't sound angry. It sounded as if...she had a very good understanding of his character.

Damn it. And it was his own damn fault, too.

He shifted to sit beside her, bracing his hand behind her back. "I shouldn't have—" He broke off, gesturing rather helplessly toward his nether regions.

"You're sorry for *that?*" She twisted her head to rest her cheek on her arms and raise her eyebrows at him, still blushing but entirely willing to challenge through a blush. "I thought most men would rather have a blow job than go to heaven."

Okay, now she was making him sound...ordinary. Like most men.

He lay back on the sand and put an arm over his forehead, frowning in the shelter of it up at the fig tree. Which gloated in a supremely phallic manner just above him. The whole damn bush was dangling testicles at him.

And if he bit into any of that brown fruit he'd find flesh that reminded him very much of...he slid a glance sideways at Jess. His gaze lingered at the curve of her butt and thigh, which currently shielded from view that lush pink flesh. He suddenly could imagine a very good way of making up for his little finale there with his damn dick.

And there was that tree trunk.

And she could just lie back down, and he would push open her thighs, and he wouldn't *bite* but...

"Ha," she said. "You're smiling. See? You did like it."

"Shut up." He shifted his arm to hide his smile. And then realizing what he'd just said, "Sorry."

She made a little noise that sounded inexplicably like laughter, given that there was no way she could find this situation funny. "I told you. No more apologies from you. I don't trust them."

"Did *you?*" he said suddenly. "Like it?"

Color flooded his face at such a stupid question. As if she could *like* having his—but she was blushing, too. This deep pink that rose right to her hairline. She turned her head away.

Merde, that made his dick start to stir. *Behave*, he told it. *Too soon.* But he *liked* that hint of soiled innocence, he liked being the source of all her dirtiness, the man who had driven her to it. He'd fallen fast and hard from that man who had loved being her prince, hadn't he?

Well, said his shameless, egotistical dick. *You did promise an afternoon of orgasms. Wouldn't want that to be just a boast.*

"Are you still mad?" she asked.

His eyebrows drew sharply together. "Did you—are you—was that some kind of *appeasement* gesture? You didn't want to, but you let me, because—" He sat up, glaring at her.

Her stare suggested he was a raving lunatic. "You flatter yourself," she said dryly. "If you think your sulks are worth my body."

Okay, well that...kind of put things in perspective. In a very reassuring perspective. He managed to lift an eyebrow. "Sulks?"

She gave a little snort of laughter. It was the most delightful sound he had heard in at least six months. A laugh. At him. "You don't realize you sulk?"

He narrowed his eyes at her.

She suddenly laughed out loud.

It was the most incredible thing. Jess, whom he'd known in various moods of romantic wistfulness and cynical flippancy and deep grief, laughed as if she was just *happy.* Happy and alive, *with him.* Like he was an essential element in that happiness.

Damn, this little fig tree cave was beautiful. He might just stay here the rest of his life. Eating figs and drinking stream water and having lots of sex. Maybe he could sex his way back to the beginning, to that dream on a terrace again. And this time make it come true.

"I most definitely do not sulk." He pushed her back on the sand, bracing himself above her on both hands. "Small, powerless boys sulk. Men, we do something ruthless when we don't get our way."

His gaze caught on her lips. Those lips that had closed around his...*ruthlessness* and...he kissed her, before he even realized he was going to, kissed her long and deep and sweet, and then kept kissing her, unable to stop telling that mouth *thank you. You are beautiful. I love your shape, your texture, the way you close around me right this second and kiss me back...*

Oh, yeah, let's just keep kissing.

He rolled them over, to spare her from the sand, but it was too late, and grains of sand fell from her body onto his. He ran his hands down her back, brushing more sand away as he smiled up at her. Her light brown hair fell in those loose waves and curls down around her face, as if reaching for him. She flushed a little—was it the things that touched closest to her heart that made her shy?—and lowered her head to hide her face under his chin. But then she kissed his collarbone.

He smiled, arms closing around her as he gazed up at those figs.

If he hadn't promised to force her to two more orgasms as revenge earlier, he might have just dozed off there, contented. But...his hand curled lazily over her bottom, which he still had not entirely bared to him. He didn't believe in empty threats. A man lost all credibility that way.

And he wanted her to believe him.

Oh, he definitely wanted her to believe in his ability to give her all the orgasms a woman could possibly stand. He smiled and slid his hand under her panties to trail his fingers down that sensitive line between her butt cheeks until he just barely brushed the open lushness of her sex. She jerked a little. Oh, she was still *highly* sensitized there, wasn't she? It wouldn't take much at all. In fact, she would need just this slow, gentle, lazy stroking, something she could stand, a tender orgasm that lapped softly through her. A long, slow, easy orgasm.

He might be able to give it to her here. Turn her over, so that her back was against his chest, hold her firm with one arm, and just gently, gently stroke her, ignoring protests, until she grew lax, until she came. But he wanted to get his own back.

So he lifted her and carried her to that tree trunk.

Her eyes came open as her butt touched its trunk and then widened in alarm. "Damien—"

"It's so cute how you say my name. As if I'm going to listen to it. I warned you, didn't I? This afternoon is mine now. You don't get to take it back."

She stared at him, eyes very wide.

He smiled. "Shh. You're feeling sleepy, aren't you?"

"I *was.*"

"Just lie back." He pushed her gently back onto it.

God, he liked that view. He pushed her legs apart. Oh, yeah. Better and better. He leaned forward and blew a long slow breath against her still-exposed clit. She jerked, and his mean streak woke up alive and hungry. Oh, *yes*, he liked the idea of doing whatever he wanted to her. And of making her like it.

"Shhhhh." He leaned forward and touched her very lightly, teasingly with his tongue.

She jerked, her thighs trying to clamp around his shoulders. He pushed them firmly back. "There you go, *chérie*. You can be as sleepy and dreamy as you want. I'll take care of this one."

"Damien—" Wondering and nervous and, yes, a little dreamy. What a beautiful mix of emotions. Especially when he caused them.

"Relax, *chérie*. I'm just playing down here. I've got all the time in the world."

And he took it, playing with her with fingers and tongue and lips, this slow, long, luxurious build as she moaned and shivered and gradually, oh so gradually, started to come, in long, shallow waves, like the kind that rolled up a flat beach that stretched out forever, gentle, not deep, but taking forever to leave. He made sure they took a long time to leave. Coaxing her to just one more ripple, and just one more, and just one more.

Until finally, finally, they all subsided away. And she covered her face with her hands and actually started to cry.

Oh, that—that hadn't been his intention. Torment, yes, and an exercise of his power, but not one that *hurt*.

He pulled her into his arms. "Shh. Shh. Okay?"

She pushed his shoulder, which he recognized as a much gentler version of his cousins' thumps of half-reproach. But she curled into him, burying her face in his shoulder. Not pushing him away, but finding refuge in him. Oh. These were different tears. Not grief or pain, but more like some women at a wedding, maybe? Just too much emotion.

He petted her, loving exactly how limp she was in his arms, as if all her will had abandoned her. And he really was a bastard, because even the way she rubbed her wet face into his shoulder made his own arousal press at him more and more insistently. He could control it, of course. But God, he didn't want to.

He stood with her in his arms. "Do you think you'd mind me taking another turn, too?"

She curled into his body and wrapped an arm around his shoulder. "Oh, God, you can do whatever you want. I think you've just made my body utterly yours."

He grinned, his arms tightening around her like his own personal pirate booty. *Yes.* He definitely liked the sound of that.

Chapter 18

"I'm sorry about your back." Damien's fingers brushed the naked curve of it, gentle over what must be scratches from the bark. His voice was deep and quiet.

Jess wrapped her arms around her knees, still naked except for panties, back on his T-shirt on the sand. Sore, tired, satiated, not at all interested in making that hike back to his car. "There you go again. Apologizing."

And you never apologize to me at all. But she had. Were they at peace now? Post-catharsis?

He sat beside her and pressed a kiss to a sting on her shoulder blade. "Your skin has marks on it from that bark. I should have made you wear a shirt for the second time."

A vision of herself as she must have looked to him, spread over that tree trunk. Adding a T-shirt to her upper body in the vision only made her sex look ten times as exposed. She flushed from her toes to her forehead again as she thought about it.

"It can't be that bad." She could only feel the brush of his fingers. They touched her left shoulder blade, then drifted to a couple of other spots on her back, the brush of those calluses making pleasure shiver through her like a sleepy smile. "I liked it," she said. "The texture. I liked *all* the textures."

She'd never felt so much texture in her life. So many senses, all at once.

Damien looked still undecided, guilty.

She shook her head a little. "You're just coasting on that reputation for meanness, aren't you?"

"What?" His eyebrows drew together a little. He rose and took a step toward the river, his head brushing fig leaves. For the first time ever, she could just take her time and enjoy the view of his naked torso without that fluttering, wild excitement and urgency taking over. Damn, he was hot. The golden tone to those broad shoulders and that lean ripple of abs belied all those business suits.

"What happened, you kidnapped one of your cousins' teddy bears and held it for ransom when you were six to get revenge for something, and the label has stuck to you ever since?"

He glanced back at her, a complicated expression startling across his face. Like she'd hit surprisingly close to home. His eyebrows drew more sternly together. "Trust me, I'm quite capable of being ruthless."

She grinned at him. "I noticed."

Damien...ha! Was that color on his cheeks? He reached up to touch a fig by his head, his hand hiding his face.

That spring of laughter inside her kept surprising her. This great, bubbling source of *happiness*. She'd been happy with him that night in New York, but a you'll-have-to-wake-up-soon happiness, rimmed around by the grief that waited just as soon as she stepped outside his sphere. Here...everything felt so *alive*. Sorrow wasn't lurking just outside, waiting to mug her as soon as it got her alone. They *were* outside. Here life waited. There was nothing to wake up from, because it was broad day.

And she'd just had maddening, greedy, life-filled, joyous *sex*. More of it than she had quite realized a person could have in one afternoon. Damien had a really interesting way of venting his grudges.

She grinned a little. His *long, hard* grudge. Made a woman kind of want to annoy him again and see how long he could keep that temper of his up the next time. She smothered her smirk in her arms.

"So is that fig you're fondling supposed to be the actual phallus or a testicle, in terms of male sex symbols?" Her grin escaped.

Laughter caught Damien completely by surprise. His face lit with it. Oh, he liked her teasing him. He liked it a lot. He dropped his hand. "I compartmentalize. Mostly, to me, they're just fruit."

"Oh, fine, ruin them for me for life while you still get to enjoy them."

He grinned, and it made him look so wickedly happy and *young*, as if life was burbling up in him, too. "Are you sure you won't eat one?" He stretched it down to her on the tips of his fingers.

She gave him a pretend indignant glower, and then grabbed it and ate it. Figs fresh off the tree were a miracle of flavor that had apparently survived being a sex symbol since the Greeks, so no sense letting him ruin them for her. She stuck her tongue out at Damien after she swallowed.

Humor and happiness startled across his face again. His eyes looked very green, as if the green river behind him and the light filtering through the great green fig leaves brought their color out.

"My reputation for ruthlessness doesn't have anything to do with sex," he pointed out to her. A wary fascination showed in his eyes, his hand curling around a fig branch for support.

She grinned. "That's a relief. When a man has an actual reputation about his sexual proclivities, it's never a good sign."

Laughter sparked in his eyes again. He took a step back toward her. "We'll keep it between us, then?"

Her breath hitched. Her eyes clung to his. "Oh, I..." *hope so. All the ways you like to have sex and I like to have sex...let's keep them just between us. Just you and me.*

What if...he was a person she could show all her dirty side to *and* all her sweet, fragile, wishing side to, too? The idea filled her with the most exquisite hope.

Hope like standing on a terrace above New York looking down at the lights of the city and still believing in stars above.

His face grew serious. He knelt in front of her on the sand and studied her face a long moment. "You look beautiful," he said suddenly. "Right now. Just"—his fingers reached toward her and then fell away— "beautiful."

Naked on the sand and God knew what going on with her hair? She wasn't *beautiful*, even when she was all dressed up for a party. Not compared to the people he was used to, certainly. She raised her eyebrows at him. "Are you sure I don't look a total mess?"

"Well, you do. But that's part of what's so beautiful."

Heat touched her cheeks. He threaded his fingers through her hair, removing bark, and then lay back on the sand, curling one hand loosely around her ankle as he drew a knee up and threw his other arm over his forehead, shielding his face from the dappling of sun.

Such a perfect, gentle cave of drooping fig branches and green leaves and filtered sunlight. The quiet rush of water. The insistent song of cicadas. A place out of time where anything was possible. She sat and he lay there for a long time, not speaking, just...quiet together.

Quiet together was a wonderful way to be. And she'd never even suspected he needed it, that quiet. Well, on the terrace that night she'd thought she'd found a kindred spirit, but the next day, she'd convinced herself that he was *Damien Rosier*, glamorous and sophisticated, and quiet moments with someone like her could not possibly be his thing.

She'd been so stupid. What a reckless, self-destructive thing, to run away from a man like him because she got scared.

"I made a wish for happiness," she said suddenly, low, gazing at the pattern of sunlight on sand. In the edge of her vision, Damien's head turned.

"That night." Her nose tickled a little. Not quite a prickle of tears but she still had to focus on breathing, on the water, on the light and shade. "In New York."

Damien watched her silently, his gaze a pressure against her cheek.

"I was so lonely and so...tired. With my father dying. And at the same time, I was *trying*, you know? I joined forces with Tara, and we were building that company, with me as its perfumer, so I could be the person he and I had always dreamed I'd be instead of the one I'd become by accident. It was almost my promise to him, that I would do that. That I would dream. That I would be happy."

Damien's hand shifted from her ankle to close over the top of her dusty foot, firm and sure.

"I'm kind of an introvert," she said. "I really don't like that kind of party. A small gathering of friends, of real friends, that's fun. But not those big, fake displays."

"Nobody likes those, Jess. It's a job we do."

Her eyebrows crinkled. She was pretty sure that a lot of people at those perfume industry parties loved every minute of them, but it was interesting that he didn't. He seemed so at ease there.

She'd been *so* stupid.

"But you know how friends always nag you when you're single? That you need to go out more, that you'll never meet anyone if you spend your Friday nights at home? I wanted to try. I didn't want to be alone. I wanted to believe that happiness existed, and that I could find some and carry it with me even through my father's death, so I'd still have some, you know? Even after he was gone." Her voice choked.

Damien sat up and wrapped his arm around her. He squeezed hard—this fierceness to his solidity and heat. *Shh. I've got you. I know it's not all right, but I've got you, if that can help.*

"I made this wish for it, in my lab, that afternoon. Almonds for Christmas, and jasmine for me and my father, and vanilla, because vanilla always makes me feel as if someone who loves me is baking me a batch of cookies. Like I still have a mom, you know? And I know it sounds stupid, from the woman who made Spoiled Brat, at a party like that, but...I sprayed it like a wish. On my wrists before I got there, but then, I couldn't last long at the party—I just really don't deal well with that kind of thing—and I stepped outside onto the terrace. But I knew that was cheating, to go to the party but spend the whole evening in hiding, so to still feel I was trying, I sprayed it at the door. A wish. For happiness. *Come find me here.*"

"I was standing by the door talking to someone, I don't remember who," Damien said. "At first I thought it was her perfume, but she was wearing this ironic floral." Yeah, Spoiled Brat's success had inspired a lot of those. "I wanted to find the person who smelled like...hope, and happiness. This private, sweet happiness that you have with those very close to you. That wish that a child makes the night before Christmas. I just wanted to see what she was like, the person who would wear that scent. I wanted to smell happiness, too."

She bent her head into her knees. "I'm sorry," she whispered, "that I got it wrong the next day. There was just so much weight on me back then. It was easier to believe I was an idiot than to believe something so perfect could actually be true."

Damien pulled her into his body to press her face into his chest. He bent his head over hers, closing her in his warmth.

Far too hot, really, on a summer day after they'd already gotten themselves very overheated. But she'd take too much heat over too little, any day.

"And then the next time I saw you, I thought you were picking up a super model, and the time after that, you were stealing my dream company right out from under me and thinking you'd bought me with it, too." She swallowed hard. "And then my father—" She broke off, and his arms tightened. "It was just a really hard time."

He didn't say anything at all. He just held her, warm and strong and there. Tears slipped out of her eyes, and for a second she tried to quell them. But it was so...quiet here. So warm. So...held. Secure. So she let them flow and somehow that made the urge to cry shorter and less painful—just this gentle wave of grief that could pass and let her focus again on the beautiful layerings of refuge around her. A great valley, the forest and river deep in its heart, the shelter of the fig tree. The strong fold of his arms.

And happiness. Life. She was still naked from the way they had seized at life and happiness so shortly before.

Naked. But protected in his arms.

"Damien," she whispered.

"Mmm?" His deep voice against her hair, the little sound that meant anything she said would be welcome.

She lifted her head to meet his eyes. "I wish..."

He waited, his eyes so close and intense.

Beautiful eyes. Beautiful face. She loved those lines of tension relaxed like this—loved what they said about the kind of man he was, that they would exist at all, and what they said about this moment, that they were all eased away.

She drew a breath and sighed, wishing she could say her wish aloud and make it come true.

This time no anger flashed in his eyes that she didn't. "Yes," he said quietly, and kissed her forehead. "I wish that, too."

Chapter 19

Kisses and kisses and kisses, in the dark against her door, with the scent of jasmine sneaking in among those kisses as if the flowers, too, wanted to touch. The night brushing cool silk around them after the heat of the day. Her hair under his fingers, her skin against his lips.

They were both tired. Ready to shower and sleep. But Damien kept kissing her because he couldn't stand to stop and walk away. Trailing kisses over her throat in under the fall of her hair, so he could take a deep breath of her scent. Brushing them across her collarbone like wishes. Finding his way to her mouth again.

I don't want to go.

But a man couldn't make love on a riverbank multiple times in the afternoon and then proceed into the evening with one hundred percent confidence that he would be able to make an excellent showing of himself if the woman invited him up to her bedroom. He wished they could just...share a shower. Undress in quiet security in each other. Share a bed, just to fall asleep.

Ask me to stay.

Her hair spilled across her face, and he chased locks of it with kisses, brushing it free of her eyes with his lips.

He could imagine it, almost. Close and yet elusive, like the scent of jasmine which could touch them but never be touched. A room with her and a bed, getting undressed and watching her undress, and it not really mattering if they were going to make love or going to sleep. They shared that bed anyway.

Because that intimate, quiet, private space of sleep was one they wanted to have together.

And he and Jess didn't have that. They had the mad trust and hope and betrayal of two strangers in New York, and from today they had...he didn't know what they had. It felt raw everywhere, what they had. Like it might be something good, if it could grow, but right now the fresh exposed skin of it was sensitive to every touch. It didn't yet allow them to move around a dark room in gentle, casual intimacy, kiss each other good night, and go to sleep.

He couldn't. It might be slightly—slightly—easier than walking into a boardroom meeting stark naked, but it still felt awkward and exposed. Like bringing handpicked wildflowers because it was all you could afford when everyone else had given the same girl hothouse roses.

He could afford hothouse roses. He just...thought the wildflowers were more precious.

He buried his face in the join of her shoulder and drew a deep breath, holding it a second before he let it out. Her arms were around his waist, and he liked that moment. He liked it a lot. Her hold of him. His resting in her.

Take it easy, the old street said. *Trust takes time.*

He drew another deep breath, easing. Of course. Of course it did. That made perfect sense.

It was easier to believe I was an idiot than to believe something that felt so perfect could actually be true.

Perfect. He had felt perfect to her, too.

He lifted his head and framed Jess's cheeks, stroking her cheekbones with his thumbs, burying his fingers in her hair. Happiness sifted across his fingers with every strand of her hair. He couldn't remember the last time he had felt so happy. He was greedy for it, afraid to spoil it by trying to cram too much of it in his mouth at once, but afraid it would all be gone tomorrow if he didn't grab it now. He'd lost it once before, after all.

"I've got to go," he murmured.

She blinked heavy eyes at him, a little wistful, but she didn't argue. She didn't say she wanted anything different. She didn't say *I wish you would come up.*

Come up to that small room over the shop, with its lavender sheets, and make her stretch out on her stomach while he stroked her back. Gave her all the tenderness that tree bark couldn't.

It would be ridiculous to put antibiotic on those little pink marks, since they hadn't even broken the skin. But he kind of wanted to minister to them. As if it would put the last healing balm on a major wound.

As if it would heal...himself.

Kind of odd, since he was impervious to harm.

Take it easy. Take your time.

Again, even the thought was easing. Right this second, given how thoroughly he had used her body that afternoon, she'd probably hold up her fingers crossed in a hex symbol if he tried to worm his way upstairs: *Down boy. Let me get some sleep.*

That made him laugh a little. He petted her hair. "You'll be okay?"

Because if you're not...if you might be scared of the dark without me or anything...feel free to say.

She gave a tiny, slumberous nod that made him want to just pick her up and carry her up the stairs to bed. Her eyes were a little wistful. But she didn't ask him to go check under her bed for monsters. Just to make her feel safe.

"You're tired." He kissed her again quickly. Trying to wean himself off this kissing.

She nodded.

He was better at talking than she was, he remembered suddenly. She had that streak of ironic wit that could sneak out when a man least expected it—like sinking his teeth into expected sweetness and encountering delicious crunch and spice—but he'd been the one, that night in New York, who had gotten her to open up, this courtship of a stranger that lured her into talking with him, telling him about stars in Texas.

While, somehow, her very quiet lured *him* into telling her about stars, too.

"Have you ever windsurfed?" he asked.

She blinked, kiss-heavy confusion. And shook her head.

"Do you want to learn?"

A little smile, a little sparkle of humor that dusted pleasure all over his heart like it was a damn beignet and she was sugar. "Right now?"

He found himself smiling back at her. Tugging the corner of her lips with his thumb, in gentle hunger for this teasing. "Tomorrow. It's Sunday. My cousins and I often go. But I can take you early, to teach you some basics before everyone else gets there."

"No harvest tomorrow?"

"It's every other day the first couple of weeks, before the jasmine starts hitting its peak bloom."

"I'll probably be terrible at it," she warned. "And look like an idiot."

"Well...yes. It's not exactly an easy sport to learn."

She smiled again, that sugar dusting of humor. Like a spritz of Christmas almond scent in the air to join the jasmine and stone. "You don't mind me looking like an idiot?"

Laughter curled up in him, wicked and delighted to wake. "Not so much, no."

Her eyes sparkled. "I'll try to return the favor some day."

He bit back a grin. Instead he raised an eyebrow in hauteur. "I think you might find that something of a challenge."

And she laughed out loud. He kissed her quickly, hard and hungry. *Damn,* he wished he hadn't started this whole conversation about him going.

She smiled up at him when he lifted his head. "You've got to go," she reminded him.

He nodded.

"You'll be okay?"

She was teasing him again. He liked it to a ridiculous degree. "Probably not," he said and took her key to open her door. He pushed her gently inside and pulled the door closed between them, then stepped to the side to make a key-in-lock motion through the window. She reached for the door, and he heard the old lock clunk into place.

He should call a locksmith and get a modern deadbolt installed on that door, now that a living person was behind it. Hell, maybe he should stay the night, just to make sure.

She smiled at him through the window that half stole the sight of her from him with its reflection of the lamplight, and then turned away and disappeared into the dark.

He stood there a long moment, and then made his way through the old twisty streets to his own apartment and climbed his narrow, winding stair.

She hadn't offered to come check under his bed for monsters either, he noticed. Because that would be ridiculous, of course. No monsters would dare mess with him. He'd slice them up and hang their body parts on the wall as a warning to others.

But he felt a little anxious to be lying in his bed by himself, just the same.

***

Jess undressed quickly. She'd learned to do that, these past two and a half years, to keep it brisk, to dive under the comforter, because sometimes grief lurked under the bed, ready to come out and grab at any toe it found peeking out from under the covers, then climb up it and settle in her heart.

She thought she was taming it, though, that monster grief. These days it was so much softer than it had been in its first wild rages. Cuddly, almost. If it climbed onto her pillow, she could tuck it into her chest and pet it, wistful but not weeping. Sometimes even smiling, as she stroked those memories, as if grief had become a tactile pleasure, or a loved one's perfume, that she kept on a shelf to open for a whiff from time to time. A way to think about and remember someone lost, to value that someone.

But tonight either that monster under her bed had gone on vacation or she had, abandoning the home where grief lurked for other climes, leaving no forwarding address.

So much life had filled up her day. Her week. Sun and stone and flowers, scent and sex. She wanted to think about Damien. The thought of him moved in the darkness. He had a little smile on his face. He was unbuttoning his shirt, taking off his watch and cufflinks. She closed her hand over the real watch on the old, scarred nightstand. It was cool and hard in the night, but he wasn't.

He smiled at her. Moonlight softened the idea of him, and shadow brought out his darkness.

She liked it. She snuggled in the sheets and closed her eyes to pretend he was really there. The sheets smelled of lavender, and the room smelled of time. Old time. Time that had been piling up there for a while, waiting for someone to come in and shake it awake, dust it off.

She breathed it in, focusing on a smile in shadow and moonlight. Dark hair blurring into darkness. Warmth. Warmth that would fill the whole bed, if he was there.

He was a really nice dream.

Cuddly, even. She touched his watch on her nightstand, that impervious, elegant titanium, and imagined his eyebrow shooting up at the suggestion he could be cuddly. A little curl of laughter teased through her as she fell asleep.

Chapter 20

"*I* think it's cute," Allegra said, hugging her knees and grinning.

"Allegra, you think everything is cute!" Layla retorted. "Which, granted, might have been justified in Matt's case. He's a teddy bear—don't tell him I said that. But Damien is most definitely *not*. That's like calling a black panther cute."

"Or James Bond," Jolie agreed. Layla gave her a delighted high five.

The women, wet from their own windsurfing, sat now on the beach, watching the men out on the waves. Léa was the only one of the women who had grown up by the sea and could have windsurfed just as long as the male cousins, but she had joined the other women when they retired exhausted to the beach, as if she enjoyed hanging out with them. Léa, with her straw blond ponytail, was a second cousin to Damien and the other Rosiers out there. Jolie, who had hair the color of something fresh baked out of the oven, had just married Gabriel Delange, whom Damien had also introduced as some kind of cousin. The restaurant owner, right. Jess was losing track of who was related how, getting tangled in this massive web of family.

"He's supposed to be getting that shop back from Jess." Allegra nodded at Jess, who sat with her arms wrapped around her knees, watching this happy group of females with some fascination. Gold strands of warmth and affection seemed to glimmer in the air around them, stretching between them in an unfamiliar web of family and support. She'd had friends, of course, but never those television-storybook friends to whom she could turn for anything and everything. And in terms of family, she had had the one thick golden cord with her father, and that was it.

The friendliness here was particularly crazy because as far as she could tell, these women barely knew each other. The heart of that network of gold threads was out on the waves. Except for Léa, all of these women had joined the family recently, by virtue of being in a relationship with one of the men currently windsurfing.

Wow.

Jealousy curled her toes into the sand. That easy, generous creation of friendship, that endless reach of family, family everywhere. It made her feel on the outside looking in and lonely.

Layla grinned at Jess. "So Damien brought you out here to drown you, is that it?"

Damien had stood waist-deep in waves, bare-chested and wet, his hot, slick physicality grappling with hers, over and over, as he righted her patiently, fall after fall. Which was why *Jess* didn't want to be hanging out with the other women on the sand. Not this morning. She wanted to drag Damien's hot wet body back to that little room over the shop and do something with it. Hell, maybe she could push *him* back on a counter or a bed and take charge. It would be fun to wrestle with him for control, that was for sure. Especially if his face lit with that sudden, flashing laughter as they struggled.

"His reputation for meanness is greatly exaggerated," Jess said.

All the women burst out laughing. "Don't go *destroying* it," Léa said. "He put a lot of work into building that reputation."

Layla shook her head. "I still remember him telling me he was the mean one. Which he claimed, of course, *while he was trying to save Matt's valley for him.* Mean right to the core." She rolled her eyes. "They've got some kind of complex, these guys. I think it comes from growing up in such intensely competitive circumstances, always trying to be the biggest and the baddest and convinced that their value *only* comes from how tough they are. Nobody cares about *anything* else at all. You want to bop them over the head." She made a headbopping gesture. "Or possibly their grandfather? But that's the way they are."

"Not Tristan," Léa said. "To be fair. He couldn't care less whether people think he's tough or not."

Out on the waves, Tristan did the most impossible flipping thing of any of them, landing with a jolt and then a smooth sail on.

"Hmm," Jess said. She had a little bit of her own experience with pretending she didn't care as a form of self-protection.

"Damien is supposed to be getting that shop back, and instead he took Jess windsurfing," Allegra said. "And *none* of you think that's cute?"

"Damien just isn't cute, Allegra," Léa said, amused. "That's like calling a sword cute. It's not going to work."

A sword, a panther, James Bond. Jess eyed Damien. As she watched, he hit a wave badly as he came off a flip and was knocked free of his board and a good ten feet through the air before he hit the water. He came up in a surge through the chop, shaking that black head, and grinned at something one of his cousins must have yelled to him. Damien laughed as he gave his cousin the finger and then cut strongly through the waves to recover his board.

The men were having the time of their lives. It was kind of beautiful to see, actually. As if tension and rivalry found a healthy outlet and they could just *play.* Challenge and compete in a way that vented an insane amount of physical energy and do it all laughing.

"You don't think Damien is cute, Jess?" Allegra challenged. The woman was like a dog with a bone with that cute thing, wasn't she?

"I'm not sure *cute* is quite the word I would use," Jess said cautiously. Hot. Dangerous. Controlled. Sexy.

With this pure core of...honor.

Care.

Hunger.

Allegra looked disappointed in her. "How many other women has he brought windsurfing with his family?" she challenged.

Jolie and Layla, recent additions to the family, glanced at Léa. Léa raised her eyebrows and then slanted a thoughtful glance at Jess. Then she smiled a slow smile. "None at all," she said.

Jess blushed to the roots of her hair. Really? *Really?*

Wow. Her arms tightened around her knees until she nearly toppled over from the squeeze. What did that mean?

"Of course, nobody brought girlfriends, until Gabe insisted on bringing you." Léa nodded to Jolie. "It was mostly our cousin time. Meaning guy time, plus me, because I could keep up."

Oh. So maybe Jess was just the first person Damien had dated—were they dating?—since the shift in the cousins' windsurfing tradition to accommodate dates?

Allegra decided to play her own devil's advocate. "It's probably all some part of a nefarious plan. Knowing Damien."

Jess flexed her toes in the sand. "No. It isn't."

All the women looked at her, definitely interested.

"Anyway, even if it was part of a plan, it wouldn't be *nefarious*, would it? He'd be doing it for all of you."

Layla blinked. And smiled at her. A relieved smile that said, *I think I might end up liking you.*

"But," Jess said slowly, "I don't think he'd sacrifice me for all of you." She thought about it a moment more. No. "He wouldn't."

Now all the women were smiling a little, settling back into the sand. Jess didn't know why, but she had the impression she'd just succeeded at some kind of initiation ceremony.

"He'd sacrifice *himself*, of course," she said suddenly. "I think he does that all the time. But...now he can't, because he'd have to sacrifice me, too. It's probably confusing for him."

"That's beautiful," Layla said suddenly, gazing out over the waves. "That for once Damien might have to do the right thing by himself because it's the only way to do the right thing by you, too. It's not cute, Allegra. It's beautiful."

"You saw that, did you?" Léa asked softly. "The sacrifice?"

"*You* saw it?" Jess asked accusingly. And Léa, his cousin, hadn't tried to change that pattern?

"That's why we have a saying, in the family: Be careful what you wish for. Damien will get it for you." Léa blotted a drop of seawater before it ran off her hair into her eyes. "So that we remember, you know—not to take too much advantage of that."

Oh. *Oh. That* was why Colette Delatour had told her the story? Because his family did see and wanted to make sure she saw, too?

"But then why—" She broke off. If his family understood him and cared for him properly, why did he have little lines at the corners of his eyes and lips when he was only thirty?

"The guys are...rougher," Léa said. "You can't underestimate the effect of having grown up with a Resistance hero for a patriarch and another for their honorary fairy godmother. Or guardian witch. And of growing up with four similarly-driven cousins for competition. They don't know *how* to be less than ruthlessly demanding of themselves and of each other. It's what they've always known. You either handle the family challenge or you leave and put yourself in some other insanely challenging situation instead, like Raoul and Lucien did, or like Raoul's father and Lucien's...not-father before them. Or there's Damien's own father for a role model—so focused on fulfilling everything he thinks everyone else needs him to be that he can hardly remember how to live otherwise." Léa was silent for a moment. And then, "Daniel's like that," she said low. "It took me a long time to understand how much. That's how I know."

"Who's Lucien?" Jess asked.

"Another cousin," Léa said. A flicker in her eyes, as if something about Lucien was painful. "Second to the oldest."

"And Daniel's your husband, right?" The husband Léa had had since she was eighteen years old? Was she keeping all these family details straight?

Léa nodded and looked out at the waves. A little smile relaxed her mouth. "He's trying to learn how to play."

"You should go play with him." Jess would be out there with Damien still, if her arms hadn't given out on her about the same time she had realized that taking care of her beginner self was preventing him from just letting himself go and glorying in the waves and the wind. That he was sacrificing his own needs to take care of hers, in other words.

That seemed to be kind of a thing with him.

"I will." Léa had such a tender smile as she watched her Daniel out there on the waves. "But this is good for him, too. Not to think about me or anything really, just to *be*. Just the pure fun."

"Isn't it good for you, too?"

Léa nodded, her eyes warming in a way that made Jess feel...almost as if there were very fine, nearly invisible golden strands stretching hesitantly through the air toward her from the other woman, a little curious, a little tentative, wondering if she would be a good person to attach to.

They reached through the air from all the women like very faint trails of scent.

"Has anyone ever made you your own perfume?" she asked them. "Customized, I mean? Unique to you?"

Various expressions of confusion at this non sequitur, except from Layla, who smiled.

"Tristan used to when we were kids," Léa said. "But not since he finished his training and grew in such demand. Now all his perfumes are *big* perfumes. For major houses."

"I'm so sick of big perfumes," Jess said. "Always having to think about *marketing* and *consumer trends* and what the company can sell instead of what is actually good." She closed her eyes a moment. Visions danced in the sunlight against them, a thousand ways to succeed twirling gaily with a thousand ways to fail. Just like every perfume she had ever made, in those moments when she held it in her head before she started trying to put a formula on paper. "I think I want to go *little*. In that shop. Make custom perfumes."

There. She'd said it. The swoop in her stomach felt as if a roller coaster had just started its dive. She was really going to take over the shop of a woman who had once literally saved lives and fought a war with her perfumes? She was?

She'd failed at her last attempt to escape big business and go out on her own. Big business, in the guise of Damien, had just reached out and caught her back, idly, without even any effort.

But the vision grew more golden in her, the sun shining bright against her eyelids. That perfume shop spoke to everything she wanted to be.

She stretched out her arms to feel the hot sand under her fingers and looked at all those potential some-kind-of-cousins.

Layla grinned at her. "I like your confidence that Damien isn't going to manage to get that shop back from you."

"*My* great-grandmother gave it to *me*," Jess said adamantly. "He doesn't have anything to say about it." She wondered if her blood great-grandmother, Élise Dubois, had frequented that shop, too. Pretended to sample different scents like an innocent shopper, bought a perfume as a gift, packaged it up, and mailed it to Paris or Berlin.

Layla gave her a tip of her sunhat.

"You go." Allegra grinned.

Léa raised an eyebrow that suddenly, vividly, showed her relationship to Damien. Who had brought his board in and was now coming up the beach.

"I could make you each one, if you like." Jess said. "To warm up. Get started."

All the women broke out into smiles. Those gold strands reaching for her grew stronger, a little more confident of their welcome.

"Be careful. She's expensive," Damien said, and she looked up at him. For a moment his body blocked the sun, making him all shadow against brightness. He dropped to a knee on the giant towel he had brought for them and reached for a smaller one to dry his dripping body. It brought his face into view, the wicked and relaxed smile on it, no tension in him anywhere. She wanted to rub his temples to savor how completely absent that migraine tension was. "She'll take you for everything you have. If you leave her shop stripped down to bare skin, don't say I didn't warn you."

Laughter lurked in his eyes as he stretched out on the towel beside her, resting on his elbows. God, he had a good body—a long, lean, ripped torso, broad, muscled shoulders narrowing down to washboard abs and a flat stomach. Paler on the abs and chest than his arms, this gradation up from the bronze at his wrists to the warm gold of his arms and the pale gold of his shoulders and chest, drops of water clinging to the dark chest hair. He hid a hell of a lot under that suit, didn't he?

"It's for *free*," Jess said firmly. "I don't charge..." She hesitated over a hugely presumptuous word.

"Family?" Damien said. "*Merde*, don't start that. There are hundreds of them running around. Make them pay through the nose. It's the only way to keep them from eating you alive."

His voice was teasing. He was still smiling, still relaxed, as he leaned back and closed his eyes against the sun. But Jess studied him sideways a moment, the sunlight fragmenting against her lowered lashes.

I think I will not *eat you alive,* she thought. *I will try not to. I'd rather you felt...whole. Not beset by ravening teeth.* She touched a hand to that strong bare wrist where his watch had left a swathe of paler skin. "You can have it back," she said softly. "Your watch. If you need it."

He opened his eyes and looked at her. The sun must have shone in his eyes, because he rolled onto one elbow to turn his back to it, gazing at her. Just this eased curve to those lips that were usually so firm. He looked down at her hand on his wrist. Then he turned his hand over and took hers. "Thank you," he said quietly.

She smiled a little, too, relaxing into the sense of him.

He played with her fingers. "Where do you keep it?"

I tried cynicism and self-protection. I want to try being honest with you now. Even if it takes more courage. "On the nightstand by my bed."

His fingers tightened gently around hers. He lifted her hand and kissed it. "Then keep it," he said, and lay back down to close his eyes again, keeping hold of her hand.

Jess was vaguely aware of the other women watching in varying degrees of delight, fascinated astonishment, and attempted discretion. Those golden threads felt very eager now, reaching, wanting to wrap around her and Damien both together.

"Did Tante Colette show you the alien photo yet?" Layla asked gleefully, watching them.

Damien did not open his eyes. He barely moved his lips. "Layla. I warned you once about messing with me. Trust me, my grandfather taught me how to dispose of bodies."

Layla laughed.

"The alien photo?" Jess asked.

"I might have a copy on my phone." Allegra dug in her beach bag.

"Allegra." Damien kept his eyes closed. "If you want to lose that phone, go ahead."

Allegra hesitated and eyed him warily. Layla clearly wasn't worried about being actually murdered, but no one seemed to doubt Damien capable of throwing a phone into the ocean. *I'll show you later,* Allegra mouthed to Jess.

Damien turned his head, opened his eyes, and raised one eyebrow.

Allegra subsided, looking faintly chastened and entirely capable still of hauling out her phone the instant Damien's back was turned. But *not* capable of doing it while he knew what she was doing.

All that gold in the air, those bright strands of interest and eagerness to accept, glinted closer and closer.

Jess lowered her lashes, peeking sideways at Damien, who had closed his eyes again. His lips were relaxed and peaceful, curving faintly upward as he lay in the sun.

I want to keep you. This man who had made her come alive everywhere, who had made her dream and wish and *fight.*

I want to reach for you. Stretch up my arms as high as I can to catch you. And if in the end she lost him— because nothing lasted, not flowers and definitely not people—she would at least have captured him in a bottle, to keep. Later, when she was lonely again, she could pull his bottle out and remember again how beautiful these days had been and know that she had given him her all. That she hadn't just wished on a star. She'd climbed up into a tree with a giant mirror and tried to catch it.

"I want to try again," she said. "With your fragrance."

He smiled without opening his eyes and folded his arm across his chest to rest her hand against his heart. "Think you can figure me out?"

His heart beat under her fingertips, still fast from all the physical exercise. The sun kissed the drops of water curling across those ripped abs and caught in the dark hair on his chest. "No. I just think that I would really like trying."

***

"You don't have to do this today," Damien murmured, slouching in that rickety chair in the old laboratory of the shop. The shadowy balm of the room stroked over skin that had felt too much sun and sea and wind that day. Generations of scent molecules seemed to dance like dust motes in the slanting light. "It's Sunday."

"I like doing it," Jess said, and he kept his lashes lowered over his eyes as he studied her. She did like doing it, he realized. She bloomed in this space. Became herself. With his cousins and extended family, she had been quiet, not in rejection but just in care, as if she was watching a wild game for a while to figure out the rules before she tried to add herself to it. Not sure of her place or of how to find it. The complete opposite of Layla or Allegra, both of whom could make themselves comfortably at home in a barrel full of monkeys.

He bit back a grin. Or maybe a barrel full of big gorillas, beating their chests at each other. His family in a nutshell.

"What's so funny?" Jess asked.

He shrugged, unable to answer, and just watched her. Yes, that reserve she had shown around his loud, large family was gone now. This was *her* space. She was at ease. In power. Sure of herself.

He never let anyone have power over him, not ever, and yet...he kind of wanted to unbutton his shirt all the way down and expose himself to even more of her power. *You can do whatever you want to me. I think you've made my body utterly yours.*

His breath moved through him deep and slow at the thought, and his eyes drifted closed.

Water ran, and the air shifted near him. A cool, damp cloth draped gently over his forehead and eyes.

Oh, hell, that felt so good. His breath caught at the force of it, and he pushed the cloth up enough to be able to see her. "I'm really fine," he said. "My headaches have been greatly exaggerated." And he never got them from sun and sea but from tension.

Also...shouldn't he be taking care of her? Given her father's long, slow passing, she must have spent much of the last few years taking care of someone else.

But she just smiled at him, a smile like a gentle, easy caress. "Of course they have," she said, as if she liked taking care of him. And he couldn't steel up the strength to resist it.

"Do you want some Vitamin E oil for your face, after all that sun and salt wind?" she asked, reaching for a jar.

Shades of his Tante Colette. Damien shook his head. His skin still felt fresh from his post-windsurfing shower, and he wanted to keep it that way. "I don't want anything that makes me unpleasant to touch."

She stilled. He kept his lashes down, his body easy. But through that veil, he saw her gaze trail the whole length of his slouched body before she pulled it away. She stared down at the bottle in her hand a moment, rubbing it once, twice, thrice.

Slow warmth moved through him, deep and strong. *I'm right here. If you want to rub me.*

"I'm glad they're not just from tension," she said suddenly.

He tried to keep his eyes half-closed as she set the bottle down and came up to him, but he couldn't. He had to see her face. He forced himself to stay slouched and vulnerable while he looked up at her, instead of rising to immediately establish *I am the biggest, most powerful person in this room. I control it.* "What isn't?"

226

"These." Her fingers brushed as delicately as a butterfly's wing beside one eye. "The little lines. They're at least partly from squinting at the sun and salt."

He gazed up at her, not sure what to say. Part of him wanted to ask, like some idiot vulnerable child, *Do you mind them?* Shit, it was hard not to stand up.

"I'm not sure about these." She brushed the corners of his lips.

His heart beat too hard for such a small touch. *Touch me some more.*

And, *Do you mind those?*

"But I like it when you smile." She pushed the corners of his lips gently up, and he couldn't smile for the life of him. The touch, the gentleness, ran too powerfully through him.

She's taking possession of me. She's touching me like she has a right to.

He wanted to grab on to something, to hold on tight, and there wasn't one damn thing strong enough in reach. The planks of a rickety folding chair. Her.

Was she strong enough now?

She was stronger than he'd understood, six months ago. Strong enough to be dealing with the long, inevitable death of the father she loved and still be starting a company, going to a party and trying to find love, reaching for stars. That took a deep-rooted core of power and dreaming and stubborn defiance, to keep wishing and working and trying, even in the darkest times.

Can I have that? That power, that dreaming, that wishing? Will you give it to me?

"I like it when you smile, too," he said.

She did smile at that. This softened look of happiness.

He caught her hand and kissed it, holding her palm curved to his cheek so that his lips rested against her palm. She stood very still. And then her free hand lifted and petted gently through his hair.

I need this so much. So much he was afraid to tell her.

He loosed her hand and was unbearably frustrated when she moved back to the counter. Instead of, say, sinking down into his lap so that their combined weight broke that rickety chair.

He watched her under his lashes. The room felt as if it should be his. Everything about it—that weightless sense of ages, the sensuality, the elusive promise of all those scents lurking in corners, the peace, and her moving around in it. "Have you figured out what you want to do with this place?"

She slanted him a glance. "I thought you were holding a court case over my head as to whether I had the right to do anything at all with it."

Her ironic defense slashed through the moment. Did his sometimes do that to her? "If you decide to sell it, of course I would ask that you sell it to me," he finally said evenly.

But it wouldn't be the same, without her in it. He wouldn't want to own it anymore. It would be just another thing he obtained on behalf of his family, while the hole in his middle grew bigger and bigger.

"I'm not selling it." She gave him a stubborn, warning glance. "It's mine."

No irritation stirred in him at her claim. No desire to prove to her the contrary, that he could take whatever he set his mind to, that she had no right to anything belonging to the Rosiers. No, instead, this deep, deep sense of reassurance. *It's yours. And you're mine.*

He wanted that so bad.

"I can see you here," he said instead. "Working here, in Grasse." *Right down the street from me.* "Making this town your own." *My town.*

"I want to make niche perfumes," she said suddenly. Her voice sounded a little suffocated, inexplicably so, until it hit him—of course. Her father had made niche perfumes and earned an excellent reputation and not

228

much financial success. She had made perfumes that sold but that no other top perfumer or critic respected, because they mocked everything the perfume industry was. And the last time she had tried to set up her own niche perfume company...he had taken it over. "And custom perfumes. Like I'm doing for you."

Somehow that made his pulse quicken, that he might have helped her start over again. That he might be here at the birth of this brave and fascinating new life she could build for herself. "Opening a business in France is hell. You might want the help of a really good businessman." He made his voice idle, almost indifferent. *I don't care if you don't ask me for help.* Yeah, right. "Someone with experience in the perfume industry."

"I know a good businessman," Jess said. "But the last time he got his hands on a dream business venture of mine, he ripped it away from me."

Fuck.

"Plus, I'm not sure he likes me."

His eyes opened wide at that. "Jasmin." What the hell?

She peeked quickly at him through her lashes, and then busied herself with jars on the counter.

Was she teasing him? Or could she genuinely not tell? Pressure tightened at his temples, like the ice that came over him any time his family said some variation of *We need someone inhuman for this. Damien, sounds like a good job for you.*

Ridiculous, that ice of anger, given that he'd chosen his own career and forged his own reputation.

He breathed through it, long and steady, rubbing the pale streak of skin on his left wrist, focusing on the cool cloth on his forehead. Color mounted in her cheeks, and...right. Right.

That thing he'd had to learn—that her rejection of him hadn't been all about him. She, herself, had been floundering, afraid to believe in anything in the cold light of day, overwhelmed by loss and grief, and could desperately have used his own strength. If he'd known. If he hadn't pulled back into himself.

What a stupid, flimsy shield that cynical flippancy of hers had been, when he thought about it. A pathetic thing to have defeated someone as ruthless, as able to cut through any opposition, as he was.

And yet her doubt defeated him still.

Hard to convince someone not to doubt you, when your own faith had been shattered.

Except that...she kept putting it back together again. Piece by careful piece as if, no matter how many shards that beautiful initial hope had been shattered into, it was still worth saving. Since she had arrived in Grasse, she had fought with him but even that had been a fight *for* him. A way of communicating, of showing anger and letting him show his, until they got down to what had hurt and what mattered and worked it out. Unlike that time in New York, when she must have been at her very lowest point, now that she was stronger and less grief-stricken, she had never once truly turned him away. She had kept fighting with him the same way he had kept fighting with her—because it gave him an excuse to keep coming back for more.

"Jasmin." He made his voice quiet, deep, something that could gently vibrate through the peace in that room without disturbing it. And when she met his eyes, he smiled at her. Just a little.

Like he'd done that first night he had met her, making himself someone she could believe in. Someone she could relax with, trust. No fighting necessary now. *I'm here. You're here. We were right about each other, that very first night.*

She came toward him slowly, as if fascinated, a test strip in one hand. "I can't get the heart notes in this thing right," she said as she came to stand between his legs.

"No?" He smiled, as his heart lightened just at the thought that she was trying. He caught the hand that held the *touche* and pressed it against his chest, angling his head to sniff at the scent.

It was sweeter, this time. The steel and stone and time held something gentler at their heart. Vanilla? He wasn't vanilla. But she was trying. He lifted her hand enough to kiss her knuckles.

She touched her free hand to his cheek. Funny how the barest graze of someone's fingers could be so sweet. "Of course, my father says there's no such thing," she said softly. "Heart, and head, and base. That those ideas suggest a separate, linear structure, when all of them really blend together."

What a...soothing idea. That the heart and the head and that deep, deep base could all blend smoothly together.

"Can I keep the trials?" he asked. "At least the ones you think are good enough for skin tests?" He'd line them up on his desk in his office just to know they were there. That she had tried and tried for him, reached for his heart over and over.

Her head tilted, her eyes pleased and searching. He wanted her to kiss him so bad. Wanted *her* to do it—to lean down, without his urging, and just brush her lips to his. It didn't matter how light the brush. He would try not to grab her and be too greedy.

He tried to make his lips soft, inviting. Did he even know how to do that? Maybe, from her point of view, his lips still held that cool, hard, ruthless line, like they did in the photos of him that Rosier SA's publicity department gave to the press.

"Do you want to try it?" He parted his collar, stroked the hollow of his own throat. "Here?" His fingertips were too damn calloused from the rock climbing. His stroking didn't have the texture he wanted at all. But a spritz of her scent would be almost close enough.

She hesitated and gave a funny little shrug. "I kind of do and yet..." Those dusk blue eyes met his, with all the promise of an early evening. "...I really like the way you smell without anything at all." A faint hint of color on her cheeks, like the last light of sunset. "Just you."

The power she had over him, that she could say something so simple and it could delight him so much. His hand curved over her butt, and he tried not to grip, tried not to pull her in close to him. *You do it. You reach for me.*

How long did he have to restrain himself, to get her to make the first move? *Were* his lips soft and inviting? No, they'd tightened in hunger again, and he bit on the inside of the lower one, trying to get them to relax.

Her thumb came and stroked beside the corner of his lips. "You have a triple A personality, don't you?"

No, he didn't, damn it. That sounded like a risk for heart disease or…migraines. Definitely a weakness. But he shook his head only a tiny, tiny bit, because if he shook it too hard it might knock her fingers away.

What was that look in her eyes? So wonderful and yet so baffling. Like tenderness, or protectiveness, just this great *caress* of a look that could not possibly be meant for him.

She bent her head and replaced the tug of her thumb with her own lips. A kiss.

She'd kissed *him.* All on her own, not him but *her.*

He drank in that kiss like a bee might drink in nectar if the crazy flower just turned upside down and started raining sweetness down on him instead of making him work for it. This glorious sense of starvation and generous fulfillment.

The cloth fell off his forehead to the floor. Her weight came more onto him, one of her hands dropping to his shoulder, the other curving around his head, the scent strip rubbing against his ear as she deepened the kiss. *Yes.* He spread his legs, urging her deeper between them. *Get lost in me.*

She rubbed her mouth away from his, nuzzling down toward the join of his shoulder, her fingers flexing into his hair as she took a deep breath, and then another. It drove him absolutely crazy when she did that, this woman who lived by her sense of smell luxuriating in his scent. His fingers flexed hard into her butt before he could stop them, and he pulled her in closer.

"I like trying to come up with fragrances for you," she murmured into his ear. "I like the idea of you collecting samples of everything I try, as if they're special to you. I like"—a little hesitation, and then, extra low, like a dirty secret—"I like *marking* you."

His head flexed back, his body lifting toward the brush of that word *marking*. The chair creaked. He tightened his hold on her, so that if he went crashing down, at least he could bring her with him in a tangle of heat and thunder on the floor. Where had all her honesty and sincerity come from? This *openness*, as if she was deliberately lowering all weapons and shields, presenting herself without armor.

"If you ever wore someone else's fragrance, I think it would drive me to a livid rage," she said.

Would it? If he got more aroused, he would combust. Just explode and burn this centuries-old stone building down. He could not possibly sit still for this much longer.

"But," she whispered, taking another deep breath of him, "I love the way you smell as *just you.*"

Oh, hell. He pulled her down onto him, finding her mouth again, his hands rubbing over her, too hard and too eager. The chair creaked again, and he lunged them to their feet before it could give under them.

The counter invited. He set her on it so that he could have his hands free, to run over her as much as he liked. "I like this skirt." Some handkerchief hem, flowing and flirty. A romantic's idea of a dress for a summer evening. His hands sank into its softness and the muscle of her thigh underneath. A man could slide and rub and play with that skirt, against her legs. He didn't have to push it up and invade.

She could wrap her legs around him and still have fabric spilling over her, not straightaway stripped bare.

She touched a finger to his third button, still buttoned, rubbing it as if she could wish it away.

"You can undo it," he murmured, sneaking kisses over her ear, through her hair, down to her shoulder, back up to her forehead. Just anywhere a kiss could fall and not take over. *I've seduced. I've taken. You take now. You take me.*

She smiled a little as she rubbed the button again. And then carefully undid it. And then the next. And then the next. There she paused, one finger sneaking in like a secret between the parted panels of his shirt, stroking his chest.

Warmth swelled in him. Not heat, not burning, but this great, massive, erotic warmth, overcoming him like sun on snow, melting everything. "You can undo all of them." He bent his head into her soft curls. "All of them, Jasmin."

She rested her forehead on his chest, between the parted panels, and took a deep breath. Savoring his scent still. Desire washed through him again, this mounting, insistent wave, like he was a sandcastle and it was going to tear him down. He stroked her back, running his fingers up and down, finding spots that made her shiver and sigh a little and take another deep breath of him.

"I'd like it," he whispered into her curls, "if you'd do that. Very much." *You have no idea how much.*

She stroked her hands over his chest, through the shirt, fisting the fabric against his skin. The touch sank hot through his body. He braced his knee against the cabinet door under the counter, to keep from driving into her.

She found a button and undid it, her head still tucked into his chest. His hand stroked firm up her back, sinking into her hair at her nape. *Don't stop.*

She didn't. Her fingertips brushed against his skin as she bared another button's worth and then another. He breathed slow, concentrating on that breathing, hands dipping down her back to her butt for something he could hold on to. *Flick*, went those fingers. And flick, and flick. Little electric teases of sensation, again and again.

He grabbed her hand as soon as the panels fell apart and pressed it against his bared ribs. She got that hint. She ran her hands over his ribs and up his chest with so much care he could have been a jasmine blossom she was afraid of crushing.

Which was ridiculous, of course. He was the very opposite of fragile. He was the one who went into battle to protect all those fragile things behind him.

"You can touch me"—*harder*, he had been going to say. *A lot harder*. But the softness and the care were so fascinating that the words changed even as he tried to say them—"any way you want." *I think you've made my body utterly yours.*

Her hands slid up over his shoulders and pushed his shirt down, and his heart pounded so hard he had to let go of her butt and grip the counter. *Steady. Steady. Let her set the pace.*

He was hungry like a child in front of a bakery window to know what she would do if she led the way.

His shirt got caught at his elbows. He pried his hand free to let her pull it off that arm, then the other. It brushed against his skin as it fell to the floor, and his breath filled his body with too much air. He felt too light and too heavy, as if he could sail across the sky and as if his gravity would suck everything about her in and crush it in his hunger.

Gripping the counter, he buried his face in the hair spilling over her shoulder, twisting through it until he could kiss the curve of her shoulder. Kiss up her throat to her ear. Slide his lips down to her shoulders, lost in the scent and fall of her hair. She drew her hands down his back, the whole length, from his shoulders to his waist, and he forgot himself and bit her.

She made a little sound.

"Sorry." He kissed the spot.

She turned her head into the join of his neck and shoulder and bit *him*. Then kissed it.

It yanked one huge thread out of his already unraveling control. "Jasmin."

She pressed her face against his shoulder, her arms tightening around his waist. "In New York, you only knew me as Jess," she whispered. "Whenever you call me Jasmin, it's like you know me whole."

He slipped his hand from the counter to her thigh, one greedy grip of skirt and her. "I like both. The *Jess* you are to your friends, and the *Jasmin* you are to the people who—" He turned his head into her hair again, stifling what he'd almost said. He drew a long breath and let it slowly out.

"There aren't any other people. You're the only one who's ever said my name quite that way."

He didn't know what to make of that. It left him feeling exposed again, as if the way he said her name stripped him naked.

She stripped him and stripped him and stripped him, didn't she? Right down to bare skin, and then she just kept going. Worse, he wasn't even sure she tried. It just happened to him, as if his clothes dissolved in her presence.

"Jasmin." Oh, damn, he'd said it again. With this huskiness in it, all raw. He bunched her skirt up toward her hip. His hand curved over the uppermost point of her thigh, his thumb stretching down inside it.

Her body flexed, her arms tightening so that her breasts pressed against him as she opened her mouth against his throat.

"Jasmin." *I love this room. But right now...I don't want to do that tree trunk over again. I don't want to push you back on this counter. Test scents on your skin.*

Oh, yes, I do. I want to do everything. But today..."Ask me up?"

He'd wanted her to ask without prompting. But arousal had surged him right past that stupid barrier.

"Yes," she whispered against his skin.

He almost hesitated. She'd skipped over asking him, just said yes to his own asking. But that would be a stupid thing to get hung up over, right now. He was Damien Rosier. He took what he wanted, he didn't wait for invitations.

Anyway...*yes* was close enough.

He picked her up, wrapping her thighs around his hips, her skirt spilling over his legs and his hands as he gripped her butt. She wrapped her arms around his shoulders, her eyes fascinated and wanting and a little shy, still, but...yes, they invited. She held on tight to him, as if she wanted to make sure he didn't get away.

Well, good. That would be absolutely shitty, if he got away.

He focused on those inviting eyes as he carried her up the dim staircase, their pelvises rubbing maddeningly with each step. *Yes. Want me. Trust me. Ask me in.*

It was a small room, with a bed in it that had been old even in the forties. Heavy furniture that had been put in here in the nineteenth century, and which, once its weight was up those stairs, no one had ever bothered to move again.

The embroidered sheets were white against that dark wood. The scents here were quieter, simpler. A rush of lavender as he laid her down on the bed. The twine of jasmine coming through the window. A base of old wood and musty time.

Her space. Hunger pounded thickly in him as he pressed his hands into the mattress on either side of her head. "You're so pretty," he said with this sense of helplessness before his own words. That was what she was, *jolie*, this lovely, rich, sweet, human pretty that made him want to kiss her forever, and yet the word seemed so inadequate to the power of the feeling.

All words were inadequate, though. Even kisses were, but he tried them anyway, kiss and kiss and kiss. *Slow down*, part of his mind tried to tell his mounting urgency. *How many times did you come yesterday? Surely only twenty-four hours later you can manage to take your time.*

All the time that filled this room, held there, like something precious.

We can take forever.

He buried his head in her hair, breathing the lavender sheets through the soft sweet scent that lingered from her shampoo. She drew her hands down his back and up, gripping and caressing over his shoulders, his arms, all the way down to his wrists, in an exploration of his body that reminded him of that first time. *He'd found his way back.*

But this time was stronger, and it was richer, and yes, it had more dirt on it, and that made it even better. Like it could survive.

"I like dirt," he said, his hand tightening in her hair, and she blinked up at him, confused.

"You like it dirty?" she murmured finally, sensual teasing.

"I—" Well, yes, also. The idea of doing dirty, kinky things to her beat at him like a full sun, heating everything, and yet... "Not right now." Dirty might have its place and time, but it wasn't this one.

Precious and careful had their space and time, too.

She wrapped her hands behind his head and twisted her hips against his, her eyes so wicked and slumberous. "Maybe a little dirty?"

She was so damn perfect for him. He scooped his hand under her butt, pressing their hips together. "Maybe a little." He rocked his hips against hers.

Her hands sank into his hair, stinging as she lifted herself until her mouth was close to his ear. "You make me feel dirty," she whispered. "I think I'd do anything with you."

Hell. It fused his brain. "Shh." He covered her mouth with his hand.

She sucked on the skin of his palm.

Hell. He shoved away from the bed and went to the window, taking a deep breath of the jasmine that grew there. He looked back.

Jess had sat up on the edge of the mattress, her hands clenching in the sheets on either side of her thighs. "You are gorgeous," she said in English, stunned. "The way you look against that window—I could *eat* you. I don't understand how you can be so gorgeous and here."

He shook his head, not sure how to tell her how beautiful she was when that wasn't even what *mattered.* He knew hundreds of beautiful women. Top model, world famous beautiful. She was different. She was her.

She made his insides shake.

He reached through the window, grabbed three tangled vines of jasmine, and yanked them free of the mass. Then started back across the room.

***

Jess's breath shortened as two long strides brought Damien back to her. That beautiful, hard body, the way he cut through a room, as if his movements were a sword's, but with a suppleness and muscle to them like a panther's. She wanted to be able to sink her hands into that tight butt of his and feel the way his muscles worked as he prowled.

She'd tousled that perfect haircut, his black hair all hers now. She'd brought that hungry glitter to his eyes. She'd gotten that shirt off his body, so that the ridged abs made her fingers itch to touch, so that her eyes could follow all those lean, hard muscles that forced the world to his will. All hers. She reached for him.

He caught her hands, the jasmine vine pressing against one wrist as he held it. His thumbs rubbed in the center of her palms. Then he pushed her back on the bed, gently, covering her body with his, kissing her.

God, she loved the power in his body and how much effort it took him to hold it in check. She dragged her hands down his arms, savoring his texture and trying to crack his control.

He let her hands get all the way to his wrists, then twisted his hands and caught hers again, pulling them above her head. He tickled her arms with the jasmine blossoms, trailing the vines up the inside of her wrists. Then he twined them around her wrists. In and out, wrapping around.

He was taking over again. He was good at that—reaching his hand down into her dark space, hauling her out of it, saving her. But this time...she wanted to be the one who stretched out her hand. She wanted to *reach*.

"Look at that." His deep voice purred dark the length of her body. "You're caught by yourself. *Jasmin.*"

"Aren't we all? Damien."

He shook his head, the hypocrite, and kissed down her forearms, his five o'clock shadow brushing against that sensitive skin. She shivered. His tongue teased at the inner bend of her elbow, and her arms stretched, jasmine-bound, to let him reach still more of her skin. He kissed and teased with tongue and teeth, brought his callused thumbs down her arms and drew patterns with his thumbnails.

"Damien." He dissolved her.

"Jasmin." He kissed over the curve of her biceps, so much subtler than the curve of his.

"Damien *Rosier*," she said. That name she hadn't known the first time. But now she thought, *What an incredible whole his past and his loyalty to his family make out of him.*

"Jasmin Bianchi." He kissed her lips, his curved. "Unspoiled. Not a brat."

She shook her head in reproach at the reference, but the movement brushed their lips together, and he slipped between hers, tongue and taking. She lifted her bound hands—carefully, so as not to lose the vine twining green and white around her wrists—to his chest. "Be careful what you wish for," she whispered.

"From me?" He held her eyes with beautiful gray-green. "Wish for anything you want."

You. "This. I wish for this."

A flicker of temper in his eyes.

She rubbed the jasmine flowers around her wrists against his chest. "I know you want me to wish for the moon and the stars, Damien. But it's the same to me. You always were like wishing for a star."

His body jerked. "Oh, hell," he muttered. "Jess." He kissed her, fierce and tender.

Damn, she wanted to touch him. Just touch him all over, not be shy, not give him the lead, just *take.* Take everything she wanted from him and trust that she could get it. She was a perfumer, damn it. At the very least, she knew how to capture the essence of something ephemeral and fragile and treasure it in a bottle.

She pushed at his shoulders, her jasmine manacles unraveling. The force in her hands startled him. That mobile black eyebrow went up a little as he rolled slowly back, searching her face. "You know what?" She sat astride him, lifting up her hands. "I don't think I *like* being caught by my own self."

She shook the jasmine free, and it fell on his chest. She caught it and drew it across his skin, tickling him with the small glossy leaves and silky flowers. "Maybe *you* can get caught by me instead." She grabbed his wrists.

Both his eyebrows were up now, but he let her take those strong wrists she couldn't possibly move without his yielding. He let her bring them together on his chest and twine the vines around them, weaving in and out, tucking in the ends to try to get the vine to hold.

Propped up a little on her headboard, he gazed down at his wrists, held captive by a garland of white flowers.

He didn't resist the slightest bit. His lashes stayed lowered, eyes impossible to read, but his mouth definitely curved. "*Volontiers*," he murmured.

Willingly. But in French, it sounded so sexy that her thighs tightened on him.

That curve of his mouth deepened. He nestled his body lower on the bed, so that the headboard no longer propped him up, and tucked his jasmine-bound hands above his head. And lifted his hips against hers, deliberately, pressing her up off the bed.

Damn, she wanted to get his pants off and feel his unabashed arousal more unabashedly still.

Well, she was on top, wasn't she? *He* was bound by *her.* So she reached for the button of his jeans, and his breath sucked in.

Ooh, nice little space there under his waistband when his stomach went concave. She bypassed the button and teased her fingers down into it, grazing as far as she could. The muscles on his arms corded, his fingers finding the edge of her pillow and gripping it hard.

"Oh, look," she murmured gleefully. "I can be mean to you, too."

"If I let you." Deep warning, even as his hips pressed up again.

She met his eyes limpidly. "I wish you would."

His eyes narrowed dangerously. "Jasmin."

"Well...you wanted something *hard* to do, didn't you, Damien?" She walked her fingers up his chest and then back down, toying around his navel. "Since just wishing for your hugs and kisses didn't seem like enough?"

"I'm not seven anymore," he said between his teeth.

She laughed and twisted her hips against his, enjoying the view of that very adult male body straining under hers. "Now how did I figure that out?"

"Can I take back what I said about you not being a brat?"

"It depends." She stroked her fingers down again, teasing that fine trail of dark hair down under the waist of his jeans. "Are you going to spoil me?"

"How about I spoil you for any other man?" He thrust his hips again. "How about that?"

"Too easy." She made a face. "You've already done that. I thought you wanted a *challenge.*"

His body stilled, his gaze locking with hers, and she realized what she had just said.

Damn honesty and daring. Her cheeks flushed under that gaze. He brought his bound hands to her hair and caught a handful of locks, pulling her head down with them until he could kiss her. He held her by her hair for his kiss, tightening his hold, kissing her and kissing her, hard, thrusting his tongue into her mouth as if *he* was on top and taking over *her.*

"Cheater," she managed when she could finally get herself to break free. She didn't break far, her head collapsing on his chest as she breathed shakily.

He brought his bound hands behind her head, capturing her. "Show me your weaknesses, and I'll exploit every one." He made it sound like the most delicious promise, all wrapped up in a warning.

"Yeah?" She braced herself up again, kneading her fingers into his shoulders. "Are you going to take me over?" A rub of her hips against his. "Buy me up?"

"Yes." He said it as matter-of-factly as he'd once taken over her company in fact. Done deal. *Mine.*

"This is *my* space," she said defiantly, just because there was something erotic about arguing, while they held each other captive.

He gave a purring, villain's laugh. "Go ahead, Jasmin. Make this little space for yourself here. I like that. Because remember, the whole town that wraps around it is *all mine.*"

Should it have made her feel helpless in his power? Because it didn't. It made her imagine the great, thick medieval walls and him as their builder and defender. With her safe behind them.

He'd always done that, this man. No matter what emotional upheaval he brought, he had always offered her safety at the same time.

I love you. She ducked her head into his chest before she could say it, this emotion that swelled up so great that it hurt not to say, as she kissed her way down his belly, the jasmine vine around his wrist tangling with locks of her hair. *God, you're so special.* He could not possibly, possibly be true, be meant for her.

He caught a fistful of it again as her lips brushed just above his waistband, his hold so tight her roots stung faintly. "No," he said. "Come back up here and kiss my mouth, Jasmin."

She loosened the button on his jeans and stroked her palm down over his briefs. "Oh, so you don't like this?"

"I think I've created a monster." But though he tried to make his voice sound put out, it was too thick with monster-creation pride.

She never had this kind of glorious self-confidence about sex. But there was something about that afternoon by the river. If he could let *himself* go, if he could take and use until all the sex was wrung out of them and they were limp on a riverbank, then...she could, too. "You make me feel a little giddy," she confessed.

His eyes lit, hot and aroused and delighted. "You make me feel one hell of a lot more than giddy. Come up here and play with me where I can reach you."

She eased his zip open, curling her hand over his cotton-veiled erection. "My arms are kind of short. I wouldn't want to not be able to reach *you.*"

"You're going to be in trouble if I get in reach of your butt at this rate," he threatened, that gorgeous tangle of laughter and frustration and arousal in his own voice.

Her butt tickled in curiosity at the idea that he might lay a spank across it. Might be fun to try once, to see if they actually liked it.

"You know, every time I have sex with you, it's completely different." She tucked her face against his belly so she could blow a breath across his skin.

"If you're still saying that when we're eighty, *then* I'll take it as a compliment," he said wryly, his erection leaping in her hand in fierce counterpoint to the light tone.

She stilled, her lashes brushing against his skin as she blinked. No, best not make too much out of a careless comment. Focus instead on the moment.

She'd learned to be very good at that, focusing on the moment.

"Come here," Damien murmured. "Jess. I'm the mean one. You're the sweet one. Come be sweet to me."

His voice was so coaxing. She couldn't resist it, kissing her way up his chest. She pressed his jasmine-tied wrists above his head again, re-tucking the ends that were loosening. "You're not very good at being mean. So I don't see why I have to be good at being sweet."

He made a kissing motion with his lips, lifting his face to her. And what else could she do with such a gorgeous man, tied up in jasmine for her, in this old bed, his golden body on her white sheets? She had to give him what he wanted. She kissed him, her hair spilling over her own shoulders and sliding down onto his.

"More," he whispered as soon as she stopped. "Kiss me more." His arms came over her head again, a circle of strength.

She brushed her lips over the prickle of his jaw.

"I should have shaved again when I took a shower."

She shook her head, her lips brushing prickles with each stroke. "You're perfect."

His chest vibrated under her hand with his pleasure at that.

"Absolutely perfect," she whispered, kissing down over his throat. Strong throat. And yet it was just as vulnerable as hers was.

He made another sound, hungry and intense. "Sweetheart." He rolled them over suddenly, his forearms above her head, the jasmine falling free over one arm, his body holding hers to the mattress in the most perfect shelter of heat and strength. "You can tie me up in you any time you want. But right now—could I just make love to you? Just like this?"

Her hands stroked down the muscles of his back, that smooth skin. His biceps framed her body, so that his weight held her captive but didn't crush. Wrapping her up in sex and strength and sweetness. So that she could wrap her arms around him and hold on tight, too. "Yes," she whispered. "Just like this."

So he did, while the jasmine vines curled over one strong forearm and tangled in her hair. While the scents of lavender and jasmine and sex and him blended all around her. He made love like that was something you could make, Love. It just took the right materials, the right blend, the right treatment, and you could make love that would last forever.

Chapter 21

"How are the migraines?" Tristan asked, grinning. Damn, Damien looked happy. How long had it been since Damien had looked *really* happy, happy like when they were kids? That shift into more and more tension had happened so gradually but inexorably over the past two decades that it had been easy to miss how great the change had been. Although these past six months had been particularly bad.

"Will you guys shut up?" Damien retorted, but he picked up a handful of jasmine and let the white flowers drift through his fingers back into the great wicker basket.

Merde, the man had lost his mind. And it didn't make Tristan want to kick things *at all* that he had never found his own woman to lose his mind over. Well, one, but that had been a different kind of losing his mind— pure outrage. Not the same thing at all.

"Are you whistling?" Tristan said. "Did you just whistle? Raoul, did you hear that?"

"Sounded more like a mouse squeaking to me," Raoul said, as he helped Matt wrestle with the vat.

"Hey." Damien turned on his oldest cousin.

"Well, if you want it to sound like a proper whistle, stop hiding it under your breath. Put some umph into it." Raoul let loose a wolf whistle that would have gotten the attention of every woman within a half-kilometer radius. Then grinned with wolfish smugness when his fiancée Allegra poked her head in through the great factory doors to see who he was whistling at. He blew her a kiss.

She rolled her eyes and laughed and blew one back, disappearing back outside. Jess stepped into the doorway with more reserve, less sure of her welcome than Allegra.

Damien gave a long, slow, low whistle, the kind that went beyond the average catcall to an awe-filled *ho-ot damn.*

Jess colored but came into the factory. She'd toured the production facility the other day, with great fascination, but Tristan had noticed she was much less confident of her place in his big family than Allegra or Layla had been. It was kind of cute to see how irresistibly she was drawn to Damien, enough to overcome all that reserve and move toward him even when all his cousins were watching.

Even difficult, saturnine Damien had found someone before Tristan did. What the hell was up with that? Tristan was the only one of the cousins who was *good* at women. Well, except for accountants. But female accountants weren't actually women, they were succubi who came to earth to suck a man's soul out of his body, and the fact that one of them wore those little pencil skirts while she did it was just further proof of evil.

"Is anybody else here actually going to help us put this damn thing in place?" Matt growled. "We've got three of these to get in. Tristan, this was your damn idea."

"The scent is much rounder coming through copper, Matt. You should be grateful to me that I pointed it out to you." For two years. Constantly. Until Matt had finally agreed to order the copper-lined vats this year, but of *course* (as Matt grumbled) the vats had gotten to the valley a month later than promised, right in the middle of the harvest, the absolute worst time to make such a switch.

Matt growled louder.

Tristan grinned—being growled at by Matt was kind of like being growled at by a big grumpy teddy bear who was terribly afraid someone would realize he was a soft, cuddly toy rather than the grizzly bear he pretended to be—and strolled over to help hook the new vat up to the overhead crane. The vat was big enough around that a fourth hand would have been helpful holding it while Matt got the hook in, but Damien had forgotten all about them. In fact—

Tristan jabbed Raoul hard in the ribs.

Over there by a stack of burlap sacks, Damien—the tough, impervious, cool, ruthless one—had lifted a hand and was letting jasmine blooms drift from his fingers all over Jess's upturned face, his expression so tender and so exposed that Tristan and Raoul immediately jerked around to put their backs to it. Then they abandoned the vat to find some excuse to stand between Damien and the factory doors, so that anyone who poked a head in wouldn't see Damien stark naked like that.

Tristan peeked over his shoulder to see if it was safe yet, and—shit. Jess had caught some of the flowers as they fell, and now was curving the handful of them against Damien's cheek, so gently that the flowers themselves rested uncrushed between her palm and his skin. Damien's expression was so—

Tristan snapped his eyes back around, horribly embarrassed. Raoul cleared his throat. Tata Véro poked her head in, and Tristan sprang forward immediately. "Tata!" he said loudly, grabbing her arm and pulling her back outside the factory. "Just the aunt I wanted to see!"

He glanced back. Raoul's body blocked Damien's mother's view of him.

"Any time on the hand with this vat," Matt growled, and Damien barely pulled himself together even with all *that* help, moving toward the vat with this slow, daydreaming step.

Tata Véro, catching sight of his expression, stopped stock still, her lips parted, the gold bracelets on her arms jingling faintly as she brought a hand to her mouth in a cross between delight and *but-is-she-good-enough-for-my-son.*

Tristan bent his head to his aunt's ear. "I think she's a little afraid he's too wonderful for her. That she can't keep him, that he'll evaporate into thin air. He might have to be careful that she doesn't try to put the memory of him into a bottle instead of holding on tight to the actual him. But she really likes him, Tata. Anyone can tell."

"Oh, that poor girl," Tata Véro said, instantly won over. "I'm sure having her father die so recently must make her insecure." She brightened, as vivid as her jewelry. "I can shake some sense into her."

"Tata." Tristan meant to be a good cousin, he really did. Deflect Damien's mother, help a guy out. But the temptation was irresistible. "You should show her some of the old albums from when we were kids. You know. So she can see how adorable he was." He grinned as Tata Véro lit up with greedy delight and headed for her potential future daughter-in-law like a duck toward a crumb cast carelessly on the water.

Bracing the vat, unable to release it without it toppling sideways on Raoul's foot, Damien looked from Tristan to his mother and Jess as Tata Véro claimed Jess's arm, leading her out of the factory. His eyes narrowed.

Tristan sighed blissfully. *Remember that time all our favorite toys disappeared and we found ransom notes in their place? That's the beauty of family. Never too late for payback.*

***

"Childhood photos?" Damien's fingers tapped once against the teak table under the old plane tree, a table currently spread with the multiple family albums his mother had dragged out from the old *mas*, the big stone house that had seen generations. Like all the other men, he had a sheen of sweat on him from the extended vat wrestling in the factory. "That was all you could think of to show her while we were working, Maman?" He gave Tristan a filthy look.

Tristan grinned.

"What's wrong?" Jess asked. "They're cute."

250

Damien's glare at Tristan should by rights have cut him into small pieces where he stood.

"This alien one is *adorable*," Jess had to admit, and there were multiple muffled chortles from the other women. Tristan looked as if he was about to burst. Raoul and Matt looked torn between the urge to tackle Tristan themselves and their own glee at Damien's expression. "You're covered in blue paint. Even your hair."

The photo was of five young boys, ranging from Tristan. age four to Raoul age nine, all of them naked except for underwear, each painted in a different color. Apparently they had been playing at alien invasion and tried to invade their parents' lazy afternoon at this very table, one summer afternoon twenty-five years ago.

She bit the inside of her lip to keep her expression innocently goo-goo eyed. "And look! Matt is wearing Superman briefs. Aww."

Matt lost his sense of humor and glared at Tristan, his cheeks flushing. Layla covered her face with her hand, tilting her head forward so that her curls helped hide how hard she was struggling with laughter. Matt growled.

"Who's this one?" Jess pointed at the boy painted in orange, as skinny as all the kids in the photo were but one of the tallest and presumably therefore one of the oldest.

Wistfulness passed over multiple faces. "Lucien," Damien said, and rested his hand on her shoulder.

Right until that second, she had never known that a hand on her shoulder might not just give support but also ask for it. What a wonderful thing the human body was, to let people seek and give comfort without ever having to admit even in their own heads that they needed it. She covered his hand with hers. "He doesn't look as much like the rest of you. Did he take after the other side of his family?"

No one said anything at all. Damien's hand tightened a little on her shoulder.

251

Okay, wrong track. She took a breath. "Purple is an interesting color choice for you," she told Tristan.

She would have named herself the woman least likely to start teasing a pack of strange family members, but sometimes a woman had to do what a woman had to do. This was Damien's world, and he seemed to need someone on his side in it. Big families were weirder than she had quite realized. Because everyone here so obviously *was* on his side, and yet there was this great tangled mass of rivalries and pressures, too.

"I was four years old and greatly abused by my elders." Tristan folded his arms and took a deep, luxurious breath, as if smelling something beautiful. "And right now, it's almost all worth it. Did you notice what's on Damien's underwear?"

"All right, that's it." Damien's hand left Jess's shoulder as he dove straight for Tristan.

Jess, Layla, and Allegra all leapt to their feet in alarm as the two bodies collided.

Damien's mother calmly petted the photo album page, beaming at it, and barely raised an eyebrow.

"It's been a long time since we've thrown them in the pond," Raoul told Matt.

"The alien photo," Matt said. "Tristan told Tata to get out the alien photo."

"You're right. We can't let him get away with that."

And then, just like that, there were *four* male bodies wrestling. "If any of you end up needing the hospital, I expect you to drive yourselves," Tata Véro said, flipping a page. "I'm retired." She winced a little at a particular thudding sound, peeked at her son in the mass, and then looked immediately back at the photo album.

Jess didn't mean to be rude and interfere in their family dynamics, but this was a lot more male violence than she was used to seeing on any given day. Or in her whole life. It wasn't that there was any punching or anything—they were wrestling and didn't seem to have any intention of actually *killing* each other. They actually seemed to be having a very good time. But still. They were at a fully operational center of agricultural production, and right there was a faucet with a hose attached.

She got up, turned it on, angled carefully so that she wouldn't hit the table with its precious family photo albums—she was *so jealous* of all those family adventures—and just aimed the hose all over them.

The men fell apart, spluttering, while Layla and Allegra fist-pumped encouragement to her.

"Fuck, that's cold," someone said, and Damien turned toward her.

He looked so damn good wet, half laughing and all menacing, that she aimed the nozzle at his chest full blast.

His grin lit his whole face as he lunged into the force of the water, straight at her, grabbing the hose. He held it up out of her reach, angling it threateningly close to her, laughing, and she ducked into his chest, scrunching her face as she braced herself and tried to make sure at least half of the spray got on him, too.

Of course, she'd kind of forgotten in that instinctive move how *wet* she had gotten him.

He laughed out loud, dropped the hose, and hugged her in hard to him, soaking her front and half her back.

"Hey!" She struggled.

He laughed and held on. Until she was laughing, too, enjoying his strength so damn much. It was a hot day. It was good to be held ruthlessly by a wet, laughing man.

His family beamed, and just as Tristan got hold of the hose and lifted it in promised revenge on her, Matt yanked it out of his hands from behind and turned the faucet off. "Wasting water in August," he grumbled. But he was grinning.

"I just want you to know," Damien said, "that *my mother* was the one who bought that damn Disney underwear. And then didn't do the laundry so that it was the only thing left in my drawer to wear that morning."

"Am I your maid?" his mother asked supremely.

"I was six, Maman!"

"You were capable of unearthing cans of paint and covering yourself and your cousins in it and organizing an alien invasion. I don't see why turning on a washing machine was so hard."

Damien sighed.

"Besides, you loved that underwear. You were always going around declaiming you were the 'never duplicated Genie of the L— '"

"Maman!"

His mother shrugged and opened innocent hands, then winked at Jess.

Damien sighed heavily and draped his arm around Jess's shoulders. "My family is a curse."

She slipped her arm around his waist and hugged herself to him. "Oh, no," she murmured, for his ears alone. "They love you so much. You're *so* lucky."

For some reason, Damien looked really, really...struck. By something that didn't hurt, quite, but it changed something about him. His arm relaxed on her shoulders, and this quiet kind of...thought...seemed to settle over his body. He kept his arm draped over her, fingers playing idly with her hair or rubbing her shoulder, long past when his clothes had dried on his body in the August evening.

And every time they looked at him, everyone in his family grinned like idiots.

Even his grandfather, when he came back out from his nap in the cool of the evening to eat with them under the plane tree, watched Damien and Jess with a faint curve of his lips. "Looks like I'm still the most ruthless man in the family," he said to Damien with considerable satisfaction.

Damien sighed. But he didn't look very put out.

Chapter 22

"It's their way of honoring you for what they think you want to be," Jess said. She stopped still on the little stone landing, where a fountain trickled, tucked against a wall. The smell of old water, of moss and wet and stone, tucked away in this ancient town of sun and flowers, grabbed at her. She had to breathe it for a moment, resting her hand on wet stone to pull in its texture.

Damien's warm, strong hand around her other hand anchored her in humanity. Perfect—this fountain made to nurture humans, and the reminder of that human hand. Her brain went off on tangents of possibilities, and she took out her moleskin journal to note down a few words and formula ideas. She'd stopped doing that a long time ago, stuck in that Spoiled Brat rut, in hopeless denial of her own career. But here, in this world, new ideas blossomed in her brain everywhere she stepped. And she noted them all down, no matter how unusable they were, just because they were beautiful anyway. Worth noting. Worth reaching for.

"What is?" Damien asked when they resumed their climb of the street of stairs.

It took her a second to remember. "Oh, the mean thing. The James Bond, panther, ruthless thing. *You* started it. And I know, I know—it must have been your way of responding to the pressures and expectations on you, of forging your own place. I can see how it would make a cycle. But they're just giving respect to who they think you've chosen to be."

They came out onto the street and headed under an arch thickly grown with fuchsia bougainvillea. She could feel Damien's gaze on her head.

"Of course, if you're *forged*," she said, "that sounds pretty immutable. Except under volcanic heat and pressures. Maybe you're something more human and supple and easier to change, but I don't know for sure how it works with families. Change might be even harder, because so many people have fit themselves to each other as they've grown that any shift affects every single person's beliefs about who they are and who you are and how you all fit together."

"For someone who doesn't have much family, you're very wise," Damien said quietly.

She shrugged, her throat tightening again at her lack of people. "I like to watch them," she said softly. "And see what they're like."

For some reason, that made him pull her in to his side for a strong hug. "You have family now," he reminded her.

Not like he did. Not solid and impossible to lose, so stuck to him that he couldn't even stretch out his arms and take a deep breath without running into family and all their expectations. But...a vision of Layla's bright, happy face flashed through her mind, and of Colette Delatour's old wisdom.

Maybe she had the beginnings of a few people. She looked up at Damien, and behind him danced little images of grinning, intrigued family members, all watching them.

Maybe more than a few. If she could figure out how to keep them, to make the relationships solid like his were.

"I don't know," she said. "I've been stuck by Spoiled Brat for years—by people's expectations of me, my expectations of them. But I was just realizing how much looser its hold is on me than all the expectations are on you. I really can just...change. Just do it. Because I want to do it. Nobody is affected by me at all."

His hand flexed on hers. "I am."

She looked up at him quickly as they came out on a terrace. He had brought her to a small town on a cliff above the sea, with a promise to show her the sunset. A minor traffic accident on the road before them had slowed them down, and now night was falling. A softer beauty than the sunset, but it filled the town everywhere.

Damien leaned his forearms on the old parapet of the terrace. "Jess. I don't know quite how it feels to be on your own. I've never done that. But if it feels...rootless to you, or risky, to give up your career in New York and try to make a go of that shop, to do your niche and custom perfumes. If it feels financially insecure, like you could lose everything and have nothing to fall back on, I just wanted you to know—that's what I'm good at. Making sure my—people—can do whatever their passion is and not have to worry about the money. I can help you with your business plan and the investments. I know how to make sure that part works out for you."

Was she one of his people? She looked down at her hand, covered by his, her throat tight. Had he just raised that financial shield of his in front of her and promised to fight her battles for her, too?

"Damien. You're already dedicating every ounce of energy you have to making sure everyone else's wishes come true. You don't have to take on mine."

He closed his eyes a moment. "You're like my mother, aren't you? You think that business and making money are bad words. I've gone down the dark path or something."

"No," she said. "I actually..." *kind of find it erotic.* That power and discipline and willingness to fight on the terms of the world to which he had been born, and to win. "I kind of like it." That was so tepid she could barely count it as the honesty she had promised herself to give to him. "It's sexy," she made herself admit.

His eyebrow went up a little, and he turned toward her.

"And when you do that thing, where you take off your cufflinks and your watch, that *see all this money and power? I'm taking it off for you* act...that's *really* hot." His eyes lit so much at that she just kept going, lifting her hands to her head to flick her fingers out. "Like, explode my head hot."

"Really," he murmured, reaching for her hips to pull her to him.

It felt hot to have admitted it, too. Like stripping herself a little bit more naked, in this awkward but determined striptease.

"Every breath you take is explode-my-head hot," he said, nestling her hips against his. "When I'm around you, there's this part of me that feels like an animal, all the time."

Wow. Talk about *hot*.

"I like the fight and the power and the money and winning," he said. "I love it. I want to stay the strongest and the most ruthless. I *like* it. That's who I *am*. It's just that—you know that shaded, quiet space you put at the heart of your last trial for me? I think I need that. That something special just for me, private, away from the battle, just *mine*. I need that, or I'm all empty."

She was unbearably touched and proud that one of her fragrance trials had managed to help him understand something he needed. It made her even more determined to give him that *something special just for him*. The *right* fragrance, the one that really got him. That showed him that someone understood him.

She turned away to lean on the parapet. They'd always had good luck understanding each other, when they leaned side by side on terraces. This time, the sea tossed against rocks below them.

"That time you fell in love," she said quietly. "What was it like?"

For a long moment, he didn't say anything. His arms braced against the terrace wall, and he gazed at the shallow waves below. "It was as if I was a falling star," he said finally, a hushed, infinite depth to his voice like the sea itself. "And she caught me."

Oh. *Oh*.

Jess stood perfectly still. It hurt so much. That someone else had made him feel that way, the way he had made *her* feel.

"Do you—do you still run into her?" she asked, her throat tightening as if someone had just grabbed her by the neck and tied a knot with her. "Is she from around Grasse?"

He cut her an odd glance, arrested. He didn't say anything.

She tried to swallow past that knot. "It must be painful," she whispered. "I'm sorry."

"It doesn't always feel good, no," Damien said. His eyebrows drew together. He slanted her another glance.

"What—what ended it?"

Damien stared at the sea. Past his head, the first star of the evening shone small and bright. "She dropped me," he said abruptly, voice clipped. "She just turned her hand upside down and let go."

Oh. It hit her like a punch in the stomach, which could be only a hint of how much worse it must have hit him. She closed her hand over the back of his. "I'm sorry." *God,* that must have hurt.

Damien turned his head and stared at her, his eyebrows pleated. "Yes, so you've said."

What?

His eyebrows slanted sharply together. "You don't even know what I'm talking about, do you?" he said suddenly, harshly. "You can't even guess."

No. Maybe not. She hadn't been dumped by someone she loved. She'd had them die on her, though. "I know what it's like to lose your heart."

His voice grew deeper, harsher. "Do you know what it's like to lose it because the other person didn't think you were *worth* it? She didn't trust you with it?"

She slowly shook her head. "No. In my case, it wasn't their choice."

He stared at her, as if she had blocked him into some kind of impasse. No outlet for him anywhere.

"She sounds like an idiot," Jess said. "And a coward."

"Jasmin. Who the hell do you think I'm talking about?"

Now it was her turn to stare.

"For God's sake, Jess." He shoved himself away from the wall. "*Idiot* about sums it up."

Her heart pounded so hard.

"Fuck." He closed his eyes and stood very still a moment. "*Fuck.*"

No, don't say that. Let me figure out first what you're trying to say. I didn't—

He opened his eyes and gave her a flat, dark look. "You make me feel so easy," he said despairingly. "You make me feel as if everything that matters is right here." He touched his hand to his heart. "Inside me. That I've *got* it. I'm not empty anymore. And no matter what I do, or how far down I think I've stripped myself, you can't even tell. Like everything that seems so good to me can't even be detected on one of your chromatographs. I'm that inhuman."

Wait! Wait, wait, wait. Don't blame yourself for me.

His voice sounded stifled, almost extinguished. "You make me feel like a wish that can come true. But you've never believed in me at all."

So many things packed into his words that she couldn't gather her wits to answer. *I'm sorry*, she wanted to say. *I'm trying. I don't—it's* hard *for me. But I didn't mean—*

"God damn it," he said bitterly, and shoved his hand through his hair once, turned, and walked away.

Chapter 23

"What are you doing to my nephew?" Colette Delatour asked.

Jess gave her newfound adoptive great-grandmother an anxious, frustrated look at that blunt beginning to the conversation and shifted away from her, pacing around the garden. "Nothing." He'd been gone to Paris "for business" for two days now. His ability to walk out had slammed across her self-confidence like a lethal blow, knocking her out of that tree with her mirror shattered around her.

But it still had some starlight in it, that mirror. And she'd be damned if she'd let it lie there without picking up the pieces. Not this time.

"So you didn't inherit Élise's courage," Colette said, disappointed.

She was using her courage *right now*. Couldn't someone as brave as Colette even tell? "It's not that! I'm working on it. I just need to *get* him. If I can get this scent for him right, that will show him."

"Or alternatively you could just tell him," Colette said.

Jesus. Some people had so much courage it gave them a completely unrealistic idea of other people's potential. "I can't do that. You don't understand."

Ninety-six-year-old eyebrows rose faintly. "Try me."

"He's too special." *He's that star in the sky that you wish for but you know you can never catch.* Not without ending up on the ground with your chin cut open on a mirror shard.

(It was as if I was a falling star. And she caught me.)

"I can't just *say* it," she said. She'd tried. That might even be the problem. When you said a wish out loud, it could never come true. "I have to show him. That I get him. That's what he wants. Something tangible. *Proof.*"

And he was going to get it, too, if she had to die still trying. Sixty-some years from now.

"Did he say that?"

"Yes," Jess said defiantly. "He asked me to make him a scent. The first day he found me in that shop. It was a challenge. It was *really* important to him." Watch, cufflinks, coat, expensive piece of armor after expensive piece of armor, all put on her counter in the determination to get that scent.

The scent that understood him.

"But I can't get the damn heart note right," she said.

"You're nowhere near the right track, if you're looking for his heart note in my gardens," Colette said.

"This is where I came the closest!" Jess pressed her face into stone, taking a deep breath. Yes, that was part of it. And the fig tree. And the lemon balm. But... "Here. When I was talking to him here."

Colette folded her arms over her pale green blouse and sighed. "You know, there's a part of you that *is* very like her. Willing to take cyanide and die rather than believe in yourself."

Hey. My great-grandmother took cyanide to escape torture, *to save you, and you're calling that a weakness?* Jess started to throw the words at Colette Delatour and then stopped.

The old woman did have a way of putting things in perspective. *In my day, we had to worry about being tortured to death, failing to resist, and betraying everyone we loved. What's your excuse for cowardice, exactly?*

Which pissed her off. *I am* trying, *thank you. Damien's the one who ran away.*

This time.

"There are only three important words in your last sentence," Colette Delatour said. "*I* and *talking* and *him.*

And you chose *here*. Because it was easier than all the others."

Jess closed her eyes a moment. And then she rested her forehead on the stone wall. A great sense of fatigue ran through her muscles, as if the stone had offered itself in their place to hold her up.

"Mémère," she said, and Colette Delatour made a little sound as if someone had hit her in the belly.

"*What* did you just call me?"

Grandmother. "I'm sorry. That was presumptuous. I just—"

"No," Colette said sharply. She was staring at Jess, her hand pressed to her stomach. "No, it's all right. That's what I am."

Jess's fingers curled into that stone. An almost weepy sense of gratitude ran through her. That the stone was there. That it was holding steady at her request for support.

Her throat tightened, and she fought that urge to tears as hard as she could. One could not show tears to Colette Delatour. Stone was a good thing to have. But it didn't always understand softness. "Mémère," she said again, and Colette's breath drew in. "I try to believe. I *wish* for it. And then right at the wrong moment, the doubt comes back. I just can't. I can't believe that I could have someone so special, and him not go away."

Her eyes stung. She pressed her head into the stone.

"You *are* very like her," Colette said, and Jess spun on her, ready to snap if the old war hero put down her great-grandmother's sacrifice again.

Colette Delatour shook her head. "She never could believe either. Not ever. Never once did she believe she could survive, she could succeed, she could do it. Thirty-six wishes she helped carry through the Alps so they could come true, and she never believed she could be good enough for them, not one single time. Thousands of people today bless that woman's name because of all the times she kept trying to do what she didn't believe."

Jess did start to cry, suddenly, this hard onslaught of tears that made her grip the stone.

"Jacky and I, we had conviction. I had my cyanide, too—I'd be damned if I'd let them have the pleasure of torturing someone else's betrayal out of *me*—but I never took it, always convinced I could get away, succeed. And I was right. And I was lucky. But she did exactly as much as I ever did. It must have cost her a hundred times more, to do all those things she couldn't believe she could do. Can you imagine the terror? But one after the other, she did them anyway."

Jess took a soft, deep breath of that stone, the tears easing out of her. God, what an amazing woman. *I want to make a scent for my great-grandmother.*

I want to make a scent for my father.

Hell, I want to make a scent for Colette Delatour. Tough down to the bone but with all these herbs and soups to nurture everyone around her.

"What I didn't have was emotional courage," said that forged steel Resistance war hero. "I'm ninety-six. You don't think I should have looked for Léo's descendants before this? Tried to heal this family sooner? I could have known your father. I could have known Layla's. I could have made up with Jacky. He's an arrogant, annoying, over-entitled brat, but he's not that hard. I'm only doing those things now, when time's got its own little cyanide pill waiting for me, so I don't have to deal with the hurt too long, if things go wrong."

Tears welled up again. Jess tried to smile through them. "You would have liked my father," she whispered. "He used to make baby stars. Dragons taking flight. He'd capture them in a bottle for me."

An old, strong hand closed over her shoulder. "I'll never know your father. Why don't you show me what you can do instead?"

***

Damien did *not* get migraines. Migraines shut people down, making it impossible for them to do anything but try to survive the agony. Damien got headaches. Something he could keep working through. Keep making perfume launch party conversation through. Keep doing whatever he had to do, until he finally got to go home and turn off all the lights.

And by Monday, if his head hurt much more, he'd put a damn bullet through it just to improve the situation. He finally even ducked out of the Paris office at noon, to go lie down at his apartment for an hour in the hope that he would die and someone would bury him in a cool, dark place free from the excruciating pain.

He could barely grit his teeth to be polite to the concierge as she handed him an express envelope on his way in. No, he did not need to deal with anyone's urgent problems right now. And—oh, crap, he could feel the vial shape in it. Some damn perfume he was supposed to give an opinion on, all he needed. Probably from Tristan, otherwise it would have been sent to the office.

He made it out of the elevator to his bed and dropped flat on it, the envelope beside him.

Fuck. He wished to God he had never bought this damn glass-walled penthouse apartment, so that he could at least shut out all the light. If he survived and his head ever stopped hurting, he was buying something in a basement. To hell with the long-term real estate investment and the need to impress everyone with Rosier power.

He rolled to the side, reaching for the nightstand drawer and Jess's little bottle of Advil, with the memory it held of her handing it to him in the garden, that moment of care slipping through their hostilities, as if he still mattered even when she was hurt and angry and they were fighting.

As he reached across the dropped envelope for the drawer, he saw the return address. *J. Bianchi.*

His breath hitched and wanted to stop there, poised between hope and fear. One of his trials? What had she done with it this time? He'd been gone for a week now. There was always so much work to do when he was in

Paris, and every single bit of that work felt safer than pulling out his phone and calling Jess. Plus, she could have called *him*, damn it. He was the one who had told her that he loved her and had her stare at him as if he was a member of an alien species who could not possibly have fallen in love.

It didn't surprise him, though, that Jess would have needed to give her reply with a perfume rather than words. He was just...deeply afraid of what those perfume-words might be.

Had she damned him to hell or maybe...made a leap of faith?

Slowly, not sure he could deal with either possibility right now, he pulled the strip to open the envelope.

A brown vial rolled into his palm, a card sliding after it. It was the first time he had ever seen Jess's handwriting, other than glimpses of her notes strewn across the counter in the perfume shop. It didn't say: *I love you, I'm sorry.* It didn't say: *You jerk for walking off like that right in the middle of an important conversation. Don't come back.* It didn't say: *I was an idiot, I agree, and so were you, let's talk.*

It said: *If you get a headache, try this.*

And for some reason—it must be his fucking head—that made his eyes sting.

He uncapped the vial, and the scent of lavender hit him immediately, spicy, fresh, optimistic. The scent of a bee sting easing. The scent of a field on the plateaus, high up, away from the world, with a wind rippling waves of purple. The scent of an afternoon making love in a small, shadowy room above an old perfume shop.

He held the vial to his nose, his eyes closed, and his breathing slowing and deepening. That tight pain eased the minutest degree at the first breath, and then a little bit more with the second, and a little bit more, like a guitar string close to snapping being slowly, slowly adjusted back to proper tightness. It eased until he almost forgot about it, his lashes growing heavy, his face muscles relaxing.

He actually fell asleep that way.

When he woke, it was pitch black outside and the vial had slipped from his hand to spill a few drops across his sheets.

His thousand-euro silky fine Paris sheets smelled of lavender. Just like the embroidered sheets carefully ironed and handed down for generations back home.

And his head didn't hurt at all.

But his heart still did, in this anxious, demanding way, like, *Get your butt up and go home.*

***

He got back to his Grasse office at eleven that morning, a short flight to Nice and the kind of driving from Nice to Grasse that his Aston Martin had been built for.

He dropped paperwork off with Fréd and stepped into his office, impatient to be gone again. To go see a woman who didn't believe in him, but she cared for him just the same. *I'm sorry I stayed so long in Paris. Merde,* that was one of his own father's techniques for dealing— not dealing—with emotional issues. *I'm back. I'm trying again.*

He hung up his coat and turned toward his desk, scrubbing his forehead at everything that awaited him on it. No matter where he went, there work was. "Fréd. What are these bottles on my desk? Did Parfumerie need my opinion on something?"

And could it wait? He knew it was eleven on a Tuesday, but...he had something important to do.

Fréd poked his red head in through the office door. "Jasmin Bianchi said you had commissioned a fragrance from her. She's been leaving things for you to test when you get back. She finally talked your address out of me and overnighted the last one, didn't you get it?"

267

Damien's heart lightened so fast. Like the whole room had been filled with that lavender oil. He moved toward the bottles as if they'd reached out and lassoed his waist, pulling him toward them. "Did she ask for me?"

He ran his fingers over the stoppers, coming to rest on that exquisite whimsy of a crystal bottle he had once set down on a counter between them just before he walked out. His thumb caressed the bottle. Once, twice, thrice. *I wonder if I ever get to make wishes.*

"Of course she did," Fréd said. "But you didn't tell me when you would be back." Clear, subtle reproach. A good assistant *hated* not knowing the schedule. "*I* kept telling her you would probably be in the next morning."

"Thank you, Fréd," he said, and Frédéric gave him a stern look just to make sure that reproach had come through properly and then disappeared, pulling the door closed.

Damien gazed at the bottles a moment. Then he slowly removed his cufflinks and turned up his sleeves, unbuttoning a button on his shirt, flexing his shoulders. He brought his bare left wrist to his nose and took a tension-easing breath of lavender. Then he picked a bottle up.

There was no note this time. Just two plain sample bottles and two elegant vintage bottles from the collection in the old shop.

He found some strips—ever present on a perfume executive's desk—and tested the first one.

Him again. The titanium and hardness. But this core of...what was it? It had this cold, far-off quality that made him think of a star out of reach. His mouth twisted, and he set the strip on his desk and tried the next one.

Him still. Titanium, hardness. The sense of time that relaxed his muscles. The sword plunged in the dirt in the shade. But there was...what was this? In that shade where the sword rested, jasmine was growing up an old wall of stone.

He smelled that one again, and then again, taking a long time before he set it aside to try the next bottle, a beautiful bottle from the Art Déco period.

His head cocked. What was *this*? It smelled...it made him think of impossible things. This clear, glimmering purity of hope, like the birth of a baby star. He loved it. It had this chest-tightening emotion packed into it, like standing beside a cradle in the dark, looking down at your firstborn child.

It took him forever to recover from that one. He couldn't keep smelling it—it was too much—but he had to pace and pace his office and go stand at the door to his balcony, clutching the jamb and gazing down the street toward her shop, before he was ready to release whatever was held in that last crystal bottle. The one he had once set on a counter precisely halfway between them.

His heart stopped. It was *her* scent. The wishing scent from New York. The almond and vanilla and jasmine, the sweetness, the hope, that naked longing for happiness. His throat tightened. His hand closed around the bottle, and he slipped it into his pocket, where it could be safe.

He went back out on the balcony, gazing toward the shop. And then...he'd been rock-climbing since he was a kid. And for his entire career at Rosier SA, he had taken the stairs inside to his office, cutting up them in cool, long strides, carrying power with every step. He shook his head, and then just went over the balcony, catching the bars, swinging himself down to the street below in one jump.

Bursting free.

Chapter 24

So many dusty corners and shelves, in a shop like this. When Jess couldn't focus, when she didn't know what to do, she cleaned a few more of them and hoped, maybe, to encounter secret, ancient treasures.

But the magic was all in the bottles. She set a box of dusty ones on the counter and began to wipe them down.

A shadowy shape moved in the doorway, and her heart leapt. But the man stepped forward, and although the lean, muscled body and the bones of his face were the same, his hair was a gold-streaked, sun-kissed texturing of blond to golden-brown.

"You must be Lucien," she said.

The man checked in the doorway, his face blanking. Then he got control of himself, in a way that reminded her *very* strongly of Damien, and moved into the room with that same prowling grace. He was of a height, with that same long, lean strength and control to his movements.

"Antoine Vallier." His voice was rather clipped.

Ah. The lawyer behind all the emails and communications and phone calls during the process as this heritage was passed to her.

"I apologize," he said. "I didn't realize you were coming at this time, and I was on vacation. Have you run into any problems with the Rosiers?"

"No, they've been very kind," she said, and his eyebrows shot to the top of his head.

"Damien's been in Paris the whole time, I take it," he said dryly. "Maybe that latest model of his is softening him."

A hitch of her heart. "No, he was here until a few days ago." *Don't react to the model, don't react, don't react.* "What latest model?"

"I can't really keep them straight. Kendall something, maybe? The one he took to the Abbaye launch Saturday night."

It felt as if she'd been punched in the stomach. For a moment, she could only stare at him. A deep breath. Another. Another. *Think this through.*

"He's not dating a model," she said. "You must have misunderstood."

Antoine Vallier looked faintly puzzled as to why she would care, then pulled out his phone, typed something, and slid it across to her. Photos from the perfume launch. Damien, standing beside a beautiful dark-haired woman, his hand at the small of her back, her smiling for the camera and him not smiling, but both of them unreadable in their ways. Giving a surface.

Jess fought physical sickness. *No, but—*

No.

That's not right.

Don't do this again, to yourself and to him.

Another breath, slow and careful.

"But most of all, I wouldn't have believed it. I would have thought, 'What's going on? Picking up another man twelve hours later doesn't fit with what I know of her.' And I would have made sure I did know what was going on, before I made any decisions to ditch you from my life."

What fit with what she knew of him? That he was socially and professionally savvy and had not only exquisite manners but a bone-deep, true-to-the-heart courtesy where women were concerned. That he was highly photogenic, and models were highly photogenic, and cameramen were always looking for the good shot. That if he was speaking to someone and suddenly they found themselves being photographed, he would hardly shove her away or humiliate her, but would pose calmly, used to that kind of thing.

She shook her head and pushed the phone back across the counter. "He's dating me," she said firmly.

"That's why the Rosiers haven't given me any trouble. That's why they've been very kind."

Because they really love Damien quite a lot, even if he's at some stage in his life where it's hard for him to understand that.

She picked up a bottle, rubbing the dust free from it in that automatic worry motion that reassured her so much. One, two, thr—

"Damien Rosier is dating you," Antoine Vallier said, startled. His green eyes flicked over her once. "*Damien* is," he repeated, as if to confirm she knew which cousin was which.

"Damien is," said a voice behind him, and relief and happiness just seemed to burst wide open inside her and fill the shop, as if she'd dropped another bottle of bitter almonds.

Antoine Vallier moved quickly to the side, turning, not like a man alarmed, but like a man who definitely didn't want Damien Rosier standing right behind him. He didn't want that kind of enemy at his back.

Damien's gaze held hers just for a second, his own somber, intent, and...and *joyful*. And then his eyes zeroed in on Antoine Vallier and went cold as ice.

Oh. Wow. And she'd thought Damien had been cold with *her*. She'd had no idea. All this time, every time, no matter how mad he was, he'd never taken out his full ruthlessness on her. "Antoine Vallier," Damien said, water-under-ice dangerous. "Are you trying to stir up trouble between me and my—Jasmin?"

"I didn't know there was trouble to stir." Cool green eyes held gray-green. "You work fast."

"It's none of your fucking business."

"Your emotional issues aren't," Antoine agreed, with a little bored moue that was *exactly* like Damien's. He inclined his head to Jasmin. "But if you need legal advice on how best to protect your ownership of this property, how to sell it, or how to set up a business in France, let me know."

"She's got me," Damien said, hard. "If she wants to establish a business. And an entire phalanx of Rosier SA lawyers I'm happy to let her consult."

"The Rosiers have infinite resources, of course," Antoine Vallier said with a thin, cool smile. "All of which are devoted to Rosier interests. No stranger to the family would come out of that kind of little favor stripped of everything, would she?"

"Are you *sure* the two of you aren't related?" Jess asked suddenly. The resemblance in the two profiles as the men faced off against each other was striking.

Antoine's face blanked. Poker face. Exactly like Damien's.

"What?" Damien recoiled. "*No.*" He stared at Jess a second, then glanced once, sharply, at Antoine, then frowned.

Antoine's face was as unreadable as it was possible to be, a faint, cool smile on his lips as if everything in this room now bored him.

"Look, I appreciate the offer," Jess said to him. "But I trust Damien."

A quick shifting in the air, as if the whole room took a breath and light slanted in.

"And I also really appreciate you stopping by to check on me. But I just—right now, I need to talk to Damien."

"I'm not your lawyer at this point," Antoine said. "But if you'll allow me one bit of advice pro bono...be careful."

Damien pivoted on him like a knife striking. "Get the hell out," he said, low and deadly.

Antoine looked to Jess.

"I'm sorry," she said quietly. "This is very private."

His lips twisted once. He nodded, held Damien's eyes a moment, and then strolled past him out through the outer shop. They heard the street door that Jess usually left slightly ajar thump closed.

Damien looked at her. Their eyes held, and already, in that long moment, the trembling tension that had filled her stomach for the past week eased a little.

"You weren't out picking up beautiful models this weekend, were you?" she said, trying for lightness.

His eyebrows slashed together. "Did that bastard claim I was? I'll fucking—"

"Journalists posted photos of the Abbaye launch."

"What, and I was in some of them? *Merde*, Jess, you know what those things are like. I must be in hundreds of photos with models from those things. Anyone would think I slept with a different model every nigh—" He broke off. His eyes searched hers.

"Yes," Jess said wryly. "A woman who grew up in the perfume industry would have to be a complete idiot and...and kind of cowardly, to believe in photos like that. Over what she really knew of the person in the photo."

Damien took a deep, slow breath and released it. He took a step forward, holding her eyes. "Or kind of sweet, and kind of shy, in her sarcastic way, and with a history of losing what she most wanted to hold onto."

She bit the inside of her lip. "I don't lose it." She held up the bottle she had been polishing. "I put it in here."

He shook his head and came toward her, both hands held out. "Terribly tight living quarters in a bottle. I know I'm a lot more trouble outside of it, but...you sure you wouldn't rather have the real thing?"

That made her eyes sting. "You know I would."

He picked her up and set her on the counter and bent his head to rest it between her breasts. And just stayed there, a deep breath moving through his body, and then another.

The anxiety that had trembled in the pit of her stomach for a week now eased all away, almost in time with the easing of his own muscles. She circled her arms around him, petting her fingertips through his hair.

He made a tiny nuzzling motion into her chest at the stroking.

Peace. Ease. Utter relief. It seeped through her bones, ran down her body from the nape of her neck in slow shivers, eased everything about her. Eased everything about *him*, so much tension running out of his body and dropping away.

"I'm sorry I didn't call," he murmured at last. "I just—I'm sorry."

Of course he was. Of course he would accept his own mistakes and apologize for them. She had never known what a special thing that was until she met him.

"You have very thin skin." She could wound him so easily.

He gave a little laugh into her chest. "No one has ever accused me of that before."

She petted him, enjoying that silky texture of his hair, the line of his back bent over her breasts. "Maybe it's only thin in this one spot."

"Right here," he agreed, sliding his arms around her.

"I could have called, to." Except that she'd needed that time to think and process just as much as he had. "But it was easier for me to make perfumes. Even though some of those perfumes—"

"Took all your heart and courage?" He kissed her collarbone.

Yes. They had. To make a baby star like her father—to offer it to Damien. To make a wish. To slip herself into his own fragrance, like its heart. That had taken every drop of courage she had.

And yet it had filled her with dreaming, with pride, with conviction, the more and more she did. She was as strong as every risk she took.

He lifted his head. "Jasmin. About the business help—I won't take over. I won't try to change what you do. You tell me what kind of business you want—a little shop where you customize perfumes for individual clients and mix your own ingredients by hand or a niche perfume company that sells all around the world—and I'll *enhance* that. I'll make sure it can work. That's what I do."

Right. And it was as important to him to give that to her as it was to her to give him baby stars caught in a bottle. She nodded, and he let his head relax back against her breasts. The last drop of tension eased from his body.

"I'm *not* just trying to strip you of all you have," he said, muffled. "No matter what that bastard Vallier says. I'm trying to give you something, too."

"You give me everything," she said quietly. It almost hurt to say it, he gave her so much. She'd had to work so hard to keep any light shining in her life until she met him—and then it was as if he had ignited her, filling her up with so much light she radiated out to the edges of the universe.

Like he was turning *her* into the star. *I love you.* "You make me feel like I…shine."

He lifted his head at that, for a quick search of her face. Then he kissed her quick and fierce and pressed his face back into her breasts again.

"Damien." She ran her hands down his back. "I think somewhere deep down I must have decided to try for you again the day I bought a ticket for Grasse. Or hoped to try again and just never admitted it to myself. And I *have* tried. I haven't backed away from one single challenge you've thrown at me—not scents and not riverbanks. But it never even crossed my mind that I could *keep* you. Maybe a memory of you"—she touched a vial holding one of his trials—"but not *you.*"

Against her throat, she could feel his eyebrows crinkling.

"I can reach for you," she said. "If I'm lucky and I stretch far enough, I can actually touch you for a while. But it's never even occurred to me that I can *hold on.* So many things have slipped through my fingers."

For a moment, he said nothing, still breathing her skin. Then he straightened slowly, gazing at her very seriously.

"But I'm going to try anyway," she said firmly. "I like trying for you. It's just believing I can get you that's the hard part. You have to be tolerant with me about that."

"Would this help?" He pulled a small box out of his pocket and held it out to her, opening the lid.

Shock ran through her. For a second she could neither think nor feel. Then her heart started to beat very hard. In the box was a diamond ring, the diamond large and absolutely flawless, catching the light even in that dim shop and radiating it back at her.

"It's not a star," Damien said regretfully. Like he *still* believed he should be able to catch actual stars for the people he loved. "But it's the best I could do."

Oh, Damien. She pressed her hands to her face. Her eyes stung.

"To show you that I know how to hold on." Damien took one hand from her cheek, linking his fingers with hers while he still held the box, tightening until their knuckles pressed together. "Hard."

She was shivering inside, this growing vibration that was going to show in a minute, crumple her to the ground like a building in an earthquake. She stared at the ring. The platinum band imitated a jasmine vine, lifting up that diamond star like a white flower.

Oh.

"If I put a ring on your finger, you can turn your hand any way you like, but you can't drop it. It's going to stay," Damien said.

Her voice shook. "I would *never* deliberately drop you again, Damien. Not now that I know you. That was a very bad time."

But that ring scared the freaking hell out of her. Like if she reached out and took it, his car would go off a cliff tomorrow and *she'd* take cyanide and die. Oh, God.

"But if you're not ready for that," he said, "I got this."
He set a businessman's leather satchel on the counter
and pulled out a long box, opening it.

A delicate diamond bracelet, with the same jasmine
motif.

What? What in the world?

But...it *did* seem kind of...safer than the ring. Was it
safer to him, too? Was that why he had bought both?

"Or this." He set the bracelet on the counter and
proffered another box. This time an exquisite necklace,
the jasmine its pendant.

What? Her heart felt like it was about to strangle
her—beating in her throat like it wanted to leap out of
her body. It pounded in her head. What was he doing?

"A handful of wildflowers isn't what you need, is it?"

"I love flowers." She was a perfumer!

"But they die. You love them, but they die. And you
have a hard time believing something beautiful can last."

"I'm trying," she said immediately. "It's not you, it's—
"

He lifted her hand and kissed it. "Right. Just like the
first time, I took it personally, but I really should have
been paying attention to you."

"You mean you didn't sacrifice yourself enough?"
She shook her head. "Damien—"

"These don't die." He took the bracelet out of its box,
so that the diamonds glinted, delicate and flawless, able
to shine even in the dim light in the workroom.
"Diamonds are forever."

She almost smiled at that, but then he fastened the
bracelet around her right wrist. It took her breath away,
more beautiful than anything she had ever imagined
gracing her body. Except maybe a twining vine of actual
jasmine as his fingers locked with hers and his body
moved inside her.

"I know I'm just using money, when you're in here
pouring your heart into your art. But...I'm good at that.

Money." He took the necklace out of the box. Calluses brushed her nape as he fastened it, stroking down the chain to settle the diamond jasmine flower halfway between the hollow of her throat and the swell of her breasts. She caught the scent of lavender oil on his wrist. "It's solid. Money. I can give you something that you can be sure you can keep."

"I want to keep *you*." It felt good to say it. *Yes. That's what I want and what I will fight to do.*

"But when you aren't sure you can," he said. "When you have those fears and doubts, and maybe I'm not around or I'm thinking of something else and not paying attention, you can touch these. Like I can smell your lavender, when I'm up in Paris and I need to remember someone cares."

The diamond bracelet fell with unfamiliar delicacy against her wrist when she set her hand on his chest. "You're giving me what you're best at."

"Isn't that what you just gave me? In those bottles you left on my desk? That's the best present anyone has ever given me in my entire life."

"I can get better," she said quickly. "I'm still trying. It never works out in the bottle like it does in my head."

"I love your trying," he said fiercely, shifting his weight so that he trapped her against the counter. "I love that you keep trying to get at me, again and again. I want that so much."

"Even if I screw up and doubt and fail?"

"Especially." His hands tightened too hard on her hips as he buried his face in her hair. "It's how much it costs you to try that makes the effort so precious." His arms flexed around her. "Me, too," he whispered into her hair. "I'm trying, too."

Yes. He was, wasn't he? Over and over, even when he screwed up and doubted and failed.

She slipped her arms around him and breathed against his chest as if she could blow ease onto his heart. "Did the lavender help your migraines?"

"It helped more than that." He tilted her head back and began to work gently at the catch of one earring.

Her eyes flew open. "Damien!"

"They had a full set in the jasmine motif," he said apologetically. "I liked them all." He laid her stud on the counter and, with the care of a man who could thread cufflinks deftly but didn't want to hurt her ear, slipped another post through her lobe, so that a delicate dangle brushed against it. She turned her head to catch sight of the other earring still in the box. A matching jasmine design, a tiny strand of diamonds with a little jasmine at the end.

His fingers moved on her other ear. "When I was in Paris, I saw this set on the Faubourg Saint-Honoré, and I thought, maybe that's what she needs. Little...proofs. Everywhere I can put them."

Jess buried her face in her hands.

"They didn't have an anklet," he said after a moment. "But maybe I could commission one."

She couldn't speak.

"I guess that's overkill," he said finally. "But all together, they're still not worth as much as that damn watch I gave you, and you didn't believe in that."

That watch was worth more than a flawless diamond bracelet, necklace, earrings, and ring? She spread her fingers to gape at him. "How much is the watch worth?"

He told her.

Good lord.

"My father tends to go overboard, too," he said. "I guess if money is what you're good at, it's important to give what you can buy with it to the people you...care about. But nobody ever gets that. They say it's just money and you're trying to buy love."

Her eyebrows drew a little together. "Somebody said that to you?" Who else's love had he tried to buy?

"My mom says it to my dad. They fought a lot when I was a kid. I told you—she didn't like what she said he was turning me into."

"I like it," she said quietly, and reached up to touch those beautiful cheekbones of his. "What you turned into."

His lips curled a little, between her palms. His eyes, holding hers, stayed very serious.

"If I liked it a little less, it would be easier," she said. "Easier to believe that...you know...I could really have you."

He stroked her back. Of all the "little proofs" that now brushed her body, that touch was the most reassuring of all. She spread her fingers against his chest.

"In their wedding photos, my parents look so happy," Damien said suddenly. "My father really loves my mother, you know. But she doesn't understand him. And they stopped being able to reach each other by the time I was old enough to notice that kind of thing."

Jess kneaded her fingers gently into his chest.

"You make me feel whole," he said. "I told you. You make my heart beat. It's as if all that great empty spot inside me...you fill it up with something sweet, just for me."

Oh. Incredible happiness filled her. And it was funny that he should put it that way, because he made her feel as if all that emptiness outside her, he wrapped himself around her and made it go away.

His breath released against her hair in a sigh. "But if you look at their wedding photos, it looks as if my parents once had the same thing. And everyone says I'm exactly like my father and my grandfather. So..."

"You, too," she realized softly. "You have a hard time believing your wish can come true, too." Because he, too, knew he couldn't catch stars. He knew he could only buy diamonds.

He nodded.

She couldn't refuse these diamonds. It would be like throwing all his worth and accomplishments back in his face, when he offered her what he thought was the best of himself. But she couldn't let him think they were what was truly important, either.

"Do you know, every single good perfume I've ever made, it's scared the hell out of me," she said. "The more it matters, the harder it is. A couple of those I left on your desk, I was sick with nerves when I forced myself to put the first concepts down on paper. But then I find my strength. While I'm doing it. And I keep going. I almost never believe I can do it. But I can keep trying."

His arms tightened on her, pulling her in close. "I love you," he said, very low and deep. The words vibrated through his chest, under her hands.

Oh. Oh. *That* was the proof. Those words rang so solid even she could believe in them. "That's better than diamonds," she whispered. "Better than flowers. And it doesn't even have a scent. Or a texture."

He drew a hand through her hair, twining it around his fingers. "It does to me."

She petted his chest. He was so right. *This* was the texture and scent of those words. "I fell in love with you on that terrace in New York," she whispered. "So hard. It was like I fell off the damn building, fifty stories up and plummeting, and you swooped in and caught me and carried me up to the stars."

He bent his head to her hair. "When I think about how you treated me the week after, when inside you felt like that, I get *so pissed off.*"

"You have a problem with grudges."

"Evidently." He kneaded his fingers into her back. Despite what he said, he didn't look angry. He looked wondering.

"It was just too dark a time." Even now her eyes filled remembering it. "I couldn't believe in that much happiness. I wanted to, I tried to, but I couldn't. I know we met on a terrace on top of the world, but in real life, I was stuck down in some dark cave."

His arms tightened on her. "God *damn it*, I wish I'd been there for you. If you'd *told* me—" But he broke off, stopping the accusation. That was water they had to let flow under its bridge.

She pressed her hand against his chest, looking up at him. "Your mother tried to tell you this when you were little, but of course little kids never understand. That all she needed for her birthday, as proof you loved her, were hugs and kisses, those were the best of all. You learned the hard way that you couldn't catch the moon and stars"—she touched the scar on his chin—"but it looks as if you decided that you sure as hell didn't have to make do with just glitter instead." She touched the bracelet and the necklace and earrings. "I love them. Thank you. I love that you took everything you were good at, and *thought* about me, and gave me something that only you could give and which has meaning to both of us."

He looked pleased, in a reserved way, like she was touching too close to something that mattered to him. Relieved. He looked a little like she had felt, when she asked him if he liked her perfume and he had said yes. Like maybe this was his equivalent of an artist's gift of self.

"They're lovely," she said again, petting his cheek. "But I think you've still never absorbed the real message. That you are the actual star."

He bent his head. Color climbed his cheeks, those hard cheekbones that she had once thought could never possibly blush. He looked heart-wrenchingly vulnerable. "Jasmin," he said, strangled.

"I was right, what I thought on that terrace. If I've caught you, then this whole world is full of magic again."

His lashes lifted, and his eyes held hers. For a moment, she thought his might have *shimmered.* "*Merde*, that's so true," he whispered. "You're my magic.

For me. But *I'm* not magic, Jasmin. I'm the hard, practical one."

She shook her head. "I told you before. You're the wish come true."

His arms tightened so hard. "I love the way you keep wishing," he murmured. "You keep trying. Even when you're sure you can't pluck the stars out of the sky, even when you're seeing them from the bottom of a well, you'll dream on them anyway. I bet you stretched your hand up, that night in Texas you told me about, and tried to see if your fingertips could brush them. I love you so damn much, Jasmin."

The words shook through her, precious and beautiful and shivering. Like he'd hung all those diamonds on a tree and set them to vibrating.

"Humans are harder than stars," she said. "Harder than perfumes. They're so...human. Things happen to them. They change. They die."

He covered her hand on his heart. "I can't promise you forever on the universe's terms. But I can promise you that while this beats, it beats for you."

Emotions strangled her. She caught a tear as it leaked from her eye, trying to be surreptitious. But since their fingers were tangled, it was his knuckle that wiped it away.

"You wore one of the scents." It was here, in the hollow of his throat. "The—"

"—wishing," he said softly. The sweet jasmine and vanilla and almond, that naïve, delicious wish for happiness like a candle against darkness.

She gasped a breath. "That's *it!*" Her whole brain sprang awake, as if she'd been hit by lightning. She pushed back away from him to clap her hands. "That's it! That's the concept!" She swung over the counter away from him, grabbing for her notebook. "Your scent. We've got the same metallic, right, but there, at the core of it, that *wishing*, that sweetness, that—" She wrote quickly, until Damien's hand closed over hers, stopping her pen.

"You're left-handed," he said.

"Yes." She tried to shake his hand loose. "One second, let me just get this down—maybe there should be a little lavender in it, too, I—"

His fingers tightened. "I have a question pending for your left hand."

She stilled. And lifted her eyes slowly to his. "You were serious about that?"

He stared at her incredulously a second. And then just lifted her up, hauled her back across the counter to him, and thunked his head in despair against hers.

Gently expressed despair, but clear nevertheless.

"Sorry. I'm sorry. I'm trying. You really are *quite* incredible, you know." She buried her face in his neck and whispered what she had been trying to say in those fragrances: "And I really, really love you."

His hands flexed on her at the words, this deep pull of her into his body. He lifted his head. "What do you wish for, Jasmin? Give it your best shot."

She took a deep breath. "This." Her thumb rubbed over the spot on his collarbone where he had spritzed her wishing scent. "Happiness." It wasn't so hard, after all, to meet those seawater eyes. It wasn't so hard, to reach for him and catch him. He was right there. "You."

His smile lit his whole face. He took her hand, sliding the ring onto her finger. "You have to be careful what you wish for around me. According to my family." His thumb rubbed possessively over the ring on her finger, and he lifted her hand enough to study the effect. His smile deepened.

"What do *you* wish for, Damien? Give it your best shot."

"I don't have to wish for it." His hand tightened on hers, enclosing the ring and her fingers in his strong grip. "I've got it."

Chapter 25

"Isn't it funny how kids can always surprise you?" Tante Colette said, rummaging in her embroidery kit. "And to think I thought you might be a good match for Tristan."

Damien glowered at his aunt but couldn't hold on to the irritation. Jess was sitting on a stool by his aunt's feet, cheerfully weeding. She seemed to have a great fascination for weeding. She'd been adding dirt to every single scent she experimented with these past two weeks, including the trials on his own fragrance.

But her teasing of him about being *dirty* could lead to all kinds of interesting places, so he was rather enjoying the theme. He picked a red flower from his aunt's beds.

"You can't inflict Tristan on someone, Mémère," Jess said, and Damien saw that little tremor of emotion that ran through his aunt at being called *grandmother*. "He's such a flirt. The poor girl would go crazy."

"He's got a very sweet heart," Tante Colette said firmly, and Damien sighed a little. His entire life, it seemed, family had been calling Tristan the sweet-hearted one, Damien the ruthless one, Matt the growly, hot-tempered one, Raoul the dangerous wild wolf, Lucien the lost, exiled warrior. They'd formed their own roles, to a certain extent, but sometimes it seemed as if family should be able to see a *little* bit more below the surface.

Jess looked across at him and met his eyes, hers warm. And he eased again. Yes, he liked this. Tough and ruthless to most of the world, but with his own tender, private space of quiet, held by her. He didn't want the world to think he was a marshmallow—*God,* he would hate for everyone to see right through his hard exterior, like they did Matt—but this, this intimate, secret sweetness, was perfect. He picked a purple flower.

"He just hides it," Tante Colette said, and Damien gazed at the sky a moment. Then he picked a white flower.

Jess smiled a little. "Hiding a sweet heart seems to run in the family."

"All the family," Damien said, fixing his aunt with a look.

Tante Colette gave him a *who-me?* stern look back and pulled some white linen out of her embroidery basket.

"Do you have any more surprises in store for the family, Tante Colette?" He picked a yellow flower.

She shook her white head at him. "You boys grew up in peacetime, financially secure, with a powerful family name behind you. And you still want me to make things easier for you. I'm just giving you a little enrichment. Like they do for zoo animals, to keep them from expiring from boredom."

"You know, I should really share with you the challenges of running an international business successfully sometime," Damien said dryly. "You might be surprised."

Tante Colette cocked her head and gave that some consideration. "When's the last time someone shot at you? Threatened to shoot an entire village if that village didn't turn you in?"

"Damn it," Damien said. "Fine. *Never*, okay?"

Colette opened her hands. "I'm just saying. A little enrichment is probably good for you."

"You know, more and more about you becomes clear every day in your family," Jess told Damien.

Damien sighed. And picked a pink flower.

"Damien's all right," Tante Colette said. "He's the tough one. Took after his grandfather."

"Or after you?" Jess said.

Tante Colette gave her a sharp look. "Not a blood relation, *petite.* Or didn't anyone tell you that yet?"

"There's a research project on nature versus nurture to be done here somewhere," Jess said.

Damien smiled and picked a jasmine vine, wrapping it around the stems of the flowers.

"Come here," Tante Colette said, and Damien walked over, sitting on the stone wall of the raised bed beside Jess.

She looked up at him with a smile. And because of that smile, he didn't feel like a complete idiot as he handed her the little bouquet of flowers.

She raised it to her face to brush her lips against it, looking so ridiculously delighted that he was deeply afraid his cheeks might be flushing. He applied a will of iron to those blood cells and resolutely did not look at his aunt.

Jess was so delighted, you'd think he'd just given her a hundred thousand dollars worth of diamonds. Hell, she liked it even better, didn't she? Her delight in the flowers was more relaxed, not overwhelmed or unnerved, just pure, glowing happiness.

He should give her bouquets of handpicked flowers all the time. It would make her deeply, deeply happy. And him, too.

He wrapped his arm around her shoulders and pulled that happiness in closer, glancing at last at his aunt.

"Young people," Tante Colette said with a shake of her head. But those wrinkled lips curved. "When's the wedding?"

Damien parted his lips to say *April*, since that was the date his extremely excited mother had thrown out, although he, personally, kind of liked the idea of a wedding day next August when they could fill the church with fresh jasmine. But he stopped suddenly, looking at his aunt. His old, old aunt who kept trying to arrange the affairs of her family. "Soon," he said. "As soon as we can."

Jess looked up at him and then at his aunt and didn't say anything. She just linked her fingers with his, the diamond jasmine shining on her finger. God, it was good to have someone who knew when your secret heart might feel tender. And he tightened his hold as he realized that hers might feel tender, too. She had lost one hundred percent of her family members, up to this point.

"You'll want this for a wedding present," Tante Colette said to Jess. "To give to the groom." She handed the white linen to Jess.

Something Tante Colette had embroidered for them, Damien thought with a tug of sweetness. Something special that—

The folds of linen fell apart in Jess's hands and revealed a set of pale kid gloves, the wide cuffs heavy with exquisite multicolored embroidery, fit for a king.

He'd never seen them, but he recognized them instantly. A sound escaped him, his gut tightening as if a cousin's punch had just landed there.

Jess lifted stunned eyes from them to Damien. "You told me about—"

"Laurianne was a glove-maker, yes." He touched the embroidery with the most delicate of fingers. Gloves centuries old, designed to protect a mercenary warrior's hands from injury and cold, and he was afraid that *his* touch would be the one that ruined them.

"And she made—"

"She made a pair of gloves for Niccolò, when he came out of Italy to win her. A gift for their wedding." Damien could barely hear his own voice. Four centuries. A revolution. Two world wars. Foreign occupation. Family feuds. And those gloves had still survived?

"Her Italian mercenary," Jess remembered softly. "Whose hands must have been so scarred from fighting everyone else's wars. She made him the softest, sweetest-smelling, most aristocratic gloves, gloves a king would wear."

"Try them on," Colette said.

"Tata—"

"They've survived since the Renaissance, Damien. Spending a few seconds on your hands won't ruin them."

Damien slowly pulled on a glove. Niccolò must have been a very big man for his time, because Damien was tall for his own generation, with strong hands, but the glove still fit him, although the leather had stiffened greatly with age. The ornate and exquisite embroidery looked, of course, kind of ridiculous, against his pants and shirt, although the gloves had probably been the ultimate in manly glory as part of the Renaissance wedding clothes Niccolò must have worn.

He could feel himself getting choked up, and he fought to keep his breathing smooth and even. "Thank you, Tante Colette."

"I thought you might want something you could actually wear, too," Colette said. "At the wedding."

He smiled at her as he eased off the gloves. "I'd love it if you would embroider me a handkerchief to wear in my tux."

Colette blinked in surprise, and then a complicated range of expressions crossed her face, but he thought one of them was touched pleasure. She looked down at her lap and cleared her throat. "Of course."

Damien smiled and laid his hand over hers. It felt so much easier to do now that he'd done it so often for Jess.

Jess squeezed his knee.

"But I was thinking of these," Tante Colette said, turning over a small embroidered bag and shaking its contents into Damien's palm.

Damien stared down at two pairs of rounded gold buttons, held together by a fine chain. Ornate etching on the gold, something from the Renaissance. They looked like—

"People would have called them sleeve buttons back then," Tante Colette said. "Probably some of the earliest preserved examples, in fact. I'm sure they should be in a museum, but that's true of most of our family heirlooms. I thought they suited you."

Cufflinks. They were cufflinks. People always gave him cufflinks when they didn't know what else to give him, but these...Damien rubbed them, incredulous emotion rising in him, adding to the overload of emotion from the gloves. "These were Niccolò's?"

"Probably. They were tucked inside one of the gloves. They would have been a sign of his rise in wealth and power and social class, at a time when only the rich wore them."

"That's perfect," Jess said. "That's *perfect* for you. You can wear them all the time. When you're out fighting for your family. When you want to remember where you belong and what matters."

"I'm going to use another bit of jewelry for that," Damien reminded her, touching his left ring finger.

She squeezed his thigh again but spoke to Tante Colette. "Thank you," she said, as heartfelt as if the gift to him had been a gift to her as well. "Thank you so much."

Damien pulled her in close to him, his hand closing around Niccolò's cuff links for safekeeping, too moved by all of it to dare speak. His voice might squeak or something equally horrible. But he dipped his head to his aunt.

"You two look very happy," Tante Colette said quietly, contented.

Jess held his handpicked bouquet up to her face to hide it. Damien nodded against Jess's hair, holding her for one more second tight before he loosed her out of respect for his aunt.

If anything, Tante Colette looked infinitely more relaxed and contented because of their public display of affection, though. She sat back in her chair—a rocking chair Damien had had imported for her from America—and stroked the arm of it, letting her eyes close against the sun.

"I'll never capture this," Jess said suddenly. She gestured with her bouquet as if to encompass everything—the bouquet itself, Tante Colette, the garden. Him. The bouquet came to rest on Damien's chest. "I'll never get it into a bottle." She took a deep breath. "But I'd like to try every day for—sixty years."

"Best make it seventy," Tante Colette said without opening her eyes. "Be hard on Damien to outlive you, and he comes from a long-lived family."

Jess smiled at her almost-napping aunt. "Go for broke?" She turned that smile up at Damien.

"Only way to shoot for the stars." He tightened his hand on hers.

She kissed his flowers, smiling at him over them.

Damn. Sometimes his heart swelled so much it squeezed all the room out of his chest. "Be kind of a challenge to give you a new diamond every day for seventy years," he said. "But I suppose Rosier SA could expand."

She laughed out loud and teased his nose with the edge of the flower bouquet. "And you called me an idiot. Hugs and kisses, Damien. Every day. No cheating and trying to give diamonds instead."

Damien smiled down at her, this great warmth spreading in his middle where once he had felt so cold and empty. "It's not cheating," he said. "But I think I can manage hugs and kisses."

And he gave her both right then. Just to practice.

After all, any idiot could make a wish. But a smart businessman knew that to make that wish come true, he had to pay attention to the details.

***

FIN

THANK YOU!

Thank you so much for reading! I hope you enjoyed Damien and Jess's story. And don't miss more Rosier stories! Sign up for Laura's newsletter (www.lauraflorand.com/newsletter) to be emailed as soon as the next one is released.

Meanwhile, if you missed Matt Rosier's story, you can find it in *Once Upon a Rose*. And you might be able to catch a teeny, tiny glimpse of a particularly elusive Rosier cousin in *All For You*. Let me know if you spot him! Keep reading for a couple of excerpts from these two books.

And I like to send out free short stories once in a while to those who sign up for my email for new releases, so let me know if there's anyone you would particularly like to see more of. You never know—my creative wheels might start turning.

Thank you so much for sharing in this new world with me! For some behind-the-scenes glimpses of the research in the south of France, check out my website and Facebook page. I hope to meet up with you there!

Thank you and all the best,

Laura Florand
Website: www.lauraflorand.com
Twitter: @LauraFlorand
Facebook: www.facebook.com/LauraFlorandAuthor
Newsletter: www.lauraflorand.com/newsletter/

LAURA FLORAND

OTHER BOOKS BY LAURA FLORAND

La Vie en Roses Series

Turning Up the Heat (a novella prequel)

The Chocolate Rose (a prequel)

A Rose in Winter, a novella in *No Place Like Home*

Once Upon a Rose

A Wish Upon Jasmine

Paris Hearts Series

All For You

Amour et Chocolat Series

All's Fair in Love and Chocolate, a novella in *Kiss the Bride*

The Chocolate Thief

The Chocolate Kiss

The Chocolate Touch

The Chocolate Heart

The Chocolate Temptation

Sun-Kissed

Shadowed Heart (a sequel to *The Chocolate Heart*)

A WISH UPON JASMINE

Snow Queen Duology

Snow-Kissed (a novella)

Sun-Kissed (also part of the Amour et Chocolat series)

Memoir

Blame It on Paris

ONCE UPON A ROSE, EXCERPT

To this valley! Matt growled, lifting his glass high. No one paid any attention, even though it was *his* thirtieth birthday, and *he* was the family patriarchal heir, no matter what Raoul and Damien wanted themselves to be.

He toasted himself while he was at it. Matthieu Rosier, Jean-Jacques Rosier's heir, owner of all he surveyed. Every petal of a rose. Every worm in the dirt trying to eat those roses. All of it.

It was all on his shoulders, but it was also all his. *J'y suis, j'y reste*, as his ancestor Niccolò Rosario had mandated over four centuries ago. *I am here and here I'll stay.*

Just for a second, that old claustrophobic feeling tried to descend on him again—that thing that had driven him to the Paris offices and into the not-so-tender embrace of a supermodel the year before, in hopes of proving that his life existed outside this valley. He drowned it in another swallow.

No, this is my place. This is where I'm *meant to be.* Here, he could handle anything the weather or people or time threw at him, do anything that needed doing. *I'm Matthieu Rosier. I know it now, and my next thirty years are going to be awesome!*

Awesome. Definitely. Grinning suddenly, he grabbed his cousin Raoul's girlfriend Allegra as she headed past him, placed her firmly behind him with her hands on his waist, and started a chain dance.

Which kind of had a bad effect on the tables, but it wasn't his fault he had so many big male cousins who danced like elephants. They'd all been trained to dance properly, too—you'd think it would come across somewhat even when they were chain dancing. *No more tuxedoes and waltzes for me, thank God. I'm never putting on a tuxedo for a woman again. From now on, I'm sticking with women who like to see a man in jeans.* He bumped into another table.

One of his aunts protested, the whole chain abandoned him and wound itself the other way, and he lurched off the table, grinning and feeling a smidge dizzy. Maybe he needed to get some air. He could probably come back in and hold still more wine afterward.

Which sounded like a great idea, because he had had *excellent* taste when he set that wine aside at twenty for his thirtieth birthday.

He turned to the door and ran straight into a guest trying to slip inside the house. Her face smashed into his chest, and he looked down at a wild mass of bronze-tipped curls and then a heart-shaped face tilting back to look up at him as she bounced backward.

"Well, *hello*," he exclaimed, delighted, picking her straight up off the floor before she fell. Then he wasn't quite sure what to do with her—maybe it had been a *tad* excessive, picking her up completely to stop her from falling? Still, he could hardly drop her now.

She was gaping at him, for one thing. And since she had the most adorable rosebud mouth, a gape was a *very* hot look on her. Her skin was this luscious sun-warmed color, as if she'd escaped from an island, and she had corkscrew honey-brown curls springing out at all angles. Even with a few of them smashed into a ponytail like that, the rest were making her head look a foot wide.

"Umm...*bonsoir*," she said carefully, wiggling her dangling toes.

Oh, and she had an *accent*. Oh, that was *hot.* "You're late," he said cheerfully. "You should have got here before I was quite this drunk."

Those rosebud lips parted again. She really shouldn't leave that mouth of hers open as if she was going to let someone else figure out what to do with it. Not when the someone else was him, anyway. Although...it *was* his birthday. He wished he could remember her name. Be shitty if she was dating one of his cousins.

He looked around, still not quite sure where to put her. At last, he crossed the great room, still carrying her by the hips, shoved some bottles out of the way on the bar, and set her butt firmly there. Nobody had hit him yet, so she probably wasn't dating one of his cousins.

Then he frowned a little bit at the bar, because it seemed a shame he'd pressed her butt against it before he had remembered to check it out. On the plus side, this set her at a level where he could just *tilt* a bit forward and end up with his face in her breasts. And he *was* feeling dizzy, and it *was* his birthday, and also, those were cute breasts. Hiding under a shirt like that. Seemed a shame. He remained upright with a valiant effort of what remained of his will. "You can talk some more," he told her, patting her on the knee. Nice muscles to her leg, there. Promising sign for her butt. "I like your accent."

"*Merci*," she said faintly, and her trouble with the R just *tickled* over his body. "Umm...do you know my name?"

Oh, damn, no. *What* was it? Shit. She was bound to get offended if he couldn't remember where they had met last. Where *had* they met last? Why didn't he remember her? She was at his birthday party, for God's sake. True, half the people around Grasse were, but you'd think he would remember the cute ones.

Some of the younger cousins tumbled against his legs while he was trying to think, and he bent down to right the littlest boy absently. The little Delange girl chasing them with confetti paused long enough to throw more of it over him and the new arrival, so that it ended up caught in that curly hair. He smiled at the little terror approvingly and felt his own hair. Yeah, there was so much confetti in it at this point that it was probably hopeless.

His aunt Annick passed by with a big tray of mostly empty glasses, persisting once again in cleaning up while the party was still going on. His grandfather and his Tante Colette had long since retired but everyone else was in full swing. And look at that, someone was wasting his good wine. He snagged the half-full glass off the tray and offered it to Curls.

"No," she said faintly, and then reached out and covered the top of it with her hand, removing it from his grasp. "And you've had enough," she said firmly.

Matt grinned. He'd been starting to have a niggle of a doubt, but that was definitely a girlfriend thing to do. Off in that surreal world where girlfriends actually cared about you enough to boss you around, like Allegra did Raoul.

"Matt. Who is this?" Aunt Annick paused long enough to ask, her eyes bright with joy at being the first to discover whom one of the cousins was dating.

"My girlfriend," he said cheerfully. He looked at his girlfriend expectantly. *Hint, hint. You can go ahead and say your name now.*

She gaped at him again. Damn, that was such a good look on her.

"Your—girlfriend?" Aunt Annick looked pretty surprised, since the aunts thought the cousins incapable of going out with someone more than once without one of them finding out about it and telling all the others. Matt grinned at her smugly. *Fooled you, didn't I?* She'd probably thought he was still brooding over Nathalie. Date just one damn supermodel in your life and no one ever thought you could get over her.

"I like to call her Bouclettes," he said grandly. It seemed plausible as a nickname. All those curls.

Aunt Annick frowned a little bit. "Half a second," she told Bouclettes. "Let me put this down. I'll be right back."

But en route instead, she crossed paths with Raoul, and Matt saw her give him the go-check-on-your-cousin poke. Damn.

"Matt," Raoul said, surging up into their space. "What the hell are you doing? Who is this?"

Oh, fine, put him on the spot. He gave Raoul a dirty look, hopefully dirty enough to encourage him to go back to Africa. And *not* laugh at him. Was Raoul laughing at him? Matt was picking up on far too much amusement. Also deep aggravation.

"A friend," he told Raoul coolly. "Back off. Go play with Allegra."

"Do you want to be his friend?" Raoul asked his guest instead, unforgivably.

Matt scowled at him. Raoul *had* a girlfriend already. What was Raoul doing trying to steal *his* girl? "He's got a girlfriend," he informed Bouclettes just to make sure she didn't get distracted. "Ignore him."

"Umm, actually..." Bouclettes began, sounding hopeful, "is your girlfriend *here*? And sober?"

"Probably not sober," Raoul said. "But better off than him. He just turned thirty."

Matt gave him an indignant look. Was it necessary to mention that? This girl looked mid-twenties, tops.

"Matt. Who is this?" his cousin Damien appeared to ask. "And why are you picking her up and carrying her around your birthday party?"

Damn it, he *knew* he only had seconds with her before all his cousins started flocking in. "Go find your own girlfriend!" he snapped at Damien. *Merde*, now Tristan was circling in, too. Tristan and Damien *liked* putting on tuxedoes. And probably liked women with corkscrew curls, too. Whose tastes *wouldn't* include those corkscrew curls? Matt wanted to squoosh those curls between his hands so bad.

"The thing is, Matt, what if she's not your girlfriend?" Raoul asked. Raoul was just being a bastard tonight, wasn't he? "You've never introduced her to us before."

"Yes, well, who wants to introduce a girl to you vultures," he retorted, sliding an arm possessively around her waist, where she still sat on the bar. It made her curls tickle his shoulder. He grinned, delighted with them. "Don't listen to them," he told her. "They're just jealous."

Damn, did he want her to know they were jealous and therefore let her realize they would be interested in her? One problem with having so many cousins nearly his size and nearly his age and sometimes with even more money was that it made for one hell of a lot of competition.

"About that girlfriend of yours," Bouclettes said to Raoul, rather desperately. She tried to sidle away from Matt's arm, but she ran into some more wine bottles packing the bar, so he tightened his arm to protect her from them.

"Right." Raoul turned, looked around the crowd of laughing, drunk dancers, and then proved he was more than a bit drunk himself by finally tilting his head back, opening his mouth, and loosening a boom that shook the rafters: "Allegra!!"

Allegra turned her dark head and shook herself free of what remained of the chain dance with some difficulty—several people kept pulling her back to dance—and appeared beside Raoul, fixing him with a minatory gaze that made Matt's heart tighten in jealousy. That chiding look was so, so...*cozy.* As if Raoul could be as annoying as he pleased and still be loved for it. Matt was annoying, too, and all he'd gotten for it so far was an astoundingly bad dating history.

He snuck a glance at Bouclettes hopefully. No time like the present for changing a man's luck with women.

"I'm not a dog," Allegra told Raoul severely.

Raoul grinned and shook his shaggy rust-and-charcoal head, instantly pseudo-meek, lifting up both her hands to kiss them. "*Pardon, bonheur.* I thought you might help us not scare Matt's new girlfriend to death."

"Or you could try backing off," Matt told him resentfully. "I was doing just fine until the three of you started crowding her." Of *course* that would be too much. Four big guys like that. He and his cousins had been pretty stubborn about trying to outgrow each other as kids. He tried, with considerable difficulty, to imagine what it might be like to be surrounded by a group of guys when your head didn't reach their shoulders, but he couldn't manage to get the angle right. In his head, he was always looking down, not up. Still, it had to be crappy, to have so many people towering over you, so he squeezed Bouclettes's waist reassuringly.

"I'll take care of you," he whispered to her. Very intriguing green eyes started to crinkle, as if she was about to laugh, which was a good sign. A man didn't get to thirty without knowing the value of making a woman laugh, so he pursued that line of attack: "Don't worry about them. Do you want me to hit one of them?"

Her eyes widened again, the laughter retreating.

"His aunts are here," Allegra told Bouclettes.

"Where are they?" Bouclettes asked rather desperately.

Allegra waved a hand to the dance floor, where Damien's mom, Tata Véro, was chopping her arms up and down in an exuberant robot dance, grinning up at his uncle Louis as she got him to try to imitate her.

"Is *she* still sober?" Bouclettes asked doubtfully. She had a really weird idea of his hospitality, if she thought his guests might still be sober at this hour of the night. What did she think he was serving people, water?

"I'm sober!" Allegra said indignantly, settling her weight against Raoul's side as if her bones might not support her by themselves. "I've only had a couple of glasses. I think." She looked up at Raoul, as if he might have kept track, but Raoul shrugged in clear indifference.

"Thanks for coming." Even if Bouclettes had gotten there a little late. They'd already sung "Joyeux Anniversaire" and everything. Matt frowned suddenly. "Are there any *choux* left? She didn't get any! Here."

He hauled Bouclettes off the bar, holding her pressed to his side as he worked his way through the crowd to a long folding table that had been pushed against a wall and was littered with remnants of the cakes that had been on it.

"Look. There are still some left." He picked one of the pastry puffs from the giant *pièce montée* they had once formed—it was about like his family to offer him a Ferrari made out of pastry puffs instead of the real thing—and proffered it right to her rosebud lips.

Well, they were gaping at him again as if she wanted him to take control of them, and even he wasn't so drunk he was actually going to do all the *other* things he kept thinking about doing to them right there with all his cousins watching. A pastry puff was a good way to sublimate.

She must have thought so, too, because those green eyes held his a moment—the pastry puff pressed against her teeth—and then she finally sighed and bit into it. Cream clung to her lips. Matt just grinned. It was probably good he was too drunk to properly articulate exactly what a good look that was on her.

She licked the cream off.

Oh, yeah. Yeah, this was a nice birthday. He bent down and kissed her to say thanks for it before he remembered he wasn't going to do *any* of the fantasies, not even the kiss one, in front of his cousins.

Her mouth was warm and—rather surprised. She pulled away from him, set her hands on his chest, and shoved.

What? He loosened his arm, deeply wounded. "What's the matter with you? Don't you like me anymore?"

"I need help," she said firmly, words that ran right through his bloodstream and made every cell in it perk up and beg to be a hero. She looked around again. As if she was trying to find some *other* knight.

He looped her straight back into him, pressing her against his chest as much as she would let him, since she was arching her upper body back. "I'll help you." *Come on, please? I want to be the one who does it. Whatever it is. Storm a castle, maybe? Climb to the top of a glass mountain?*

"Matt." Allegra reappeared and poked at him. "Do you actually know her at all?"

Would people quit asking him questions like that? It was getting annoying. She was at his birthday party, wasn't she?

"No," Bouclettes said, wounding him to the heart. "He doesn't. My car broke down, and this was the nearest house."

"Oh, my God." Allegra clapped her hands to her mouth. "Matt, *let go of her.*"

"You need me to fix your car?" Matt asked, his tongue feeling fuzzy. He could do that. He could fix just about anything. Seemed odd in the middle of the night when he was trying to celebrate his birthday, but then again...if one of the damn machines on this place wanted to break down, it *never* did it at a convenient moment. "All right." He looked around, trying to remember where he had put his tools. "The *atelier d'extraction,*" he remembered. "They're probably in the extraction plant. I'll be right back."

He started to haul Bouclettes with him, because he was not at all fond of the idea of leaving her alone with Damien and Tristan, but Allegra reached in and grabbed his waist. He gave Raoul an appalled look. *Hey, that's not my fault. She started it. I never touched her.*

Raoul grabbed his other arm, which made Matt wince, because he was sure as hell too drunk to stop the punch that was coming. "Matt," Raoul said, instead of hitting him. "You cannot fix a car in the dark while you're this drunk. You'll undo her brake cable or something by accident, and she'll run off a cliff. I don't think any of us are in a state to work on it, really. You'll have to wait until morning," he told Bouclettes.

Morning. "You want to go to bed?" Matt asked her helpfully.

She wrenched out of what was left of his hold.

"Matt!" Allegra wedged her body with great determination between him and Bouclettes, and Raoul *still* didn't hit him. Raoul must be drunk, was all Matt could figure. "He's harmless," she told Bouclettes. "Or he's trying to be. But seriously—you can see everyone is wasted. They have mattresses filling the old attic for all the people who can't drive home tonight. Why don't you sleep on one of those, and in the morning we'll get you going again. Matt can fix your car in minutes, when he's not this drunk."

"Depends," Matt corrected conscientiously. "Is it a Ferrari?" The Ferrari he didn't get for his birthday? "I wouldn't want to rush it, if so."

Bouclettes looked at him, looked at Allegra so rudely wedging her body between Matt's and hers, looked around at the party, and finally spread her fingers across her face and began to laugh. She laughed so hard Matt started to worry she might be too drunk to drive, too. "Best to sleep it off," he told her, which brought another wave of semi-hysterical laughter.

"You need food," Allegra decided. "Also something to drink."

"*Not* wine," Bouclettes said firmly.

"It's good wine," Matt told her. "Been in our *cave* for ten years, this one, I think. One of the first wines I ever stocked in the *cave* myself."

"No, no, no," Allegra agreed with Bouclettes. "We must have fizzy water somewhere. Would a sealed bottle make you feel more comfortable?"

"A little bit, at this point," Bouclettes said, for no reason Matt could figure out.

But Allegra grinned in wry sympathy, as if women had some secret language concerning sealed bottles of water. Which would just figure, with women. And she indicated the much-diminished cheese platters. "Here, have some cheese. Raoul, can you haul Matt into one of the bathrooms and put him under the shower?"

"It's my birthday!" Matt protested.

"Hose would be easier," Raoul said. "But that's a myth, you know. It won't really do any good, just make him wet."

"I'll take care of it," said Damien, who *always* had to prove he could fulfill people's wishes better than anyone else. He grabbed Matt. Matt decided not to hit him, so as not to make a bad impression on Bouclettes. Also, Damien might duck, and then you never knew which of the people packed around him his fist might hit instead. If it was Allegra or Bouclettes, his cousins probably wouldn't let him live to see his thirty-first year, and who would want to, with that on his conscience?

"Allow me." His cousin Léa appeared beside them, blonde hair caught back in one of her matter-of-fact ponytails, and Matt looked at her with some relief because she always showed good sense. Actually a second cousin and one of the few girls to play with the five male first cousins growing up, she'd kind of been forced into that sensible role. "Come on, Matt, here." She took his arm from Damien and slipped it around her own waist.

What *was* it with the women tonight? Was it because it was his birthday? Léa's husband Daniel gave him a look of rather steely patience, but also didn't hit him. Somebody should have told him the guys would let him hug their women on his birthday. He would have been taking greater advantage.

"But—don't you want to come?" he asked Bouclettes wistfully as he let Léa lead him away. He might not be quite the putty Daniel was in Léa's hands, but Léa was hard to say no to.

"I'm good right here," Bouclettes said firmly, holding up a hand. He really wanted to kiss her right in the center of that adamant palm and see what she did with that.

But he let Léa boss him, because it was Léa. And when he got back, Bouclettes was gone.

Gone.

Just plain gone. Like he had imagined her or something.

What the fuck? It was his *birthday*. He didn't get to keep her?

That was so damn lousy he had to open up the bottles he had put aside on his twenty-first birthday and which he was supposed to be saving for next year.

Available now!

And don't miss the all new Paris Hearts series! Keep reading for an excerpt.

ALL FOR YOU, EXCERPT

Paris, near République

Célie worked in heaven. Every day she ran up the stairs to it, into the light that reached down to her, shining through the great casement windows as she came into the *laboratoire*, gleaming in soft dark tones off the marble counters. She hung up her helmet and black leather jacket and pulled on her black chef's jacket instead and ran her fingers through her hair to perk it back out into its current wild pixie cut. She washed her hands and stroked one palm all down the length of one long marble counter as she headed to check on her chocolates from the day before.

Oh, the beauties. There they were, the flat, perfect squares with their little prints, subtle but adamant, the way her boss liked them. Perfect. There were the ganaches and the pralinés setting up in their metal frames. Day three on the mint ganache. Time to slice it into squares with the *guitare* and send them to the enrober.

She called teasing hellos to everyone. "What, you here already, Amand? I didn't expect you until noon." Totally unfair to the hardworking caramellier, but he had slept in once, after a birthday bash, arriving to work so late and so horrified at himself that no one had ever let him forget it.

"Dom, when's the wedding again?" Dominique Richard, their boss, was diligently trying to resist marrying his girlfriend until he had given her enough time to figure out what a bad bet he was, and the only way to handle that was tease him. Otherwise Célie's heart might squeeze too much in this warm, fuzzy, mushy urge to give the man a big hug—and then a very hard shove into the arms of his happiness.

Guys who screwed over a woman's chance at happiness because they were so convinced they weren't good enough did *not* earn any points in her book.

"Can somebody work around here besides me?" Dom asked in complete exasperation, totally unmerited, just because the guy had no idea how to deal with all the teasing that came his way. It was why they couldn't resist. He was so big, and he got all ruffled and grouchy and adorable.

"I want to have time to pick out my dress!" Célie protested, hauling down the *guitare*. "I know exactly what you two are going to do. You'll put it off until all of a sudden you wander in some Monday with a stunned, scared look on your face, and we'll find out you eloped over the weekend to some village in Papua New Guinea. And we'll have missed the whole thing!"

Dom growled desperately, like a persecuted bear, and bent his head over his éclairs.

Célie grinned and started slicing her mint ganache into squares, the guitar wires cutting through it effortlessly. *There you go.* She tasted one. Soft, dissolving in her mouth, delicately infused with fresh mint. *Mmm. Perfect. Time to get it all dressed up.* Enrobing time.

She got to spend her days like this. In one of the top chocolate *laboratoires* in Paris. Okay, the top, but some people over in the Sixth like a certain Sylvain Marquis persisted in disputing that point. What*ever*. He was such a classicist. *Boring.* And *everyone* knew that cinnamon did not marry well with dark chocolate, so that latest Cade Marquis bar of his was just ridiculous.

And she didn't even want to think about Simon Casset with his stupid sculptures. So he could do fancy sculptures. Was that real chocolate? Did people eat that stuff? No. So. *She* did important chocolate. Chocolate that adventured. Chocolate people wanted to sink their teeth into. Chocolate that opened a whole world up in front of a person, right there in her mouth.

Chocolate that was so much beyond anything she had ever dreamed her life would be as a teenager. *God,* she loved her day. She stretched out her arms, nearly bopped their apprentice Zoe, who was carrying a bowl of chocolate to the scale, grinned at her in apology, and carried her mint ganaches over to the enrober.

She'd been loving her day for a little over three hours and was getting kind of ready to take a little break from doing so and let her back muscles relax for fifteen minutes when Guillemette showed up at the top of the stairs. Célie cocked her eyebrows at the other woman hopefully. Time for a little not-smoke break, perhaps? Were things quiet enough downstairs? Célie didn't smoke anymore, not since some stupid guy she once knew made her quit and she found out how many *flavors* there were out there when they weren't being hidden by tobacco. But sometimes she'd give just about anything to be able to hold a cigarette between her fingers and blow smoke out with a sexy purse of her lips and truly believe that was all it took to make her cool.

Because the double ear piercings and the spiky pixie hair were a lot less expensive over the long-term, but they could be misinterpreted as bravado, whereas—

A teenager slouching against a wall and blowing smoke from her mouth was *always* clearly genuine coolness, no bravado about it, of course. Célie rolled her eyes at herself, and Guillemette, instead of gesturing for her to come join her for the not-smoke break, instead came up to her counter where she was working and stole a little chocolate. "There's a guy here to see you," Guillemette said a little doubtfully. "And we're getting low on the Arabica."

Célie glanced at the trolley full of trays where the Arabica chocolates had finished and were ready to be transferred to metal flats. "I'll bring some down with me. Who's the guy?" Maybe that guy she had met Saturday, Danny and Tiare's friend? She tried to figure out if she felt any excitement about that, but adrenaline ran pretty high in her on a normal day in the *laboratoire*, so it was hard to tell.

"He didn't say."

And Guillemette hadn't asked? Maybe there had been several customers at once or something.

"I'll be down in a second," Célie said, and Guillemette headed back while Célie loaded up a couple of the metal flats they used in the display cases with the Arabica, with its subtle texture, no prints on this one. Dark and exotic and touched with coffee.

She ran down the spiral metal stairs with her usual happy energy, and halfway down, the face of the big man waiting with his hands in his pockets by the pastry display counter came into view, and she—

Tripped.

The trays flew out of her hands as her foot caught on one of the metal steps, and she grabbed after them even as they sailed away. Her knuckles knocked against one tray, and chocolates shot off it, raining down everywhere just as she started to realize she was falling, too.

Oh, *fuck*, that instant flashing realization of how much this was going to hurt and how much too late it was to save herself, even as she tried to grab the banister, and—

Hard hands caught her, and she *oofed* into them and right up against a big body, caught like a rugby ball, except it was raining chocolates during this game, and—

She gasped for breath, post impact, and pulled herself upright, staring up at the person who still held her in steadying hands.

Wary, hard, intense hazel green eyes stared back down at her. He looked caught, instead of her, his lips parted, as if maybe he had meant to say something. But, looking down at her, he didn't say anything at all.

Strong eyebrows, strong stubborn forehead and cheekbones and chin—every single damn bone in his body stubborn—and skin so much more tanned and weathered than when she had last seen it. Brown hair cropped military-close to his head and sanded by sun.

Célie wrenched back out of his hands, her own flying to her face as she burst into tears.

Just—burst. Right there in public, with all her colleagues and their customers around her. She backed up a step and then another, tears flooding down her cheeks, chocolate crushing under her feet.

"Célie," he said, and even his voice sounded rougher and tougher. And wary.

She turned and ran back up the staircase, dashing at her eyes to try to see the steps through the tears, and burst back up through the glass doors into the *laboratoire*. Dom looked up immediately, and then straightened. "Célie? *What's wrong?*"

Big, bad Dom, yeah, right, with the heart of gold. He came forward while she shook her head, having nothing she could tell him, scrubbing at her eyes in vain.

The glass door behind her opened. "Célie," that rough, half-familiar voice said. "I—"

She darted toward the other end of the *laboratoire* and her ganache cooling room.

"Get the fuck out of my kitchen," Dom said behind her, flat, and she paused, half turning.

Dom Richard, big and dark, stood blocking the other man in the glass doorway. Joss locked eyes with him, these two big dangerous men, one who wanted in and one who wasn't about to let him. Célie bit a finger, on sudden fear, and started back toward them.

Joss Castel looked past Dom to her. Their eyes held.

"Célie, go in the other room," Dom said without turning around. And to Joss: "You. *Get out.*"

Joss thrust his hands in his pockets. Out of combat. Sheathing his weapons. He nodded once, a jerk of his head at Célie, and turned and made his way down the stairs.

Dom followed. Célie went to the casement window above the store's entrance and watched as Joss left the store, crossed the street, and turned to look up at the window. She started crying again, just at that look, and when she lifted her hand to swipe her eyes, he must have caught the movement through the reflection off the glass, because his gaze focused on her.

"What was that all about?" Dom asked behind her. She turned, but she couldn't quite get herself to leave the window. She couldn't quite get herself to walk out of sight. "Célie, who is that guy and what did he do?"

She shook her head.

"Célie."

She slashed a hand through the air, wishing she could shut things down like a *man* could, make her hand say, *This subject is closed.* When *Dom* slashed a subject closed with one move of his hand like that, no one messed with *him.* Well, except for her, of course. "Just someone I knew before. Years ago. Before I worked here."

"When you lived in Tarterets?" Their old, bad *banlieue.* "And he was bad? Did he hit you? Was he dealing? What was it?"

She gazed at Dom uneasily. For all that he was so big and bad and dark, always seeming to have that threat of violence in him, it was the first time she had ever seen him about to commit violence.

"No," she said quickly. "No. He didn't."

"Célie."

"No, he really didn't, damn it, Dom! *Merde.* Do you think I would *let* him?"

"You couldn't have been over eighteen."

"Yeah, well—he didn't."

Dom's teeth showed, like a man who didn't believe her and was about to reach out and rip the truth out of her. "Then *what*—"

"He left me! That's all. He fucking left me there, so that he could go make himself into a better person. Yeah. So *fuck you*, Dom. Go marry your girlfriend instead of playing around with this *I-need-to-be-good-enough* shit and leave me alone!"

And she sank down on her butt, right there in the cooling room, between the trolleys full of chocolate and the marble island, in the slanting light from the casement window, and cried.

Just cried and cried and cried.

It sure as hell put a damper on chocolate production for a while, but for as long as she needed it, people did leave her alone.

Available now!

A WISH UPON JASMINE

ACKNOWLEDGEMENTS

Once again, a huge thank you goes to author Virginia Kantra for her insight into story here as well as to Mercy and Dale Anderson, Lisa Chinn, and Deborah Rines, who volunteered to read early drafts and give me invaluable feedback. This book would be far lesser without them.

And an enormous thanks to perfumer Lynne de R. in Grasse, who invited me into her perfume shop in Grasse one day and thus started me down the path of this story. It is also Lynne who introduced me to Joseph Mul, to whom I once again owe many, many thanks for allowing me to explore his fields outside of Grasse during the harvest and question him and everyone who works there relentlessly about all aspects of the rose and jasmine harvests. Of course any inaccuracies that have slipped into the story are all mine, but I owe much of the richness of texture in this story to their willingness to let me experience it myself.

And thank you once again to Sébastien and Mia for their patience and support when I am deep in story.

LAURA FLORAND

ABOUT LAURA FLORAND

Laura Florand burst on the contemporary romance scene in 2012 with her award-winning Amour et Chocolat series. Since then, her international bestselling books have appeared in ten languages, been named among the Best Books of the Year by *Romantic Times* and Barnes & Noble, received the RT Seal of Excellence and numerous starred reviews from *Publishers Weekly, Library Journal,* and *Booklist,* and been recommended by NPR, *USA Today,* and *The Wall Street Journal,* among others.

After a Fulbright year in Tahiti and backpacking everywhere from New Zealand to Greece, and several years living in Madrid and Paris, Laura now teaches Romance Studies at Duke University. Contrary to what the "Romance Studies" may imply, this means she primarily teaches French language and culture and does a great deal of research on French gastronomy, particularly chocolate.

A WISH UPON JASMINE

COPYRIGHT

Copyright 2015, Laura Florand

Cover by Sébastien Florand

ISBN-13: 978-1-943168-09-5